Praise for #1 *New York Times* bestselling author Debbie Macomber

"Debbie Macomber tells women's stories in a way no one else does."

—*BookPage*

"Macomber is a skilled storyteller."

—*Publishers Weekly*

"No one writes stories of love and forgiveness like Macomber."

—*RT Book Reviews*

Praise for *New York Times* bestselling author Shannon Stacey

"[Stacey's] hunky firefighters will make readers hot under the collar. This sexy, engaging tale will prime readers for the next offering."

—*Publishers Weekly* on *Fully Ignited*

"[This] contemporary tale is full of the love (and requisite family high jinks) that readers have come to expect from Shannon Stacey. The chemistry between Emma and Sean positively sizzles."

—*RT Book Reviews* (4½ stars) on *Yours to Keep*

Debbie Macomber is a #1 *New York Times* bestselling author and a leading voice in women's fiction worldwide. Her work has appeared on every major bestseller list, with more than 170 million copies in print, and she is a multiple award winner. Hallmark Channel based a television series on Debbie's popular Cedar Cove books. For more information, visit her website, debbiemacomber.com.

New York Times and *USA TODAY* bestselling author **Shannon Stacey** lives with her husband and two sons in New England, where her two favorite activities are writing stories of happily-ever-afters and driving her UTV through the mud. You can contact Shannon through her website, shannonstacey.com, where she maintains an almost daily blog, visit her on Twitter, Twitter.com/shannonstacey, and on Facebook, Facebook.com/shannonstacey.authorpage, or email her at shannon@shannonstacey.com.

To find out about other books by Shannon Stacey or to be alerted to new releases, sign up for her monthly newsletter at bit.ly/shannonstaceynewsletter.

#1 *New York Times* Bestselling Author

DEBBIE MACOMBER

WANTED: PERFECT PARTNER

 HARLEQUIN® BESTSELLING AUTHOR COLLECTION

ISBN-13: 978-1-335-97273-6

Wanted: Perfect Partner

Copyright © 2018 by Harlequin Books S.A.

The publisher acknowledges the copyright holders of the individual works as follows:

Wanted: Perfect Partner
Copyright © 1995 by Debbie Macomber

Fully Ignited
Copyright © 2016 by Shannon Stacey

Recycling programs for this product may not exist in your area.

HARLEQUIN®
www.Harlequin.com

Printed in U.S.A.

CONTENTS

Also available from Debbie Macomber

WANTED:
PERFECT PARTNER

Debbie Macomber

For Arlene Tresness, a grandma like me,
a lover of books, a devoted reader of mine. Thank
you for your unfailing support and enthusiasm.
(Your grandchildren think the world of you!)

Prologue

"Is our ad there?" Fifteen-year-old Lindsey Remington whispered to her best friend. She glanced nervously at her bedroom door. Lindsey's biggest fear was that her mother would find her and Brenda scanning the Dateline section of the Wednesday paper and discover what they'd done.

Okay, so it was a bit…dishonest to write an ad on Meg Remington's behalf, but it was clear to Lindsey that her mom needed help. She was convinced that Meg *wanted* to remarry, whether she knew it or not.

It wasn't as if Lindsey could pull a potential husband out of nowhere. So she wrote the ad, with her best friend advising her.

"Here," Brenda said excitedly, pointing to the middle of the page. "It's here. Oh, my goodness! It's really here, just the way we wrote it."

Lindsey found the ad. She read aloud:

"Wanted: Perfect partner. I'm dating-shy, divorced and seeking a man with marriage in mind. I look like a beauty queen, cook like a mom, kiss like a woman in love. Box 1234."

"It sounds even better in print," Brenda said.

"Do you think anyone will actually respond?" Lindsey asked.

"I bet we get lots of letters."

"I still think we should've said her kisses taste better than chocolate."

"It didn't fit. Remember?" They'd worked long and hard on the wording. Lindsey had wanted to describe her mother as "stunning," and Brenda was afraid it might not meet the truth-in-advertising rules.

All right, so her mother wasn't fashion model material, but she was very pretty. Or she could be, with a little assistance from the magazines Lindsey had been reading lately. Luckily Meg had a daughter who knew the ropes.

"Don't worry, Linds," Brenda said with a romantic sigh. "This is the best thing you could ever have done for your mother."

Lindsey hoped her mom appreciated her efforts. "Just remember, this guy has to be *perfect*. We'll need to be careful who we pick."

"No problem. If we don't like the sound of one guy, we'll choose someone else," Brenda said, as if they were guaranteed to have tons of applicants. "That's the beauty of our plan. We'll screen all the applicants before your mother has a chance to date them. How many teenagers get to choose their own stepfathers? Not many, I bet."

Lindsey returned her attention to the ad, gnawing on the corner of her lip. She was experiencing a twinge of pride along with a mild case of guilt.

Her mother wasn't going to like this. When Meg learned what she and Brenda had done, she'd probably get all bent out of shape.

As for the ad, Lindsey figured if she were a man inclined to read the Dateline section, the ad would intrigue her.

"Some men will write just because your mom's pretty, but it's the part about her being a good cook that'll really work," Brenda assured her. "My grandma says Grandpa married her because her German potato salad was so good. Can you believe it?"

Brenda brought up a good point. "How will we know if a man is marrying her for her looks or her meat loaf or 'cause he loves her?"

"We won't," Brenda said, "but by then we'll be out of the picture. Your mother will be on her own."

Lindsey wished she knew more about men. Unfortunately her experience was limited. She'd only gone on two real dates, both times to school dances. And her mother had been a chaperone.

"The day will come when Mom will appreciate what we've done for her," Lindsey said. "She's the one who's always saying how important it is to go after your dreams. Well, this is my dream for her. She wants a man. She just doesn't know it yet."

"All she needs is a little help from us."

"And she's got it," Lindsey said, smiling broadly.

Chapter 1

Those girls were up to something. Meg Remington peeked in her fifteen-year-old daughter's bedroom to see Lindsey and her best friend, Brenda, crouched on the floor beside the bed. They were speaking in heated whispers.

Meg cleared her throat and instantly both girls were silent.

"Hi, Mom," Lindsey said, her bright blue eyes flashing.

Meg knew the look, which generally spelled trouble. "What are you two doing?"

"Nothing."

"Nothing," Brenda echoed with angelic innocence.

Meg crossed her arms and leaned her shoulder against the doorjamb. She had all the time in the world, and she wanted them to know it. "Tell me why I don't believe that. You two have the *look*."

"What look?" Lindsey repeated, turning to Brenda.

"The one every mother recognizes. You're up to something, and I want to know what." She crossed her ankles, indicating that she'd make herself comfortable until they were ready to let her in on their little secret. She could outwait them if need be.

"All right, if you *must* know," Lindsey said with a shrug of defeat. She leapt to her feet and Brenda followed suit. "But we haven't finished planning everything yet."

"I must know." Meg was struck by how beautiful her daughter had become over the past few years. She'd gone from the gangly, awkward, big-teeth stage to real beauty almost overnight. Meg's ex-husband, Dave, had commented on the changes in Lindsey when she'd flown from Seattle to Los Angeles to visit over spring break. Their little girl was growing up.

"We've been doing some heavy-duty planning," Brenda explained.

"And exactly what are the two of you working on? I haven't seen you all evening." Generally, when Brenda stayed over, which was at least one night of every weekend, the two of them were up until all hours playing music, watching television or DVDs. The house had been suspiciously quiet all evening. Come to think of it, they'd been spending a lot of time in Lindsey's bedroom of late. Far too much time.

The girls glanced at each other before answering.

"You tell her," Brenda urged, "she's your mother."

"I know." Lindsey brushed back the long strands of hair. "But it might be a little easier coming from you."

"Lindsey?" Meg was more curious than ever now.

"You'd better sit down, Mom." Lindsey took Meg by the hand and guided her to the bed.

Meg sat on the edge. Both girls stood in front of her and each seemed to be waiting for the other to speak first.

"You're such an attractive woman," Lindsey began.

Meg frowned. This sounded like a setup to her, and the best way to handle that was to get straight to the point. "You need money? How much, and for what?"

With her usual flair for the dramatic, Lindsey rolled her eyes. "I don't need any money. I meant what I said—you're beautiful."

"It's true," Brenda piped up. "And you're only thirty-seven."

"I am?" Meg had to think about that. "Yeah, I guess I am."

"You're still so young."

"I wouldn't go that far…"

"You've still got it, Mrs. Remington," Brenda cut in, her voice intense. "You're young and pretty and single, and you've got *it*." Her fist flew through the air and punctuated the comment.

"Got what?" Meg was beginning to feel a bit confused.

"You're not in bad shape, either," Lindsey commented, resting her chin on one hand.

Meg sucked in her stomach, feeling pleased with the girls' assessment.

"Of course you'd look even better if you lost ten pounds," her daughter said thoughtfully.

Ten pounds. Meg breathed again and her stomach pouched out. Those ten pounds had first made their appearance when Meg was pregnant with Lindsey nearly sixteen years earlier. She was downright proud of having maintained her post-pregnancy weight for all these years.

"Ten pounds isn't too much to lose," Brenda said confidently.

"It won't be hard at all—especially with the two of us helping you."

Meg stared into their eager, expectant faces. "Why is it so important for me to lose ten pounds? I happen to like the way I look."

"There's more."

Meg glanced from one girl to the other. "More? What is that supposed to mean?"

"You need to be physically fit. Think about it, Mom. When's the last time you ran an eight-minute mile?"

Meg didn't need to consider that at all—she already knew the answer. "Never." She'd jogged around the track during high school, only because it was required of her. The lowest grade she'd ever received was in phys ed.

"See?" Lindsey said to Brenda.

"We'll work with her," Brenda answered. "But we'll have to start soon."

Lindsey crossed her arms and carefully scrutinized Meg. "About your clothes, Mom."

"My clothes?" Meg cried, still astonished that her daughter wanted her to run an eight-minute mile. She owned a bookstore, for heaven's sake. In the eight years since she'd bought out Mr. Olsen, not once had she been required to run for anything.

"I want to know what's going on here," Meg said. "Now."

"I promise we'll answer all your questions in a minute," Brenda explained. "Please be patient, Mrs. Remington."

Lindsey sighed. "Mom, I don't mean to be rude or anything, but when it comes to your clothes, well... you need help."

"Help?" And to think Meg had been dressing herself for the past thirty-some years. Until now, no one had bothered to tell her what a poor job she'd done.

"I'm here to see you don't ever wear high-waisted jeans again," Lindsey said, as though pledging her life to a crusade. "They're called mom jeans," she whispered.

"So you two are official members of the fashion police?" Meg asked. Apparently they'd issued an APB on her!

Lindsey and Brenda giggled.

"That's what it sounds like."

"We're here to help you," Brenda said in loving tones.

"We're here to keep you from committing those fashion sins."

"What sins?" Meg should've known. "Do you mind telling me what this little heart-to-heart is all about?"

"*You*, Mom," Lindsey said, in a voice that suggested the answer should've been obvious.

"Why now? Why me?"

"Why not?" Lindsey responded.

Meg started to get up, but Lindsey directed her back onto the bed. "We aren't finished yet. We're just getting to the good part."

"Honey, I appreciate what you're doing, but..."

"Sit down, Mom," Lindsey said in stern tones. "I haven't told you the most important thing yet."

Meg held up both hands. "Okay, okay."

"Like we already said, you're still young," Brenda began.

Lindsey smiled sweetly. "You could have more children if you wanted and—"

"Now wait a minute!" Meg cried.

"What we're really saying is that you're quite attractive."

"Or I could be," Meg amended, "with a little assistance from the two of you."

"Not all that much," Brenda added sympathetically. "We just want to get you started on the right track."

"I see," Meg muttered.

"Together," Lindsey said, slipping her arm around Brenda's waist and beaming a proud smile, "we're going to find you a husband."

"A husband." Meg's feet went out from under her and she slipped off the bed and landed with a solid whack on the carpet.

Lindsey and Brenda each grabbed one arm and pulled her off the floor. "Are you all right?" Lindsey asked, sounding genuinely concerned.

"You should've been more subtle," Brenda said accusingly. "There was no need to blurt it out like that."

Meg rubbed her rear end and sat back down on the bed. "What makes either of you think I want a husband?" she demanded angrily. She'd already been through one bad marriage and she wasn't eager to repeat the experience.

"When's the last time you went out on a date?" Lindsey asked.

"I don't remember," Meg snapped. "What does it matter, anyway?"

"Mother, it's clear to me you aren't thinking about the future."

"The future? What are you talking about?"

"Do you realize that in three years I'll be in college?"

"Three years," Meg repeated. "No-o, I guess I hadn't given it much thought." Although at the moment sending her daughter away actually seemed appealing.

"You'll be all alone."

"Alone isn't such a bad thing," Meg told them.

"At forty it is," Lindsey said dramatically. "I'll worry myself sick about you," she continued.

"She will," Brenda confirmed, nodding twice.

Meg figured it was a good thing she was sitting down.

"Tell me, Mother," Lindsey said, "what would it hurt to start dating again?"

"Honey, has it ever occurred to you that I'm happy just the way I am?"

"No," Lindsey returned. "You aren't happy. You're letting life pass you by. It's time to take action. I don't know what went wrong between you and Dad, but whatever it was must've been traumatic. You haven't had a relationship since—have you?"

Meg didn't answer that question, but wanted to reassure Lindsey about the break-up of her marriage. "It was a friendly divorce." In fact, Meg got along better with Dave now than she had when they were married.

Brenda shook her head. "There's no such thing as a friendly divorce. My dad's an attorney and he should know."

"I don't want to talk about the divorce," Meg said

in her sternest voice. "It happened a long time ago and bringing it up now isn't going to help anyone."

"It might help *you*," Lindsey said, her eyes intense, "but I can understand why you don't want to talk about it. Don't worry," she said, and a bright smile transformed her face, "because you're going to get all the help you need from Brenda and me."

"That's what I was afraid of." Meg stood up and moved toward the door.

"Your diet starts tomorrow," Lindsey called after her.

"And your exercise regime," Brenda added. "You haven't got a thing to worry about, Mrs. Remington. We're going to find you a man before you know it."

Meg closed her eyes. If thirty-seven was so young, why didn't she have the energy to stand up to these two? She wasn't going on any diet, nor did she have time for exercising.

As for having Lindsey as a wardrobe consultant... That was ridiculous, and Meg intended to tell her daughter and Brenda exactly that.

First thing in the morning.

Meg soon learned exactly how serious Lindsey and Brenda were about finding her a husband. She woke Saturday morning to the sound of a workout DVD playing loudly on the television in her bedroom.

She lay facedown, awakened from a pleasant dream about a sunny beach. Her arm hung over the side of the bed, her fingertips dangling an inch or so above the carpet.

"You ready, Mrs. Remington?" Brenda called from the doorway.

She tried to ignore the girl, but that didn't work.

"You ready?" Brenda called a second time. She seemed to be jogging in place. "Don't worry, we'll go nice and slow in the beginning."

"I'm not doing anything without speaking to my attorney first," Meg muttered. She stuck out her arm and searched blindly for the phone.

"Forget it, Mom. That isn't going to work." Lindsey walked into the bedroom and set a coffee mug on the nightstand.

"Bless you, my child," Meg said. "Ah, coffee." She'd struggled into a sitting position before she realized caffeine had nothing to do with whatever Lindsey had brought her. "What *is* this?" she barked.

"It's a protein supplement. The lady at the health food store recommends it for toning skin in women over thirty."

"Are you sure you're supposed to drink it?" Meg asked.

Lindsey and Brenda looked at each other blankly.

"I'd better check the instructions again," Lindsey said and carried it away.

"Don't worry, Mrs. Remington, we'll have you whipped into shape in no time."

"Coffee," she pleaded. She couldn't be expected to do anything, let alone exercise, without caffeine.

"You can have your coffee," Brenda promised her, "but first…"

Meg didn't bother to listen to the rest. She slithered back under the covers and pulled a pillow over her head. Although it did block out some of the noise, she had no trouble hearing the girls. They weren't accepting defeat lightly. They launched into a lively discussion about the pros and cons of allowing Meg to drink coffee. She had news for these two dictators. Let either one of them try to stand between her and her first cup of coffee.

The conversation moved to the topic of the divorce; Brenda apparently believed Meg had suffered psychological damage that had prevented her from pursuing another relationship.

It was all Meg could do not to shove the pillow aside and put in her two cents' worth. What she should've done was order them out of the bedroom, but she was actually curious to hear what they had to say.

Her divorce hadn't been as bad as all that. She and Dave had made the mistake of marrying far too young. Meg had been twenty-two when she'd had Lindsey, and Dave was fresh out of college. In the five years of their marriage there hadn't been any ugly fights or bitter disagreements. Maybe it would've helped if there had been.

By the time Lindsey was four, Dave had decided he didn't love Meg anymore and wanted a divorce. It shouldn't have come as a surprise, but it did—and it hurt. Meg suspected he'd found someone else.

She was right.

For a long time after the divorce was final, Meg tried to convince herself that her failed marriage didn't matter. She and her husband had parted on friendly terms. For Lindsey's sake, Meg had made sure they maintained an amicable relationship.

Dave had hurt her, though, and Meg had denied that pain for too long. Eventually she'd recovered. It was over now, and she was perfectly content with her life.

She'd started working at Book Ends, an independent bookstore, and then, with a loan from her parents she'd managed to buy it.

Between the bookstore and a fifteen-year-old daughter, Meg had little time for seeking out new relationships. The first few years after the divorce she'd had a number of opportunities to get involved with other men. She hadn't. At the time, Meg simply wasn't interested, and as the years went on, she'd stopped thinking about it.

"Mother, would you please get out of this bed," Lindsey said, standing over her. Then in enticing tones, she murmured, "I have coffee."

"You tricked me before."

"This one's real coffee. The other stuff, well, I apologize about that. I guess I misunderstood the lady at the health food store. You were right. According to the directions, you're supposed to use it in the bath, not drink it. Sorry about that."

Meg could see it wasn't going to do the least bit of good to hide her face under a pillow. "I can't buy my way out of this?" she asked.

"Nope."

"You'll feel much better after you exercise," Brenda promised her. "Really, you will."

An hour later, Meg didn't feel any such thing. She couldn't move without some part of her anatomy protesting.

"You did great, Mrs. Remington," Brenda praised.

Meg limped into her kitchen and slowly lowered herself into a chair. Who would've believed a workout DVD, followed by a short—this was the term the girls used—one-mile run, would reduce her to this.

In the past hour she'd been poked, prodded, pushed and punished.

"I've got your meals all planned out for you," Lindsey informed her. She opened the refrigerator door and took out a sandwich bag. She held it up for Meg's inspection. "This is your lunch."

Meg would've asked her about the meager contents if she'd had the breath to do so. All she could see was one radish, a square of cheese—low-fat, she presumed—and a small bunch of seedless grapes.

"Don't have any more than the nonfat yogurt for breakfast, okay?"

Meg nodded, rather than dredge up the energy to argue.

"Are you going to tell her about dinner?" Brenda asked.

"Oh, yeah. Listen, Mom, you've been a real trouper about this and we thought we should reward you. Tonight for dinner you can have a baked potato."

She managed a weak smile. Visions of butter and sour cream waltzed through her head.

"With fresh grilled fish."

"You like fish, don't you, Mrs. Remington?"

Meg nodded. At this point she would've agreed to anything just to get the girls out of her kitchen, so she could recover enough to cook herself a decent breakfast.

"Brenda and I are going shopping," Lindsey announced. "We're going to pick out a whole new wardrobe for you, Mom."

"It's the craziest thing," Meg told her best friend, Laura Harrison, that same afternoon. They were unpacking boxes of books in the back room. "All of a sudden, Lindsey said she wants me to remarry."

"Really?"

Laura found this far too humorous to suit Meg. "But she wants me to lose ten pounds and run an eight-minute mile first."

"Oh, I get it now," Laura muttered, taking paperbacks from the shipping carton and placing them on a cart.

"What?"

"Lindsey was in the store a couple of weeks ago looking for a book that explained carbs and fat grams."

"I'm allowed thirty fat grams a day," Meg informed her. "And one hundred grams of carbohydrates." Not that her fifteen-year-old daughter was going to dictate what she did and didn't eat.

"I hope Lindsey doesn't find out about that submarine sandwich you had for lunch."

"I couldn't help it," Meg said. "I haven't been that hungry in years. I don't think anyone bothered to tell Lindsey and Brenda that one of the effects of a workout is a voracious appetite."

"What was that phone call about earlier?" Laura asked.

Meg frowned as she moved books onto the cart. "Lindsey wanted my credit card number for a slinky black dress with a scoop neckline." Lindsey had sounded rapturous over the dress, describing it in detail, especially the deep cuts up the sides that would reveal plenty of thigh. "She said she found it on sale— and it was a deal too good to pass up." She paused. "Needless to say, I told her no."

"What would Lindsey want with a slinky black dress?"

"She wanted it for me," Meg said, under her breath.

"You?"

"Apparently once I fit the proper image, they plan to dress me up and escort me around town."

Laura laughed.

"I'm beginning to think you might not be such a good friend after all," Meg told her employee. "I expected sympathy and advice, not laughter."

"I'm sorry, Meg. Really."

She sounded far more amused than she did sorry.

Meg cast her a disgruntled look. "You know what your problem is, don't you?"

"Yes," Laura was quick to tell her. "I'm married, with college-age children. I don't have to put up with any of this nonsense and you do. Wait, my dear, until Lindsey gets her driver's license. *Then* you'll know what real fear is."

"One disaster at a time, thank you." Meg sat on a stool and reached for her coffee cup. "I don't mind telling you I'm worried about all this."

"Why?" Laura straightened and picked up her own cup, refilling it from the freshly brewed pot. "It's a stage Lindsey's going through. Trust me, it'll pass."

"Lindsey keeps insisting I'll be lonely when she leaves for college, which she reminded me is in three years."

"Will you be?"

Meg had to think about that. "I don't know. I suppose in some ways I will be. The house will feel empty without her." The two weeks Lindsey spent with her father every year seemed interminable. Meg wandered around the house like a lost puppy.

"So, why *not* get involved in another relationship?" Laura asked.

"With whom?" was Meg's first question. "I don't know any single men."

"Sure you do," Laura countered. "There's Ed, who has the insurance office two doors down."

"Ed's single?" She rather liked Ed. He seemed like a decent guy, but she'd never thought of him in terms of dating.

"The fact that you didn't know Ed was single says a lot. You've got to keep your eyes and ears open."

"Who else?"

"Buck's divorced."

Buck was a regular customer, and although she couldn't quite understand why, Meg had never cared for him. "I wouldn't go out with Buck."

"I didn't say you had to go out with him, I just said he was single."

Meg couldn't see herself kissing either man. "Anyone else?"

"There are lots of men out there."

"Oh, really, and I'm blind?"

"Yes," Laura said. "If you want the truth, I don't think Lindsey's idea is so bad. True, she may be going about it the wrong way, but it wouldn't hurt you to test the waters. You might be surprised at what you find."

Meg sighed. She'd expected support from her best friend, and instead Laura had turned traitor.

By the time Meg had closed the bookstore and headed home, she was exhausted. So much for all those claims about exercise generating energy. In her experience, it did the reverse.

"Lindsey," she called out, "are you home?"

"I'm in my room," came the muffled reply from the bedroom at the top of the stairs.

Something she couldn't put her finger on prompted Meg to hurry upstairs to her daughter's bedroom despite her aching muscles. She knocked once and opened the door to see Lindsey and Brenda sitting on the bed, leafing through a stack of letters.

Lindsey hid the one she was reading behind her back. "Mom?" she said, her eyes wide. "Hi."

"Hello."

"Hello, Mrs. Remington," Brenda said, looking decidedly guilty.

It was then that Meg saw the black dress hanging from the closet door. It was the most provocative thing she'd seen in years.

"How'd you get the dress?" Meg demanded, angry that Lindsey had gone against her wishes and wondering how she'd managed to do it.

The two girls stared at each other, neither one eager to give her an answer. "Brenda phoned her mother and she put it on her credit card," Lindsey said at last.

"What?" Meg felt ready to explode.

"It was only a small lie," Brenda said quickly. "I told my mom it was perfect and on sale and too cheap to resist. What I didn't tell her was that the dress wasn't for me."

"It's going back right this minute, and then the three of us are paying Brenda's parents a visit."

"Mom!" Lindsey flew off the bed. "Wait, please." She had a panicked look in her eyes. "What we did was wrong, but when you wouldn't agree to buy the dress yourself, we didn't know what to do. You just don't have anything appropriate for Chez Michelle."

Chez Michelle was one of the most exclusive restaurants in Seattle, with a reputation for excellent French cuisine. Meg had never eaten there herself, but Laura and her husband had celebrated their silver wedding anniversary at Chez Michelle and raved about it for weeks afterward.

"You're not making any sense," Meg told her daughter.

Lindsey bit her lip and nodded.

"You have to tell her," Brenda insisted.

"Tell me what?"

"You're the one who wrote the last letter," Lindsey said. "The least you could've done was get the dates right."

"It's tonight."

"I know," Lindsey snapped.

"Would someone tell me what's going on here?" Meg asked, her patience at its end.

"You need that dress, Mom," Lindsey said in a voice so low Meg had to strain to hear her.

"And why would that be?"

"You have a dinner date."

"I do? And just who am I going out with?" She assumed this had something to do with Chez Michelle.

"Steve Conlan."

"Steve Conlan?" Meg repeated. She said it again, looking for something remotely familiar about the name and finding nothing,

"You don't know him," Lindsey told her. "But he's really nice. Brenda and I both like him." She glanced at her friend for confirmation and Brenda nodded eagerly.

"You've met him?" Meg didn't like the sound of this.

"Not really. We exchanged a couple of letters and then we e-mailed back and forth and he seems like a really great guy." The last part was said with forced enthusiasm.

"You've been writing a strange man."

"He's not so strange, Mom, not really. He sounds just like one of us."

"He wants to meet you," Brenda put in.

"Me?" Meg brought her hand to her throat. "Why would he want to do that?"

The girls shared a look, reminiscent of the one she'd caught the night before.

"Lindsey?" Meg asked. "Why would this man want to meet me?"

Her daughter lowered her eyes, refusing to meet Mcg's. "Because when we wrote Steve…"

"Yes?"

"Brenda and I told him we were you."

Chapter 2

Steve Conlan glanced at his watch. The time hadn't changed since he'd looked before. He could tell it was going to be one of those nights. He had the distinct feeling it would drag by, one interminable minute after another.

He still hadn't figured how he'd gotten himself into this mess. He was minding his own business and the next thing he knew… He didn't want to think about it, because whenever he did his blood pressure rose.

Nancy was going to pay for this.

He was early, not because he was so eager for tonight. No, he was only eager to get it over with.

He tried not to check the time and failed. A minute had passed. Or was it a lifetime?

His necktie felt as if it would strangle him. A tie. He couldn't believe he'd let Nancy talk him into wearing a stupid tie.

Because he needed something to occupy his time, he took the snapshot out of his shirt pocket.

Meg Remington.

She had a nice face, he decided. Nothing spectacular. She certainly wasn't drop-dead gorgeous, but she wasn't plain, either. Her eyes were her best feature. Clear. Bright. Expressive. She had a cute mouth, too. Very kissable. Sensuous.

What was he supposed to say to the woman? The hell if he knew. He'd read her letters and e-mails a dozen times. She sounded—he hated to say it—immature, as if she felt the need to impress him. She seemed to think that because she ran an eight-minute mile it qualified her for the Olympics. Frankly, he wondered what their dinner would be like, with her being so food conscious and all. She'd actually bragged about how few fat grams and carbs she consumed. Clearly she wasn't familiar with the menu at Chez Michelle. He couldn't see a single low-fat or low-carb entrée.

That was another thing. The woman had expensive tastes. Dinner at Chez Michelle would set him back three hundred bucks—if he was lucky. So far he'd been anything but...

Involuntarily his gaze fell to his watch again, and he groaned inwardly. His sister owed him for this.

Big-time.

"I refuse to meet a strange man for dinner," Meg insisted coldly. There were some things even a mother wouldn't do.

"But you have to," Brenda pleaded. "I'm sorry, Mrs. Remington, I feel really bad springing this on you, but Steve didn't do anything wrong. You've just *got* to show up. You have to…otherwise he might lose faith in all women."

"So?"

"But he's your date," Lindsey said. "It would've worked out great if—" she paused and scowled at her best friend "—if one of us hadn't gotten the days mixed up."

"Exactly when did you plan on telling me you've been communicating with a strange man, using *my* name?"

"Soon," Lindsey said with conviction. "We had to… He started asking about meeting you almost right away. We did everything we could to hold him off. Oh, by the way, if he asks about your appendix, you've made a full recovery."

Meg groaned. The time frame of their deception wasn't what interested her. She was stalling, looking for a way out of this. She could leave a message for Steve at the restaurant, explaining that she couldn't make it, but that seemed like such a cowardly thing to do.

Unfortunately no escape plan presented itself. Brenda was right; it wasn't Steve's fault that he'd been duped by a pair of teenagers. It wasn't her fault, either, but then Lindsey was her daughter.

"He's very nice-looking," Brenda said. She reached behind her and pulled out a picture from one of the envelopes scattered across Lindsey's bed. "Here, see what I mean?" Meg swore she heard the girl sigh. "He's got blue eyes and check out his smile."

Meg took the photo from Brenda and studied it. Her daughter's friend was right. Steve Conlan was pleasant-looking. His hair was a little long, but that didn't bother her. He wore a cowboy hat and boots and had his thumbs tucked into his hip pockets as he stared into the camera.

"He's tall, dark and *lonesome*," Lindsey said wistfully.

"Has he ever been married?" Meg asked, curiosity getting the better of her.

"Nope." This time it was Brenda who supplied the information. "He's got his own business, same as you, Mrs. Remington. He owns a body shop and he's been sinking every penny into it."

"What made him place the ad?" she asked the girls. A sudden thought came to her. "He *is* the one who advertised, isn't he?"

Both girls looked away and Meg's heart froze. "You mean to say you two advertised for a husband for me?" She spoke slowly, each word distinct.

"We got lots of letters, too," Brenda said proudly. "We went through them all and chose Steve Conlan."

"Don't you want to know why?" Lindsey prodded.

Meg gestured weakly, still too shocked to react.

"Steve says he decided to answer your ad because one day he woke up and realized life was passing him by. All his friends were married, and he felt like something important was missing in his life. Then he knew it wasn't *something* but someone."

"What about female friends?" Meg asked, thinking he didn't look like a man who'd have to find companionship in the classifieds.

"He said in his letter that..." Lindsey paused and rustled through a sheaf of papers, searching for the right envelope. "Here it is," she muttered. "He doesn't have much opportunity to meet single women unless they've been in an accident, and generally they're not in the mood for romance when they're dealing with a body shop and an insurance company." Lindsey grinned. "He's kind of witty. I like that about him."

"He said a lot of women his age have already been married and divorced and had a passel of kids."

This didn't sound too promising to Meg. "You did happen to mention that I'm divorced, too, didn't you?"

"Of course," Lindsey insisted. "We'd never lie."

Meg bit her tongue to keep from saying the obvious.

"Just think," Brenda said, "out of all the women who advertised, Steve chose you and we chose him. It's destiny."

The girls thought she'd feel complimented, but Meg was suspicious. "Surely there was someone younger and prettier, without children, who interested him."

The two girls exchanged a smile. "He liked the fact that you count carbs and fat grams," Brenda said proudly.

So much for their unwillingness to stretch the truth. "You actually told him that?" She closed her eyes and groaned. "What else did you say?"

"Just that you're really wonderful."

"Heroic," Brenda added. "And you are."

Oh, great. They'd made her sound like a thin Joan of Arc.

"You will meet him, won't you?" Lindsey's dark eyes pleaded with Meg.

"What I should do is march the two of you down to that fancy restaurant and have you personally apologize to him. You both deserve to be grounded until you're forty."

The girls blinked in unison. "But, Mom..."

"Mrs. Remington…"

Meg raised her hand and stopped them. "I won't take you to Chez Michelle, and as for the grounding part…we'll discuss it later."

Two pairs of shoulders sagged with relief.

"But I won't have dinner with Steve Conlan," she said emphatically. "I'll go to the restaurant, introduce myself and explain what happened. I'm sure he'll agree that the best thing to do is skip dinner altogether."

"You'll wear the dress, won't you?" Lindsey asked, eyeing the slinky black concoction hanging outside her closet door.

"Absolutely not," Meg said. She refused to even consider it.

"But you don't have anything special enough for Chez Michelle. Just try it on, Mom."

"No. Well…"

"Come on, Mom. Brenda and I want to see how it looks."

An hour later Meg pulled up at Chez Michelle in the very dress she'd sworn she'd never wear. It fit as if it'd been designed just for her, enhancing her figure and camouflaging those stubborn ten pounds. At least that was what Lindsey and Brenda told her.

"Hello." The hostess greeted her with a wide smile. "Table for one?"

"I'm…meeting someone," Meg said, glancing around the waiting area looking for a man who resembled "tall, dark and lonesome" in the photo. No one did. Nor was there a single male wearing a cowboy hat.

The only man who looked vaguely like the one in the photograph stood in the corner of the room, leaning indolently against the wall as if he had all the time in the world.

He straightened and stared at her.

Meg stared back.

He reached inside his suit pocket and took out a picture.

Meg opened the clasp of her purse and removed the photo the girls had given her. She looked down at it and then up again.

He appeared to be doing the same thing.

"Meg Remington?" he asked uncertainly.

She nodded. "Steve Conlan?"

He nodded, too.

He wore a suit and tie. A suit and tie. The guy had really gone all out for her. Meg swallowed uncomfortably. He'd invited her to this ultrafancy restaurant expecting to meet the woman who'd exchanged those letters and messages with him. Meg felt her heart settle somewhere in the vicinity of her knees. She couldn't very well introduce herself and immediately say it had all been a mistake and cancel dinner. Not when he'd gone to so much trouble.

"I believe our table is ready," Steve said, holding out his arm to her. His hand touched her elbow and he addressed the hostess. "We can be seated now."

The woman gave him an odd look, then picked up two huge menus. "This way."

Meg might've been wrong, but she thought she heard some reluctance in his voice. Perhaps she was a disappointment to Steve Conlan. After the fitness drill Lindsey and Brenda had put her through, Meg was feeling her advancing age.

Pride stiffened Meg's shoulders. So she hadn't

signed any modeling contracts lately. What did he expect from a thirty-seven-year-old woman? If he wanted to date a woman in her twenties, he shouldn't have answered her ad. Lindsey's ad, she corrected. It was all Meg could do not to stop Steve Conlan right then and there and tell him this was as good as it got.

Especially in this dress. It was simply gorgeous. Meg knew now the girls had made the perfect choice. She was glad she'd given in to them on this one. Besides, Lindsey was right; she didn't own anything fancy enough for Chez Michelle. Before she could stop herself she'd agreed to wear it. Soon both girls were offering her fashion advice.

They were escorted to a linen-covered table next to the window, which overlooked Elliott Bay and Puget Sound. The moon's reflection on the water sent gilded light across the surface, and the restaurant's interior was dimly lit.

Meg squinted, barely able to read her menu. She wondered if Steve was having the same problem. Originally she hadn't intended to have dinner with him. Wouldn't even now, if he hadn't gone to so much trouble on her behalf. It seemed crass to drop in, announce it had all been a misguided attempt by her daughter to play matchmaker, ask his forgiveness and speedily disappear.

"I believe I'll have the chicken cordon bleu," she said, deciding on the least expensive item on the menu. "And please, I insist on paying for my own meal." It would be unforgivable to gouge him for that, as well.

"Dinner's on me," Steve insisted, setting his menu aside. He smiled for the first time and it transformed his face. He studied her, as if he wasn't sure what to make of her.

"But..." Meg lowered her gaze and closed her mouth. She didn't know where to start and yet she didn't know how much longer she could maintain the pretense. "This is all very elegant..."

"Yes," he agreed, spinning the stem of his water glass between his thumb and index finger.

"You look different than your picture." Meg had no idea why she'd told him that. What she *should* be doing was explaining about Lindsey and Brenda.

"How's that?"

"Your eyes are much bluer and you've cut your hair."

He gave a slight grin. "And your picture didn't do you justice."

Meg hadn't thought to ask Lindsey which one she'd mailed Steve. "Can I see?"

"Sure." He pulled it out of his pocket and handed it over.

Meg took one look and rolled her eyes. She couldn't believe Lindsey had sent this particular photograph to anyone. It'd been taken just before Christmas a year earlier. She was standing in front of the Christmas tree wearing a white dress that drained all the color from her face. The flash from the camera made her eyes appear red. She looked like she was recovering from a serious ailment.

"This is one of the worst pictures ever taken of me," she said impatiently. "The one of me at the bookstore is *much* better."

Steve's brow creased with a frown. "I see. You should've sent that one."

Meg realized what she'd said too late. "You're right, I should have… How silly of me."

The waitress came and they placed their orders, both declining a drink, Meg to keep down the cost and Steve, no doubt, to hurry the meal along.

Once the server had left the table, Meg carefully smoothed the napkin across her lap. "Listen, Steve…"

"Meg…"

They both stopped.

"You go first," he said, gesturing toward her.

"All right." She cocked her head to one side and then the other, going over the words in her mind. "This isn't easy…"

Steve frowned. "It's been a pleasure to meet me, but the chemistry just isn't there and you'd like to let me down gently and be done with it."

"No!" she hurried to assure him.

"Oh."

The disappointment in his tone came as a mild shock. Then she understood. "You…expected a different kind of woman and—"

"Not in the least. If the truth be known, I'm pleasantly surprised."

She swallowed. "I wish you hadn't said that."

"Why not?"

"Because…" She dragged in a deep breath. "Because I'm not the person you think I am. I mean…" This was proving even more difficult than it should have. "I didn't write those letters."

Steve's eyes narrowed. "Then who did?"

"My daughter and her friend."

"I…see."

Meg's fingers crushed the linen napkin in her lap.

"You have every reason to be upset. It was an underhanded thing to do to us both."

"You didn't know anything about this?"

"I swear I didn't. I would've put a stop to it immediately if I had."

Steve reached for his water and drank thirstily. "I would have, too."

"I want you to know I intend to discipline Lindsey for this. I can only apologize…" She stopped midsentence when she saw his shoulders moving with suppressed laughter. "Steve?"

"I didn't write those letters, either. The ones from me."

"What?" Disbelief settled over Meg. "You mean to say you didn't respond to the ad in Dateline?"

"Nope. My romantic little sister did. Nancy's on this kick about seeing me married. I don't understand it, but—"

"Just a minute," Meg said, raising her hand. "Let me see if I've got this straight. You didn't respond to the ad in Dateline."

"You've got it."

"Then why are you here?"

He shrugged. "Probably for the same reason you are. I figured you were some lonely heart seeking companionship and frankly I felt bad that Nancy had led you on like this. It isn't your fault my crazy sister thinks it's time I got married."

He paused when their meals were delivered.

Meg dug into her chicken with gusto. Irritation usually made her hungry. She stabbed a carrot slice with her fork.

"So you felt sorry for me?" she said, chewing the carrot vigorously.

He looked up, apparently sensing her irritation. "No sorrier than you felt for me."

He had her there.

"It's the reason you showed up, isn't it?" he pressed.

She agreed with a nod. "When did you find out about this dinner date?"

"This morning. You?"

She glanced at her watch. "About two hours ago."

Steve chuckled. "They didn't give you much opportunity to object, did they?"

"Actually they got the days mixed up and went into a panic. I don't suppose you happened to read any of the letters or e-mails they wrote?"

"As a matter of fact I did. Interesting stuff."

"I'll bet." She stabbed one of the potato pieces with her fork. "You should know that not everything they said was the truth." She put the potato in her mouth and chewed.

"So you don't actually run an eight-minute mile."

"No…"

"Nine minutes?"

"I don't exactly run, and before you ask me about carbs and fat grams, you can forget everything Lindsey told you about those, too. And for the record, my appendix is in great shape."

Steve chuckled. "What did Nancy tell you about me?"

"Since I've only read tidbits of your letters and e-mails, I can't really say."

"Oh?" His voice fell noticeably.

"As I recall, your sister did suggest that your life's

quite empty and you're looking for something to fill your lonely nights—" she paused for effect "—until you realized it wasn't *something* you were searching for but *someone*."

His jaw tightened. "She said that?"

"Yup." Meg took some pleasure in telling him that.

"Well, that's a crock of bull. I certainly hope you didn't believe it."

Meg smiled. "Not really. Lindsey didn't mean any harm, you know."

"Nancy, either, although I'd like to throttle her. The kid's nineteen and she's got romance and marriage on her mind. Unfortunately, it's me she's trying to marry off."

"Lindsey thinks I'm lost and lonely, but I'm perfectly content with my life."

"Me, too."

"Why ruin everything now?"

"Exactly," Steve agreed with conviction. "A woman would want to change everything about me."

"A man would string me along until he found someone prettier and sexier. Besides," Meg added, "I have no intention of becoming a pawn in some ploy of my daughter's."

"Nancy can take a flying leap into Green Lake before I'll let her arrange my love life," Steve told her adamantly. "I certainly intend to marry, but on *my* time—not when my kid sister ropes me into a lonely-hearts-club relationship."

"I feel the same way."

"Great." Steve grinned at her, and Meg had to admit he had a wonderful smile. It lit up his eyes and softened his features. "Shall we drink to our agreement?"

"Definitely."

Steve attracted the waitress's attention and ordered a bottle of wine.

Meg was astonished by the ease with which they could talk, once all the pretense between them had been resolved. She told him about her bookstore and liked hearing about his body shop. They lingered over coffee and dessert, and not until it became apparent that the restaurant was about to close did they get up to leave.

"I enjoyed myself," Meg said as they strolled to the door.

"Don't sound so surprised."

"Frankly, I am."

He laughed. "I guess I am, too."

The valet brought her Ford Escort to the front of the restaurant and held open her door.

"Thank you for a lovely dinner," she said, suddenly feeling shy and awkward.

"The pleasure was all mine."

Neither of them made an effort to move. The valet checked his watch and Meg glanced at him guiltily. Steve ignored him and eventually so did Meg.

"I guess this is goodbye," she said, wishing now that she hadn't made such a big issue about not being her daughter's pawn.

"Looks that way."

She lowered her eyes, fighting the enticement she read in his. "Thanks again."

Steve traced his finger along her jaw. His work-calloused fingertip felt warm against her skin. If they hadn't been standing under the lights of a fancy French restaurant with a valet looking on, Meg wondered if he would've kissed her. She wanted to think he might have.

On the drive home, she dismissed the idea as fanciful. It had been a long time since she'd been wined and dined, that was all. And an even longer time since she'd been kissed...

Sensation after sensation traveled across her face where he'd touched her. Smile after smile flirted with her mouth at the memory of his lips so close to hers. She wouldn't forget the date or the man anytime soon. That was for sure.

"Well, how'd it go?" Nancy demanded. His teenage sister met Steve at the door. Her eyes were wide with curiosity as she followed him inside.

Steve looked at his watch and frowned. "What are you still doing up?"

Nancy's face fell. "You asked me to wait for you, so we could talk."

Steve slid his fingers through his hair. "I did, didn't I?"

"You're much later than you thought you'd be."

He didn't respond, unwilling to let his sister know how much he'd enjoyed himself. "I'm furious with you for what you did," he said, forcing his voice to sound gruff with irritation.

"I don't blame you," she agreed readily enough.

"Haven't you got an exam to study for or something?" he asked, although he knew very well she didn't. Nancy attended the nearby University of Washington. She was staying with Steve for the summer, since their parents were now living in Montana.

"You liked her, didn't you?"

Nancy sounded much too smug to suit Steve.

"And no, I don't have any exams to study for, and you know it. They ended two weeks ago." Since then, she'd taken a summer job at the university library.

"So you've decided to stay in Seattle and make my life miserable."

"No, I've decided to stay in Seattle and see you married. Come on, Steve, you're thirty-eight! That's getting up there." She flopped down on the sofa and sat with her legs underneath her, as if she planned to plant herself right there until he announced his engagement.

The problem, Steve decided, was that Nancy was the product of parents who'd never expected a second child and had spoiled her senseless. He was partially to blame, as well, but he'd never thought she'd pull something like this.

"You work too hard," she said. "Loosen up and enjoy life a little."

"You're going to write Meg Remington a formal letter of apology." He refused to back down on this.

"Okay, I'll write her." All at once she was on her feet. "When are you seeing her again?"

"I'm not."

Nancy fell back onto the sofa. "Why not?"

Darned if Steve could give her an answer. He and Meg had made that decision early on in their conversation, and for the life of him he couldn't remember why.

"Because," he growled. "Now leave me alone."

Nancy threw back her head and laughed. "You like her. You really, really like her."

Meg sat in the back storeroom and rubbed her aching feet. The new shoes pinched her toes, but this was what she got for buying them half a size too small. They were on sale and she loved them, although the store had been out of size eights. Even knowing her feet would pay the penalty later, Meg had chosen to wear them today.

Laura stuck her head through the door and smiled when she saw her. "A beautiful bouquet of flowers just arrived for you," she said.

"For me?"

"That's what the envelope said."

"Who from?"

"I didn't read the card, if that's what you're asking, but Lindsey's here and she grabbed it and let out a holler. My guess is the flowers are from Steve."

"Steve." Pain or no pain, Meg was on her feet. She hobbled to the front of the store and found her fifteen-year-old daughter grinning triumphantly.

"Steve Conlan sent flowers," she crowed.

"So I see." Meg's fingers shook as she removed the card from the small envelope.

"He said, and I quote, 'You're one special woman, Meg Remington. Love, Steve.'"

The bouquet was huge, with at least ten different varieties of flowers all arranged in a white wicker basket. It must have cost him easily a hundred dollars.

"We agreed," she whispered.

"Agreed to what?" Lindsey prodded.

"That we weren't going to see each other again."

"Obviously he changed his mind," Lindsey said, as excited as if she'd just discovered a twenty-dollar bill in the bottom of her purse.

Unwilling to trust her daughter's assessment of the situation, Meg stared at her best friend.

"Don't look at me," Laura said.

"I'm sure you're wrong," Meg said to Lindsey, her heart still beating a little too fast.

"Why else would he send flowers?" Lindsey asked calmly.

"He wanted to say he was glad we met, that's all. I don't think we should make something out of this," she said. "It's just…a courtesy."

"Call him," Lindsey pleaded.

"I most certainly will not!"

"But, Mom, don't you see? Steve's saying he likes you, but he doesn't want to pressure you into anything unless you like him, too."

"He is?" Whatever confidence she'd felt a moment earlier vanished like ice cream at a Fourth of July picnic.

"The next move is yours."

"Laura?"

"I wouldn't know," her fickle friend said. "I've been married to the same man for twenty-six years. All this intrigue is beyond me."

"I agree with your daughter," a shy voice said from the other side of the counter. "You should call him."

It was Meg's customer, Judith Wilson. Meg wasn't sure she should listen to the older woman who faithfully purchased romance novels twice a month. Judith was a real romantic and would undoubtedly read more into the gesture than Steve had intended.

"See?" Lindsey said excitedly. "The ball's in your court. Steve made his move and now he's waiting for yours."

Meg didn't know what to do.

"It's been three days," Lindsey reminded her. "He's had time to think over the situation, and so have you."

"Call him," Laura suggested. "If for nothing more than to thank him for the flowers."

"Yes, call him," Judith echoed, clutching her bag of books.

"It's the least you can do." Once more it was her daughter offering advice.

"All right," Meg said reluctantly. The flowers were gorgeous, and thanking him would be the proper thing to do.

"I'll get his work number for you," Lindsey volunteered, pulling the Yellow Pages from behind the cash register.

The kid had Steve's shop number faster than directory assistance could have located it.

"I'll use the phone in the back room," Meg said. She didn't need several pairs of ears listening in on her conversation.

She felt everyone's eyes on her as she hurried into the storeroom. Her hand actually shook as she punched out the telephone number.

"Emerald City," a gruff male voice answered.

"Hello, this is Meg Remington calling for Steve Conlan."

"Hold on a minute."

"Of course."

A moment later, Steve was on the line. "Meg?"

"Hello, Steve. I know you're busy, so I won't take up much of your time. I'm calling to thank you for the flowers."

A long pause followed her words. "Flowers? What flowers?"

Chapter 3

"You mean you don't know anything about these flowers?" Meg cried, her voice raised. Steve could see that he hadn't done a very good job of breaking the news, but he was as shocked as she was.

"If you didn't send them, who did?" Meg demanded.

It wasn't difficult to figure that one out. "I can make a wild guess," he said with heavy sarcasm. He jerked his fingers through his hair, then glanced at the wall clock. It was close to quitting time. "Can you meet me?"

"Why?"

Her blatant lack of enthusiasm irritated him. He'd been thinking about her for three days. Nancy was right—he liked Meg Remington. She was a bit eccentric and a little on the hysterical side, but he was willing to overlook that. During their time together, he'd been struck by her intelligence and her warmth. He'd wished more than once that they'd decided to ignore the way they'd been thrown together and continue to see each other. Apparently Meg suffered no such regrets and was pleased to be rid of him.

"Why do you want to meet?" she repeated, lowering her voice.

"We need to talk."

"Where?"

"How about a drink? Can you get away from the store in the next hour or so?"

She hesitated. "I'll try."

Steve mentioned a popular sports bar in Kent, and she agreed to meet him there at five-thirty. His spirits lifted considerably at the prospect of seeing her again. He must've been smiling as he hung up because his foreman, Gary Wilcox, cast him a puzzled look.

"I didn't know you had yourself a new girlfriend," Gary said. "When did this happen?"

"It hasn't." The last thing Steve needed was Gary feeding false information to his sister. Nancy and her outrageous ideas about marrying him off was enough of a problem, without Gary encouraging it.

"It hasn't happened *yet*, you mean," Gary said, making a notation in the appointment schedule.

Steve glanced over his shoulder, to be sure Gary wasn't making notes about the conversation he'd had with Meg. He was getting paranoid already. A woman did that to a man, made him jumpy and insecure; he knew that much from past experience.

An hour later Steve sat in the bar, facing a big-screen television with a frosty mug of beer in his hand.

The table he'd chosen was in the far corner of the room, where he could easily watch the front door.

Meg walked in ten minutes after him. At least Steve thought it was Meg. The woman carried a tennis racket and wore one of those cute little pleated-skirt outfits. He hadn't realized Meg played tennis. He knew she didn't run and disliked exercise, but...

Steve squinted and stared, unsure. After all, he'd only seen her the one time, and in the slinky black dress she'd looked a whole lot different.

Meg solved his problem when she apparently recognized him. She walked across the room, and he noticed that she was limping. She slid into the chair beside him, then set the tennis racket on the table.

"Lindsey knows," she announced.

Steve's head went back to study her. "I beg your pardon?"

"My daughter figured it out."

"Figured what out?"

"That I was meeting you," she said in exasperated tones. "First, I called you from the back room at the store, so our conversation could be private."

"So?"

She glared at him. "Then I made up this ridiculous story about a tennis game I'd forgotten. I haven't played tennis in years and Lindsey knows that. She immediately had all these questions. She saw straight through me." She pulled the sweatband from her hair and stuffed it in her purse. "She's probably home right now laughing her head off. I can't do this... I could never lie convincingly."

"Why didn't you just tell your daughter the truth?" He was puzzled by the need to lie at all.

Meg's look of consternation said that would've been impossible. "Well…because Lindsey would think the two of us meeting meant something."

"Why? You told her I didn't write those letters and e-mails, didn't you?"

"No."

"Why not?"

Meg played with the worn strings of the tennis racket as her eyes avoided his. "I should have… I mean, this is crazy."

"You can say that again." He tried to sound nonchalant and wondered if he'd managed it. He didn't think so. He was actually rather amused by the whole setup. Her daughter and his sister. The girls were close in age and obviously spoke the same language.

"Lindsey's still got romantic ideas when it comes to men and marriage, but…" Meg paused and chanced a look at him. "She really stepped over the line with this stunt."

"What did you say about our date?"

Meg's hands returned to the tennis racket. "Not much."

Steve hadn't been willing to discuss the details of their evening together with Nancy, either. Nothing had surprised him more than discovering how attractive he'd found Meg Remington. It wasn't solely a sexual attraction, although she certainly appealed to him.

Whenever he'd thought about her in the past three days, he'd remember how they'd talked nonstop over wine and dessert. He remembered how absorbed she'd been in what he was saying; at one point she'd leaned forward and then realized her dress revealed a fair bit of cleavage. Red-faced, she'd pulled back and attempted to adjust her bodice.

Steve liked the way her eyes brightened when she spoke about her bookstore and her daughter, and the way she had of holding her breath when she was excited about something, as if she'd forgotten to breathe.

"Your sister—the one who wrote the letters—is the same one who sent the flowers?" Meg asked, breaking into his thoughts.

Steve nodded. "I'd bet on it."

Meg fiddled with the clasp of her purse and brought out a small card, which she handed him.

Steve raised his arm to attract the cocktail waitress's attention and indicate he wanted another beer for Meg.

"I shouldn't," she said, reaching for a pretzel. "If I come home with beer on my breath, Lindsey will know for sure I wasn't playing tennis."

"According to you, she's already figured it out."

She slid the bowl of pretzels closer and grabbed another handful. "That's true."

Steve opened the card that had come with the flowers and rolled his eyes. "This is from Nancy, all right," he muttered. "I'd never write anything this hokey."

The waitress came with another mug of beer and Steve paid for it. "Do you want more pretzels?" he asked Meg.

"Please." Then in a lower voice, she added, "This type of situation always makes me hungry."

She licked the salt from her fingertips. "Has my daughter, Lindsey, been in contact with you?"

"No, but then I wouldn't know, would I?"

Meg was holding the pretzel in front of her mouth. "Why wouldn't you?"

"Because Lindsey would be writing to Nancy."

Meg's head dropped in a gesture of defeat. "You're right. Much more of this craziness and heaven only knows what they could do to our lives."

"We need to take control," Steve said.

"I totally agree with you," was her response. She took a sip of her beer and set the mug down. "I shouldn't be drinking this on an empty stomach—it'll go straight to my head."

"The bar's got great sandwiches."

"Pretzels are fine." Apparently she'd realized that she was holding the bowl, and she shoved it back to the center of the table. "Sorry," she muttered.

"No problem."

He saw her wince and recalled that she'd been limping earlier. "Is there something wrong with your foot?"

"The shoes I wore to work were too tight," she said, speaking so quietly he had to strain to hear.

"Here," he said, reaching under the table for her feet and setting them on his lap.

"What are you doing?" she asked in a shocked voice.

"I thought I'd rub them for you."

"You'd do that?"

"Yes." It didn't seem so odd to him. The fact was, he hated to see her in pain. "Besides, we need to talk over how we're going to handle this situation. I have a feeling that we'll have to be in top mental form to deal with these kids."

"You're right." She closed her eyes and purred like

a well-fed kitten when he removed her tennis shoes and kneaded her aching feet.

"Feel better?" he asked after a couple of minutes.

She nodded, her eyes still closed. "I think you should stop," she said, sounding completely unconvincing.

"Why?" He asked the question, but he stopped and bent down to pick up her shoes, which he'd placed on the floor.

"Thank you," Meg said. She looked around a little self-consciously as she slipped her shoes back on and tied the laces.

Feeling somewhat embarrassed by his uncharacteristic response to her, Steve cleared his throat and picked up his beer. "Do you have any ideas?" he asked.

She stared at him as if she didn't know what he was talking about, then straightened abruptly. "Oh, you mean for dealing with the kids. No, not really. What about you? Any suggestions?"

"Well, we're agreed that we've got to stop letting them run our lives."

"Exactly. We can't allow them to force us into a relationship."

He nodded. But if that was the case, he wondered, why did he experience the almost overwhelming desire to kiss her? All of a sudden, it bothered him that they were discussing strategies that would ensure the end of any contact between them.

He imagined leaning toward her, touching his lips to hers...

There's something wrong with this picture, Conlan, he said to himself, but he couldn't keep from studying her—and picturing their kiss.

He'd been wrong about her face, he decided. She was beautiful, with classic features, large eyes, a full mouth. He'd trailed his finger down the curve of her cheek the first time they'd met, and now he did so a second time, mentally.

She knew what he was thinking. Steve swore she did. The pulse in her throat hammered wildly and she looked away.

Steve did, too. He didn't know what was happening, didn't want to know. He reached for his beer and gulped down two deep swallows.

What on earth was he doing? Rubbing her feet, thinking about kissing her. He didn't need a woman messing up his life!

Especially a woman like Meg Remington.

"So you met Steve again," Laura said. They sat on a bench in Lincoln Park enjoying huge ice-cream cones. A ferry eased toward the dock at Fauntleroy.

"Who told you that?" Meg answered, deciding to play dumb.

"Lindsey, who else? You really didn't think you fooled her, did you?"

"No." Clearly she had no talent for subterfuge.

"So tell me how your meeting went."

Meg didn't answer. She couldn't. She wasn't sure what, if anything, she and Steve had accomplished during their meeting at the bar. They'd come up with a plan to dissuade his sister and her daughter, but the more hours that passed, the more ridiculous it seemed. And Meg's willingness, indeed her eagerness, to see Steve again was disturbing.

In retrospect she saw that it'd been a mistake for

them to get together. All she could think about was
how he'd lifted her legs onto his lap and rubbed the
tired achiness away. There'd been a sudden explosion
of awareness between them. A living, breathing, throbbing awareness.

Rarely had Meg wanted a man to kiss her more.
Right in the middle of a sports bar, for heaven's sake!
It was the craziest thing to happen to her in years. That
of itself was distressing, but what happened afterward
baffled her even more.

Melting ice cream dripped onto her hand and Meg
hurriedly licked it away.

"Meg?" Laura said, studying her. "What's wrong?"

"Nothing," she said, laughing off her friend's concern. "What could possibly be wrong?"

"You haven't been yourself the last couple of days."

"Sure I have," she said, then deciding it was point-
less to go on lying, she blurted out the truth. "I'm
afraid I could really fall for this guy."

Laura laughed. "What's so awful about that?"

"For one thing, he isn't interested in me."

This time Laura eyed her suspiciously. "What
makes you think that?"

"Several things."

Laura bit into her waffle cone. "Name one."

"Well, he wanted to meet so we could figure out
a way to keep the kids from manipulating our lives."

"That sounds suspiciously like an excuse to see you
again," Laura murmured.

"Trust me, it wasn't. Steve did everything but come
right out and say he's not interested in me."

"You're sure about this?"

"Of course I am! There was ample opportunity for

him to suggest we get to know each other better, and
he didn't." She'd assumed Steve had experienced the
same physical attraction she had, but maybe she'd been
wrong.

Lindsey and Brenda had insisted she still had it.
All Meg could say was that recent experience had
proven otherwise. Whatever *it* was had long since deserted her.

"Did it occur to you that he might've been waiting
for *you* to suggest something?" Laura asked.

"No," Meg told her frankly. Steve wasn't a man who
took his cues from a woman. If he wanted something
or someone, he'd make it known. If he wanted to continue to see her, he would've said so.

"There's got to be more than that."

"There is." Meg took a deep breath. "I was just
getting ready to tell you. Steve came up with the idea
originally, but I agreed."

"To what?"

Meg stood and found the closest garbage receptacle
to dump what remained of her ice cream. "Before I
tell you, remember I'd been drinking beer on an empty
stomach." Okay, she'd had the pretzels.

"This doesn't sound promising," Laura said.

"It isn't." Drawing in another deep breath, she sat
down on the park bench again. "We realized that the
louder we protested and the more often we said we
weren't attracted to each other, the less likely either
Lindsey or Nancy will believe us."

"There's a problem with this scenario," Laura muttered.

"There is?"

"Yes. You *are* interested in Steve. Very interested." Laura gave her a look that said Meg hadn't fooled her.

Meg glanced away. "I don't want to confuse the issue with that."

"All right, go on," Laura said with a wave of her hand.

"Steve thinks the only possible way we have of convincing Lindsey that he's not the right person for me is if he starts dating me and—"

"See?" Laura said triumphantly. "He's interested. Don't you get it? This idea of his is just an excuse."

"I doubt it." Meg could see no reason for him to play games if he truly wanted a relationship with her. "You can come over this evening if you want and see for yourself."

"See what?"

"Steve's coming to meet Lindsey."

"To your house?"

"Yes."

Laura grinned widely. "R-e-a-l-l-y," she said, dragging out the word.

"Really. But it isn't what you think." Because if Laura did believe Steve wanted to pursue something with Meg, her friend was in for a major disappointment.

Meg got home an hour later. Lindsey had taken Steve's visit seriously. She'd cleaned the house, baked cookies and wore her best jeans. A dress would've been asking too much.

"Hello, sweetheart."

"Mom," Lindsey said, frowning at her watch. "Do you have any idea what time it is?"

"Yeah."

"Don't you think you should shower and change clothes? Steve will be here in an hour and a half."

"I know." She supposed she should reveal more enthusiasm, if only for show, but she couldn't make herself do it. This had been Steve's idea and she'd agreed, but she still wasn't convinced.

"I was thinking you should wear that sundress we bought last year with the pretty red-rose print," Lindsey suggested. "That and your white sandals." She studied her mother critically. "I wish you had one of those broad-brimmed sun hats. A pretty white one would be perfect. Very romantic."

"We'll just have to make do with the sombrero Grandpa bought you in Mexico," Meg teased.

"Mother," Lindsey cried, appalled. "That would look stupid!"

Meg sighed dramatically, for effect. "I don't know how I managed to dress myself all these years without you."

She thought—or hoped—that her daughter would laugh. Lindsey didn't. "That might be the reason you're still single. Have you considered that?"

This kid was no help when it came to boosting her confidence.

"You're a great mother," Lindsey said, redeeming herself somewhat, "but promise me you'll never go clothes-shopping without me again."

Rather than make rash pledges she had no intention of keeping, Meg hurried up the stairs and got into the shower. The hot water pulsating against her skin refreshed her and renewed her sense of humor. She could hardly wait to see Lindsey's face when she met Steve.

With a towel tucked around her, Meg wandered

into her bedroom and examined the contents of her closet. In this case, Lindsey was right; the sundress was her best choice. She wore it, Meg told herself, because it looked good on her and *not* because Lindsey had suggested it.

Her daughter was waiting for her in the living room. The floral arrangement Steve, or rather Nancy, had sent was displayed in the middle of the coffee table.

Lindsey had polished the silver tea set until it gleamed. The previous time Meg had used it was when Pastor Delany came for a visit shortly after Meg's father died.

The doorbell chimed. Lindsey turned to her mother with a grin. "We're ready," she said, and gave her a thumbs-up sign.

Meg had assumed she knew what to expect, but when she opened the front door her mouth sagged open.

"Steve?" she whispered to the man dressed in a black leather jacket, tight blue jeans and a white T-shirt. "Is that you?"

He winked at her. "You expecting someone else?"

"N-no," she stammered.

"Invite me in," he said in a low voice. As she stepped aside, he walked past her and placed his index finger under her chin, closing her mouth.

He stood in the archway between the entry and her living room, feet braced apart. "You must be Lindsey," he said gruffly. "I'm Steve."

"You're Steve?" Lindsey sounded uncharacteristically meek.

"Lindsey, this is Steve Conlan," Meg said, standing next to him.

Steve slid his arm around Meg's waist and planted a noisy kiss on her cheek. He glanced at Lindsey. "I understand you're the one who got us together. Thanks."

"You're welcome." Lindsey's eyes didn't so much as flicker. She certainly wasn't about to let them read her thoughts. "You, uh, don't look anything like your picture."

Steve refused to take his eyes off Meg. He squeezed her waist again. "The one I sent was taken a while back," he said. "Before I went to prison."

Lindsey gasped. "Prison?"

"Don't worry, sweetheart. It wasn't a violent crime."

"What…were you in for?" Lindsey asked, her voice shaking.

Steve rubbed the side of his jaw, shadowed by a dark growth of beard. "If you don't mind, I'd rather not say."

"Sit down, Steve," Meg said from between gritted teeth. Talk about overkill. Any more of this and everything would be ruined.

"Would you care for coffee?" Lindsey asked. Her young voice continued to tremble.

"You got a beer?"

"It's not a good idea to be drinking this early in the afternoon, is it?" Meg asked sweetly.

Steve sat down on the sofa, balancing his ankle on the opposite knee. He looked around as if he were casing the joint.

Meg moved to the silver service. "Coffee or tea?"

"Coffee, but add a little something that'll give it some kick."

Meg poured coffee for him and added a generous dollop of half-and-half. He frowned at the delicate bone china cup as though he wasn't sure how to hold it.

Lindsey sat down on the ottoman, her eyes huge. "I…you never said anything about prison."

"Don't like to mention it until people have a chance to meet me for themselves. Some of 'em tend to think the worst of a person when they hear he's had a felony conviction."

"A…felony." Lindsey snapped her mouth shut, inhaled deeply, then said in a subdued tone, "I see."

"The flowers are lovely." Meg fingered a rosebud from the bouquet.

Steve grinned. "My probation officer told me women like that sort of thing. Glad to know he was right." He sipped his coffee and made a slurping sound. "By the way, you'll be glad to hear I told him about you and me, and he did a background check on you and said it was fine for us to see each other."

"That's wonderful," Meg said with enthusiasm that wasn't *entirely* faked.

Steve set aside the delicate cup and leaned forward, his elbows on his knees. He stared at Lindsey and smiled. "Yup, I got to thank you," he said. "I realize your mother's upset with you placing that ad and everything. It's usually not a good idea to fool someone like that, but I wasn't being completely honest with you, either, so I guess we're even."

Lindsey nodded.

"Your mother's one special woman. There aren't a lot of females who'd be willing to overlook my past. Most women don't care that I've got a heart of gold. Your mama did. We sat down in that fancy restaurant and I took one look at her pretty face and I knew she was the woman for me." He rubbed the side of his unshaven jaw and laughed. "I do have to tell you, though, that when you suggested Chez Michelle, I was afraid Meg might be too high-maintenance for someone like me."

"I'm sorry…" Lindsey floundered with the apology. "I didn't know."

"Don't you worry. Your mama was worth every penny of that fancy dinner. Just getting to know her and love her—why, a man couldn't ask for a prettier gal." He eyed her as if she were a Thanksgiving feast, then moistened his lips, implying it was all he could do to keep from grabbing her right then and there and kissing her.

"Steve…" Meg muttered.

"Sorry," he said, and seemed to pull himself together. "Earl Markham, my probation officer, says I've gotta be careful not to rush things. But I look at your beautiful eyes and I can't help myself."

"Yes, well…"

"You didn't tell me how good-looking your daughter is," he said, as though Meg had purposely been holding out on him.

"Lindsey's my pride and joy," Meg said, beaming her daughter a smile.

"I got plenty of friends who wouldn't mind meeting a good-looking girl like you." He winked at Lindsey, suggesting that all he needed was one word from her and he'd make the arrangements immediately.

"Absolutely not!" Meg said, forgetting this was just a game. "I won't have you introducing my daughter to your friends."

Steve's eyes widened with surprise and he held up his right hand, as if taking an oath. "Sorry, I didn't mean to offend. You don't want Lindsey dating any of my buddies, fine, I'll see it never happens."

"Good." Meg had to acknowledge that Steve was an excellent actor. He almost had *her* believing him. She suspected that was because he'd turned himself into the man she'd half expected to meet that night.

Steve smacked his lips. "I gotta tell you when I first saw Meg in that pretty black dress, my heart went all the way to the floor. She's the most beautiful woman I've seen since I was released." His eyes softened as his gaze fell on Meg.

"Released?" Lindsey squeaked.

"From prison," Steve clarified, his gaze immediately returning to Meg.

It would help considerably if he didn't look so sincere, Meg thought.

"Yes, well…" she said, standing. But once she was on her feet, she wasn't sure what to do.

"I'll bet you want me to take you on that motorcycle ride I been promising you," Steve said, downing the last of his coffee.

"Mom's going on a motorcycle with you?" Lindsey asked, swallowing visibly.

"I'd better change clothes," Meg said, eager to escape so she could speak to Steve alone.

"No need," Steve said. "You can ride sidesaddle if you want. I brought my Hog. There's plenty of room, although I gotta tell you, I been dreaming about you sitting behind me, wrapping your arms around my waist. You'll need to hold on tight, honey, real tight." His eyes didn't waver from hers, and the sexual innuendo was unmistakable.

"Yes, well…" Either the room had grown considerably warmer or Meg was in deep trouble.

Judging by the look of disgust Lindsey cast her, she could see it was the latter.

"I think I'll change into a pair of jeans, if it's all the same to you."

"Sure," Steve said, wiping the back of his hand across his mouth. "Just don't keep me waiting long, you hear?"

"I won't," she promised.

Meg rushed toward the stairs, anxious to get away.

Steve reached out to stop her. His hand closed over her shoulder and he brought her into his arms. She gasped in shock. Without giving her time to recover, he lowered his mouth to hers.

It was all for show, but that didn't keep her heart from fluttering wildly. Her stomach muscles tightened at the unexpectedness of his kiss.

Her lips parted and she slid her arms tightly around his narrow waist.

Steve groaned and Meg was afraid the hunger she felt in him was a reflection of her own. By the time he dragged his lips from hers they were both panting. Speechless, they stared at each other.

"I'll… I'll be right back," she managed to whisper. Then she raced up the stairs as if demons were in hot pursuit. On the way she caught a glimpse of Lindsey staring after her, open-mouthed.

Chapter 4

The minute they were alone outside, Meg hit Steve across his upper arm, hurting her hand in the process. Biting her lip, she shook her fingers several times, then clutched her aching hand protectively with the other.

"What was that for?" Steve demanded, glaring at her.

"You overdid it," she snapped, barely understanding her own outrage.

"I had to convince her I was unsuitable, didn't I?"

Meg bristled. "Yes, but you went above and beyond what we discussed. All that business about me being so beautiful," she muttered as she walked to the driveway where he'd parked the Harley-Davidson. She climbed onto the leather seat without thinking.

"I thought I did a great job," Steve argued. A smile raised the edges of his mouth.

"That's another thing," she said, unable to stop looking at him. "Was that kiss really necessary?"

"Yes," he said calmly, but Meg could tell that he didn't take kindly to her rebuke. "Lindsey needed to see me in action," he insisted.

"You frightened my daughter half out of her wits as it was. There was no need to…"

Steve's eyes widened, then softened into a smile. "You liked the kiss," he said flatly. "You liked it and that scared you."

"Don't be ridiculous! It…it was disgusting."

"No, it wasn't." His smile was cocky. He laughed, the timbre low and mildly threatening. "Maybe I should prove how wrong you are."

Meg shifted uncomfortably on the seat. "Let's get this over with," she said, feigning boredom. "You're going to take me out for an hour or so and then drive me back. Right? By the way, where did you get the motorcycle?"

He advanced a step toward her. "It's mine."

"Yours?" He was exactly the kind of man her mother had warned her about, and here she was flirting with danger. He moved a step closer and she held herself rigid.

"You don't know much about men, do you?" he asked, his voice low and husky.

"I was married for nearly six years," she informed him primly. He was close now, too close. She kept her spine stiff and her eyes straight ahead. If the motorcycle was his, it was reasonable to assume the leather jacket belonged to him, as well. The persona he'd taken on, the criminal element, might not be too far from the truth.

"You haven't been with a man since, have you?"

She felt his breath against her flushed face. "I refuse to answer questions of a personal nature," she returned, her voice hoarse and low.

"You haven't," he said confidently. "Look at me, Meg."

"No. Let's get this ride over with."

"Look at me," he repeated.

She tried to resist, but the words were warm and hypnotic. Against her better judgment, she twisted toward him. "Yes?" she asked, her heart pounding so hard she thought it might leap right through her chest.

He wove his hands into her hair and tilted her head back so that she couldn't avoid staring up at him. His gaze bored relentlessly into hers.

"Admit it," he whispered. "You enjoyed the kiss." His eyes were compelling, she admitted reluctantly, resisting him every step.

"How like a man—everything's about ego," she said in an effort to make light of what had happened. "Even a silly little kiss."

Steve frowned.

There was a fluttery feeling in the pit of her stomach, the same feeling that had attacked her when he'd kissed her by the staircase. She felt vulnerable and helpless.

"It wasn't little and it wasn't silly. But it was what we both wanted," he said in a deceptively normal voice.

"You're crazy," she murmured, hurrying to assure him that he'd been wrong. Very wrong. She lowered her eyes, but this proved to be a tactical error. Before she realized what he intended, he was kissing her again.

Meg wanted to protest. If she'd fought him, struggled, he might have released her. But her one weak objection came in the form of a moan, and it appeared to encourage rather than dissuade him.

All at once it was important to get closer. A moment later she was kneeling on the leather cushion and Steve had slipped his arms around her middle. They didn't stay there long. He glided his hands along her back, urging her more tightly against him.

Meg didn't require much inducement. Her body willfully molded itself to his. Then, abruptly, her eyes fluttered open and with a determined effort she broke free. Steve's arms tightened before he relaxed and finally released her.

The look on his face was one of shock.

For her own part, Meg was having a difficult time breathing. Sensations swarmed through her. Unwanted sensations. Steve made her feel as if she'd never been kissed before, never been held or loved. Never been married or shared intimacies with a man.

She blinked, and Steve backed away. He frowned and raked his fingers through his hair, apparently sorting out his own troubled emotions.

"I suppose you expect me to admit I enjoyed that," she said with more than a hint of belligerence. These feelings frightened her. The fact that she'd reacted to him could easily be explained. Good grief, she was a normal woman—but this giddy, end-of-the-world sensation wasn't anything she'd ever experienced.

"You don't have to admit to a damned thing," he

said. He climbed onto the Hog and revved the engine aggressively.

"Stop," she cried, shouting above the noise. She waved a hand to clear away the exhaust.

"What's wrong now?" he snapped, twisting around to look at her.

"Nothing… Just go slow, all right?"

Separated by only a couple of inches, Meg felt him tense. "I'm not exactly in a slow mood."

"I guessed as much."

She didn't know what he intended as he expertly maneuvered the motorcycle out of her driveway. Mortified, Meg glanced up and down the street, wondering how many of her neighbors had witnessed the exchange between her and Steve. Fortunately Lindsey wasn't at the front window watching as Meg had half feared.

"Hang on," he shouted.

She placed her hands lightly on either side of his waist, hoping to keep the contact as impersonal as possible—until they turned the first corner. From that moment on, she wrapped her arms around him as tightly as she could.

Meg was grateful that he chose not to drive far. He stopped at a park less than a mile from her house. After he'd eased into a parking space, he switched off the engine and sat motionless for a couple of minutes.

"You okay?" he asked after a while.

"I'm fine. Great. That was…fun." She was astonished at her new talent for telling white lies. She was far from fine. Her insides were a mess, although that had almost nothing to do with the motorcycle ride. Her heart refused to settle down to a normal pace, and she

couldn't stop thinking about their kisses. The first time
had been traumatic, but it didn't compare to her nearly
suffocating reaction to his second kiss.

Steve checked his watch. "We'll give it another five
minutes and then I'll take you back to the house. That
should give Lindsey enough time to worry about you
without sending her into a panic."

"Perfect," she said brightly—a little too brightly.

"Then tomorrow afternoon I'll pick you up after
work and you can do your thing with my sister."

Although he couldn't see her, she nodded. Meg only
hoped her act for Nancy would be as convincing as
Steve's had been with Lindsey.

"After that, we won't need to see each other again,"
Steve said. "As far as I'm concerned, it isn't a minute too soon."

Meg felt much the same way. She was just as eager
to get him out of her life.

Wasn't she?

It hadn't been a good day. Steve would've liked to
blame his foul mood on work-related problems, but
everything at Emerald City Body Shop had run like
clockwork. The one reason that presented itself was
Meg Remington.

He'd known from the first night that getting involved with her would mean trouble. Sure enough, he
was waist-deep in quicksand, and all because he hadn't
wanted to hurt the woman's feelings.

Okay, that accounted for their dinner date, but afterward…what happened was no one's fault except his
own. Donning his leather jacket and jeans and playing

the role of the disgruntled ex-con had been fun. But then he had to go and do something stupid.

The stupid part was because of the kiss. He'd been a fool to force Meg to admit how good it had been. This was what he got for allowing his pride to stand in the way.

Well, Steve had learned his lesson. The next time he was tempted to kiss Meg, he'd go stand in the middle of the freeway. Man, oh man, she could kiss. Only she didn't seem to realize it. Much more of that kissing and he would've been renting a hotel room.

Not Meg, though. Oh, no. She acted as outraged as a nun. Apparently she'd forgotten that men and women did that sort of thing. Enjoyed it, too. Looked forward to doing it again.

The woman was insane, and the sooner he could extract her from his life, the better. He didn't need this. Who did?

One more night, he assured himself. He was taking Meg to meet Nancy this evening, and when they were finished, it would be over and they'd never have to see each other again. If she played her cards right. He'd done his part.

Despite his sour mood, Steve grinned. He'd never forget the look of shock and horror in Lindsey's eyes when he walked into the house. Her jaw had nearly hit the carpet when he put his arms around Meg's waist and announced that he was an ex-con. He wouldn't forget the look in Meg's eyes, either.

Steve laughed outright.

"Something funny?" Gary Wilcox asked.

Steve glared at his foreman. "Not a thing. Now get back to work."

At six o'clock, Steve pulled into the parking space in the alley behind Meg's bookstore. He didn't like the idea of sneaking around and going to her back door, but that was what Meg wanted and far be it from him to argue. He'd be well rid of the woman—at least that was what he kept trying to tell himself.

He knocked and waited a few minutes, growing impatient.

The door opened and a woman in black mesh nylons and the shortest miniskirt he'd seen in years stood in front of him. She vaguely resembled Tina Turner. She wore tons of makeup and she'd certainly had her hair done at the same salon as Tina.

"I'm here for Meg Remington," he said, annoyed that Meg had made such a fuss about his coming to the back door and then sent someone else to answer it.

"Steve," Meg whispered, "it's me."

"What the hell?" He jerked his head back and examined her more thoroughly. "We're meeting my sister," he reminded her stiffly, "not going to some costume party."

"I took my cue from you," she said. "Good grief! You arrived at my door looking like a Hell's Angel— what did you expect *me* to do?"

Steve rubbed his face. Darned if he knew anymore. All he wanted was to get this over with. "Fine. Let's get out of here."

"Just a minute. I need to change shoes."

She slipped out of a perfectly fine pair of flats and into spiky high heels that added a good five inches to her height. Steve wondered how she'd manage to walk in those things. She might as well have been on stilts.

He led her around to his car and opened the door.

He noticed that she sighed with what sounded like relief once she was inside the car.

"I didn't know what I was going to do if you brought that motorcycle again." She tugged down her miniskirt self-consciously.

"For the record, I don't often take it out."

She looked relieved, but why it should matter to her one way or the other, he had no idea.

"Just remember," he said, feeling obliged to caution her. "Nancy's a few years older than Lindsey. She won't be as easily fooled."

"I'll be careful about overkill," she mumbled, "unlike certain people I know."

The drive took an eternity, and it wasn't due to heavy traffic, either. In fact, when Steve looked at his watch he was surprised at what good time they'd made. What made the drive so troublesome—he hated to admit this—was Meg's legs. She'd crossed them, exposing plenty of smooth, shapely thigh. Her high heels dangled from the ends of her toes.

Steve appreciated women as a whole—some more than others, of course. He didn't focus on body parts. But it was torture to sit with Meg in the close confines of his car and keep his eyes off her legs. The woman looked incredible. If only she'd keep her mouth shut!

Nancy was standing on the porch when Steve pulled into the driveway.

"This is where your sister lives?" Meg asked.

"It's my home," Steve answered, certain she was about to find something wrong with it.

"Your home?" She sounded impressed. "It's very nice."

"Thanks." He turned off the engine. "Nancy's quite

a bit younger than I am—a surprise for my mom and dad. She attends college at the University of Washington nine months out of the year. Our parents retired to Montana a couple of years back."

"I see. Does Nancy live with you?"

"Not on your life," he said, climbing out of the car. "She's in residence during the school year. She got a job here this summer and I agreed to let her stay with me a few months. A mistake I don't plan to repeat anytime soon."

Steve was watching for his sister's reaction when he helped Meg out of the car. To her credit, the nineteen-year-old didn't reveal much, but Steve knew her well enough to realize she was shocked by Meg's appearance.

"You must be Nancy," Meg said in a low, sultry voice.

"And you must be Meg," Nancy said, coming down the steps to greet her. "I've been dying to meet you."

"I hope I'm not a disappointment." This was said in a soft, cooing tone, as if she couldn't have tolerated disillusioning Steve's little sister. She clasped Steve's arm and he noticed for the first time that her nails—now two inches long—were painted a brilliant fire-engine red.

Nancy held open the door and smiled in welcome. "Please, come inside."

Meg's high heels clattered against the tile entryway. Steve looked around, pleased to note that his sister had cleaned up the house a bit.

"Oh, Stevie," Meg whined, "you never told me what a beautiful home you have." She trailed one finger along the underside of his jaw. "But then, we haven't had time to discuss much of anything, have we?"

"Make yourself comfortable," Steve said and

watched as Meg chose to sit on the sofa. She sat, crossing her legs with great ceremony. Then she patted the empty space beside her, silently requesting Steve to join her there. He glanced longingly at his favorite chair, but moved across the room and sat down next to Meg.

The minute he was comfortable, Meg placed her hand possessively on his knee and flexed her nails into his thigh. Inch by provocative inch she raked her nails up his leg until it was all Steve could do not to pop straight off the sofa. He caught her hand and stopped her from reaching what seemed to be her ultimate destination.

Her expression was mildly repentant when she looked at him, but Steve knew her well enough to know the action had been deliberate.

"I thought you might be hungry before Steve takes you to dinner, so I made a few hors d'oeuvres," Nancy said and excused herself.

"What are you doing?" Steve whispered the minute his sister was out of the room.

"Doing? What do you mean?" She had wide-eyed innocence down to an art.

"Never mind," he muttered as Nancy returned from the kitchen carrying a small silver platter.

"Those look wonderful," Meg said sweetly when his sister put the tray on the coffee table in front of them. "But I couldn't eat a thing."

To the best of his knowledge it was the first time his sister had cooked from the moment she'd moved in with him, and he wasn't about to let it go to waste. He chose a tiny wiener wrapped in some kind of crispy dough and tossed it in his mouth.

"You shouldn't have gone to all this trouble," Meg told his sister.

Nancy sat across the room from them, apparently at a complete loss for words.

"I suspect you're wondering about all these letters and e-mails I wrote," Meg said, getting the conversation going. "I hope you aren't unhappy with me."

"No, no, not at all," Nancy said, rushing the words together.

"It's just that I've come to know what people *really* want from me by the things they say." She turned, and with the tip of her index finger wiped a crumb from the corner of his mouth. Her tongue moistened her lips and Steve's insides turned to mush.

"I learned a long time ago what men want from a woman," Meg continued after a moment, "especially when I went to work for a phone sex line. Most of the guys are just looking for a woman to talk dirty to them."

"I see." Nancy folded her hands primly in her lap.

"There was the occasional guy who was looking for a good girl to shock, of course. I got very talented at acting horrified." She made a soft, gasping sound, then laughed demurely.

"Why…why would someone like you place an ad in Dateline?" Nancy asked, nervously brushing the hair from her face.

"Well, first," Meg said, holding his sister's gaze, "it's just about the only way someone like me can meet anyone decent. But it wasn't your brother who answered the ad, now, was it?"

"No, but—"

"Not that it matters," Meg said, cutting her off. "I

was tired of my job and all those guys asking me to say those nasty things, and I didn't want to start working on my back again."

"On your…back," Nancy repeated.

"I'm sorry, sugar. I didn't mean to shock you. I've got a colorful past—but that doesn't mean I'm a bad girl. I've got a heart just brimming with love. All I need is the right man." Her gaze wandered to Steve and was long and deliberate. "Your brother's given me a reason to dream again," Meg said softly. "Lots of people think women like me don't have feelings, but they're wrong."

"I'm sure that's true," Nancy said tentatively.

"I knew I chose right when I found out your brother has his own business."

"He's struggled financially for years," Nancy was quick to tell her. "It's still touch and go. He lives from one month to the next." Nancy glared at him pointedly. "Don't you, Steve?"

"Not anymore. I'm more than solvent now," Steve tossed in for good measure, struggling not to laugh. He was enjoying this.

Meg tightened her arm around his. "I can see how well Stevie's doing for himself. He's wonderful," she said, refusing to look away. The adoration on her face embarrassed him.

"Why, Steve here could make enough money to keep me in the lifestyle to which I'd like to become accustomed." She laughed coyly.

"Ah…" It sounded to Steve as if his sister was close to hyperventilating.

"Of course, I wouldn't take anything from him without giving in return. That wouldn't be fair." She snuggled closer to his side and gave him a look so purely sexual Steve was convinced he'd embarrass them all.

"There are things I could teach your brother," Meg said in a husky voice full of sexual innuendo. She acted as though she was eager to get started right that moment and the only thing holding her back was propriety. Her breathing grew heavy—and if he didn't know better he'd think she actually *had* worked for one of those disreputable phone services.

Soon he was having a problem controlling his own breathing.

"Steve!" Nancy snapped.

He turned his attention back to his sister, staring at her blankly.

"Didn't you hear Meg?" she asked.

He shrugged. He knew the two women were talking, but he'd barely noticed their conversation.

"Meg's talking about moving in with you," Nancy said through clenched teeth.

"I don't mean to rush you, darlin'," Meg whispered. Leaning forward, she licked his earlobe with the tip of her tongue.

Hot sensation shot down his spine.

Meg threw back her head and laughed softly, then whispered just loudly enough for Nancy to hear, "I have an incredibly talented tongue."

Nancy closed her eyes as if she couldn't bear to watch another minute of this. Frankly, Steve didn't know how much more he could take himself.

"I think it's time we left for dinner," he said. Otherwise he was going to start believing all the promises Meg was making. Heaven knew, he *wanted* to believe them. The demure bookseller had turned into something completely different. All traces of innocence had disappeared and in their place was the most sexually provocative female he'd ever met. Just being in the same room with her made his blood sizzle.

"You want to leave already?" Meg gave the impression that she was terribly disappointed.

"That's probably best," Nancy muttered, and then realizing what she'd said, hurried to add, "I mean, you two don't want to waste your evening with me, do you?" She frowned at Steve. "You won't be late, will you?"

"No."

"Unfortunately, I'm still working for the phone people," Meg said, "so I won't keep him too long, but I can't promise he'll have much kick left in him when I'm finished." Apparently thinking herself exceptionally clever, Meg laughed at her own joke.

It wasn't until they were back in the car and on the freeway that Steve recognized how angry he was. It made no sense, but he wasn't exactly rational just then.

"Why are you so mad?" Meg asked about halfway back to the bookstore. They hadn't spoken a word from the time they'd left his house.

"Talk about overkill," he muttered.

"I thought I did a good job," she said.

"You came off like a—"

"I know. That's what I wanted. After meeting me, do you honestly think your sister's going to encourage our relationship?"

"No," he growled.

"I can guarantee you that Lindsey doesn't want me

to see you, either. I thought that's what this whole scheme of yours was about."

"It sounded like a good idea at the time." He tightened his hands on the steering wheel. "It seemed like a surefire way to convince your daughter that I was the wrong man for you."

"And your sister that I was equally wrong for you."

Silence settled over them like nightfall. Neither of them seemed inclined to talk again.

Steve edged his car into the alley behind Meg's store and parked his car behind hers.

"I'm not so sure anymore," he said without looking at her.

"About what?"

"The two of us. Somewhere in the middle of all this, I decided I kind of like you." It hadn't been easy to admit, and he hoped she appreciated what it had cost his pride. "It probably wouldn't have been as obvious if you hadn't made yourself out to be so cheap. That isn't you any more than the rebel without a cause is me."

He wished she'd say something. When she did speak, her voice was timid and small. "Then there was the kiss."

"Kisses," he corrected. "They were pretty great and we both know it," he said with confidence. He knew what his own reaction had been, and she hadn't fooled him with hers.

"Yes," she said softly.

"Especially the one on the motorcycle," he said, prompting her to continue.

"Especially the one on the motorcycle," she mimicked. "Honestly, Steve, you must've known."

His smile was full blown. "I did."

"I... I didn't do a very good job of disguising what I was feeling."

She hadn't, but he was in a gracious mood.

"How about dinner?" he suggested. He was eager to have the real Meg Remington back. Eager to experiment with a few more kisses—see if they were anything close to what his memory kept insisting they'd been.

She hesitated. "I want to, but I can't," she eventually said.

He bristled and turned in the driver's seat to face her. "Why not?"

"I promised Lindsey I'd be home by seven and it's nearly that now."

"Call her and tell her you're going out to dinner with me."

She dragged in a deep breath and seemed to hold it. "I can't do that, either."

"Why not?"

"After meeting you, I promised her we'd talk. She wanted to last evening, and we didn't... That was my fault. You kissed me," she said, "and I didn't feel like a heart-to-heart with my daughter after that."

"And it's all my fault?"

"Yes," she insisted.

"Do you know what Lindsey wants to discuss?"

"Of course, I know. You. She doesn't want me seeing you again, which is exactly the point of the entire charade. Remember?"

"Yeah," Steve said, scowling.

"Are...are you telling me you've changed your mind?" she asked.

"Yes." He hated to be the one to say it first, but one of them had to. "What about you?"

"I think so."

Steve flattened his hand against the steering wheel. "I swear you're about the worst thing that's ever happened to my ego."

She laughed and rested her hand on his shoulder. The wig she had on tilted sideways and she righted it. "That does sound terrible, doesn't it?"

He smiled. "Yeah. The least you could do is show some enthusiasm."

"I haven't dated much in the last ten years. But if I was going to choose any man, it would be you."

"That's better," he said. He wanted to kiss her. He'd been thinking about it from the moment he'd picked her up.

"Only..." Meg said sadly.

"Only what?" he repeated, lowering his mouth to hers.

Their lips met and it was heaven, just the way he'd known it would be. By the time the kiss ended, Steve was leaning his head against the window of the car door, his eyes closed. It was even more wonderful than he'd remembered, and that seemed impossible.

Meg's head was on his chest, tucked beneath his chin.

"It's too late," she whispered.

"What's too late?"

"We've gone to all this trouble to convince Lindsey that you're all wrong for me."

"I know, but..."

"Do you think Nancy will believe this was all a silly joke?"

"No."

"I think we should end everything right here and now, don't you?" she asked.

Steve stiffened. "If that's what you want."

She moved away from him. "I guess it is," she said, with just a hint of regret.

Chapter 5

Lindsey was pacing the living room, waiting for Meg when she walked in the front door.

"Hi, honey," Meg said, trying to sound cheerful yet exhausted—since she'd led Lindsey to believe she was taking inventory at the bookstore and that was why she'd come home so late.

"It's way after seven!" her daughter cried, rushing toward her. "You weren't with Steve, were you?"

"Ah…" Meg wasn't willing to lie outright. Half-truths and innuendos were about as far as she wanted to stretch this.

Lindsey closed her eyes and waved her hands vaguely. "Forget it. Don't answer that."

"Honey, what's wrong?" Meg asked as calmly as she could. Unfortunately, she didn't think she sounded all that reassuring. She'd left Steve only moments earlier and was already feeling some regret. After following through with this ridiculous charade, Steve wanted to change his mind and continue seeing Meg. She'd quickly put an end to *that* idea. Now she wasn't sure she'd made the right decision.

"Mom," Lindsey said, her dark eyes challenging, "we need to talk."

"Of course." Meg walked into the kitchen and took the china teapot from the hutch. "My mother always made tea when we had something to discuss." Somehow, the ritual of drinking tea together put everything in perspective. Meg missed those times with her mother.

Lindsey helped her assemble everything they needed and carried it into the dining room. Meg poured them each a cup, once the tea had steeped, and they sat across from each other at the polished mahogany table.

Meg waited, and when Lindsey wasn't immediately forthcoming she decided to get the conversation started. "You wanted to talk to me about Steve, right?"

Lindsey clasped the delicate china cup with one hand and lowered her gaze. "Do you really, really like him?" she asked anxiously.

Meg answered before she took time to censor the question. "Yes."

"But why? I mean, he's nothing like what I thought he'd be." She hesitated. "I suppose this is what Brenda and I get for pretending we were you," she mumbled. "Maybe if you'd read his stuff, you would've been able to tell what kind of guy he really is."

"Steve is actually a fine person." And he was. Or at least the Steve Meg knew.

Lindsey risked a glance at her. "You've said hundreds of times that you don't want me to judge others by outward appearances, but sometimes that's all there is."

"You're worried about me and Steve, aren't you?" Meg said gently.

Lindsey rubbed her finger along the edge of the teacup. "I realize now that what Brenda and I did was really stupid. We linked you up with a guy who has a prison record. We sure were easy to fool," Lindsey said with a scowl. "We're only fifteen years old!"

"But I like Steve," Meg felt obliged to tell her.

Lindsey looked as if she didn't know how to account for that. "I'm afraid he's going to hurt you."

"Steve wouldn't do that," Meg assured her, "but I understand your concern, honey, and I promise you I won't let the situation get out of hand."

Lindsey frowned, stiffened her shoulders and blurted out, "I don't want you to see him again."

"But..."

"I mean it, Mom. This guy is trouble."

Talk about role reversal!

"I want you to *promise* me you won't see Steve Conlan again."

"Lindsey..."

"This is important. You may not understand it now, but I promise you will in the future. There are plenty of other men, law-abiding citizens, who'd give their right arms to meet a woman like you."

Meg stared. She couldn't be hearing this. This sounded exactly like something her mother had said back when Meg was in high school.

The intense look in Lindsey's eyes softened and

she gestured weakly. "The time will come when you'll thank me for this."

"Really?" Meg couldn't resist raising her eyebrows.

"There'll be a boy in my life that you'll disapprove of and I won't understand why," Lindsey went on. "When that happens, I want you to remind me of now."

Meg shook her head—in bafflement and disbelief. "Are you telling me you'd break up with a boy simply because I didn't like him?"

"No," Lindsey said carefully. "But I'd consider it because I know how I feel about you seeing Steve, and I'd understand how you might feel about someone I was dating. Don't get me wrong," she hurried to add, "I don't dislike Steve… He's kind of cute. It's just that I feel you could do a whole lot better."

"I'll think about it," Meg promised.

Lindsey nodded. "I can't ask for more than that."

Her daughter had behaved just as Meg had predicted. This had gone precisely according to plan. But Meg didn't feel good about it. If anything, she felt more depressed following their conversation than before.

She didn't have any talent when it came to relationships, Meg decided, as she finished putting away the dinner dishes later that evening. Steve had come right out and told her he'd had a change of heart, and she'd bungled everything. Instead of admitting that she felt the same way he did, she'd trampled all over his ego.

Meg turned to the kitchen phone, tempted to call him. It couldn't end like this, with such confusion, such uncertainty about what she really wanted. What *they* wanted.

Never had an evening passed more slowly. It seemed

to take Lindsey hours to go to bed, and by then Meg was yawning herself.

As soon as Meg could be reasonably sure that her daughter was asleep, she tiptoed toward the kitchen phone and dialed Steve's number, her heart pounding. Finally she heard his groggy voice.

"Steve?" she whispered. "Thank goodness it's you. I didn't know what I was going to do if Nancy answered."

"Meg? Is that you?" He sounded surprised to hear from her, and none too pleased.

She bristled. "How many other women do you have phoning you at eleven o'clock at night?"

He didn't respond right away, and when he spoke his voice definitely lacked welcome. "I thought you said it wasn't a good idea for us to see each other."

"I… I don't know what I want."

"Do you expect me to make your decisions for you?"

"Of course not." This wasn't going well. In fact, it was going very badly. She probably should've waited until she'd had time to figure this out a little more clearly.

"Is there a reason you called?" he asked gruffly.

"Yes," she said, sorry now that she'd phoned him. "I wanted to apologize for being abrupt earlier. I…can see now that I shouldn't have called."

Having said that, she carefully replaced the receiver. For a long moment she stared at the phone, feeling like an idiot.

She'd turned away to head up the stairs when the phone rang, jolting her. Quickly she grabbed it before the noise could wake Lindsey.

"Hello," she whispered.

"Meet me." It was Steve.

"I can't leave Lindsey."

"Why not? She's in bed, isn't she?"

"Yes, but…"

"Write her a note. Tell her you're going to the grocery store."

How reasonable he made it sound—as if she usually did her shopping in the middle of the night.

"She won't even know you're gone," Steve said.

Meg closed her eyes. They'd been together only a few hours earlier, and yet it felt as if they'd been apart for weeks.

Her stomach twisted. Then—before she could change her mind—she blurted out, "All right, but I can't stay long."

"Fair enough."

They agreed to meet in the Albertson's parking lot. The huge store was open twenty-four hours a day. Meg had been shopping there for years. The note she left Lindsey said she'd gone to pick up some milk— that classic excuse—but it was exactly what she intended to do.

She sat in her car until she saw Steve pull into the nearly empty lot. Uncertain she was doing the right thing, she got out and waited for him.

Steve parked in the spot next to hers. They stood facing each other for a moment, neither speaking.

"I can't believe we're doing this," she said.

It appeared she wasn't the only one with doubts. Steve's face was blank, emotionless. "Me neither."

They walked into the store together and reached for

grocery carts. Meg's had a squeaky wheel. The sound echoed through the cavernous store.

The deli was closed, but Steve was able to get them each a cup of coffee from the friendly night manager. They parked their empty carts and sat at a small white table in the deli section. Neither seemed inclined to speak.

She felt encouraged that Steve had phoned her back, but she suspected he regretted it now.

"You know what you said earlier?" she began.

"I said lots of things earlier. Which particular thing are you referring to?"

Meg guessed his sarcasm was warranted. After all, she'd wounded his ego, and he wasn't giving her the chance to do it again. "About the two of us, you know, dating."

"You said Lindsey wouldn't like it."

"She doesn't," Meg said. "She asked me not to see you again."

His gaze pinned hers. "Did you agree?"

"Not...entirely."

His eyes narrowed with a frown. "You'd better explain."

"Well, as you've already surmised, Lindsey isn't keen on me seeing you. Which is exactly the reason you stopped by the house and did your biker routine, right? Well, it worked. She's worried that you're the wrong man for me." It would've helped if he hadn't bragged about his prison record and mentioned his parole officer's name. But now didn't seem to be the time to bring that up.

"Did you or did you not promise her you wouldn't see me again?"

"Neither." Meg sipped from the disposable cup and grimaced at the taste of burned coffee.

"Then what *did* you say to her?"

Meg lifted one shoulder in a shrug. "That I'd think about it."

"Have you?"

Propping her elbows on the table's edge, Meg swirled the black liquid around the cup and avoided looking at Steve. "I called you, didn't I?"

"I still haven't figured out why."

That was the problem: she hadn't, either. Not really. "I guess it's because you have a point about seeing each other again."

"Oh, yeah?" He gave her a cocky grin.

Her anger flared. "Would you stop it?"

"Stop what?" he asked innocently.

"The next thing I know, you're going to ask me how much I enjoyed kissing you."

Steve smiled for the first time. "It wouldn't hurt to know."

"All right, since it means so much to you, I'll admit it. No man's ever kissed me the way you do. It scares me—but at the same time I wish it could go on forever." Having admitted this much, she supposed she might as well say it all. "My marriage left me wondering if I was…if I was capable of those kinds of feelings…" She paused and lowered her eyes. "I was afraid I was, you know, frigid," she said in a choked whisper.

She stared down at her coffee, then took a sip, followed by several more, as if the vile stuff were the antidote to some dreaded illness.

The last thing she expected her small confession to provoke in Steve was a laugh. "You're joking!"

She shook her head forcefully. "Don't laugh. Please."

His hand reached for hers and their fingers entwined. "I wasn't laughing at you, Meg," he said gently. "You're one of the most sensual women I've ever met. Trust me, if you're frigid—and there's a word I haven't heard in years—then I'm a monk."

Meg looked up and offered him a fragile smile. It astonished her that this man who'd known her for only a few days could chase away the doubts that had hounded her through the years after her divorce.

He cleared his throat. "I, uh, don't think you should look at me like that."

"Like what?"

"Like you want me to kiss you."

Her eyes drifted shut. "Maybe I do... That's what makes everything so complicated. I'm really attracted to you. I haven't felt like this before—not ever, not even with my ex-husband, and like I said, that scares me."

He stood up, still holding Meg's hand, and tugged her to her feet.

"Where are we going?" she asked.

"Someplace private," he said, scanning the store. He led her through the frozen food section, past the bakery and into a small alcove where the wine was kept. With her back to the domestic beer, he brought her into his arms and covered her mouth with his.

Their kiss was rough with need, but she wasn't sure whose need was greater. Meg could feel Steve's heart racing as hard as her own. She supposed she should've pulled away, ended the kiss, stepped out of his arms. But Meg didn't want that.

* * *

Steve yawned. He was *so* tired. With good reason. It'd been almost three before he'd gone to bed and four before he'd been able to fall asleep. His alarm had gone off at six.

He arrived at the shop and made a pot of coffee. He mumbled a greeting when Gary got in.

"I hope you're in a better mood than you were yesterday," his foreman told him. "What's wrong with you, anyway?"

Steve checked over the job orders for the day. "Women," he muttered in explanation and apology.

"I should've guessed. What's going on?"

"You don't want to hear this," he said and headed for the garage.

"Sure I do," Gary said, following him. "I don't suppose this has anything to do with Nancy, does it?"

Steve glared at him. "What do you know about my sister?"

"Not much," Gary said and held up both hands. "Just what you said about her fixing you up with some woman. It's none of my business, but you and this woman seem to be hitting it off just fine."

Steve continued to glare at him. "What makes you say that?"

Gary laughed. "I haven't seen you this miserable in years. Which probably means you've fallen for her. Why don't you put yourself out of your misery? Shoot yourself and be done with it."

Frowning, Steve turned away. The kid was a smart-ass, although now that Steve thought about it, Gary might have come up with the perfect solution.

* * *

It was noon before Steve had a chance to go into his office. He made sure no one was looking, then closed the door and reached for the phone.

"Book Ends, Laura speaking," a woman said in a friendly voice.

"Is Meg available?" he asked, sounding as businesslike as possible.

"May I ask who's calling?"

Steve hesitated. "Steve Conlan."

"One minute, please."

It took longer than that for Meg to get on the line. "Steve, hi." She seemed tired but happy to hear from him. That helped.

"How are you?" he asked, struggling to hold back a yawn.

"Dead on my feet. I'm not as young as I used to be."

"Does Lindsey know you slipped out of the house last night?"

"No, but I should never have stayed out that late."

Steve didn't have any argument there. They'd left the Albertson's store when a stock boy stumbled upon them in the wine section, embarrassing Meg no end— although Steve had rather enjoyed the way her blush had brightened her cheeks.

With no other idea of where to take her at that hour, Steve had driven down to Alki Point in west Seattle, where they sat on the beach and talked.

They hadn't discussed anything of earth-shattering importance, but he discovered that they had a great deal in common. Mostly, he discovered that he liked Meg. He was already well aware of what Meg, the sensuous and beautiful woman, was capable of doing to him physically. Last night, he learned about Meg, the person.

They hadn't kissed again. Steve was convinced they both knew how dangerous kissing had become. It wouldn't take much for their kisses to lead to more... a *lot* more. And when that happened, he didn't plan to have it take place on a public beach.

He didn't know where the time had gone, but when he'd looked at his watch he'd been shocked. Meg, too. It was after three in the morning. They'd rushed their farewells without making arrangements to see each other again.

"When can we get together?" he asked.

"I don't know..."

Was this how it was going to be? Would they have to start over each and every time they met? "Would you rather we didn't meet again?" he asked.

"No," she said immediately.

"We've got to make some decisions," he said, angry with himself for not saying anything about it on that moonlit beach. They'd discussed so many different things, from politics to movies to lifelong dreams, yet hadn't talked about their own relationship.

"I know."

"Would tonight work?" he asked. "Same time?"

She hesitated and he gritted his teeth with impatience.

"Okay." The longing in her voice reassured him.

"Fine," he said, relieved. "I'll pick you up at your house at eleven."

"I have to go now."

"Yeah. Me, too."

Steve replaced the receiver and glanced up to find

Nancy standing in his office doorway, her arms folded in disapproval.

"Was that Meg?" she demanded.

"That's none of your business," Steve said sharply.

"We need to talk about her and I'm tired of you putting me off."

"I'm not discussing Meg Remington with you."

"How could you date someone like her?" Nancy asked, her face wrinkled in disgust.

"Might I remind you that you were the one who introduced us?"

"Yes, but she deceived me. Steve, be serious! Can you honestly imagine introducing her to Mom and Dad?"

"Yes," he answered calmly.

Nancy threw her arms in the air. "This is your problem. You're thinking with your you-know-what."

"Nancy!"

"It's true!"

"Stay out of my business. Understand?"

"But…"

"I make my own decisions," Steve said forcefully.

"And your own mistakes," Nancy muttered, walking out of the room.

"We're both crazy," Meg said, sitting next to Steve in his car. She sipped from a can of cold soda, enjoying the sweet taste of it.

"Candidates for the loony bin," he agreed.

"I wasn't sure I'd be able to get away," Meg confessed. "Brenda's spending the night with Lindsey, and those two are going to be up half the night."

"Did you tell them you were leaving the house?"

"No," she said, "but I left them a note. Just in case... Although I'm hoping they won't come downstairs. Oh, and this time I should remember to bring home some milk."

"I was thinking Lindsey and I should have another meeting," Steve began. "Only this time I want you to bring her to the shop. I'll show her around and explain that the whole biker, ex-con routine was a joke." He waited, then looked at Meg. "What do you think?"

"I'm afraid hell hath no fury like a teenager fooled."

"That's what I was afraid you were going to say." Steve finished his drink and placed his arm around her shoulder. "One thing's for sure. I'm through with sneaking around in the middle of the night."

Meg covered her mouth as she yawned. "I'm too old for this."

"You and me both."

Meg finished her soda, too, and leaned back against Steve, his chest supporting her back. She didn't dare close her eyes for fear she'd fall asleep.

"Nancy isn't any too happy about me seeing you, either."

"I'll talk to her, explain everything." Except that, like Lindsey, Steve's sister probably wouldn't be too pleased.

"It's settled, then," Steve said. "I'll talk to Lindsey and you'll talk to Nancy. Neither one of them is going to enjoy being the butt of a joke, but it wasn't like we planned this. Besides, it serves them right for manipulating us like they did."

"You'd think they'd be pleased," Meg inserted. "Their plan worked—not the way they wanted, mind you, but we're seeing each other and that's the whole point. Right?"

Steve chuckled and stroked her hair. "Right."

"I wish it wasn't like this," Meg whispered.

Steve kissed the top of her head. "So do I."

Meg smiled, twisting in his arms so they faced each other.

Steve's hands lingered on her face. His mouth was so close she could feel his breath against her cheek. A shiver of awareness skittered down her spine.

Meg closed her eyes and lifted her mouth to Steve's. He hesitated for a fraction of a second, as if he had second thoughts about what might happen next.

His kiss was warm and gentle. But his gentleness didn't last long. There was a hunger in Steve, a hunger in Meg that flared to life like a fire stoked.

"Meg…"

"I know… I know."

"Tomorrow," he said and drew in a deep, even breath.

"Tomorrow," she repeated, but she had no idea what she was agreeing to. She opened her eyes and leaned back. "What about tomorrow?"

"We'll talk to Lindsey and Nancy."

"Okay."

Fifteen minutes later, Steve dropped her off at the house.

It wasn't until he drove away that she realized she'd left her purse in his car. Her purse with the key to her house…

"Damn," she muttered, hurrying into the backyard, hoping Lindsey had forgotten to lock the sliding glass door. She hadn't; it was locked tight.

No help for it—she searched until she found the spare key, hidden under one of the flowerpots on her porch. It'd been there for so many years she wasn't sure it would work.

Luckily it did. As quietly as she could, Meg slipped into the house.

She climbed the stairs and tiptoed into her room. She undressed without turning on the light and was in bed minutes later.

The neighbor's German shepherd barked, obviously from inside their house, and Lindsey looked up from painting her toenails. "There it is again," she said.

"I heard it, too," Brenda said.

"Wolf doesn't bark without a reason."

Ever curious, Brenda walked over to the bedroom window and peered into the yard below. After a moment, she whirled around. "There's someone in your backyard," she whispered, wide-eyed.

"This isn't the time for jokes," Lindsey said, continuing to paint her toenails a bright shade of pink. "We were discussing my mother, remember?"

Brenda didn't move away from the window. "There *is* someone there."

"Who?"

"It's a man… Oh, my goodness, come and look."

The panic in her friend's voice made Lindsey catapult to a standing position. Walking on her heels to keep her freshly painted toenails off the carpet, she hobbled toward the window.

Brenda was right; she *did* see someone in the yard. "Turn the lights off," she hissed.

Lindsey's heart lodged in her throat as she recognized the dark form. "It's Steve Conlan!" She saw him clearly in the moonlight; he wasn't even making any attempt to hide.

"What's that in his hand?"

Lindsey focused her attention on the object Steve was carrying. It looked like a purse. Gasping, she twisted away from the window and placed her back against the wall. She gestured wildly toward the phone.

"What's wrong?" Brenda cried. "Are you having an asthma attack?"

Lindsey shook her head. "He broke in to the house and stole my mother's purse." Brenda handed her the phone and Lindsey dialed 911 as fast as her nervous fingers would let her.

She barely gave the operator time to answer. "There's a man in our backyard," she whispered frantically. "He took my mother's purse."

The emergency operator seemed to have a thousand questions she wanted Lindsey to answer. Lindsey did the best she could.

"He's a convicted felon... I can give you the name of his probation officer if you want. Just hurry!" she pleaded.

"Officers have been dispatched."

"Please, please hurry." Lindsey was afraid that unless the police arrived within the next minute Steve would make a clean getaway.

Steve debated whether he should leave Meg's purse on the front porch. It would be easy enough to tuck it inside the mailbox, but then she might not find it until much later the next day.

He walked around the house to the backyard, thinking there might be someplace he could put it where she'd find it in the morning.

There wasn't.

The only thing he'd managed to do was rouse the neighbor's dog. He would've rung the doorbell and given her the silly thing if there'd been any lights on, but apparently she'd gone to bed. He wasn't especially eager to confront Lindsey, either. Not yet.

He still hadn't made up his mind, when he heard a noise from behind him.

"Police! Freeze!"

Was this a joke? Maybe not—whoever it was sounded serious. He froze.

"Put the purse down and turn around slowly."

Once more Steve did as instructed. With his arms raised, he turned to find two police officers with their weapons drawn and pointed at him.

"Looks like we caught ourselves a burglar," one of them said, switching on a huge flashlight.

"Caught him redhanded," the other agreed.

Chapter 6

"If you'd let me explain," Steve said, squinting against the light at the two officers. A dog barked ferociously in the next-door neighbor's yard. A man in pajamas had let the dog out and joined the audience.

"Do you always carry a woman's purse?"

"It belongs to—"

"My mother."

Although Steve couldn't see her face, he recognized the righteous tones as belonging to Meg's daughter. Lindsey and her friend stood beside the two officers and looked as if they'd gladly provide the rope for a hanging.

"Wolf." The neighbour silenced the German shepherd, but made no move to go inside.

"My name's Steve Conlan," Steve said, striving to come across as sane and reasonable. This was, after all, merely a misunderstanding.

"I wouldn't believe him if I were you," Lindsey advised the officers. "It might not be his real name." Then in lower tones she added, "He has a criminal record. I happen to know for a fact that he's a convicted felon."

"I'm not a felon," Steve growled. "And it *is* my real name. Officers, if you'd give me the opportunity to—"

"His parole officer's name is Earl Markham." Lindsey cut him off, her voice indignant. "He told me himself!"

"I know Earl Markham," the younger of the two policemen said. "And he is a parole officer."

"I know him, too," Steve barked impatiently. "We went to high school together."

"Yeah, right."

The scorn in Lindsey's voice reminded Steve of Meg when she was furious with him. Like mother, like daughter, it seemed.

"If you'd let me explain." Steve tried again, struggling to stay calm. It wasn't easy with two guns aimed at him and a man in pajamas clutching the collar of a huge dog—thank goodness for the fence. Not to mention a couple of teenage girls accusing him of who knew what.

"Don't listen to him," the other girl was saying. "He lies! He had us believing all kinds of things, and all because he thought we were Lindsey's mother."

A short silence followed her announcement. "Say that again?" the older officer muttered. "How well do you know this man?"

"My name's Steve Conlan." Steve tried yet again.

"Which may or may not be his real name." This, too, came from Lindsey's friend.

"If you'll let me get my wallet, I'll prove who I am," Steve assured them. He made an effort to sound vaguely amused by the whole situation. He lowered one arm and started to move his hand toward his back pocket.

"Keep your hands up where I can see them," the older cop snapped.

"What's going on?" The voice drifted down from the upstairs area of the house. A sweetly feminine, slightly groggy voice.

Steve glanced up, and to his great relief saw Meg's face framed in the second-floor window.

"Meg," Steve shouted, grateful that she'd finally heard the commotion. "Tell these men who I am, so they can put their weapons away."

"Steve?" she cried, shocked. "What are you doing at my house?"

"Do you know this man?" the cop asked, tilting his head back and shouting up at Meg.

"Ma'am, would you mind stepping outside?" the second officer asked. He mumbled something Steve couldn't hear under his breath.

"I'll be right down," Meg told them, and Steve watched her turn away from the window.

"Have you been sneaking around seeing my mother?"

"Lindsey, it's not like it seems," Steve said, experiencing a twinge of guilt at the way he'd misled the girl. He'd planned to talk to Meg's daughter soon, but he hadn't intended to do it in front of the police.

"I'd be more interested to find out why he has your mother's purse, if I were you," the second teenager said.

"I already know why he's got Mom's purse," Lindsey said loudly. "He stole it."

"No, I didn't!" Steve rolled his eyes. "I was trying to return it."

"You have my purse?" This was from Meg. "Oh, hello, Mr. Robinson. Hi, Wolf. I think everything's under control here." Man and dog went back inside a moment later.

"My purse!" she said again.

Steve relaxed and lowered his arms. "You left it in my car," he said.

"Thank goodness you found it." Meg, at least, displayed the appropriate amount of appreciation. "I didn't know when I'd get it back."

Now that the flashlight wasn't blinding him and the officers had returned the guns to their holsters, Steve saw Meg for the first time. In fact, he couldn't take his eyes off her. She'd thrown a flimsy cotton robe over her baby-doll pajamas but despite that, they revealed a length of sleek, smooth thigh whenever she moved. The top was low-cut and the robe gaped open and... Meg grabbed the lapels and held them together with both hands. It didn't help much.

Steve was afraid he wasn't the only one who'd noticed Meg's attire. Both officers looked approvingly in her direction. Steve was about to ask the younger of the two to wipe the grin off his face, but he held his breath and counted backward from ten.

He got to five. "Lindsey, go get your mother a coat."

"I don't have to take orders from you," the girl snapped.

Meg blinked and seemed to realize that despite the robe, such as it was, her nightwear left little to the imagination.

In an apparent effort to deflect a shouting match,

one officer asked Lindsey a few questions, while the other engaged Steve and Meg in conversation.

"You know this man?" he asked Meg.

"Yes, of course. His name's Steve Conlan."

"Steve Conlan." The officer made note of it on a small pad. "That's what he said earlier."

Steve pulled out his wallet and flipped it open, silently thrusting it out. The cop glanced at it and nodded.

"He didn't steal my purse, either," Meg went on.

Steve cast the other man an I-told-you-so look, but said nothing.

"You went out with Steve behind my back?" Lindsey cried, peering around the second policeman. Her eyes narrowed. "I can't *believe* you'd do something like that—after our talk and everything."

Meg cast her a guilty look. "We'll discuss this later."

But Lindsey wasn't going to be so easily dissuaded. "After our talk, I really, really thought I was getting through to you. Now I see how wrong I was."

"If you'd give me a chance to explain…" Steve began, wanting to avoid an argument between Meg and her daughter.

Static from the police officer's walkie-talkie was followed by a muffled voice. The two men were obviously being dispatched to another location.

"Everything okay here?" the policeman asked Meg.

"It's fine."

"Young lady?"

Lindsey folded her arms and pointed her nose toward the night sky. "All I can say is that my mother's a serious disappointment to me."

"I'm afraid I can't help you there."

"I didn't think you could," she said, shaking her head. "I thought better of her than this—sneaking out at night to see a man of…of low moral fiber."

"Lindsey!"

"Why don't we all go inside and discuss this," Steve suggested. He felt more than a little ridiculous standing in Meg's yard, and he was eager to clear the air between Lindsey and him.

"I have nothing to say to either of you," Lindsey said. She marched into the house, with Brenda scurrying behind.

Steve watched them stomp off in single file and released a deep breath. He was about to apologize for having made such a mess of things, when Meg whirled around to face him.

"I can't believe you!"

Steve ran his fingers through his hair. Meg didn't seem to grasp that this ordeal hadn't exactly been a pleasure for him, either.

"I apologize, Meg." He did feel bad about all the trouble he'd caused, but he'd only been trying to help. When he'd found her purse, returning it had seemed the best thing to do. He didn't want her wondering where it was, and he'd honestly thought he could do it without ending up in jail.

"How dare you tell my daughter to get me a coat."

Steve's head jerked up. His throat tightened with the strength of his anger. "I nearly got myself arrested— thanks to your daughter, I might add—and *you're* upset because I objected to you traipsing around in front of the neighborhood half-naked?"

Meg opened her mouth and then closed it.

"Okay," he amended, "you are wearing a robe, although it's not much of one. Neither of those cops could take their eyes off you. I supposed you enjoyed the attention."

"Don't be ridiculous! I came downstairs as fast as I could, in order to help you."

"You call parading in front of those men like that *helping* me? All I needed was for you to identify me so I could leave. That's all." His words grew louder. He was close to losing his cool and he knew it.

"I think you'd better go," Meg said, pointing in the direction of the street. Steve noticed with satisfaction that her finger shook.

"I'm out of here," he told her, "and not a minute too soon. You might have appreciated the embarrassment I endured trying to do you a favor, but I can see you don't. Which is fine by me."

"Like *you* didn't embarrass *me*?" she shouted.

"You weren't the one who had a gun pointed at you and a kid claiming you were a menace to society."

"Lindsey was only repeating what you'd told her." Meg pushed the hair away from her face, using both hands. "This isn't working."

"Wrong," he said sharply. "It's working all too well. You make me crazy, and I don't like it."

"But…"

"If I'm going to get arrested, I want it to be for someone who's willing to acknowledge the trouble I've gone through for her." Certain he was making no sense whatsoever, Steve stalked over to his car and drove away.

Meg squared her shoulders and drew her flimsy robe more tightly around her as she opened the screen door and walked back inside. The exhaust from Steve's car lingered in the yard, reminding her how angry he'd been when he left.

She was angry, too. And confused.

It didn't help to find Lindsey and Brenda sitting in the darkened living room waiting for her.

"You should both be in bed," Meg told them.

"We want to talk to you first," Lindsey announced, her hands folded on her knees.

"Not tonight," she said shortly. "I'm tired and upset."

"You!" Lindsey cried. "Brenda and I are exhausted, but that doesn't matter. What does is that you broke your word."

"I didn't promise not to see Steve again," Meg told her. She'd been careful about that.

Meg went back to the door and stood in front of the screen, half hoping Steve would return—not knowing what she'd say or do if he did.

"You've been sneaking out of the house to see him, haven't you?"

Meg lifted one shoulder in a shrug.

"You have!" Lindsey was outraged. "When?"

Meg lifted the other shoulder.

"Can't I trust you anymore?"

"Lindsey, Steve's not exactly what he said he was."

"I'll just bet," she muttered. "He's got you fooled, hasn't he? You'd believe anything he says because that's what you *want* to believe. You're so crazy about this guy you can't even see what's right in front of your face."

If she'd been a little less upset herself, Meg might've been willing to set the record straight then and there.

"We want to talk to you," Meg told her daughter. "Steve and I, together, and explain everything."

"Never!"

"Mrs. Remington, don't let him fool you," Brenda threw in dramatically.

"Let's not worry about this now," she said as defeat settled over her. "It's late and I have to be at the store early in the morning."

Lindsey stood, her hands clenched at her sides. "I want you to promise me you won't see him again."

"Lindsey, please."

"If you don't, Mom, I'll never be able to trust you again."

"It's time we had a little talk," Nancy said, bringing a steaming cup of coffee to the breakfast table. After the night he'd had, the last thing Steve wanted was a tête-à-tête with his troublesome younger sister.

"No, thanks."

Nancy left the table, taking the coffee with her.

"Hey, I want the coffee."

"Oh." She brought it back and slipped into the chair across from him. "Something's bothering you."

"Nothing gets past you, does it?" He almost scalded his mouth in his eagerness to get some caffeine into his system.

"Can you tell me what's wrong?" She stared at him with big brown eyes that suggested she could solve all his problems, if only he'd let her.

"No."

"It has to do with that Meg, doesn't it?"

Steve mumbled a noncommittal reply. He didn't

care to discuss Meg Remington just then. What he'd told Meg was the simple truth—she made him crazy. No woman had ever affected him as powerfully as she did. After the way they'd parted, he doubted they'd see each other again, and damn it all, that wasn't what he wanted.

"She's not the woman for you," Nancy said, her eyes solemn.

"Nancy," he said in a low voice, "don't say any more. Okay?"

She closed her eyes, shaking her head. "You're falling in love with her."

"No, I'm not," he muttered. Cradling the mug in both hands, he tried the coffee again, sipping from the edge to avoid burning his mouth.

"Thou protest too much," she told him, with a sanctimonious sigh. "I'm afraid you've made it necessary for me to take matters into my own hands. Someone's got to look out for your best interests."

Steve lowered the mug and glared at his sister. "What did you do *this* time?"

"Nothing yet. There's this woman, a widow I met on campus, and I'd like you to get to know her. She's nothing like Meg, but as far as I'm concerned…"

"No!" He wasn't listening to another word. The last time his sister had roped him into her schemes he'd met a crazy woman with an even crazier daughter. No more.

"But Steve…"

"You heard me." The chair made a scraping sound against the tile floor as he stood. "I won't be home for dinner."

Nancy stood, too. "When will you be back?"

Steve regarded her suspiciously. "I don't know. Why?"

"Because the least you can do is meet Sandy."

Steve gritted his teeth. "You invited her to the house?"

"Don't worry—I didn't mention you. I wanted the two of you to meet casually. She's nervous about dating again, and I was afraid if I told her about my big, bad brother she'd run in the opposite direction."

"That's what I'm going to do. If you want to work on anyone's love life, you might try your own."

"All right, all right," Nancy said, sounding defeated. "Just stay away from Meg, okay? The woman's bad news."

Steve's laugh was humorless. "You're telling me."

A week passed. Steve refused to dwell on his confrontation with Meg. He didn't call her and she didn't phone him, either.

He hated to end it all, but he didn't see any other option.

He missed her, though. He tried to tell himself otherwise. Tried to convince himself a man has his pride. Tried not to think about her.

And failed.

Early one afternoon, Nancy came by the shop with a friend. They were on their way to a movie, or so Nancy claimed.

Nancy smiled a little-sister smile and cheerfully asked Steve if he'd give Sandy an estimate on repairing her fender.

Sandy was petite. Cute. A little fragile.

It didn't take Steve long to figure out that this Sandy was the same one Nancy had wanted him to meet. The widow. The woman who'd save him from Meg's clutches.

"Pleased to meet you," Steve said, wiping his greasy hands on the pink cloth he had tucked in his hip pocket.

Nancy smiled innocently, looking pleased with herself.

"I'll have a written estimate for you by the time you two get back here."

"You don't have to work late again, do you?" Nancy asked, not even attempting to be coy.

Steve could already see what was coming. His conniving sister was about to wrangle a dinner invitation out of him. One that meant he'd be stuck entertaining Sandy.

"I'm afraid I'm tied up this evening," he said stiffly.

"Oh, darn. I was hoping you could take Sandy and me to dinner."

"Sorry," he said. "Now, if you'll excuse me…"

"It was a pleasure to meet you, Mr. Conlan."

"The pleasure was mine," he said and turned away.

Unfortunately, it didn't end with Sandy. His sister had several other friends with dented fenders or cracked windshields. They all seemed to need estimates in the days that followed.

"The next time a woman comes in and asks for me, I'm unavailable," he told his crew. Steve made sure that on her next visit Nancy would know he didn't have time for her matchmaking games. He told her as much when she stopped by—alone—a couple of days later.

"I was only trying to help."

"Thanks, but no thanks." He sat at his desk, making

his way through the piles of paperwork stacked in front of him.

Nancy expelled a sigh. "You aren't seeing Meg again, are you?"

His hand tightened around the pen. "That's none of your business."

"Yes, it is! A woman like that could ruin your life."

In some ways she already had, but Nancy wouldn't understand. Whenever he met another woman, Steve found himself comparing her to Meg. Invariably everyone else fell short. Far short. He was miserable without her.

Nancy left, and Steve leaned back in his chair, studying the phone. All it would take was one call. He wouldn't have to mention the incident with the police. He could even make a joke of it, maybe buy her a pair of flannel pajamas. The kind that went from her neck to her feet. They'd both laugh, say how sorry they were and put an end to this stalemate.

Then he'd take her in his arms, hold her and kiss her. This was the part he dwelled on most. The reconciliation.

"Steve." Gary Wilcox stuck his head in the office door.

Steve jerked his attention away from the phone.

"There's someone here to see you. A woman."

Impatience made Steve's blood boil. "What did I say earlier? I gave specific instructions to tell any of my sister's friends that I'm unavailable."

"But—"

"Is that so hard to understand?"

"Nope," Gary said without emotion. "I don't have

a problem doing that, if it's what you really want, but I kinda had the feeling this one's special."

Knowing his foreman had cast an appreciative eye at the widow, Steve suspected it was Sandy who'd dropped by unannounced. "You talk to her."

"Me?"

"Yeah, you."

"What am I supposed to say?"

Steve rubbed a hand down his tired face. Did he have to do everything himself? "I don't know, just say whatever seems appropriate. I promise you Nancy won't be sending any more eligible women to the shop."

"Nancy didn't send this one."

The pen slipped from Steve's hands and rolled across the desk. "Who did?"

"She didn't say. All I got was her name. Meg Remington. I seem to recall hearing it mentioned a time or two—generally when you were upset."

Steve pushed back his chair and slowly stood. His heart reacted with a swift, furious pace. "Meg's here?"

"That's what I've been trying to tell you for the last five minutes."

Steve sank back into the chair. "Send her in."

A mischievous grin danced across Gary's mouth. "That's what I thought you'd say."

Steve stood, then sat back down and busied himself with things on his desk. He wanted Meg to think he was busy. The minute she walked into the room, he'd set everything aside.

A full five minutes passed and still she didn't show up. Steve came out of his office and ran into Gary, who frowned and shook his head. "She's gone."

"Gone?"

Gary nodded. "The only thing I can figure out is that she must've overheard you say you weren't available and left."

Steve muttered a four-letter word and hurried out. He wasn't sure where he'd find her, but he wasn't going to let her walk out of his life.

She wasn't at the bookstore and he didn't see her car at home. He tried the grocery store, too, for good measure. Without success.

It wasn't until nearly seven that he drove to her house again. That he was willing to confront her daughter was a sign of how desperate he'd become.

He stood on her front porch and rang the doorbell. Waiting for someone to answer, he buried his hands deep in his pockets. A preventive action, he realized, to keep from reaching for her the instant she appeared.

"Just a minute," he heard her call.

Then the door opened and Meg was standing there.

His gaze drifted over her. He'd planned to play it cool, casually mention that he was in the neighborhood and heard she'd stopped by the office. Their eyes met, held, and Steve forgot about hiding his feelings. She wore a pretty pale blue summer dress.

"Hello, Steve."

"Hello."

The screen door stood between them.

They continued to stare at each other.

"Can I come in?" he asked. Pride be damned. It'd been cold comfort in the past two weeks. If he had to apologize, or grovel or beg forgiveness, then so be it. He wanted her back in his life.

"Of course." She unlatched the door and pushed it open.

Steve stepped inside. He could barely breathe, never mind think. Pulling her into his arms didn't seem appropriate, but that was all he wanted to do.

"Where's Lindsey?" he managed to ask.

Meg's voice was breathy and uneven. "She's out for the evening."

He needed to touch her. Reaching up, he cupped her cheek in his rough palm. Slowly, Meg closed her eyes and leaned her head into his hand.

"I had to come here," he whispered.

"I'm so sorry. About everything."

"Me, too."

Unable to wait a second longer, Steve folded her in his arms and brought her mouth to his. Gentleness was beyond him, his hunger as great as any he'd ever known.

Meg grabbed his shirt as if she needed an anchor, something to secure her during the wild, sensual storm. He backed her against the door.

Meg gasped, and Steve moved a few inches away. With his hands framing her cheeks, he studied her beautiful face. Her shoulders were heaving, and he realized his own breathing was just as labored.

He rubbed the pad of his thumb across her moist, swollen lips. The action was unhurried—an apology for his roughness, his eagerness.

She moaned softly and he kissed her again. Gently. With restraint. Her arms were around his neck, and Steve had never tasted a sweeter kiss.

"I was going to call," he told her, burying his face

in the slope of her neck. "A thousand times I told my-self I'd call. Every minute apart from you was torture."

"I wanted to call you, too."

"I'm glad…"

"You were right," Meg confessed. "I should've been wearing something more…discreet."

"I was jealous, pure and simple." He felt her smile against the side of his face and smiled, too.

"I would've been jealous if the situation had been reversed."

"Don't worry. I didn't date a single one of the women Nancy arranged for me to meet."

Meg jerked back. "What women?"

"Ah…it's not important."

"It is to me."

He knew it would've been to him, as well, so he explained. "Nancy felt it was necessary to save me from a loose woman, so she introduced me to some of her friends."

"And you refused to go out with them." Meg sounded pleased.

"All I want to do is talk to Lindsey. Get things straightened out."

"Me, too. But we can't right now."

"So I see."

"Hold me," she said, nestling in his arms. "I don't want you to leave for a long, long time."

Steve planted tiny kisses along the side of her neck, marking his way back to her lips. "When will Lindsey be back?" he whispered.

"She's spending the night at Brenda's."

His hold tightened. "Meg," he said, then kissed her with a hunger he couldn't deny. "I want to make love to you. There's a lot we have to discuss before we make that kind of commitment, but we have an opportunity to do that now, don't we?"

"Mmm."

He kissed her again, pacing himself. "Thank God you dropped in at the office. I don't know how long it would've taken me to come to my senses otherwise."

"The office?" Meg repeated, breaking away from him. "I was never at your office."

Chapter 7

"It doesn't matter if you were at my office or not," Steve said, kissing Meg again. Slowly. Thoroughly.

She couldn't manage even a token resistance, although her mind whirled with questions.

She was starved for the taste of him. Starved for his touch. Starved for *him*. The loneliness had been suffocating. Before she'd met Steve, her life had seemed just fine. Then within a matter of weeks she'd realized how empty everything was without him.

"I've missed you so much," she told him between deep kisses.

"Me, too."

"You should've phoned," she whispered.

"You, too."

"I know."

"I'm crazy about you."

She was so tempted to throw caution to the wind and make love with this man who excited her so much. Who made her feel alive.

If ever the moment was right it was now, with Lindsey gone until morning.

But...

The questions returned. There'd only been one man in her life, her ex-husband, Lindsey's father, and by the time they'd divorced Meg had felt like a failure as a wife. Inadequate. Unresponsive.

"Steve... Steve." Her fingers were in Steve's hair as his mouth roamed over her throat. "Stop, please."

He went still, his lips pressed against the hollow of her throat. "You want me to stop? Now?"

"Please...for just a minute. Did you say you thought I'd been to your office?" She wanted that confusion cleared up first.

"It's what Gary told me." He raised his head, eyes clouded with passion. "It doesn't matter—I'm here now. I've missed you so much. I can't believe either of us let this go on so long."

"But it does matter," she argued. "Because I wasn't there."

Steve shut his eyes and seemed to be fighting something in himself. Finally, he straightened and eased away from her.

"I'm glad you're here," she whispered. "I've missed you, too. It's just that before we..." She felt as though her face was on fire. How she wished she was more experienced, more sophisticated. "You know."

"Make love," he finished for her.

"Yes... We should come to some sort of understanding. It's like you said—we should talk first."

Steve took her by the hand. He led her into the living room and chose the big overstuffed chair that was her favorite.

He sat and, reaching up, pulled her onto his lap. "So let's talk."

"Okay," she said, hating the way her voice trembled.

"First I want to clear something up. You say you *didn't* stop by my office this afternoon?"

"No. I was at the store until after six."

"I didn't see you there."

"I was in the back room, processing orders." Because she was afraid he'd think she was lying in order to save face, she added, "You can check with Laura if you want."

Steve frowned. "I believe you. Why wouldn't I?" He studied her. "But that isn't why you stopped us just now, is it?"

Meg lowered her gaze. "No," she whispered.

"I didn't think so. Are you going to tell me?"

"Tell you what?" Steve's arm went around her waist. It felt good to be this close to him.

"I suspect your reluctance has to do with your marriage."

"My marriage?"

"It doesn't take a detective to figure out that your ex-husband hurt you badly."

"No divorce is easy," Meg admitted, "but I'm not an emotional cripple, if that's what you mean."

"It isn't." He drew her even closer and kissed her again. She kissed him back, offering him her heart, her soul, her body...

"I can't seem to keep my hands off you," he murmured. "I wanted to talk to you about your marriage. Instead, I'm a second away from ravishing you."

And she was a second away from letting him.

"It was a friendly divorce," Meg insisted, returning to the subject he'd introduced. It wasn't a comfortable one—but it was safer than touching and kissing and where that would lead.

Steve eyed her suspiciously. "How friendly?" he asked.

"We parted amicably. It was a mutual decision."

"What caused the divorce?"

Meg closed her eyes and sighed. "He had a girl-friend," she said, trying not to reveal her bitterness. For years she'd kept the feelings of hurt and betrayal buried deep.

In the beginning, that had been for Lindsey's sake. Later, she was afraid to face the anger for fear of what it would do to her. "Dave didn't love me anymore," she said, in an unemotional voice. As if it didn't matter. As if it had never mattered.

"What about Lindsey? He abandoned her, too?"

"He knew I'd always be there for her, and I will. He lives in California now."

"What about his commitment to you and his daughter? That wasn't important to him?"

"I don't know—you'd need to ask Dave about that."

"How long did this business with the girlfriend go on before he told you about her?"

"I don't know," she said again. She had her suspicions, plenty of them, but none she was willing to discuss with Steve. "I do know that when Dave got around to telling me he wanted a divorce, she was pregnant."

"In other words, you felt there was nothing you could do but step aside?"

"I had no problem doing that." Maybe if she'd loved Dave more, she would've been willing to fight for him. But by the time Dave told her about Brittany, she wanted out of the marriage. Just plain out.

"So you got divorced."

"Yes, with no fuss at all. He gave me what I wanted."

"And what was that?"

"He was willing to let me raise Lindsey." She shook her head. "It's not what you're thinking."

"And what am I thinking?"

She placed the back of her hand against her forehead and gave him a forlorn look, like the heroine of a silent movie. "That the divorce traumatized me."

"I wasn't thinking that at all," he assured her. "Your marriage had already taken care of that."

Meg dropped her hand, then raised it again to brush away her tears. How well Steve understood.

"It wasn't enough that your husband had an affair. When he walked out on you and Lindsey, he made sure you blamed yourself for his infidelity, didn't he?" She didn't respond, and he asked her a second time, his voice gentle. "Didn't he?"

Meg jerked her head away for fear he'd read the truth in her eyes. "It's over now… It was all a long time ago."

"But it isn't over. If it was, we'd be upstairs making love instead of sitting here talking. You haven't been able to trust another man since Dave."

"No," she whispered, her head lowered.

"Oh, baby," he said tenderly, gathering her in his arms. "I'm so sorry."

She blinked rapidly in an effort to forestall more tears. "I trust you," she told him, and she knew instinctively that Steve would never betray his wife or walk away from his family.

"You do trust me," he said, "otherwise you wouldn't have let me get this close to you. Just be warned. I intend to get a whole lot closer, and soon."

With anyone else Meg would have felt threatened, but with Steve it felt like a promise. A promise she wanted him to fulfill.

"It's better that we wait to make love," he surprised her by adding.

"It is?" Her head shot up.

"I want to clear the air with Lindsey first," he told her. "Get things settled between us. I'd much rather be her friend than her foe."

"And I'd like to be Nancy's friend, too," Meg said.

He smiled. "Those girls don't know what they started—or where it's going to end."

"Exactly where are we going?" Lindsey asked, staring out the car window.

"I already told you." Meg was losing patience with her daughter.

"To see Steve at work?"

"Yes."

"Work release, you mean."

"Lindsey!" Meg said emphatically. She'd never known her to be this difficult. "Steve has his own business. We both thought if you could see him at work, you'd know that what he told you about being an ex-con was all a farce."

Lindsey remained sullen for several minutes, then asked, "Why'd he say all those things if they weren't true?"

Her daughter had a valid point, but they'd gone over this same ground a dozen times. "We wanted you to dislike him."

Unfortunately Steve's plan had worked all too well. And Meg had obviously done an equally good job with Nancy, because his sister didn't want him continuing to see her, either. What a mess they'd created.

"Why wouldn't you and Steve want me to like him?" Lindsey asked.

"I've already explained, and I don't feel like repeating the story yet again," Meg said. "Suffice it to say I'm not especially proud of our behavior."

Lindsey pouted, but didn't ask any more questions.

Meg pulled into the parking lot at Steve's business and watched as Lindsey took in everything—the well-established body shop, the customers, the neat surroundings.

There were three large bays all filled with vehicles in various states of disrepair. Men dressed in blue-striped coveralls worked on the cars.

"They *all* look like they came straight from a prison yard," Lindsey mumbled under her breath.

"Lindsey," Meg pleaded, wanting this meeting to go well. "At least give Steve a chance."

"I did once, and according to you he lied."

Once more, Meg had no argument. "Just listen to him, okay?"

"All right, but I'm not making any promises."

The shop smelled of paint and grease; the scents weren't unpleasant. There was a small waiting area with a coffeepot, paper cups and several outdated magazines.

"Hello," Meg said to the man standing behind the counter. "I'm Meg Remington. Steve is expecting me."

The man studied her. "*You're* Meg Remington?" he asked.

"Yes."

"You don't look like the Meg Remington who was in here last week."

"I beg your pardon?"

"Never mind, Gary," Steve said, walking out from the office. He smiled warmly when he saw Meg. Lindsey sat in the waiting area, reading a two-year-old issue of *Car and Driver* as if it contained the answers to life's questions.

"Hello, Lindsey," Steve said.

"Hello," she returned in starched tones.

"Would you and your mother care to come into my office?"

"Will we be safe?"

A hint of a smile cracked Steve's mouth, but otherwise he didn't let on that her question had amused him. "I don't think there'll be a problem."

"All right, fine, since you insist." She set aside the magazine and stood.

Steve ushered them into the spotlessly clean office and gestured at the two chairs on the other side of his desk. "Please, have a seat."

They did, with Lindsey perched stiffly on the edge of hers.

"Would you like something to drink?" he asked.

"No, thanks."

Meg didn't think she'd ever seen Lindsey less friendly. It wasn't like her to behave like this. Presumably she thought she was protecting her mother.

"I have a confession to make," Steve said, after an awkward moment. He leaned back in his chair.

"Shouldn't you be telling this to the police?" Lindsey asked.

"Not this time." His eyes connected with Meg's. She tried to tell him how sorry she was, but nothing she'd said had changed Lindsey's attitude.

"I did something I regret," Steve continued undaunted. "I lied to you. And as often happens when people lie, it came back to haunt me."

"I'm afraid I was a party to this falsehood myself," Meg added.

"How do you know it's really a lie?" Lindsey demanded of Meg. "Steve could actually be a convicted criminal. He might be sitting behind that desk, but how do we know if what he says is true?"

Meg rolled her eyes.

"Who are you *really*, Steve Conlan?" Lindsey leaned forward, planting both hands on the edge of his desk.

"I'm exactly who I appear to be. I'm thirty-eight years old. Unmarried. I own this shop and have ten full-time employees."

"Can you prove it?"

"Of course."

A knock sounded on the door.

"Come in," Steve called.

The man who'd greeted her when she first arrived stuck his head inside the door. He smiled apologetically. "Sorry to interrupt, but Sandy Janick's on the phone."

Steve frowned. "Are we working on Sandy's vehicle?" he wanted to know. "I don't remember seeing a work order."

"No, she's that friend your sister was trying to set you up with. Remember?"

"Tell her I'll call her back," Steve said without hesitating.

Meg bristled. He'd admitted that his sister had been playing matchmaker. So Nancy had set him up with another woman. Probably one without a troublesome teenager and a bunch of emotional garbage she was dragging around from a previous marriage. Meg tried to swallow the lump forming in her throat.

"Gary," Steve said, stopping the other man from leaving. "Would you kindly tell Lindsey who owns this shop?"

"Sure," the other man said with a grin. "Mostly the IRS."

"I'm serious," Steve said impatiently.

Gary chuckled. "Last I heard it was Walter Milton at Key Bank. Oops, there goes the phone again." He was gone an instant later.

"Walter Milton," Lindsey said skeptically. "So you really *don't* own this business."

"Walter Milton's my banker and a good friend."

"So is Earl Markham, your parole officer," Lindsey snapped. "A high school friend, correct?" She shook her head. "I'm afraid I can't believe you, Mr. Conlan. If you were trying to get me to change my mind about you seeing my mother, it didn't work." Then turning to Meg, she said, "I wouldn't trust him if I were you. He's got a look about him…"

"What look?" Meg and Steve asked simultaneously.

"You know—a criminal look. I'm sure I've seen his face before, and my guess is that it was in some post office."

Meg ground her teeth with frustration. "Lindsey, would you please stop being so difficult?"

"I don't think it's a good idea for you to date a man who lies."

"You're right," Steve surprised them both by saying. "I should never have made up that ridiculous story about being a felon. I've learned my lesson and I won't pull that stunt again. All I'm asking is that you give me a second chance to prove myself."

"I don't think so."

Meg resisted throwing her arms in the air.

"You know what really bothers me?" Lindsey went on. "That you'd involve my mother in this stupid scam of yours. That's really low."

"I don't blame you for being angry with me," Steve said, before Meg could respond. "But don't be upset with your mother—it was my idea, not hers."

"My mother wouldn't stoop to anything that underhanded on her own."

Meg's eyes met Steve's and she wanted to weep with frustration.

"I was hoping you'd find it in your heart to forgive me," Steve said contritely, returning his attention to Lindsey. "I'd like us to be friends."

"Even if we were, that doesn't mean I approve of you seeing my mother."

"Lindsey," Meg began. "I—"

"Mom, we can't trust this guy," Lindsey interrupted. "We know how willing he is to lie. And what about that phone call just now?" She pointed at Steve. "Another woman calls and he can hardly wait to get back to her. You saw the expression on his face."

"Don't be ridiculous," Steve snapped. "I'm crazy about your mother. I wouldn't hurt her for the world."

"Yeah, whatever. That's what they all say." Lindsey had perfected the world-weary tone so beloved of teenagers everywhere.

"I've had enough, Lindsey," Meg said sternly. "I think you'd better go wait in the car."

Lindsey leapt eagerly out of her chair and rushed from the office, leaving Steve and Meg alone.

"I'm sorry," she whispered, standing.

"I'll try to talk to her again." Steve walked around the desk and pulled her into his arms. "All she needs is a little time. Eventually she'll learn to trust me." He raised her hand to his mouth and kissed the knuckles. "But one thing's for sure…"

"What's that?"

"I'm through with sneaking around meeting you. I'm taking you to dinner tonight and I'm coming to the front door. Lindsey will just have to accept that we're dating. In fact, I'll ask her if she'd like to join us."

"She won't," Meg said with certainty.

"I'm still going to ask. She may not like me now, but in time I'll win her heart, just the way I intend to win her mother's."

What Steve didn't seem to understand was that he'd already won hers.

At seven that night, Meg was humming softly to herself and dabbing perfume on her wrists. Steve was due any minute.

The telephone rang, but Meg didn't bother to answer. There was no point. The call was almost guaranteed to be for Lindsey. She heard the girl racing at breakneck speed for the phone, as if reaching it before the second ring was some kind of personal goal.

"Mom!" Lindsey screeched from the kitchen downstairs, reaching her in the master bath.

"I'll be right there," she called back, checking her reflection in the bathroom mirror one last time.

Lindsey yelled something else that Meg couldn't hear.

"Who is it?" Meg asked, coming out of her bedroom and hurrying downstairs.

"I already told you it's Steve," Lindsey said indifferently as she passed her leaving the kitchen.

Meg glanced at her watch and reached for the phone. "Hello."

"Hi," he said, sounding discouraged. "I ran into a problem and it looks like I'm going to be late."

"What kind of problem?" It was already later than her normal dinnertime, and Meg was hungry.

"I'm not sure yet. Sandy Janick phoned and apparently she's got a flat tire…"

"Listen," Meg said with feigned cheerfulness, "why don't we cancel dinner for this evening? It sounds like you've got your hands full."

"Yes, but…"

"I'm hungry right now. It's no big deal—we'll have dinner another night."

Steve hesitated. "You're sure?"

"Positive." She was trembling so badly it was difficult to remain standing. Steve and Sandy. She suspected Nancy had arranged the flat tire, but if Steve couldn't see through that, then it was obvious he didn't want to. "It's not a problem," Meg insisted.

"I'll give you a call tomorrow."

"Sure… That would be great." She barely heard the rest of the conversation. He kept talking and Meg hoped she made the appropriate responses. She must have, because a couple of minutes later he hung up.

Closing her eyes, Meg exhaled and replaced the receiver.

"Mom?"

Meg turned to face her daughter.

"Is everything okay?"

She nodded, unable to chase away the burning pain that attacked the pit of her stomach and radiated out.

"Then how come you're so pale?"

"I'm fine, honey. Steve and I won't be going out to dinner after all." She tried to sound as if nothing was amiss, but her entire world seemed to be collapsing around her. "Why don't we get a pizza? Do you want to call? Order whatever you want. Okay?"

She was overreacting and knew it. If Steve was doing something underhanded, he wouldn't tell her he was meeting Sandy Janick. He'd do the same things Dave had done. He'd lie and cheat.

"I'm going to change my clothes," Meg said, heading blindly for the stairs.

She half expected Lindsey to follow her and announce that she'd been right all along, that Steve wasn't to be trusted. But to Meg's astonishment, her daughter said nothing.

"I knew if anyone could help Sandy with her flat tire it would be you," Nancy said, smiling benevolently at her older brother.

Steve glanced at his watch, frustrated and angry with his sister—and himself. She'd done it again. She'd manipulated him into doing something he didn't want to do. Instead of spending the evening with Meg, he'd been trapped into helping these two out of a fix.

Leave it to his sister. Not only had Nancy and Sandy managed to get a flat, but they'd been on the Mercer Island floating bridge in the middle of rush-hour traffic. Steve had to arrange for a tow truck and then meet them at his shop. From there, they'd all ended up back at the house, and Sandy had made it clear that she was looking for a little male companionship. There was a time Steve would've jumped at the chance to console the attractive widow. But no longer.

"I can't tell you how much I appreciate your help," Sandy told him now. "Thank you so much."

"You're welcome." He looked pointedly at his watch. It was just after nine, still early enough to steal away and visit Meg. Lindsey would disapprove, but that couldn't be avoided.

The girl was proving to be more of a problem than Steve had expected. She was downright stubborn and unwilling to give him the slightest bit of credit. Well, she was dealing with a pro, and Steve wasn't about to give up on either of the Remington women. Not without a fight.

"You're leaving?" Nancy asked as Steve marched to the front door.

"Yes," he said. "Is that a problem?"

"I guess not." His sister wore a downtrodden look, as if he'd disappointed her.

"I have to be going, too," Sandy Janick said. "Again, thank you."

Steve walked her to the door and said a polite good-bye, hoping it really *was* goodbye. He wished her well, but wasn't interested in becoming her knight in shining armor. Not when there was another damsel whose interest he coveted.

He closed the door as he went to retrieve his car keys from the hall table and grab his jacket.

Nancy got up and followed him as he prepared to leave. "Where are you going?" she asked.

Steve glared at his sister. "What makes you think it's any of your business?"

"Because I have a feeling that you're off to see that…that floozy."

"*Floozy?* What on earth have you been reading?" Shaking his head, he muttered, "Meg isn't a floozy or a woman of ill repute or a hussy or any other silly term you want to call her. She's a single mother and a businesswoman. She owns a bookstore. She—"

"That's not what she told me."

"Listen. I'm thirty-eight years old and I won't have my little sister running my love life. Now, I helped you and your friend, but I had to break a dinner date with Meg to do it."

"Then I'm glad Sandy got that flat tire," she said defiantly.

Steve had had enough. "Stay out of my life, Nancy. I'm warning you."

His sister raised her head dramatically, as if she'd come to some momentous decision. "I'm afraid I can't do that. I'm really sorry, Steve."

"What do you mean, you *can't*?"

"I can't stand idly by and watch the brother I've

always loved and admired make a complete fool of himself. Especially over a woman like *that*."

Steve's patience was gone. Vanished. But before he could say a word, Nancy threw herself in front of him.

"I won't let you do this!" she said, stretching her arms across the door.

The phone rang just then, and Steve knew he'd been saved by the bell. Nancy flew across the room to answer it.

Hoping to make a clean getaway, Steve opened the door and dashed outside. As he'd suspected, Nancy tore out after him.

"It's for you," she called from the front porch.

Steve was already in his car and he wasn't going to be waylaid by his sister a second time.

"Tell whoever it is I'll call back."

"It's a woman."

"What's her name?"

"Lindsey," she called at the top of her voice. "And she wants to talk to you."

Chapter 8

The last person Steve expected to hear from was Meg's standoffish teenage daughter. He climbed out of his car and ran up the porch steps. He walked directly past his sister and without saying a word went straight to the phone.

"Lindsey? What's the problem?" he asked. He was in no mood for games and he wanted her to know it.

"Are you alone?" Lindsey asked him.

Steve noticed that her voice was lower than usual. He assumed that meant Meg wasn't aware of her daughter's call.

"My sister's here," he answered. Nancy stood with her arms folded, frowning at him with unconcealed disapproval.

"Anyone else?" Lindsey asked, then added snidely, "Especially someone named Sandy."

It sounded as if Lindsey was jealous on her mother's behalf, which was ridiculous. The kid would be glad of an excuse to get rid of him. "No. Sandy left a few minutes ago."

"So you *were* with her," she accused.

In light of the confrontation he'd just had with his sister, Steve's hold on his patience was already strained. "Is there a reason for your call?" he asked bluntly.

"Of course," Lindsey muttered with an undignified huff. "I want to know what you said that upset my mother."

"What I said?" Steve didn't understand.

"After you called, she told me to order pizza for dinner and then she said I could have anything on it I wanted. She knows I like anchovies and she can't stand 'em. Then," Lindsey said, after a short pause, "the pizza came and she looked at me like she didn't have a clue where it came from. Something's wrong and I want you to tell me what it is."

"I have no idea."

"Mom's just not herself." Another pause, a longer one this time. "You'd better come over and talk to her."

An invitation from the veritable dragon of a daughter herself? This was a stroke of luck. "You sure you can trust me?" he couldn't resist asking.

"Not really," she said with feeling. "But I don't think I have a choice. My mom likes you although I can't figure out why."

The kid was a definite hazard to his ego, but Steve decided to let the comment pass.

"You think your mother's upset because I broke our dinner date?" he asked. "Well, I've got news for you—she's the one who called it off. She said it was no big deal."

"And you believed her?"

"Shouldn't I?"

Steve could picture the girl rolling her eyes. "Either you aren't as smart as you look, or you've been in prison for so long you don't know anything about women."

Steve didn't find either possibility flattering. "All I did was phone to tell her I was going to be late. What's so awful about that?"

"You were late because you were meeting another woman!"

"Wrong," Steve protested. "I was *helping* another woman. Actually two women, one of whom was my sister."

"Don't you get it? My dad left my mother because of another woman. He made up all these lies about where he was and what he was doing so he could be with her."

"And you're worried that your mother assumes I'm doing the same thing? Lindsey, isn't that a bit of a stretch?"

"Yes…no. I don't know," she said. "All I know is you canceled—"

"*She* canceled."

"Your dinner date because you were meeting another woman—"

"Helping another woman and my sister."

"Whatever. All I know is that Mom hasn't been the same since, and if you care about her the way you keep saying…"

"I do."

"Then I suggest you get over here, and fast." The line was abruptly disconnected.

Steve stared at the receiver, then replaced it, shaking his head as he did.

"What's wrong with Meg?" Nancy asked.

Steve shrugged. "Darned if I know. No one ever told me falling in love was so complicated." Having said that, he marched out the door.

Nancy ran after him. "You're in love with her?"

"I sure am."

A huge smile lit up his sister's face. Steve stood next to his car, wondering if he was seeing things. A smile was the last reaction he would've expected from Nancy.

He muttered to himself on the short drive to Meg's house. He didn't stop muttering—about women and daughters and sisters—until he rang the doorbell.

The door was opened two seconds later by Lindsey. "It took you long enough," she said.

"Lindsey, who is it?" Meg asked, stepping out from the kitchen. She'd apparently been putting away dishes, because she had a plate and a coffee mug in her hand. "Steve," she whispered, "what are you doing here?"

"Have you had dinner yet?"

"Not really," Lindsey answered for her mother. "She nibbled on a slice of pizza, but that was only so I wouldn't bug her. I ordered her favorite kind, too." She paused and grimaced. "Vegetarian. Even though *I* like anchovies and pepperoni."

"Weren't you hungry?" Steve asked, silencing Lindsey with a look.

Meg raised one shoulder in a shrug. "Not really. What about you? Did you get anything to eat?"

"Nope."

"There's leftover pizza if you're interested."

"I'm interested," he said, moving toward her. Lindsey was right—Meg seemed upset.

"You're not going to *eat*, are you?" Lindsey demanded.

"Why not?" Steve asked.

The girl sighed loudly. "What my mother needs here is reassurance. If you had a romantic thought in that empty space between your ears, you'd take her in your arms and...and kiss her."

All Steve could do was stand there and stare. This was the same annoying girl who'd been a source of constant irritation from the moment they'd met. Something had changed, and he didn't know what or why.

"Lindsey?" Meg obviously had the same questions as Steve.

"What?" Lindsey asked. "Oh, you want to know why I changed my mind. Well, I've been thinking. If Steve really meant what he said about being friends, then I guess I'm willing to meet him halfway." This was said as if it had come at great personal sacrifice. She turned to Steve. "Actually, I can't see any way around it. It's clear to me that my mother's fallen in love with you."

"Lindsey!"

Steve enjoyed the way Meg's blush colored her pale cheeks.

"And it's equally clear to me that Steve feels the same, especially if he was willing to put up with all my insults. Frankly, I can't see fighting it any longer. What's the point? And really, I can't keep a constant eye on you two. I do have my own life."

Lindsey's change of heart was welcome news to Steve. The kid held the all-important key to Meg's heart. He'd never win her love, if he didn't gain Lindsey's approval first.

"Don't get the idea I *like* any of this," Lindsey added—to salvage her pride, he guessed. "But I can learn to live with it."

"Great," Steve said, offering her his hand. "Let's shake on it."

Lindsey studied his hand as if she wasn't sure she wanted to touch him. But once she did, her shake was firm and confident.

"You're nothing like you were supposed to be," she muttered under her breath.

"I apologize for being such a disappointment," he said out of the corner of his mouth.

"Can't do anything about that now. Mom's crazy about you."

"I think she's pretty terrific, too."

Lindsey sighed. "So I noticed."

"What are you two talking about?" Meg asked.

"Nothing," Lindsey answered with exaggerated innocence. She looked at Steve and winked.

He returned her wink, pleased to be on solid ground with the girl. "Did someone say something about pizza?"

"I did," Meg told him. "Come into the kitchen and I'll microwave the leftovers."

"Mother," Lindsey groaned. "I thought I could count on you to be a little more romantic. Or do I have to do everything myself?"

"What did I do wrong now?"

"Couldn't you make Steve something special?"

Meg took a moment to think this over. "I've got chicken I could make into a salad. If he doesn't like that, there's always peanut-butter-and-jelly sandwiches."

"I'd rather have the pizza," Steve interjected. He didn't want Meg wasting her time preparing a meal, all in the name of some romantic fantasy. He wanted her to talk—and to listen.

Before Lindsey could protest, Steve followed Meg into the kitchen. "Do you know what that was about?"

Meg smiled and opened the refrigerator. "Nope." She took out the pizza box and set it on the counter.

Steve climbed onto the stool. "So what happened earlier?" he asked.

Meg hesitated, separating a piece of the pizza. "I suppose Lindsey called you?"

"Yes, but I was already on my way over here."

He saw that she avoided his eyes, as she made busywork of setting two huge slices of pizza on a plate and heating them in the microwave. "After your phone call, I had kind of a panic attack."

"About?" he prompted.

"You... Us."

"And?"

"And I worked it out myself. I felt pretty foolish afterward. I realized you aren't the same kind of man Dave was...is. If you call to say you're helping another woman, then that's exactly what you're doing."

"You thought I was seeing someone else?" Lindsey had implied as much, but he hadn't taken it seriously.

"I feel silly now," she said, setting the sizzling pizza slices in front of him. She propped her elbows on the counter and rested her chin in her palms. "It was as if the craziness of my marriage was back. You see, at one time I tried to believe Dave. He'd make up the most outrageous stories to account for the huge periods of time he was away from home, and like a naive idiot, I'd believe him." She paused. "I guess because I wanted to. But Dave's not my problem anymore."

"A leopard doesn't change his spots," Steve said, finishing off the first slice. "If Dave cheated on you, he'll cheat on his present wife, too. It stands to reason."

"I know. From what Lindsey said after her last visit to California, Dave's marriage is on shaky ground. I'm sorry for him and for his wife."

Steve offered Meg the second slice, which she declined. He'd just taken a bite when the low strains of soulful violin music drifted toward them. Steve glanced at Meg and she shrugged, perplexed.

Lindsey appeared in the kitchen, looking thoroughly disgusted. "You two need my help, don't you?"

"Help?" Steve repeated. "With what?"

"Romance." She walked into the room and took Steve's hand and then her mother's. She led them both into the living room. The furniture had been pushed to one side and the lights turned down low. Two crystal glasses and a bottle of red wine sat on the coffee table, ready to be put to good use.

"Now, I'll disappear into my room for a while," she said, "and you two can do all the things I've read about in novels."

Steve and Meg stared blankly at each other.

"Don't tell me you need help with that, too!"

"We can take it from here," Steve was quick to assure her.

"I should hope so," Lindsey muttered. With an air of superiority she headed up the stairs.

The music was sultry. Inviting. Once Lindsey was out of sight, Steve held his arms open to Meg. "Shall we dance?"

Steve could've sworn she blushed, very prettily, too, before she slipped into his embrace. He brought her close and sighed, reveling in the feel of her.

"I'm not very good at dancing," she murmured.

"Hey, don't worry. All we have to do is shift our feet a little." He laid his cheek next to hers.

He'd never had the time or the patience for romance. Or so he'd believed. Then he'd met Meg and his organized, safe, secure world had been turned upside down. Nothing had been the same since, and Steve suspected it never would be again.

Even Gary Wilcox seemed to recognize the difference between Steve's attitude toward Meg and his attitude to the other women he'd dated over the years. Steve didn't know how his foreman had figured it out, but he had. Of course, inviting Meg and Lindsey to the shop might have given Gary a clue. The idea of letting Lindsey see him at work had been an excuse; in reality he'd been trying to impress Meg, show her how successful he was. Prove to her that he was worthy of her attention.

Steve had always kept his personal life separate from the business. His personal life—that was a joke. He'd worked for years, dedicating his life to building a thriving business. He'd been successful, but that success had come at a price. There was very little room in his life for love.

But there was room for Meg and Lindsey.

Meg's lithe body moved with the music provocatively, seductively, against his. He wanted to hold her even tighter, kiss her, caress her...

They stopped moving, the pretense of dancing more than he could sustain. "I want you so badly," he whispered.

Meg sighed and raised her head so their eyes met in the dim light. "I want you, too. It frightens me how much..."

He ran his fingers up through her hair and held his breath as he slowly lowered his mouth to hers. "Oh, Meg." He kissed her over and over, unable to get enough of her.

The sound of a throat being cleared suddenly penetrated his brain.

Lindsey. Again.

Steve groaned inwardly. Slowly, reluctantly, he loosened his grip on Meg and eased his body away from hers.

She resisted. "Don't stop."

"Lindsey's back," he whispered.

Meg buried her face in his sweater.

"Hello, again," Lindsey said cheerfully from the stairs. "It looks like I returned in the nick of time." She pranced down the steps, walked over to the wine bottle and sadly shook her head. "You didn't even open the wine."

"We didn't get a chance," Steve muttered.

"I gave you twenty minutes," she said. "From what I can see, that was about five minutes longer than I should've waited. You're a fast worker."

"Lindsey," Meg said, in what was obviously meant to be her sternest voice. Unfortunately, the effect was more tentative than severe.

"I know I'm making a pest of myself—and I apologize, I really do. But we've been talking about this stuff in my sex-ed. class, and there's a case to be made for abstinence."

"What's that got to do with your mother and me?" Steve made the mistake of asking.

"You don't really want me to answer that, do you?" Lindsey asked. "Mom's flustered enough as it is."

"I guess not."

"We could discuss safe sex, if you want."

Steve watched in fascination as Meg's face turned a deep shade of red. "Lindsey!" This time her mother's voice was loud and clear. "You're embarrassing me."

"Sorry, Mom, but I figured we should raise the subject now instead of later." She dropped down on the sofa, then reached for the wine bottle and examined the label. "It's a good month, too. September. Brenda's uncle bought it for us. He said it wasn't a great wine, but it'd get the job done."

Steve's hand gripped Lindsey's shoulder. "It was, uh, thoughtful of you."

"Thanks." She smiled broadly. "But we were going for the romantic element."

"Now," Steve said, "would you mind if your mother and I talked? By ourselves? We didn't get much of a chance to do that earlier."

"I suppose that'd be all right—only I need to know something first." She set the wine bottle down and looked intently at Steve. "Are you going to marry my mother?"

Meg made a small mewling noise that suggested she was mortified beyond words. She sank onto the ottoman and covered her face with both hands.

"Well, are you?" Lindsey pressed, ignoring her mother entirely.

Steve couldn't very well say he hadn't been thinking along those lines. There'd been little else on his mind for the past few days. He loved Meg. When he wasn't with her, it felt as if something was missing from his life. From his heart.

Steve had never imagined himself with a ready-made family, but he couldn't see himself without Meg and Lindsey. Not now.

"I believe that's a subject your mother and I need to discuss privately, but since you asked I'll tell you."

Lindsey got to her feet and Meg dropped her hands and looked up at him.

"You're going to marry us, aren't you." Lindsey's words were more statement than question. A satisfied smile lit up her face. "You're really going to do it."

"If your mother will have me."

"She will, trust me," Lindsey answered, looking gleeful. "I've known my mother forever and I've never seen her this gaga over a man."

"I can do my own talking, thank you very much," Meg said. "This is the most humiliating moment of my life—thanks to you, Lindsey Marie Remington." She stood, hands on her hips. "Go to your room and we'll talk when I've finished begging Steve to forgive you."

"What did I do that was so terrible?" Lindsey muttered.

Meg pointed to the stairs.

It looked as though Lindsey was about to argue; apparently she thought better of it. Her shoulders slumped forward and she moved slowly toward the stairs.

"I was just helping," she said under her breath.

"We'll talk about that later, young lady."

Lindsey's blue eyes met Steve's as she passed him. "I know I'm in trouble when she calls me *young lady*. She's mad. Be careful what you say. Don't ruin everything now."

"I'll try my best," Steve promised.

Meg waited until her daughter had reached the top of the stairs before she spoke. "I can't begin to tell you how sorry I am about that." Although her voice was calm, Steve wasn't fooled. Meg was angry, just as Lindsey had said.

"I'll have Lindsey apologize after I've had a chance to cool down," Meg was saying. "I don't dare speak to her now." She paced the carpet. "I want you to know I absolve you from everything that was said."

Steve rubbed his jaw. "Absolve me from what, precisely?"

"I want it understood, here and now, that I don't expect you to marry me."

"But I like the idea."

"I don't," she flared. "Not when my daughter practically ordered you to propose. Now," she said with a deep breath, "I think it might be best if you left."

Steve tried to protest, but Meg ushered him to the door and he could see that this wasn't the time to reason with her.

"I've never been so mortified in my life," Meg told Laura. She counted the change and put it in the cash register. The store was due to open in ten minutes and she felt far from ready to deal with customers.

"But he said he wanted to marry you, didn't he?"

"It was a pity proposal. Good grief, what else could he say?"

Laura restocked the front display with the latest bestsellers. "Steve doesn't look like the kind of guy who'd propose if he didn't mean it."

"He didn't mean it."

"What makes you so sure?"

Meg wanted to find a hole, crawl inside and hide for the rest of her natural life. No one seemed to appreciate the extent of her humiliation. Steve certainly hadn't. He'd tried to conceal it from her, but he'd viewed the incident with Lindsey as one big joke.

She hadn't intended to mention it to anyone. Laura knew because she'd sensed something was wrong with Meg, and in a moment of weakness, Meg had blurted out the entire episode.

"Have you talked to Lindsey about what she did?" Laura asked.

"In my current frame of mind," Meg told her, "I thought it better not to try. I'll talk to her when I can do so without screaming or weeping in frustration."

"What I don't understand," Laura said, hugging a book to her chest, "is what happened to bring about such a reversal in her attitude to Steve. The last time we talked, you were pulling out your hair because she refused to believe he wasn't a convicted felon."

"I don't know what's going on with her. I just don't get it."

"You've got to admit, this romance between you and Steve has taken some unexpected twists and turns," Laura said. "First, you didn't even *want* to meet him, then once you did you agreed not to see each other again. It would've ended there if not for the flowers."

"Which didn't even come from Steve. He was just glad to be done with me."

"That's not the way I remember it."

"I doubt I'll ever see him again," Meg said, slamming the cash drawer shut.

"Now you're being ridiculous," Laura said.

"I wouldn't blame him. No man in his right mind would want to get tangled up with Lindsey and me."

"I'm sure that's not true."

Laura sounded so definite about that. Meg desperately wanted to believe her, but she knew better. When she closed the shop at six that evening, she still hadn't heard from Steve, which convinced Meg that he was relieved to be free of her.

Lindsey was sitting in the living room reading when Meg got home from work. "Hi," she said, taking a huge bite out of a big Red Delicious apple.

Meg set aside her purse and slipped off her shoes. The tiles in the entryway felt cool against her aching feet.

"You're not mad at me anymore, are you?" Lindsey asked. She got off the sofa and moved into the kitchen, where Meg was pouring herself a glass of iced tea.

"You embarrassed me."

"Steve wasn't embarrassed," Lindsey said. "I don't understand why you're so upset."

"How would you feel if I called up Dale Kotz and told him you wanted to go to the ninth-grade dance with him? He'd probably agree, because he likes you, but you'd never know if Dale would've asked you himself."

"Oh." Lindsey didn't say anything for several minutes.

"But it's more than that, Lindsey. I was mortified to the very marrow of my bones. I felt like you pressured Steve into proposing."

Lindsey sat in one of the kitchen chairs. "Would you believe me if I told you I was sorry?"

"Yes, but it doesn't change what happened."

"You are still angry, aren't you?"

"No," Meg said, opening the refrigerator and taking out lettuce for a salad. "I'm not angry anymore, just incredibly embarrassed and hurt."

"I didn't mean to hurt you, Mom," Lindsey said in a low voice. "I was only trying to help."

"I know, honey, but you didn't. You made everything much, much worse."

Lindsey hung her head. "I feel just awful."

Meg didn't feel much better herself. She sat down at the table, next to her daughter, and patted Lindsey's hand.

Lindsey managed a weak smile, then fell into her mother's arms and hid her face against Meg's shoulder. "Men are so dumb sometimes," she murmured. "Brenda says love is like a game of connect the dots. Only with men, you have to make the dots and then draw the lines. They don't get it."

Meg stroked her daughter's hair.

"Do you love him, Mom?"

Meg smiled for the first time that day. "Yeah, I think I do. I certainly didn't plan on falling in love with him, that's for sure. It just sort of…happened."

"I don't think he expected to fall in love with you, either."

The doorbell chimed, and horrified that she might

be caught crying, Lindsey broke away from her mother and hurriedly brushed the tears from her face.

"I'll get it," Meg said. She padded barefoot into the hallway and opened the door.

Steve stood on the other side, holding a dozen long-stemmed roses. He grinned. "Hello," he said, handing her the flowers. "I thought we'd try this marriage-proposal thing again, only this time we'll do it my way—not Lindsey's."

Chapter 9

"Marriage proposal?" Meg repeated, staring down at the roses in her arms. "Really, Steve, there's no need to do this." Her throat was closing up on her; she could barely speak and she couldn't meet his eyes.

"I know exactly what I'm doing," Steve said.

"Is it Brenda?" Lindsey called from the kitchen.

"No, it's Steve."

"Steve!" Lindsey cried excitedly. "This is great. Maybe I didn't ruin everything after all."

"Hello, Meg," Steve said softly.

"Hi." She still couldn't look him in the eye.

"I'd like to talk to you."

"I... I was hoping we could do that," Meg told him. "They're lovely, thank you."

She handed Lindsey the flowers. "Would you take care of these for me?" she asked her daughter. "Steve and I are going to talk and we'd appreciate some privacy. Okay?"

"Sure, Mom."

Lindsey disappeared into the kitchen and Meg sat down on the sofa. Steve sat beside her and took her hand. She wished he wasn't so close. The man had a way of muddling her most organized thoughts.

"Before you say anything, I have a couple of things I'd like to talk to you about," she began. She freed her hand from his and clasped her knees. "I've been doing a lot of thinking and...and I've come to a few conclusions."

"About what?"

"Us," she said. Dragging in a deep breath, she continued. "Laura reminded me this afternoon that our relationship has taken some unexpected twists and turns. Neither one of us wanted to meet the other—we were thrown into an impossible situation.

"We wouldn't have seen each other again if it wasn't for the flowers your sister sent me. From the moment we met, we've had two other people dictating our lives."

"To some extent that's true," Steve agreed, "but we wouldn't have allowed any of this to happen if we hadn't been attracted to each other from the beginning."

"Maybe," she admitted slowly.

"What do you mean, maybe?" Steve asked.

"I think we both need some time apart to decide what we really want."

"No way!" he said. "I've had thirty-eight years to look for what I want and I've found it. I'd like to make you and Lindsey a permanent part of my life."

"Ah, yes. Lindsey," Meg said. "As you might have noticed, she's fifteen going on thirty. I have a feeling this is what the rest of the teen years are going to be like."

"So you could use a gentle hand to help you steer her in the right direction." Steve leapt to his feet and jerked his fingers through his hair. "Listen, if you're trying to suggest you'd rather not marry me, just say so."

Meg straightened, keeping her back stiff. For a moment she couldn't speak. "That's what I'm saying," she finally managed.

Steve froze, and it was clear to Meg that he was in shock. "I see," he said after a long pause. "Then what do you want from me?"

Meg closed her eyes. "Maybe it'd be best if we—"

"Don't say it, Meg," he warned in low tones, "because we'll both know it's a lie."

"Maybe it'd be best if we—" she felt she had to say the words "—didn't see each other for a while."

Steve's smile was filled with sarcasm. "Let me tell you something, Meg Remington, because someone obviously needs to. Your husband walked out on you and your daughter. It happens. It wasn't the first time a man deserted his family for another woman and it won't be the last. But you've spent the past ten years building a wall around you and Lindsey.

"No one else was allowed in until Lindsey took matters into her own hands. Now that I'm here, you don't know what to do. You started to care for me and now you're scared to death."

"Steve…"

"Your safe, secure world is being threatened by another man. Do you think I don't know you love me?"

he demanded. "You're crazy about me. I feel the same way about you, and to be fair, you've done a damned good job of shaking up my world, too.

"If you want it to end here and now, okay, but at least be honest about it. You're pushing me away because you're afraid of knocking down those walls of yours. You're afraid to trust another man with your heart."

"You seem to have me all figured out," she said, trying—without much success—to sound sarcastic. To sound as if her emotions were unaffected by his words.

"You want me to leave without giving you this diamond burning a hole in my pocket, then fine. But don't think it's over, because it isn't. I don't give up that easily." He stalked out of the room and paused at her front door. "Don't get a false sense of security. I'll be back and next time I'm bringing reinforcements." The door closed with a bang.

"Mom," Lindsey asked, slipping into the room and sitting down next to Meg. "What happened?"

Meg struggled not to weep. "I…got cold feet."

"But you told me you were in love with Steve."

"I am," she whispered.

"Then why'd you send him away?"

Meg released her breath. "Because I'm an idiot."

"Then stop him," Lindsey said urgently.

"I can't… It's too late."

"No, it isn't," Lindsey argued and rushed out the front door. A part of Meg wanted to stop her daughter. Meg's pride had taken enough of a beating in the past few days. But her heart, her treacherous heart, knew that the battle had already been lost. She was in love with Steve Conlan.

A minute later Lindsey burst into the house, breathing hard. Panting, she said between giant gulps of air, "Steve says…if you want to talk to him…you're going to have to come outside…yourself."

Meg clasped her hands together. "Where is he?"

"Sitting in his truck. Hurry, Mom! I don't think… he'll wait much longer."

With her heart pounding, Meg walked onto the porch and leaned against the column. Steve's truck was parked at the curb.

He turned his head when he saw her. His eyes were cold. Unfriendly. Unwelcoming.

Meg bit her lip and met his gaze squarely. It took every ounce of resolve she had to move off the porch and take a few steps toward him. She paused halfway across the freshly mowed lawn.

Steve rolled down the window. "What?" he demanded.

She blinked, her heart racing.

"Lindsey said you had something you wanted to tell me," he muttered.

Meg should've known better than to let Lindsey do her talking for her. She opened her mouth, but her throat was clogged with tears. She tried to swallow, refusing to cry in front of him.

"Say it!"

"I…don't know if I can."

"Either you say it or I'm leaving." He turned away from her and started the engine.

"Mom, we're going to lose him," Lindsey cried from the porch. "Don't let him go…"

"I…love you," she whispered.

Steve switched off the engine. "Did you say something?"

"I love you, Steve Conlan. I'm scared out of my wits. You're right—I have built a wall around us. I don't want to lose you. It's just that I'm…afraid." Her voice caught on the last word.

His eyes held hers and after a moment, he smiled. "That wasn't so difficult, now, was it?"

"Yes, it was," she countered. "It was incredibly hard." He didn't seem to realize she was standing on her front lawn with half the neighborhood looking on as she told him how much she loved him.

"You're going to marry me, Meg Remington."

She sniffled. "Probably."

He got out of his truck, slammed the door and with three long strides eliminated the distance between them. "Will you or will you not marry me?"

"I will," she said, laughing and crying at the same time, then she ran to meet him halfway.

"That's what I thought." Steve hauled her into his arms and buried her in his embrace. He grabbed her about the waist and whirled her around, then half carried her back into the house.

Once inside, he kicked the door shut and they leaned against it, kissing frantically.

Lindsey cleared her throat behind them. "I hate to interrupt, but I have a few important questions."

Steve hid his face in Meg's neck and mumbled something she couldn't hear, which was no doubt for the best.

"Okay, kiddo, what do you want to know?" Steve asked when he'd regrouped.

"We're getting married?" Lindsey asked. Meg liked the way she'd included herself.

"Yup," Steve assured her. "We're going to be a family."

Lindsey let out a holler that could be heard three blocks away.

"Where will we live? Your house or ours?"

Steve looked at Meg. "Do you care?"

She shook her head.

"We'll live wherever you want," Steve told the girl. "I imagine staying close to your friends is important, so we'll take that into consideration."

"Great." Lindsey beamed him a smile. "What about adding to the family? Mom's willing, I think."

Once more Steve looked at Meg, and laughing, she nodded. "Oh, yes," she murmured, "there'll be several additions to this family."

Steve's eyes grew intense, and Meg knew he was thinking the same thing she was. She wanted his babies as much as she wanted this man. She loved him, desired him, anticipated all they could discover together, all they could learn from each other.

"One last thing," Lindsey said.

It was hard to pull her eyes away from Steve, but she wanted to include Lindsey in these important decisions. "Yes, honey?"

"It's just that I'd rather you didn't go shopping for your wedding dress alone. You're really good at lots of things, but frankly, Mom, you don't have any fashion sense."

As it turned out, Lindsey, Brenda and Steve's sister, Nancy, were all involved in the process of choosing the all-important wedding dress. Steve, naturally, wasn't allowed within a hundred feet of Meg and her dress until the day of the ceremony.

The wedding took place three months later, with family and friends gathered around. Lindsey proudly served as her mother's maid of honor.

Steve endured all the formality because he knew it mattered to Meg and to Lindsey. Nancy and his mother seemed to enjoy making plans for the wedding, too. All that was required of him was to show up and say, "I do," which suited Steve just fine.

In his view, this fuss over weddings was for women. Men considered it a necessary evil. Or so he believed until his wedding day. When he saw Meg walk down the aisle, the emotion that throbbed in his chest came as a complete and utter surprise.

He'd known he loved her—he must, to put up with all the craziness that had befallen their courtship. But he hadn't realized how deep that love went. Not until he saw Meg so solemn and so beautiful. His bride. She stole his breath as he gazed at her.

The reception was a blur. Every time he looked at Meg he found it difficult to believe that this beautiful, vibrant woman was his wife. His thoughts were a jumbled, confused mess as he greeted those he needed to greet and thanked those he needed to thank.

It seemed half a lifetime before he was alone with his wife. He'd booked the honeymoon suite at a hotel close to Sea-Tac airport. The following morning they were flying to Hawaii for two weeks. Meg had never seen the islands. Steve suspected he didn't need a tropical playground to discover paradise. He would find that in her arms.

"My husband." Meg said the word shyly as Steve fumbled with the key card to unlock their suite. "I like the way it sounds."

"So do I, but not quite as much as I like the sound of wife." With the door open, he swept Meg into his arms and carried her into the room.

He hadn't taken two steps before they started to kiss.

Meg tasted of wedding cake and champagne, of passion and love. She wound her arms around his neck and enticed him to kiss her again. Steve didn't need much of an invitation.

At the unbridled desire he read in her eyes, Steve moaned and carried her to the bed. After he'd set her feet on the floor, he kissed her again, slowly, with all the pent-up desire inside him.

He reached behind her for the zipper of her dress. "I haven't made any secret of how much I want to make love to you."

"That's true," she whispered, kissing his jaw. "Thank you for agreeing to wait. It meant a lot to me to start our marriage this way."

He slipped the sleeve down her arm and kissed the ivory perfection of one shoulder. Then he kissed the other, his lips blazing a trail up the side of her neck to the hollow of her throat.

"You make my knees go weak," she told him in a low voice.

"Mine are, too."

Together they collapsed on the bed. Steve kissed her and loosened his tie. With their lips joined, Meg's fingers worked at his shirt, undressing him.

Soon they were lost in each other, loving each other,

immersed in a world of their own. A world from which they didn't emerge until the summer sun had been replaced by a glittering moon and a sky full of stars.

Back at the reception, Lindsey sat with Steve's sister, Nancy, and licked the icing off their fingertips. "Do you suppose they'll ever figure it out?"

Nancy sipped champagne from a crystal flute. "I doubt either of them is thinking about much right now—except each other."

"We made some real mistakes, though."

"We?" Nancy said, eyeing Lindsey.

"Okay, me. I'll admit I nearly ruined everything by pushing the marriage issue. How was I to know my mother would take it so personally? Jeez, she just about had a heart attack, and all because I suggested Steve marry her."

"It worked out, though," Nancy said, looking pleased with herself. "And I made a few blunders of my own. Getting my friend to go to the shop and say she was Meg wasn't the smartest thing I've ever done. Steve was bound to find out sooner or later that it wasn't Meg."

"But we had to do something," Lindsey insisted. "They were both being so stubborn. One of them had to give in. Besides, your ploy worked."

"Better than the flowers I sent."

Lindsey sampled another bite of wedding cake. "You know what was the hardest part?"

"I know what it was for me. I had one heck of a time keeping a straight face when your mother came to the house dressed in a Tina Turner wig and five-inch heels. Oh, Lindsey, if you could've seen her."

"Steve was pretty funny himself, with his leather jacket and that bad-boy smirk."

"Neither one of them's any good at acting," Nancy said, still grinning.

"Not like us."

"Not like us," Nancy agreed.

* * * * *

Also available from Shannon Stacey and Carina Press

Holiday Sparks
Mistletoe and Margaritas
Slow Summer Kisses
Snowbound with the CEO
A Fighting Chance
Holiday with a Twist
Alone with You
Heart of the Storm
Hold Her Again

The Kowalski Series

Exclusively Yours
Undeniably Yours
Yours to Keep
All He Ever Needed
All He Ever Desired
All He Ever Dreamed
Love a Little Sideways
Taken with You
Falling for Max
What It Takes

The Boston Fire Series

Heat Exchange
Controlled Burn
Fully Ignited
Hot Response

Don't miss the next book in the Boston Fire series:

Under Control

Visit the Author Profile page
at Harlequin.com for more titles.

FULLY IGNITED

Shannon Stacey

For Megan. As your eldest sister, I have to admit that seeing a photograph of you in your firefighting gear struck a little fear in my heart, but I am immensely proud of you. Be brave, be safe and know that I love you.

And though she be but little, she is fierce.
—Shakespeare

Chapter 1

"The street's probably going to be full of people, so try not to run anybody over."

Scott Kincaid ignored the helpful instruction from Simmons since driving the big-ass fire engine through the narrow backstreets of Boston was hard enough without looking over to roll your eyes at the asshole officer riding shotgun.

Chemistry in a fire company mattered, and Engine 59 had it. Or they used to. And it wasn't a surprise they'd been a close group. Their lieutenant, Danny Walsh, was Scott's brother-in-law. Aidan Hunt, his best friend for years, was going to marry his other sister very soon. Even Grant Cutter, who was the kid of the bunch, had fit right in. And their pumper always rolled out with Ladder 37, and they meshed with that company, too, which was good since they shared the old brick fire station.

Things had gone south about six weeks ago, though, when Danny got hurt. Besides smoke inhalation, he'd suffered a concussion, a busted arm and a leg broken in two places. Having guys fill in here and there wasn't easy, even short term, and then they'd heard the news Danny needed surgery on the leg. They'd found a temporary lieutenant solution with Simmons, but it wasn't really working out.

Mostly because Simmons was such an asshole.

Scott turned onto the side street and rolled up in front of the function hall that had called in the alarm. He didn't have to worry about running anybody over because there was nobody on the street.

"Did the Rapture come and nobody told us?" Grant asked, leaning between the front seats to peer out at the empty street.

Aidan snorted. "Shit, the Rapture could hit and it would probably be a month before Boston noticed."

"Hey, anybody seen Mrs. Broussard lately?" Scott joked.

"Maybe we can save the stand-up routine for after we clear the scene," Simmons barked.

"Do you think everybody went home?" Grant asked.

"Dispatch said it's a wedding reception and they weren't sure what set the alarm off, so it's more likely they're all still inside," Aidan said.

"I want this building cleared," Simmons said, and he gestured for Aidan to go first. Simmons was never first through any door.

Scott was familiar with feeling as if he'd just

stepped through a door into hell. But walking into the function hall was a special kind of hell.

Unable to silence the fire alarm, it sounded as if they'd simply cranked the music higher and kept dancing. For a few seconds he wondered how they'd managed to dim the lights more than the code would allow, but then he figured out some genius had plugged in a smoke machine.

"They weren't sure what set the alarm off?" he asked Aidan, watching fake smoke billow up from the dance floor to hover at ceiling level. At least the sprinkler system hadn't gone off, since it was triggered by heat.

"Everybody out," Simmons tried to shout over the music. Everybody ignored him.

Welcome to the party, Scott thought. As Aidan went to deal with the alarm, Scott sent Grant over toward the corner to pull the plug on the smoke machine. They'd have to clear everybody out and do a quick sweep of the building, but it wouldn't take long.

The guys from Ladder 37 came in on their heels, with their lieutenant, Rick Gullotti, in front. Gavin Boudreau, who was only a little older than Grant, stood in the shadow of big Jeff Porter, and Chris Eriksson—the oldest of all of them, barring Chief Cobb—pulled up the rear.

"You owe me ten bucks, kid," Chris said.

Gavin rolled his eyes at Scott. "I bet him it was somebody smoking in the bathroom."

"Hell, half the people in here could be smoking right now and nobody would know." Scott shook his head. "Simmons wants us to get everybody outside."

Rick nodded. "I only saw one cruiser out there, so

we'll have to send Cutter and Boudreau outside with them. As drunk as these people are, they'll want to play with the shiny fire trucks."

Before they could move, a woman in a frilly hot-pink dress clearly marking her as a bridesmaid stepped up to Scott and ran her hand down the front of his bunker coat. "Well, hello, sexy."

"I'm going to have to ask you to go outside, ma'am," he said, taking a step back.

Instead, she looked over her shoulder and waved at a friend. "I think they're strippers!"

It wasn't the first time they'd been mistaken for strippers, but it was the first time it had happened to Scott at a wedding reception. Who expected strippers to show up at a wedding? Luckily, the alarm and the music both cut off, and Simmons's voice boomed through the speakers.

"Everybody needs to evacuate the building so we can do our jobs. The sooner we can verify there's no threat to your safety, the sooner you can get back to your party."

It didn't take them long to sweep the building once everybody had cleared out, even with two of their guys tied up keeping drunk people from climbing on the trucks. Then they stood around while Simmons rounded up the people in charge and threatened them with all kinds of dire consequences if the smoke machine was turned back on.

"It's too bad you swore off women," Aidan said. "A drunk bridesmaid who thinks you're a stripper is just your type."

"*Was* my type." Scott snorted. "Except the drunk part."

"Lydia was just talking about how we should reconsider having a small wedding because there won't be any single bridesmaids. Just Ashley as her matron of honor."

"Oh, hell no. When the wedding's for your sister, you don't mess around with the bridesmaids."

"How long's it been since you went on a date?"

As his best friend, Aidan knew he hadn't been on a date in months. "Not long enough to tangle with a drunk bridesmaid."

After it had become clear his last girlfriend—who he'd actually felt something for—had been chasing his benefits and even hinted she might get pregnant so he'd have to marry her, Scott had decided to take a hiatus from the relationship scene. Seeing Aidan and Lydia together, as well as what Ashley and Danny had gone through—from their separation and reunion to his injuries—had just driven home that he wanted the real thing. Love, marriage and a baby carriage.

But he hadn't found the right woman and he didn't want to miss her because he was hooking up with women he knew weren't in it for the long run.

"We're outta here," Rick Gullotti yelled to them, and they all headed for the door.

By the time they were backing the engines under the brick arches at the station, Scott was feeling the exhaustion set in. Even though they only worked two shifts per week—barring extra time to cover for somebody or events like the St. Patrick's Day parade last week—twenty-four hours was a long time. Hopefully, even though it was Friday night, he'd have time to hit his bunk for a quick power nap.

"Who the hell gets married at the end of March,

anyway?" Grant asked while they went through the process of checking over the engines and putting their turnout gear on the racks for the next run. "It's too cold for a nice wedding, but not cold enough to be a winter wedding. Maybe you get a discount if you get married when nobody else wants to."

"Judging by the bride's extreme lack of sobriety, I'm going to guess it wasn't a shotgun situation," Aidan said.

Scott snorted. "She was pretty near that tipping point where one drink makes the difference between the groom having the best wedding night ever or the worst wedding night ever."

They all laughed, which annoyed Simmons. They knew he didn't like chitchat when they were going through a procedure list because he thought things got missed when they were distracted. Like they weren't capable of lining their boots up in a neat row while telling a few jokes.

"I'm going upstairs," Simmons said, disgust practically dripping from his voice. "I'm so glad after tonight, you idiots will be somebody else's problem."

Nobody was as glad as they were, Scott thought, though he wasn't so much an idiot that he voiced the thought out loud. He felt bad for the guys at Simmons's usual house, who were stuck with him on a regular basis, unless they all had sticks up their asses, too.

They'd just finished up and were ready to head up to the third-floor living quarters when a woman walked through the open bay door. Scott, who'd been just about to hit the button to lower the big overhead, dropped his hand.

For a few seconds, all his mind registered was an

attractive brunette who was a little on the tall side and had a smoking body, and he assumed she was stopping by to see one of the guys or bring baked goods. Homemade cookies and muffins, and even the occasional pie, were definitely perks of the job.

Then he noticed the Boston Fire logo on her T-shirt, peeking out from behind her unzipped sweatshirt. The folded papers in her hand. The way she stood with her feet slightly apart and her back straight, her gaze sweeping around the engine bays in a way that didn't strike him as curiosity. She was appraising. Judging.

She stared at Engine 59 for a long moment, her gaze sweeping over the apparatus. And then she turned that same steady scrutiny on the guys, looking each of them in the eye for a few seconds before moving on to the next.

When she got to Scott, he looked into eyes that were a pretty shade of green and found himself surprised. He was expecting them to be brown. He grinned, a reflexive reaction to making eye contact with a pretty woman.

"I'm looking for Chief Cobb," she said, and the truth of the situation hit Scott like a hydrant wrench.

Holy shit. The new guy wasn't a guy.

Jamie Rutherford knew that look, since she'd seen it a few times before. It was the look that said somebody hadn't gotten the memo that Jamie wasn't short for James, and that they were about to share their firehouse with a woman.

She'd been in this situation before and, as long as there wasn't a straight-up misogynistic jerk in the building, she'd be fine. The guys would be awkward and stiff around her for a few days, but once she'd been out on some runs with them and done her job, that would wear off.

And if there was a misogynistic jerk in the bunch, she'd deal with that, too.

Since there were still guys moving around on the other side of the truck marked Ladder 37, she'd guess these men in front of her were with Engine 59. While she'd probably crossed paths with all or some of them, there were almost fifteen hundred firefighters in Boston and she didn't recognize any of them. She'd been sent some basic information ahead of time, though, so she knew their names and didn't have any trouble matching the photographs to the real faces.

"Is he expecting you?"

It was Aidan Hunt who'd spoken, and she wasn't surprised to see he was standing next to Scott Kincaid. They'd been best friends for years, although the relationship had gotten rocky when Aidan started secretly dating Scott's sister. Scott and his sisters, Lydia and Ashley, were the kids of Tommy Kincaid, a retired firefighter who owned Kincaid's Pub, and Aidan was like a second son to Tommy.

None of that had been in the file she'd received, of course. But she'd been to Kincaid's a few times, with a group, and she'd heard some gossip. So she also knew that the guy who'd been hurt and whose job she was taking—even temporarily—was more than just a coworker to these guys. He was literally family.

"He said I could stop by tonight and look around," she said. "I'll be filling in for Walsh and I wanted to get the lay of the land before Tuesday. Jamie Rutherford, by the way."

They each said their name, stepping forward to shake her hand. Scott was last and maybe it was her imagination, but his touch seemed to linger for a few seconds longer than expected. "Welcome to E-59."

"Thanks." She'd heard he had a reputation for being a ladies' man, but if he thought he could charm his way into her good graces, he was wrong. His thick dark hair and dark eyes, with a little sexy scruff on his jaw, would have put him squarely in "her type" territory, but the E-59 logo on his T-shirt was like an electrified boundary fence.

The ladder company guys walked over and introduced themselves before heading upstairs, and Jamie was thankful she'd taken so much time memorizing the brief bios in the file. She'd probably be overwhelmed as hell if she hadn't had a head start on putting names with faces.

"I'll take you upstairs," Grant said. "Cobb's probably in his office."

After she'd met the older guy, whose job consisted mostly of running herd on a pack of firefighters while slowly drowning in paperwork, she was handed back over to Grant for the grand tour.

The narrow but tall brick station house was pretty typical for some parts of the city. The two engine bays and equipment and personnel lockers on the ground floor. The second floor was offices, a half bath and a small bunk room for the officers. The third floor was the living space. Two old couches and a couple of older chairs were in the main room, facing a big television. An open door led into a bigger bunk room, which was empty at the moment. There was a shower room and a couple of bathrooms in the back, along with a space for working out. The kitchen was big and she noticed right away how clean it was.

When she mentioned it, Grant opened the pantry door to show the sheets of paper tacked to the inside of it. "We have a pretty strict checklist now because one of the other companies was slacking. It still says Walsh because so many different guys were filling in for him, but I can change it and print new copies."

"No sense in wasting the time and paper," she said. "I'll just do the things with his name on them."

"Okay." He paused, and his eyebrows furrowed as if he was trying to figure out how to ask an awkward question. "Where will you sleep?"

"In a bunk downstairs. Probably in Walsh's until he's ready to take it back."

"What about the bathroom? Well, the bathroom's separate, but we just have a big shower room, like a locker room type because the building's so old and they had to make it fit."

She liked the way the younger guy laid his concerns on the table so she could address them, rather than whispering with the other guys when they thought she couldn't hear them. "I'll probably use the half bath on the second floor most of the time. But if I want a shower, I'll make sure nobody needs it and then I have a hanger for the doorknob so you guys know I'm in there."

"Okay." He didn't seem to have any more questions. "Are you hungry?"

"No, but thanks."

Scott Kincaid walked into the kitchen, and looked at her before heading to the fridge. "What do you think?"

"Not too different from any other house, except a little cleaner."

"He show you the lists?"

"Yeah."

Jamie watched him pop open a soda and chug some of it, his throat working as he swallowed. She'd worked in this so-called man's field a long time and had had her share of attractive coworkers, so she knew her body language and expression remained totally neutral. But inside, she felt a sizzle of sexual attraction that was strong enough she knew she'd have to be careful around this guy.

He lowered the can and grimaced. "I hate this crap."

"So why are you drinking it?" She'd caught a glimpse of the wide variety of beverages in the refrigerator, so his choice had been deliberate.

"Looking for a caffeine and sugar double whammy. I was going to hit the bunk room for a nap, but there's a fully involved commercial fire and if they strike more alarms, we'll have to go."

A sugar high wasn't going to sustain him long, but he already knew that and *den mother* wasn't the first impression she wanted to make. "I should probably get out of the way, then. I guess I'll see you guys Tuesday."

"How's your commute look?" Scott asked after suffering a few more gulps of the soda.

"Believe it or not, I found a place only a few blocks from here because the price was right. Boston's not cheap, but I didn't want roommates, so it's just a studio. I had a bitch of a commute at my last assignment, though, so I'd live in a closet to be able to walk to work."

"But just temporarily," Grant said. "Danny's coming back."

She didn't take any offense, since she knew he hadn't intended any. "The rent's month to month instead of a lease, so if I end up back across the city, I can move again."

Scott rinsed out his empty can and dumped it into the recycling bucket. "Guess I'll see you Tuesday."

"Yeah. See you then." Because Scott was walking away and Grant was behind her, Jamie let her gaze drop to Scott's ass.

Fortunately, she managed to stifle the sigh of appreciation before it escaped, but she had a feeling she'd be giving herself a stern talking-to in the mirror later. Scott Kincaid might not mind being known around the neighborhood as a ladies' man, but people tended to be harder on women. The only reputation she cared to have was the one she'd built—a damn good firefighter who showed up, did her job well and went home.

Chapter 2

Scott pulled open the glass door of Kincaid's Pub and stepped inside. His dad had chosen not to update all the old brick and wood, and the building still had antique fixtures, so it took his eyes a few seconds to adjust to the dim lighting.

He wasn't surprised to see it was on the slow side for a Saturday night. Besides the fact everybody was still partied out from St. Patrick's Day, the bar didn't get a lot of off-the-street traffic. The plain brick building didn't look like much, there were no neon or beer signs in the two big windows, and the only sign was a small one screwed over the door. While anybody was welcome at Kincaid's, Scott had always gotten the feeling his dad preferred it the way it was—a local watering hole catering mostly to firefighters.

His sister Lydia was behind the U-shaped bar, and

he didn't see any sign of Ashley. After she and Danny had gotten back together, they'd spent time rebuilding their marriage. Then, shortly after she found out she was expecting their first child, Danny had gotten hurt working a fire. It was no surprise she'd been spending less and less time at the bar.

Fortunately for their father, who believed a Kincaid should man the bar at Kincaid's Pub, but who also didn't want to work too hard, Lydia was not only great at it, but didn't mind the job. Because of Aidan's schedule, they were free to work around the bar's hours. Even those weren't set in stone, since they opened around lunchtime and were generally closing up by nine or ten. Tommy wasn't into the late-night bar-hopping crowd so if the locals went home early, so did they. Occasionally a big game would keep them in front of the television past close, but it was at the whim of whoever was working the bar.

His father's best friend, Fitz Fitzgibbon, sat on his usual stool in the back corner of the bar, near the ancient scanner that barely worked. Not only had Scott known the man his entire life—he'd even called him Uncle Fitz when he was a kid—but Fitz had retired from Ladder 37 a few years after Tommy Kincaid retired from Engine 59, so there was a sense of kinship that went beyond being family.

When Fitz waved him over, Scott didn't need a crystal ball to know what was on the guy's mind. He'd been hoping to have a beer first, but Lydia was delivering food to one of the tables. Just as he reached Fitz, his dad stepped out from the back room.

Tommy Kincaid had always been a big man, but now he was made up of a lot less muscle and not as strong as he used to be. He could be a real son of a bitch at times and had a temper—which he'd passed on to both Scott and Lydia—but he grinned when he saw Scott and joined them.

Fitz set his mug down on the bar with a thump. "Scotty, what's this bullshit I hear about a girl being assigned to Engine 59?"

Tommy snorted. "Fitzy, as the father of two adult daughters, I can tell you they don't like being called *girls* these days."

"What the hell am I supposed to call them?"

"Women," Scott snapped. "Seriously. Have you moved off that stool in the last century at all? You know they can vote now, too, right?"

"I'll move off this stool and teach you a lesson about respect if you don't watch your tone, boy."

If any other old guy gathering moss on a bar stool threatened him, Scott would have laughed in his face. But when it was your old man's best friend, you had to watch your tone. He wasn't too worried about his physical well-being, but it would suck if his dad threw him out of the bar and he had to go somewhere else for a beer.

"It's bad luck to have a *woman* around," Fitz grumbled.

"I think that's only on ships," Scott said. He wasn't sure about bad luck, but he had a feeling having Jamie Rutherford around was going to be a distraction.

He couldn't quite put his finger on what it was about her that made him want to sit across a table from her and ask her a million questions about herself. The hard punch of sexual attraction had taken him by surprise with its intensity, but it was more than that. She had an air of calm confidence that intrigued him—like she was a woman who really had her shit together—and that was something he must find attractive because he'd thought about her more than a few times in the last twenty-four hours.

It was too bad that they not only worked together, but that she was his superior.

Fitz gave a mournful shake of his head. "Can't talk about stuff of a sexual nature with your buddy when there's a woman around, if you know what I mean."

"Since *my* buddy's doing stuff of a sexual nature with my *sister*, trust me, that ship has already sailed," Scott replied, trying to keep the annoyance he felt from creeping into his tone. The old guy was really scraping the bottom of the barrel looking for a reason to disapprove of a woman being on the job.

"What do you guys talk about, then?"

"Sports and how much taxes suck, like everybody else."

As intended, the mention of taxes set Fitz off like a wind-up toy. Once he got going, dragging Tommy into a tirade about the government, Scott made his escape. "I'm going to grab a beer. I'll be back."

Not any time soon, if he could help it, but they probably wouldn't even notice. He walked around to the other side of the bar, which had no stools. Tommy had figured out a long time ago nobody ever sat on that side, but would stand around and talk, so he'd taken the stools out to make more space.

Lydia set a mug on a napkin in front of him and smiled. "I would have brought one to you, but I thought you might need a reason to escape."

"Thanks." He took a long sip and sighed. "I knew

they'd have some opinions about a woman in the company, but I thought they'd go with PMS or women having less upper body strength or something, not the fact we can't indulge in locker room talk around her."

"Aidan said it kind of sucks that he can't talk to his best friend about his sex life ever again."

Scott grimaced. "I don't even want to talk *about* talking about Aidan's sex life."

"How do *you* feel about having a woman in the company?"

"I don't know." He shrugged. "It'll be weird, I guess. None of us have ever worked with a woman before. But she's not only a firefighter, she's an officer, so I guess she's probably good at the job."

"What's she like?"

"Don't really know yet. I talked to her for like maybe five minutes."

When his sister just looked at him, one eyebrow arched, he wondered what Aidan had said about Jamie. Or, more specifically, what Aidan had said about what Scott thought of Jamie. While he had no intention of sharing his reaction to her with anybody because he'd never hear the end of it, Aidan was like a brother to him. If anybody would pick up on a look or body language or any other sign Scott was attracted to their new lieutenant, it would be him.

"I'm going to need better gossip from you guys if I'm going to be stuck behind this bar all the time," she said, letting him off the hook for now. "Aidan's out back with Chris. I guess the mother-in-law's in town, so his wife let him sneak out for a few minutes."

Scott chuckled and carried his beer back to the small alcove that held a pool table and a few tables.

Chris Eriksson had been married a long time and they'd all spent more than a few hours hanging around the station, listening to his mother-in-law war stories.

The room was empty except for the two guys, who were sitting at one of the tables with their feet up on empty chairs. "Well, this is one helluva party."

"If by *helluva party*," Chris said, "you mean quiet and nagging-free, then yes. Pull up a chair."

Scott had been thinking about playing a couple games of pool, but neither of them looked like they'd be able to muster enough ambition to stand that long, so he pulled over a chair and sat down. Then he put his feet up on the edge of the chair Aidan was using as an ottoman.

"Heard your mother-in-law's visiting," he said to Chris.

"Yeah. And guess what moron made the mistake of mentioning the fact our new lieutenant is a woman?"

"Why's that a big deal? It's not your wife or her mother who have to carry the line if she can't handle it. Which I'm pretty sure she can."

"They don't even care about her pulling her weight. They want to know how old she is and if she's married and what she looks like, and shit like that."

Aidan laughed. "I guess young, attractive and single didn't go over well."

"She's older than we are," Scott said.

"She ain't older than me," Chris said. "And she ain't older than my wife so, in her eyes, Jamie Rutherford is a pretty young thing. Probably wouldn't have been so bad if it was just Cindy, but her mom wouldn't let it go. Wanted to know if she sleeps with us—you know, in the same bunk room—and about the shower situation and shit."

It hadn't occurred to Scott that some of the wives or girlfriends might take issue with a woman being assigned to the company. It was tight quarters and they tended to form a strong bond, so he could see how some of them would be insecure about it.

"Lydia asked me what she's like," Scott said.

Aidan laughed. "Oh, she already interrogated the hell out of me, but she knows I'm not going home to anybody but her."

Since the guy had been willing to sacrifice their friendship, his relationship with Tommy Kincaid *and* his job for Lydia, Scott wasn't too worried about Aidan straying. "Plus, when your coworker and best friend is your future brother-in-law, you know that's a one-way street to getting your ass kicked."

Aidan lifted his beer in a mock toast. "True story."

Scott nodded and drank his own beer, listening as Chris went back to telling them how dinner with his mother-in-law had gone. But he was only partly paying attention because his mind kept wandering to Jamie Rutherford.

He wasn't sure how having a woman in the company was going to work out, but he had no doubt it was going to be interesting.

Jamie pulled open the tucked flaps on another cardboard box with a weary sigh. She'd gotten pretty good at moving over the years, but this was her first time moving into a studio apartment that didn't feel a whole lot bigger than the box she was unpacking.

She'd already seen to the most important stuff. The television had cable. The Keurig was on the counter and her favorite mug was next to it. The modem was hooked up, her laptop was on the small kitchen table, and her phone charger was plugged in next to the bed.

The rest she was chipping away at a little bit at a time. Having very few cupboards and only one closet was a challenge, but she'd picked up some under-the-bed plastic bins at the store. She'd also grabbed some picnic hamper–style baskets at the same time. They'd be good for storing things in the living room area while being somewhat decorative. As long as she didn't have cardboard boxes or piles of stuff in corners, she'd be happy.

Her cell phone, which was sitting on the counter, chimed to let her know she had a new text message. After hitting the button to heat up water for a cup of decaf, she picked it up and smiled when she saw it was from Steph Lawson. She worked at her family's pizza place around the corner from Jamie's old station and was the closest friend she'd made in Boston.

According to my app, it will take me five hours to visit you.

Jamie laughed. Stop exaggerating.

At least she thought Steph was exaggerating. It was hard to tell with Boston. When she'd first arrived in the city, she'd felt like a rat in a maze tightly packed with cars, angry people, construction and one-way streets, and she still hadn't quite mastered driving there yet. She could do it, but her knuckles would ache for an hour after from clutching the steering wheel. And she still had no idea how to calculate how long it would take to get anywhere. Sometimes it took fifteen minutes to get to the dentist and sometimes it took an hour and twenty minutes.

At least she didn't have to drive the fire trucks. She was perfectly content to ride shotgun when it came to getting a thirty-five- to forty-five-foot-long truck through the rat maze.

I want to see your apartment but the only day I have off is Tuesday and you have to work every Tuesday.

There's not much to see. Literally.

Give me a tour. I'm on break.

Jamie made herself a coffee while her laptop booted up, and then she initiated a video chat with Steph. After doing one slow swivel with the computer's camera, she laughed and set it on the counter.

"That's it?"

"Yup." Jamie laughed at her friend's scowl. With her blond hair pulled back tightly into a bun for work and her glasses on because she'd once had an incident with contact lenses and hot pepper juice on her hands, the frown made Steph look like a disapproving school principal. "Easy to clean, though."

There was a blue leather love seat and a glass coffee table in the living room area. A small glass kitchen table with two chairs between that space and the kitchen space. And toward the back was the queen bed, with an oak dresser nearly hiding the door to the bathroom. She could have had more floor space if she got a smaller bed, but she refused to compromise when it came to sleeping and she'd spent a small fortune on the mattress set.

She didn't even want to think about how much it

had cost her to have what little furniture she had carried up to the fourth floor. Hopefully her next assignment would be in commuting distance because she did *not* want to move again any time soon.

"Tell me more about the new job," Steph said. "I have five more minutes to kill."

"I told you everything. I got the tour, met the guys and left. I won't have anything more to add until after tomorrow, I guess."

"You didn't say much."

"Because you were working and I hate texting entire conversations."

Steph shrugged. Because she worked for the family business and hadn't yet fulfilled her mother's dream for her of marrying a nice man and bearing a pack of grandchildren, she worked long hours and texting was sometimes the only way she ever got to talk to people who weren't related to her or ordering food. "Are any of them hot?"

Yes. Actually, a few of them were, but it was Scott Kincaid's face that popped into her head. "I guess. I'm not there looking for a boyfriend."

Her own fire company was the *last* place she'd look for a boyfriend, even if she wanted one. She'd never experienced a workplace romance, but she could only imagine how messy they got. Gossip and tension and, God forbid, the potential for a sexual harassment situation. Everything she'd worked her ass off for could be gone, or at the very least tainted. She wanted nothing to do with any of that.

"You never know where you'll meet your true love," Steph said.

"I'm hanging up on you. Go back to work."

Once she'd ended the chat, Jamie looked at the boxes still remaining and then carried the laptop and her coffee to the table. Pulling up her Facebook account, she settled in to catch up on things. Her sisters' kids were all still being cute and her mother was still sharing every knitting joke that crossed her feed. Jamie's best friend from school was at Disney World with her family, and Jamie hit the like button on a few of those photos. Her aunt was really hitting some online game or another hard, and the rest of her feed was full of political memes she skimmed past.

After privately sending her mom a picture of the apartment—which she'd taken from the door, so it showed almost the entire place—she closed the laptop and sighed. She really wanted to have everything in order before she left, but she'd also need to get to bed early. Nerves were always a bit of an issue before starting with a new company, and she knew she'd have trouble falling asleep, which would make the twenty-four-hour shift even harder.

It was time to get up off her butt and get stuff done. Tomorrow would be a big day.

Scott showed up for his shift on Tuesday with his game face on. Jamie Rutherford was going to be working with them for at least six weeks, and probably longer, and he was going to treat her no differently than he'd treated any of the other temporary replacements for Danny Walsh. Scott might have a reputation for liking women a little too much and having a bad temper, but he was also a professional firefighter. He could handle having a woman in the company, whether he'd had a particularly steamy sex dream about her or not.

Thinking about that dream as he walked through the open bay door wasn't a good move, so Scott turned his attention to the truck. He knew the guys who'd just wrapped up their tour took good care of her, but looking over E-59 was how he started every day. She was one of the older trucks in service, since she took care of a primarily residential neighborhood without the industrial buildings or densely populated high-rises other areas did, and so got less of the budget. But she was solid and dependable and looking her over always calmed him down.

When he passed through the second floor, he resisted the urge to look through the open office door and see if Jamie was in there. He never stopped to say hello to Danny, knowing he'd see him upstairs at some point, so he wasn't going to stop and say hello to Jamie.

When he reached the third floor and heard a woman's laughter, he paused. She had a really great laugh, and he listened until whatever had been going on quieted before walking into the living room.

It looked like he was the last one there, which wasn't surprising. He was never late, but the other guys had an annoying tendency to be early, which just made him look late. Everybody had coffee, most of them still in the slow stages of coming fully awake.

"Hey, Scotty," Aidan said. "You awake yet?"

"Not by choice. I hope you guys didn't drink all the coffee."

"We did."

"But I made another pot," Gavin said, probably guessing it was his coffee Scott would steal.

Jamie was just finishing making her own coffee when he walked into the kitchen, so she left the stuff on the counter for him. Her hair was in a French braid—which he knew because every time the school had sent a lice notice around his mom had put his sisters' thick hair into French braids so tight they'd whine. He guessed Jamie wore it that way because it kept her hair out of the way while not making a ponytail lump under her helmet.

"Good morning," she said, and he realized he'd been staring at her hair.

"Morning. So it sounded like I missed the party." She frowned at him over the rim of her mug. "The laughing, I mean. I heard you laughing."

"Oh, I was laughing at Jeff's reaction to me telling the guys I'm a vegetarian."

Scott almost dropped his mug. "You are? Seriously?"

She laughed again, the sound seeming to fill the kitchen. "No, I'm not. I just wanted to see what they'd say about not having meat with any meals for the next two months or so."

"That's...wow, that's mean. What did Jeff say?"

"He said there was probably some law that said she had to be accommodated and then told Grant to put a dozen steaks and a bag of carrot sticks on the grocery list."

Scott laughed. "Yeah, nobody cares if you get the shower to yourself, but we're not giving up meat."

He probably shouldn't have brought up her in the shower if he was trying to stay in a purely professional head space, because his mind immediately wanted to picture her naked and covered in bubbly lather.

Rick Gullotti chose that moment to come in and wash out his empty mug. "Hey, Scotty, when you get home, do me a favor and ask Tommy if he knows anybody who wants to buy a snowblower. I know it's the wrong time of year and it's a bit of a beater, but we'll give somebody a good deal on it. Joe used it to do the walkways while I did the driveway with the bigger one, but now that he and Marie have moved into senior living with a grounds crew, I don't need two."

"I'll ask him. You and Jess move downstairs yet?"

Rick shook his head. "We're going to take our time and remodel it the way we want it, and with her still traveling between here and San Diego a lot, that's not high on our priority list."

"You live with your dad?" Jamie asked when Rick had gone back into the other room.

"Yes and no. I rent the apartment upstairs, so I'm around if he needs me and I get a family discount on the rent, but I still have my own space. There's no way we could actually live together."

"I've heard a lot about your dad, actually. He's pretty well respected."

"Yeah." He wasn't always the best father and he certainly hadn't been a great husband, but he'd been a damn good firefighter. "You should come to Kincaid's Pub sometime. It's where we hang out and relax. Drink a beer. Shoot some pool."

"That's your family's bar, right?"

"No, we just stuck our name on the sign for grins." When she rolled her eyes, he laughed. "Yeah, my old man owns it. My sisters, Lydia and Ashley, usually run the bar, though mostly Lydia these days."

"And Ashley's married to Danny Walsh."

"You're pretty well-informed."

She shrugged. "People talk. Especially Danny."

"What do you mean?"

"He reached out to me last night to see if I had any questions or concerns, which was really nice. You can tell he's bored and sick of being cooped up."

"Talk for a while, did he?" She nodded. "He fill you in on everybody?"

Jamie smiled, her eyes crinkling at the corners. "Yeah, he did."

He waited, but she didn't say anything else. Usually he'd shrug it off, but for some reason he really wanted to know what Danny had told this woman about him. The seconds ticked by, and he was about to ask when the alarm sounded and everybody started toward the engine bays.

"Suspicious odor in a residential unit. Haz-Mat en route."

Scott paused on his way to the racks holding their turnout gear and looked at Rick. "Tell me it's not a damn meth lab."

"Won't know until Haz-Mat goes in."

Once they were geared up, Scott climbed into the driver's seat and fired the engine. As soon as he had confirmation they weren't forgetting anybody, he hit the siren and waited a few seconds for pedestrians and drivers to catch on and get out of the way before rolling out.

Jamie was riding shotgun and she seemed calm as she monitored the radio while keeping an eye on any potential hazards on that side of the road, but he didn't miss her sharp intakes of breath or her fingernails digging into her leg or her right hand tightening on the door handle as he navigated the narrow streets and tight corners.

"Somebody's double-parked," she said as he swung

wide around a right-hand turn. "Flashers on, but it looks like somebody's in it."

Scott laid on the horn, since the sirens obviously weren't enough, and slowed down enough to let the idiot move.

"Don't hit him," she warned. "I'm pretty brutal when it comes to payback for any extra paperwork."

He chuckled, but didn't respond as he squeezed the truck down a narrow one-way with parking on both sides. They arrived right after the Haz-Mat truck, with Ladder 37 right behind them.

They'd stage for now, ready to offer support if something went wrong—like, God forbid, the odor was some asshole cooking meth—but nobody would go in until Haz-Mat cleared it or there was a confirmed fire.

"I will *never* get used to these streets," Jamie said as they stood and waited, and he looked over at her. She wasn't shaken, exactly, but he could see that she was trying to relax.

"I was born and raised here, so if I didn't want to spend my life walking or taking the T, I had to learn to drive in it."

"You're pretty good at it," she said, and he felt a weird rush of pride. "I like that, because it lessens the paperwork load."

"Worst paperwork ever was probably the time Gullotti moved a cruiser with L-37's front bumper. I'm still glad it was them and not us because the ass chewing lasted for *days*."

"I can't even imagine."

"Rookie cop thought he could do double the traffic control by blocking the road with his car and then going down to the other end of the street. There were kids trapped on the third floor and it was fully involved, so Gullotti moved it himself. Wrecked the hell out of it, too."

"And the kids?"

"Everybody got out. Jeff Porter, the big guy over there? He printed out a photograph of the kids being hugged by their mom that one of the news guys took, and pinned it to the bulletin board so every time somebody gave them shit about the police car, they could look at it and not give a shit."

She nodded, her lips curving into a smile. "I think I'm going to like you guys."

It was a simple, casual statement that anybody new to the company might have made, but something about the words coming out of Jamie's mouth seemed to set Scott's blood on fire. He wanted her to like him, and that was a problem.

He realized they'd gravitated toward each other while talking, slightly separated from the other guys. While nobody else probably even noticed, he was suddenly self-conscious about it and stepped away from Jamie. "I just remembered I wanted to talk to Grant about something."

She just nodded, her attention on the voices coming through her radio, and Scott walked all the way back to the end of Ladder 37, where Grant was talking to Gavin Boudreau, the youngest guy in the ladder company. But he'd been lying about needing to talk to the kid, so he just stood there and listened to them talk about a video game and waited for an update from Haz-Mat.

Chapter 3

Jamie was relieved when the word came through that the second-floor residents were trying to strip the varnish from their old wooden floors without proper ventilation, which caused the chemical smell throughout the building. Everything was under control and the fire companies could return to quarters.

She liked having the opportunity to respond to a call with them and see how they did things outside of a critical life-or-death situation. Not that she was worried about being able to handle that. Her training and experience would get her through. But it was nice to get a feel for the company in action first.

Once the trucks were backed into the bays, Jamie quietly stowed her turnout gear while keeping an eye on the guys. There was obviously a strong sense of camaraderie, and a lot of banter and laughter went on, but she didn't see any of them slacking or trying to take shortcuts. She could see that they took the care of the trucks and their gear very seriously, which was a relief. It was hard enough being in charge when you were the "new guy" without having to crack down on lax procedures right off the bat.

She and Rick went into their shared office and went through some paperwork. Luckily it was all standardized stuff, which didn't vary much from station to station, and Walsh had been good about staying on top of it, so Jamie didn't have to do much in the way of catching up.

After glancing at the clock, she pulled out her cell phone and called her dad. Every time she moved to a new station, he worried about her having a new group of guys in her life, so she usually called to fill him in.

"Hi, Dad," she said when he answered.

"Hey, honey. How are you? I have a client coming in about five minutes, so I'll take the abridged version now and you can have a nice long chat with Mom later."

She laughed, leaning back in her chair. Her dad had always worked out of a home office, so his daughters had grown up having access to him all the time, but in quick bursts in between appointments. "I'm good. I'm working with great guys here, and it's probably been one of the smoothest transitions I've had."

"I'm glad to hear it. I know you haven't had many problems—that you've told me about, at least—but I always worry. How's your apartment? You haven't had any problems with the neighborhood, have you?"

If he had his way, she'd live in a place with security and a doorman, but those weren't easy to come by in that part of the city, especially if you didn't want roommates to help float the extra cost. "No problems. And there are two locked doors and three flights of stairs between me and the street, so I'm not worried."

"Your mom showed me the pictures you sent. You'll definitely get your exercise." She heard papers shuffling in the background, since he'd put her on speakerphone. "Tell me about your new coworkers."

She filled him in, giving him a very brief character sketch of each of the guys. He seemed impressed when she told him about the chore list, maybe because he remembered the long venting session she'd subjected him to when she'd been a rookie and got assigned to a company that assumed, because there was a woman on hand, they didn't have to make coffee or scrub toilets anymore.

"You sound happy," he said.

"I am." She chuckled. "Tentatively, of course. It's still early, but I have a good feeling about this company."

"You're a good judge of character, so I'm happy for you."

"It must be time for your client, so I'll let you go. Give my love to Mom and tell her I'll chat with her soon. Maybe tomorrow. Love you, Dad."

"Love you, too, honey. Talk to you soon."

Once the call ended, she went upstairs to find the guys scattered around the third floor, ticking things off the day's to-do list.

When she went into the kitchen, Gavin and Chris were in there. "Hey, guys."

"Hey," they said in unison.

She opened the pantry door and scanned for Walsh's name on the list. "Food purge duty, huh? That sounds fun."

"You and I can do the fridge and Chris has the pantry," Gavin told her. "It doesn't take long, since we try to do it every week."

They started by putting a fresh trash bag in the garbage can, while Chris took a second bag into the pantry. Then Gavin, who had a better idea of how long things had been in there, opened the fridge and started on the top shelf.

"I'll hand off to you," he said. "Anything disposable, you can toss the whole thing. If something's in a dish or whatever, dump the contents and we'll wash the dishes after."

"I guess if you try to do it every week, there shouldn't be anything too bad in there."

"Are you married?" Gavin asked, handing her a plastic bag of fruit definitely past its prime to toss. "Have any kids?"

"Nope. You?"

"No. Jeff and Chris are both married. Aidan and Rick are both engaged, and Grant and I are single, so we date and stuff. He's been seeing this girl for like a month, so it might get serious." He paused. "And Scotty's on a break right now."

"A break?"

"Yeah, from dating. He's not seeing anybody right now, and hasn't for at least a couple of months, I think."

"Wow, a couple of months." He was practically a monk, she thought, though she chose to keep that bit of sarcasm to herself.

"He's dated some real winners, let me tell ya. I guess now he's looking for somebody to marry, so he's not dating until he finds the right woman."

"How do you find out if you want to marry a woman if you don't date her first?"

Grant looked confused for a minute, and then he laughed. "No, if he meets a woman he thinks he might want to marry in the future, he'd probably date her a couple of times to see. But he's not dating women he knows he won't marry just to have a girlfriend anymore because then he might miss out on the right woman."

"I guess people reach a point in their lives when they know what they want and what they don't want and their priorities shift."

"Scotty definitely knows what he *doesn't* want now," Chris said, his deep voice startling Jamie. He was so quiet, she'd almost forgotten he was in the pantry. "Now he's looking for a TV wife."

She laughed. "He wants a wife on television? Like an actress?"

"No, like a wife from one of those old shows, with the wife in the apron and pearls, making dinner while helping the kids do their homework. Meeting him at the door with his slippers and all that."

"Probably going to be a long break for him, then." If Scott was holding out for some idealized Suzy Homemaker version of a wife, he'd be spending a lot of time alone.

"He's exaggerating," Gavin said. "A little. And I think that's everything from the fridge and freezer."

"Not much," Chris responded, pulling the full trash bag out of the can and tying it off.

"Are you guys making food?" Aidan asked, walking in with Scott and Jeff on his heels.

"No, we're throwing food away," Jamie said, gesturing to the garbage can.

"I was thinking about eating that leftover American chop suey," Scott said, peering over her shoulder.

He was close enough so she could smell his shampoo, and she tried to ignore the goose bumps that tickled her skin. "I opened the container and smelled it. Trust me when I tell you tossing it was for the best."

His laughter was almost a physical touch, and she picked up the garbage can so she had an excuse to step away from him. After putting it in its place, she pulled the bag out and shoved the contents down so she could tie it off.

"I'll take that for you," Scott said, reaching for it. His hand brushed hers and it took all of her willpower to simply let go and move her hand instead of yanking it back as though she'd been burned.

"Thanks."

"Nobody's making more dirty dishes until we're done in here," Gavin said, making a shooing motion back toward the living room.

Jamie was surprised when the other guys listened to him. He and Grant were not only the youngest, but the lowest on the seniority totem pole, so it was clear to her that everybody in both companies respected the chore list.

Scott was the last one to leave the kitchen, and he turned back as he reached the door, giving her a grin that threatened to short-circuit her common sense. "Thanks for saving me from the American chop suey."

She felt herself smiling back at him and could only

hope the heat flooding her body didn't show on her face. "Can't be going a man down on my first tour."

Once he was gone, she started filling the sink with hot, soapy water to give herself a moment. She'd never been attracted to a guy she worked with before, and she had no coping skills for the way her pulse quickened every time she saw Scott.

Dumping the dishes they'd taken from the fridge into the sink, she turned the water off, wishing she could turn the attraction off just as easily. It was time to start exploring the neighborhood and finding good hangout places. Maybe she'd get lucky and feel that same zing for a guy she *didn't* work with.

"You okay?" Gavin asked, and she realized she'd been standing there, gripping the edge of the sink and staring at the soap bubbles.

"Yeah, I just got lost in thought. You drying?"

She'd just pulled the plug after washing the last dish when the alarm sounded.

Scott rang the doorbell of his sister's house and then waited, zipping his sweatshirt against the chill in the air. When Ashley opened the door, he couldn't help grinning at her. It had become a habit—almost an involuntary reflex—since she and Danny had told him she was pregnant.

That had been mere days before the fire they almost lost Danny to, and Scott would never forget the gut-wrenching fear that he was going to have to tell his sister her husband and the father of her unborn child had died.

That was behind them now, though, and every time he saw his sister, Scott had a *holy crap, she's having a baby* moment. She wasn't showing yet, and wouldn't for a while, but she was already glowing.

"Hey, you. Come on in."

He stepped into the house the couple had bought cheap and then remodeled over time. They'd planned ahead and now, while their first child was still just a speck of a thing, they had a nice home in a great neighborhood for a lot less than most of their neighbors had paid.

"Hey, Danny, Scotty's here," she called, and Scott heard what sounded like a recliner being folded back into a sitting position.

Danny was almost on his feet by the time Scott walked into the living room, and he was glad to see him moving with less pain than the last time he'd stopped by. His leg was in a cast, and he tucked crutches under his arm as he stood up on his good leg.

"You didn't have to get up."

"Yes, he did," Ashley said. "He's supposed to get up and move around a lot, actually. He just can't put weight on the leg yet."

Danny rolled his eyes, but the warm smile he gave his wife made it more affectionate than annoying. "I have to stop taking her to my appointments."

"Good luck with that," Scott said. "How you doing?"

"Better."

"Want to get out of the house?"

Danny's face brightened, but then he looked at Ashley. "Is that okay with you? Just for a little while, maybe?"

She chuckled. "Who do you think called Scotty and

told him to get you the hell out of the house before I smother you with a pillow?"

"We'll just go to the bar for a bit and hang out, since you can't wear real clothes," Scott told him.

Danny looked down at the sweatpants with one leg cut off above the cast. "Sounds good to me."

"No beer, though," Ashley said. "Decaf or soda or something. I know you haven't been taking the pain-killers they gave you if you can help it, but going out and sitting in those chairs might be a lot and you'll want a pill to help you sleep."

"Yes, dear."

Scott found a fascinating spot on the wall to stare at, bracing himself for an awkward family moment. Their communication issues had been one of the biggest reasons their marriage had hit the skids and, while Ashley didn't have as hot a temper as he and Lydia did, that was exactly the kind of platitude that would make her pop off.

But then Danny slapped Ashley on the ass and they both laughed when the action made him wobble, almost falling off his crutches. Scott kept staring at that spot on the wall, though, because then there was kissing. He was happier for his sister than he'd been about almost anything in his life, but that didn't mean he wanted to watch the reconciliation in action.

"You're presentable enough for a bar," she said. "But you should at least brush your hair."

Scott chuckled when Danny ran his hands through his hair and grinned at his wife. "How's that?"

She gave him an affectionate eye roll, and then she smiled when Danny rested his hand on her stomach for a second. "I won't be too late."

Scott felt a pang of something—yearning, maybe—at the gesture and went back to the foyer to grab Danny's sweatshirt off the hook. There was a lot of love going on around him, what with Danny and Ashley making up, Aidan and Lydia falling in love, and then Rick Gullotti falling for his landlords' granddaughter.

He wanted it. All of it. The love, the having a person to go home to at the end of the day. The holding hands and secret glances. The babies. Not just because the people around him had it, but because when he lay down at night, he felt the emptiness. He felt incomplete.

"You're going to have to take my car," Ashley said, taking her keys out of a dish on a side table near the door. "Unless you think you can catch him when he falls out of your truck."

"I could just drop the tailgate and hoist him into the bed. It's not far."

"The seat's all the way back on the passenger side, so he can get in okay. He'll need a hand getting out, though. The crutches fit if you wedge them between the front seats and…you'll figure it out."

Scott figured it out without putting the end of the sticks through the car's display console, which he considered a win. Then, after locking his truck, he slid into his sister's car and started the engine.

"It's a four-cylinder, so don't try to beat any lights," Danny warned. "You won't make it."

Scott laughed and backed out onto the street. "Too bad I don't have long enough ramps. I could put you in this car, drive it up into the back of my truck and then drive that."

"We'd be legendary." Danny laughed and then looked over at him. "I really appreciate this, Scotty. I'm losing my freaking mind at home. I mean, I get out with Ashley, but I know she'd like a break and I need a break."

"Hey, any time."

It took longer to get Danny out of the car, onto his crutches and into the bar, and then to go park the car, than it had taken to drive there, and Scott managed to break a sweat despite the dropping temperature.

By the time he got back inside, Danny had disappeared, but Lydia waved him toward the back room. Danny was sitting at a table against the wall, with his leg propped up on a second chair. He was talking to Gavin, who seemed to be there alone.

"Hey, I was hoping you'd show up," he said to Scott. "I had some time to kill, so I figured I'd see if anybody was around for a game."

"Since you got me a beer, I guess it would be rude to say no."

"I got you two beers, since Danny can't drink his."

Danny held up a soda. "If I can get enough of a sugar rush, I might be able to lean against the table and shoot some pool. For now, I'll watch."

Scott broke and the game was on. He won the first game, pausing occasionally for a sip of beer while Gavin analyzed potential shots. The kid was a math whiz and sometimes mumbled to himself, as if he was doing fancy geometry equations in his head to line up his shots.

Scott happened to be standing at the end of the pool table that offered a view of the door when it opened and a woman walked in. It was Jamie, and he was glad she went the other way—toward the bar—because he couldn't take his eyes off of her.

"Hey, it's your shot," Gavin said just as Jamie passed beyond his view from the alcove.

"You got somewhere to be?" he asked, turning back to the table.

"Yeah, I've got a date tonight. I'm meeting her at nine."

Scott bent over the table and considered the angle. "Who goes on a date at nine o'clock on a Wednesday night?"

"Two people who have Thursdays off. Was that Jamie who walked in just now?"

He asked the question midshot and Scott swore as the ball rebounded off the bumper, a fraction of an inch from the pocket. "Yeah, I guess."

Gavin sank his last two balls, putting an end to the game. "You must have something on your mind tonight. You're not usually this easy to beat."

"I read somewhere you're supposed to allow kids to win things once in a while. Good for your self-esteem."

A few guys wandered in, each carrying a full mug of beer. Scott recognized two of them as firefighters from a nearby station, though not nearby enough so they were regulars at Kincaid's.

"Hey, boys. How's it going?"

Scott felt his temper rise at the arrogant tone, but he shrugged. "Just finishing up. Feel free."

Gavin was heading out anyway, and he had no desire to shoot pool with this group. They'd been at a table when he showed up, so he knew they'd had a head start on the drinking, and he didn't like the one guy very much. Randy, he thought his name was.

He joined Danny at the table and took a long swallow of his beer before grimacing. A fresh cold one would be nice, but Lydia didn't wait on him when he was in the back room, so he'd have to go to the bar. And Jamie was at the bar.

Danny leaned across the table so he could keep his voice low. "Speaking as both your brother-in-law and your lieutenant, you don't want to go there."

"Go where?"

"I saw you, man. It was pretty obvious you were checking out a woman you thought was hot, and then a minute later Gavin says Jamie Rutherford had walked in."

Scott managed not to squirm on the chair, but he didn't look at Danny. Instead he watched Randy whatever-his-name-was breaking, and he winced. The guy was sloppy and if he ripped the felt, Tommy would tear him a new one.

"Scotty."

He shrugged. "Yeah, so I looked. Nothing wrong with that."

"You don't exactly have a reputation for self-control when it comes to women." His brother-in-law held up his hand when he turned to frown at him. "Yeah, I know you're reformed and all that happy horseshit. I'm just saying you shouldn't go there. It's a bad idea."

"I know that." He also knew that changing his ways as far as women were concerned wasn't just happy horseshit. He was serious about taking relationships more seriously and finding the woman he wanted to spend the rest of his life with.

That didn't mean he couldn't appreciate a beautiful woman, though, as long as he was more careful to keep his appreciation to himself.

Jamie called herself every synonym for *idiot* she could think of as she walked across Kincaid's Pub to the bar.

Yesterday, she'd told herself she needed to find some hangout spots and meet a guy who wasn't a firefighter and would hopefully distract her from Scott Kincaid. Today, she was walking into his family's bar.

She knew it was stupid, but she'd done her best to rationalize the decision, anyway. What better way to get to know her coworkers than to have a beer with them?

As soon as she reached the bar, she would have guessed the woman behind it was one of Scott's sisters even if he hadn't told her they primarily did the bartending. The woman with the dark hair pulled into a thick ponytail gave her a polite smile, and then did a double-take when she saw the E-59 logo on Jamie's T-shirt.

"You must be Jamie," she said, extending her hand over the bar. "I'm Lydia, Scott's sister and Aidan's fiancée."

Jamie shook her hand, smiling. "Nice to meet you. I've been in with friends a couple of times, though it's been a while and I don't think you were here."

"I was living in New Hampshire for a while. What can I get you to drink?"

Jamie told her she'd take whatever Lydia recommended on tap, noticing there were no stools on her side of the bar, though a couple of guys were sitting on the other side. They were in business suits, so she guessed it was an after-work meet-up and their work wasn't fighting fires.

Lydia set a frosted mug on a paper coaster in front of her. "You're not a New Englander, judging by the accent. How'd you end up in Boston?"

She shrugged, swirling her drink in the glass. "Classic story, I guess. I moved here for a guy. Then the guy moved on and I didn't."

"Was he from here?"

"No. He got offered a job in pharmaceutical sales and we'd been together long enough so he asked me to go with him the first time. Once you do that, you're pretty much an official couple, so every time he moved to a bigger city and a bigger company for work, I moved, too. Things were going south between us about the time he realized he hated being away from his parents and I like Boston, so he went home without me."

"Where's home?"

Jamie hated this part—all the questions—though she knew there was no way around it. The firefighting community was close-knit, and she was going to be part of if whether she wanted to be or not. "Nebraska."

Lydia frowned. "Really?"

"Really."

"I don't think I've ever met anybody from Nebraska."

Jamie laughed. "You'd be surprised how often I hear that."

"You guys don't even have a hockey team, do you?"

"Not a professional one, no."

"Nothing to stop you from being a Bruins fan, then. Some of the guys are out back, playing pool. It's that room off to the side over there."

Wondering if one of the guys was Scott, Jamie picked up her beer and looked in the direction Lydia pointed. "Thanks. I guess I'll say hi, at least."

As she walked across the bar, she took a few deep breaths. If Scott was in there, she'd be ready for that spark she felt every time she saw him and make sure she didn't look at him any differently than she looked at the other guys.

It wasn't easy, though. There were four guys around the pool table, none of whom she recognized. But there, at a table against the wall, was Scott. He was sitting with a guy in a cast who had to be Danny Walsh, and they both smiled when they saw her.

Her stomach did a little flip-flop at Scott's smile, so she focused on his companion. "You must be Danny."

"Nice to meet you in person. I'd get up, but…" He waved a hand at the cast. "You'd probably be gone by the time I managed it."

She stepped forward and shook his hand, before backing up. Unfortunately, in trying to put a little space between her and Scott, she backed up too far and bumped into one of the guys playing pool.

"Oh, sorry," she said, turning to apologize.

The guy's smile turned sleazy when he looked her over and his gaze caught on her T-shirt. "Who'd you sleep with to get the shirt, honey?"

"Excuse me?"

"Does he know you took it or did you sneak out in it?"

"The shirt belongs to me." She turned her back on him because he wasn't worth her time.

"Aw, don't be like that, honey. You can play with my hose if you want."

Jamie turned to give the guy *the look*. It was a look that had served her well over the years and, more often than not, ended with the person on the receiving end dropping his or her gaze and muttering an apology.

But the asshole wasn't looking at her. He was looking over her shoulder, and before she could grasp what that meant, somebody rushed by her to the right.

Jamie dropped her beer as she reached for Scott, but he was too fast. He grabbed the douche bag by the shirt, but the guy had seen him coming and managed to get his fist in Scott's face. It didn't slow him down, though, and Scott landed a punch of his own.

"Scotty!" Danny yelled, and through the corner of her eye, Jamie saw him trying to get his cast off the chair. "Goddammit, Kincaid!"

The two guys went to the ground and Jamie saw the douche bag's buddies moving in. This was going to get messy, especially if Danny decided to be a hero and wade in on his crutches.

"That's enough," she yelled, bending to grab the back of Scott's collar.

When the douche bag's arm flopped out for a second, she put her foot on it, pinning it to the floor. That put her slightly off balance, though, so pulling at Scott's collar didn't accomplish anything.

She threaded her hands into Scott's hair and yanked hard. "I said that's enough."

He let go of the douche bag to reach for her hand. "Ow. Let go."

"Get up." When he resisted, she pulled harder. "Get. Up."

He struggled to his feet as his sister rounded the corner, a softball bat in her hand. She looked at Jamie and, for a second, she thought Lydia was going to smile. Then she looked at the guy on the floor before narrowing her eyes at his friends.

"Get your buddy and get out of my bar."

"He started it."

"Yeah, but his name's over the door, so get out and don't bother coming back."

Once they were gone, Scott batted at Jamie's hand again. "You can let go now. And you didn't have to do that."

She released her grip on his hair. "I wouldn't have had to do that if you'd listened to me."

"This isn't the station."

"No, it's not," Lydia broke in, pointing the bat at him. "It's our bar and if you pull this stupid shit again, you can find another place to hang out. Now go put some ice on that eye for a few minutes and then clean up that beer."

"That's mine," Jamie said. "Just tell me where the mop is."

"He can do it."

Lydia walked away, and Jamie might have smiled at the exasperated look Scott sent after his older sister, but she was too annoyed with him. And with the way Danny was watching them.

"Show me where the mop is," she said. "I'll clean this up while you put ice on that eye."

"You okay for a few minutes, Danny?" he asked.

"I'm good."

Jamie followed him, her eyes on the back of his head. Because he'd gotten sweaty in the tussle with the douche bag, she could still see the ruffled area where her fingers had been buried in his hair.

It was tempting to reach out and smooth the strands so she wouldn't be distracted, but she curled her hands into fists instead. No more touching Scott Kincaid.

Chapter 4

Scott's head was pounding, his eye socket was throbbing, and he imagined he could still feel Jamie's fingers wrapped in his hair. Later, when he was alone, he might reimagine that scenario without the fight and her throwing her authority around. Just him and Jamie and her hand buried in his hair.

He walked into the back room and turned to face her. "You're not mopping the floor, dammit. I'll clean it up. And I don't need any ice."

"What the hell were you thinking?"

Even though she'd just dragged him to his feet by his hair, her anger set him back a step. "What do you mean?"

"Did I ask for your help?"

"Did you hear what that asshole said to you?"

"Yeah, I did. And I didn't give a shit. You think

that's the first time I've heard sleazy comments about playing with hoses?" God, she was gorgeous when she was pissed. "If a guy puts his hands on me, then I'll take care of it. Otherwise, the shit coming out of their mouths isn't worth my time."

"I'm not letting some asshole talk to women like that in here."

"It's different, Scott. Because we work together."

"So? That's even more reason not to let somebody disrespect you."

She blew out an exasperated breath, which he knew was a woman's way of calling him an idiot without wasting words. "Everybody's going to assume you popped off on that guy because you and I are hooking up."

"Or maybe they'll assume I'm not going to stand there and let a woman be disrespected in my family's bar."

She cocked her head sideways, arching an eyebrow. "You really believe that's what they're going to think?"

No, they weren't. They were going to jump to the conclusion he was parking his boots under the hot lieutenant's bed. "The only guy in that room whose opinion matters is Danny's and he knows we're not hooking up."

"Does he?"

"Yeah, because I told him we're not."

She looked at him, her eyes narrowing. "And why would he ask?"

Busted. He didn't want to tell her Danny had warned him off after catching him watching her walk into the bar. "I guess I just have a reputation for not being able to resist a single woman."

"Sit down on that stepladder and look up at the light so I can see your eye."

"You're very bossy, you know that?"

"It came with the promotion. Sit."

He sat, and then he sucked in a breath when Jamie stepped close and took his chin between her fingers. She tilted his head back, scowling at his eye under the glare of the bare bulb. Her hand was warm, and he reacted immediately to her touch. Trying not to shift around on the stool to ease the discomfort of his jeans, he dropped his gaze because meeting hers wasn't helping. But he found himself eye level with her breasts, which was even worse.

"For a guy who runs his mouth like that, he doesn't throw much of a punch," she said finally.

"He barely made contact. His hand glanced off, mostly."

She didn't let go of his chin, though. "As for your reputation, I heard you *are* resisting single women and have been for a while. So tell me again why your usual lieutenant would ask you if we're hooking up."

"He was asking as my brother-in-law. Mostly." Since her hand was still touching his face, he didn't feel it was too out of line to rest his hands on her hips as he raised his gaze back to hers. "Fine. He might have caught me looking at you a certain way."

"That's a bad idea." She let go of his chin, but her hand didn't fall away. Instead, her fingertips trailed over his jaw.

"It's a really bad idea," he agreed.

Without moving his hands, Scott stood. She didn't take a step back, so their bodies were so close one of them only had to shift and they'd be touching. Jamie's hand dropped from his face to his shoulder before trailing down his arm.

"I've never been involved with anybody at work. Ever."

He tightened his grip on her hips, his gaze on her mouth. "We're not *at* work."

"And when we are?"

"Then we do our jobs."

They were so close, he felt the rush of her sigh over his mouth. "You make it sound so simple."

"It doesn't have to be complicated."

The tightening of her fingers on his arm and the subtle lift of her chin were all the invitation he needed. He closed his mouth over hers, forcing himself to rein in the hunger he felt for her and be gentle.

Her lips were soft and he moved his hands from her hips to her waist so he wouldn't be tempted to pull her hard up against him as he kissed her.

When her fingers threaded through his hair again—not pulling this time, but not gentle, either—he deepened the kiss. Her lips parted as his tongue dipped between them, and he groaned as she pressed her body to his. Her breasts pressed against his chest and for one crazy second, he thought about kicking the door closed.

He felt her yank his T-shirt free of his jeans and her hands sliding up his naked back. Damn the door. Damn the bar. He wanted this woman so badly his entire body ached with it.

"Scotty, get the damn mop out here before somebody slips in that beer and sues Dad and I end up having to find a new job!"

Jamie jerked away from him, her chest rising and

falling as fast as his was. She raised her hand to her mouth, her eyes wide. "I forgot where we were for a minute."

"I forgot everything but you for a minute." It was the truth, and it made her cheeks turn pink.

"I can't believe this." She blew out a breath and ran her hands through her hair as if smoothing it, even though he hadn't even gotten a chance to mess it up yet. "There's no way we're getting out of here without them thinking we were up to no good."

"There's an employee bathroom across the hall. Go hang in there for a few minutes. I'll tell Lydia you helped me with the ice and that you're dumping the rest of it."

"Okay. I'm going to head out, by the way, so... good night."

He didn't want her to go yet. It felt as if there was still unfinished business between them. Not sexually, since that would be an incredibly stupid thing to do, but he wanted to get an idea of how she felt about the kiss. She'd obviously been as into it as he was, but that didn't mean she wouldn't be mad at herself—or both of them—or have regrets. Or maybe she'd decided it really wasn't that complicated and the incredibly sexy kiss was okay. Maybe they could even do it again.

He'd like to know what was going on in her head.

"Dammit, Scott!" Lydia bellowed again, and he sighed.

"Gimme a minute!" He turned to Jamie, but she was already slipping across the hallway and into the staff bathroom. "Good night."

Cursing under his breath, he grabbed the mop bucket. The mop and the cleaning spray they used were already in it, so he wheeled it down the hall and into the bar.

"Where's Jamie?" Lydia asked as he passed by, because God forbid his sister should ever be too busy to be up his ass about every little thing.

"She's taking care of the ice so I can wipe up the beer before we get sued and you have to find another job." She arched an eyebrow at his tone and he wasn't in the mood to get into a verbal tangle with her, so he moderated it. "She said she was going to dump the ice and then she's leaving, and that's all I know."

Danny was still where they'd left him, sitting against the wall with his leg propped on a chair. "I was beginning to wonder if you forgot about me and went home."

"I probably would have remembered when I got outside and didn't have my truck because it's parked in your driveway."

"True. Where's Jamie?"

"She's heading out after she takes care of the ice pack."

"Uh-huh." Danny crunched his empty soda can and set it on the table. "You're asking for trouble, Scotty."

He bent to pick out the larger pieces of the broken mug. "What are you talking about?"

"You didn't put any ice on that eye, your hair's even more messed up than it was, and now your shirt's untucked."

"You've been cooped up too long with bad detective shows, dude."

When Danny just made a noncommittal sound, Scott yanked the old metal dustpan off the hook of the mop bucket handle and dumped the glass into it.

He wasn't very good at getting anything over on his family, so maybe that kiss was going to end up being more complicated than he'd thought.

Jamie dabbed at her face with a paper towel, staring at her reflection in the mirror. The cold water hadn't helped much and she still looked like a woman who'd just been kissed senseless in a supply room.

What were the chances she could walk through the bar and out the front door without Scott's sister seeing her face?

What a stupid thing to do, she told herself. After years of proving herself and building a reputation based on nothing but being good at fighting fires, she'd made it through one damn tour with Scott before her self-control crumpled like a napkin.

Balling up the paper towel and tossing it into the trash, Jamie took a deep breath and reached for the doorknob. There was nothing for it but to walk out there and hope Lydia was busy with a customer. At most she could offer a casual wave goodbye as she walked out the door.

She should have known better. Lydia was leaning against the bar, her eyes on the television screen when Jamie walked out into the main bar area. Obviously Tuesdays weren't their busy night.

"Hey, sorry tonight turned into a circus sideshow for you," Lydia said when she saw her. "We don't usually have problems in here, and very rarely are punches thrown. Leave it to Scotty."

"The other guy had it coming, though it should have been me who got to smack him one."

Lydia laughed. "You've gotta be pretty fast to beat

Scotty's temper to the draw, though he's been a lot more mellow lately."

"I'm just glad it wasn't worse. I guess I'm going to head home."

"You sure you don't want a beer? You never got to drink yours."

"I'm all set. I'm actually not a big beer drinker, anyway. It's just the easiest thing to order in a bar."

"I hear you." Lydia picked up a towel and wiped at a spot on the bar. "I hate to pile on whatever impression we're making tonight, but you need to kiss Bobby Orr."

Jamie heard the word *kiss* and her stomach clenched, but then the rest of the words caught up. What the hell was Lydia talking about? "Who's Bobby Orr and why would I need to kiss him?"

"You don't know who... Oh, that's right. You're from Nebraska." She pointed to a huge photo of a guy in a hockey uniform. It was in a frame that was literally screwed to the wall, and a signature was scrawled near the bottom.

Jamie had noticed all of the sports paraphernalia hanging around the bar when she walked in, but none of it really meant anything to her. Even if she were a big sports fan—which she wasn't—this was Boston and other than a vague recognition of the logos because she didn't live under a rock, she had no idea what any of it was.

"Bobby Orr is a Bruins legend," Lydia explained. "And if you break a dish or a glass, you have to kiss the picture. If you don't, you're jinxed and who knows what'll happen next."

Jamie stared at her, wondering if this was some kind

of firehouse hazing ritual, but Lydia looked more embarrassed than expectant. "You're serious."

"Yeah. It's a tradition. Or a superstition. Whatever you want to call it."

"I've noticed that's a big thing in Boston." Lydia shrugged, not denying it. "As much as I'd like to be free of jinxes, I'm not kissing that picture. This is a bar and if somebody's lips are on that glass every time a glass breaks, mine won't be."

"You don't have to put your mouth on it. Just kiss your fingertips and touch the glass. That's close enough, and it's what most people do. The sober ones, anyway."

"You know, it was technically your brother who made the mug fall."

"It fell out of your hand." Lydia folded her arms, waiting. "But a woman who refused to do it a few years back tripped after she left here and needed stitches in her knee, but she couldn't get to the hospital because her car had been towed."

Laughing—though she wasn't sure if it was at the superstition or herself—Jamie walked around the bar to the photo. After kissing her fingertips, she reached up and pressed them to the glass covering the man's cheek.

"Boston's a strange place," she said.

Lydia nodded. "But you chose to stay because you fit right in."

Jamie smiled. "Good point. Is it safe for me to leave now?"

"Yeah. I'm sure I'll see you again, though, right? We didn't scare you off?"

If she was smart, she wouldn't come within a mile

of Kincaid's Pub for the rest of her time with E-59. "I don't scare easily."

"I didn't think so. We'll have to drag you out for a girl's night sometime. Ashley and I. It's probably good to get away from the guys now and then."

"Yeah, maybe."

Jamie had walked to the bar, which meant she had plenty of cold, fresh air to help clear her head on the way back to her apartment. Her head refused to be cleared, however, and her thoughts ran in circles all the way home.

She was glad she'd kissed Scott because it was fun and hot and everything she wanted in a kiss. And there was no harm in it because her stay was temporary and he was killing time while on the lookout for his television wife, as Chris had called the future Mrs. Kincaid.

She shouldn't have kissed him because she was going to have to show up at the station in a couple of days and not only work side by side with him, but be his superior. It wasn't 1955 anymore and her record was pretty impeccable, so her career would survive kissing a fellow firefighter. But she didn't need the side-eye looks and the snickers behind her back.

A mug of hot chocolate didn't help. Nor did repeats of one of her favorite shows, about dropping naked people into the jungle to test their survival skills. And when she finally gave up and went to bed, she wasn't surprised when closing her eyes turned her thoughts right back to Scott.

She wanted to kiss him again. She wanted to kiss him longer, somewhere his sister wasn't yelling for a mop and there was a soft surface for them to collapse onto when her knees finally gave out. That one kiss had been like running her finger through frosting. Now she wanted the whole slice of cake.

It was a long time before she finally drifted off.

Because it had been Danny's turn to go on a grocery store run, Jamie got up the next morning—usually an off day—and, after showering under cool water to force herself awake after a rough night of tossing and turning, headed to the station to meet Grant Cutter and one of the guys from another E-59 group, who typically worked Wednesdays and Saturdays. Grant had told her they could manage without her and she could have a pass, since she was new, but she not only didn't shirk her duties, she had nothing better to do. If nothing else, it would keep her from thinking too much about kissing Scott in the back room of the bar.

It was all she'd thought about since she walked out of Kincaid's Pub last night, including during the hours she should have been sleeping. Standing in front of him, she'd been stupid enough to think she could kiss him and then, curiosity satisfied, they could move on.

Instead, the kiss had jacked her sexual attraction up to sexual hunger and she didn't have a lot of willpower when it came to denying herself something she *really* wanted.

"Hey, Jamie." Grant waved to her from the back of the bay. "This is Derek Gilman."

"Nice to meet you," she said, extending her hand when she was close enough.

Tall and blond, with a scar down his jaw, the other man shook her hand. "Welcome to the house."

"Thanks." She didn't see any sign of him having a problem with her gender, which was a relief. "Are we ready?"

"In a sec." Grant looked over his shoulder. "I think I hear him coming now."

She frowned. "Who? I thought it was just the three of us."

"Oh, Scotty showed up because he got his wires crossed and thought you weren't going. Since he doesn't have anything better to do, he said he'd still tag along."

Shit. She'd thought she had another day before she'd have to see him again. Because his sister had yelled for the mop, there hadn't really been a resolution between them. No *hey, what are we going to do about this* conversation so she could be absolutely sure they were on the same page. And that page was nobody on the job knowing there might be something going on between her and one of the firefighters in her company.

When Scott stepped out of the stairwell and into the bay, she swallowed hard and focused on keeping her expression neutral. He stopped when he saw her and their eyes locked for a few seconds, but then he lifted in his chin in a casual nod. "Morning, Jamie."

"Good morning."

He turned to the other guys. "Hey, Gilman. Good to see you."

"You, too."

"I guess I'll drive," Scott said. "My truck will fit all four of us and it's a nice day, so we can throw the groceries in the back."

"Shotgun," Jamie said, smiling when Grant groaned.

She'd said it out of reflex, but it didn't seem like such a good idea when she was sitting next to Scott, separated only by a center console between the bucket seats. Grant and Derek were talking hockey in the backseats, while silence and classic rock reigned in the front seats. Through the corner of her eye, Jamie could see Scott's thumb tapping the steering wheel with the rhythm of the music, and she wondered if he was the kind to sing along if he'd been alone.

It took them almost forty minutes to drive to the big chain supermarket, but Jamie knew it would be worth the time. Supporting the local businesses and small markets in a fire station's neighborhood was something they all tried to do on a day-by-day basis, but when it came to stocking up for the month, they had to try to keep the prices down.

As they walked across the parking lot, Jamie asked, "So how do we do this? Is the list divided up?"

Scott shook his head. "That would be far too organized. We wander up and down the aisles together, looking for the stuff on the list, and then eventually we'll start splitting up as we remember things that aren't on the list and they're almost always back in aisles we already hit."

She laughed. "That explains why we volunteer to come on our own time."

"That and the probability we won't have to abandon the carts to put out a fire."

Scott and Derek each pushed a cart. Grant had the list, and he and Jamie kept an eye out for the items they were looking for. And she kept her mouth shut about the fact they were starting in the refrigeration section, which made no sense to her. But the fact they'd all turned to the left without a discussion told her it was just the backward way they always did it, and she didn't want to nag. After grabbing a variety of sliced and shredded cheeses, a product on the list caught her eye, and she lifted the box out of the cooler with a frown.

"What is this stuff? Yogurt in squeeze tubes?" She'd seen some odd snack requests on house grocery lists, but this stuff looked like it was meant for the kindergarten crowd. "For the firefighters too lazy to wash a spoon?"

"Oh, we're not getting those," Derek said. "Mikey G. is the only one who eats those. His kid got him hooked on them, I guess. But he's behind on throwing his share of money into the kitty, so if he wants them, he can bring them from home."

"Harsh," Grant said. "Poor guy won't have his squeeze yogurt."

"Third month in a row this has happened," Derek replied. After a short pause, he chuckled. "He's lucky we don't make him eat bread and water at mealtime."

"Is he doing okay?" Scott asked.

Jamie had been thinking the question, but she wasn't sure how to phrase it. She liked that Scott was concerned being late on his firehouse fund payments three months in a row might indicate Mike G. was in some financial trouble. If he was and could swallow his pride enough to admit it, there were ways for him to get help.

"Yeah. We let him slide when he went through the divorce because getting his own place was expensive and then the child support and everything. But we get the feeling he's taking advantage now, so we'll start small. No yogurt for Mikey."

Jamie put it back and leaned over Grant's shoulder to see how much stuff was left on the list. "Maybe I should have packed a lunch."

"We kill the supplies in March," Grant said. "A lot of slow cooker meals because we get so many nuisance calls. People forget in March that it's still winter and it can be slippery out there. Plus, around St. Patrick's Day we've got extra guys on hand and we're busy and the pantry suffers."

"We should split the list," Derek said. After scanning it, he carefully tore a chunk out of the side of the paper. "We'll take these staple-type items. Coffees, spices, flour, sugar and crap. Plus paper goods. You guys keep working on the rest of it and then we'll go from there."

When Derek handed the paper to her, Jamie realized he'd naturally drawn the teams based on where they were standing at the time. Grant was standing next to him, while Jamie was in front of Scott's cart.

Great. Unexpected alone time.

They made it to the cans of fruit, where they needed to grab pineapple rings for ham, according to the list. Then Scott leaned on the handle of the shopping cart while she was reading labels. "Hey, while we're alone, I wanted to say something to you."

She tensed, fighting an urge to look around and see if they really *were* alone. Just because Grant and Derek weren't in Scott's sight line didn't mean they weren't still in earshot. "In the grocery store?"

"Yeah. I wanted to apologize for losing my temper last night and hitting that guy."

She hadn't been expecting that, and had braced herself for talking about the kiss while standing in front of canned fruit. "Oh. I should probably apologize for pulling your hair, then."

"I've worked on controlling my temper, but the way

he was talking to you was… I should have let you handle it." Then he looked sideways at her, grinning. "I didn't mind the hair pulling too much, though."

"Stop that," she said in an urgent whisper.

He leaned closer to her and her fingers itched to bury themselves in his hair again. "We're still not at work."

"We're here in a professional capacity, though." She needed a stronger argument because the kiss at the bar was pretty solid evidence her current tactics weren't working. "Besides, you're supposed to be on a break from dating, remember?"

He shrugged. "Maybe I need a break from taking a break. A temporary relapse, like six to eight weeks long."

It was incredibly tempting. And also incredibly risky, because that was treading dangerously close to real relationship territory. "There's no possible way we could keep even a supercasual relationship a secret for two months, and it won't be *you* who suffers the brunt of the gossip or ends up with the tarnished reputation. It'll be me because I'm the officer and, most importantly, because I'm a woman."

"You're not good at secrets?"

"*Me?* Your company is like the freaking Brady Bunch or something. One big happy family—literally, almost—and I'd bet you a hundred dollars right now that some combination of Danny, Ashley, Lydia or Aidan have already had a conversation about us. Your life's part of a family game of Telephone right now."

It seemed as though he wanted to deny it for a few seconds, but then he gave her a chagrined look. "Yeah, secrets are tough. *But*, Aidan managed to date Lydia without me knowing for a while. It can be done."

"Would he have been able to if she'd been working at the station and sharing living quarters with you guys for twenty-four-hour tours?"

"No. Shit, all you did was walk by me in the bar and Danny's radar pinged."

"You said at the bar it doesn't have to be complicated, but it already *is*. We don't need to make our jobs complicated on top of it."

"But—"

"Hey, Kincaid! Catch!"

Scott turned and got his hands up in time to catch the bulk package of paper towels Grant threw at him.

"Did you hear me?" she asked quietly, while they still had a few seconds.

He looked at her, his gaze holding hers in an intense way that made her shiver. "Yeah, I heard you."

It was for the best, Jamie knew. Their relationship needed to go back to being strictly business. But that determination she was doing the right thing didn't stop her from sneaking a huge bag of chocolate candies into the cart. A woman could only deprive herself of so many delicious things.

Chapter 5

Scott usually hung out with his dad in the evening if it wasn't a night Scott had anything going on and Tommy wasn't going to the bar to sit and swap the same old stories with Fitz. It seemed stupid for Tommy to sit and watch television alone while Scott was one floor up, watching the same shows alone.

But tonight, Scott felt restless and he lingered in his own apartment. It didn't have too much of a homey feel, with most of the personal touches being limited to the leather sofa and love seat in front of his enormous TV. But he'd redone the floors from carpet to wood laminate himself, and repainted the entire apartment. He'd also sunk a lot of money into the bathroom, but none of that made him feel particularly bonded to the place. It was just where he lived, and he got a great deal on the rent.

It wasn't a home, though, and he wondered if that's what was nagging at him. Was it stuff that made a home? Or was it the wife and kids he didn't have? He was only twenty-seven, so he wasn't sure why he felt such a strong desire to finally settle down, but he couldn't deny it was there.

Maybe he should buy some stuff. He wasn't sure what. Wicker baskets? Or maybe some plants. He'd get a pet, but it wasn't like he was asking a dog to make it through an eight-hour workday without him. He was gone twenty-four hours at a time, and that wouldn't be fair to anything except maybe a fish, and he didn't see the point in that.

When he realized his dad was probably scowling up at his ceiling, wondering why he hadn't come down, Scott stepped through the sliding glass doors onto his deck. One flight of stairs down, he walked through his dad's back door.

"I was beginning to wonder if you were coming down tonight," his dad called from his ancient recliner.

"Yeah, I was on the phone," he lied. As he walked through the kitchen toward the living room, Scott looked around him.

Was it the stuff that made it feel like home, or just the fact he'd grown up in this house? Unlike the second and third floors, nothing had changed in the three-bedroom first-floor apartment, and there was definitely an '80s feel about it.

He had really vague memories of his mom nagging his dad to start remodeling, room by room. He'd always promised he'd get around to it soon and she'd roll her eyes. Then she'd been diagnosed too late with breast cancer. Scott was nine when she died, and giving away her personal possessions had been heart-breaking enough. The remodeling never happened.

Scott plopped down on the sofa and put his feet up on the old wooden coffee table. "I'm beat. I almost went to bed instead of coming down. I volunteered for supermarket duty today."

"I'd rather scrub floors. Speaking of the house, how's Danny's fill-in doing?"

"Jamie? Okay, I guess." He wondered if his dad's curiosity was related to the job, or if one of his sisters had said something to him.

"Pulling her weight?"

"Yeah. There hasn't been much weight to pull, other than some odor and medical calls."

His dad shook his head. "It's never made sense to me for fire to respond to medical calls. Especially both trucks."

Scott knew that, since they'd had this conversation many times at the bar. "I know, but E-59 and L-37 roll together, and we can be almost anywhere in four minutes. More fire truck coverage than ambulance coverage, which you know. But anyway, we haven't worked an active fire yet, but I don't have any doubts about her ability to pull her weight."

"You sound pretty sure of that."

Scott shrugged. "If I was worried about her doing her job, everybody would know."

His dad chuckled. "Yeah, you've never been shy about giving your opinion. We should invite her over for dinner. I'd like to get to know her some."

Oh, there was no way in hell could Scott let that happen. Jamie had made it pretty clear in the grocery store that she wanted to keep a wall of professionalism between them. Turning around and inviting her home to meet the parent probably wasn't what she was going for.

"I'm sure she'll stop by the bar some night and you can meet her," he said.

"The bar's loud and people are always interrupting my conversations to talk to me. Here we can have a nice meal and relax."

"It's just not a good idea, Pop. And she won't be around long, anyway. Once Danny's cleared to come back, she'll be gone."

"So? She's here now. And I wouldn't mind meeting the woman, seeing as how my son started a brawl in my bar over her."

Dammit. Somebody—maybe Lydia, or maybe anybody else who'd been there that night—had ratted him out. "It wasn't a brawl."

"I told you what would happen if you started a fight in the bar again."

"Yeah. You'd throw me out. But that was years ago, and I didn't start the fight. He threw the first punch."

His dad turned the television down a couple of notches and turned to give him a stern look. "From what I heard, he threw the first punch because you went flying across the room, knocking Jamie's beer out of her hand, and grabbed hold of him."

Unless one of the douche bag's friends had gone back to the bar when Tommy was there and complained, the only people who knew that were Danny and Jamie. Since Danny hadn't ratted him out directly to the old man, he must have told Ashley the details. And either Ashley had told their dad, or Ashley had told Lydia, who told their dad. He was guessing the latter.

Jamie hadn't been wrong about his life being the subject of a family game of Telephone.

"He had it coming."

Tommy chuckled. "The only reason I'm not pissed is the sheer enjoyment I'm getting out of picturing you being hauled off the guy by a woman with a fistful of your hair."

There was a time Scott would have leaped to his own defense, trying to protect his ego. But he just laughed with his dad. "I'm glad those security cameras in the pool room are just for show."

"I'm not. I would have liked to see it." His dad nodded. "She sounds like quite a woman, which is why I want to meet her."

"Like I said, Pops, she'll probably show up at the bar some night."

"Okay." Tommy shrugged, and Scott felt a rush of relief. "I'll make it a group thing and tell your sister to have Aidan invite her."

Scott wasn't going to win this one. "Fine. Do what you want. You always do."

"I think I'm going to like her."

"You probably will, not that it matters one way or the other."

His dad shrugged. "You never know."

Scott wasn't sure what he meant by that, but he was damn sure his family was a pain in the ass. His brother-in-law was trying to warn him off getting involved with Jamie, while his father sure seemed to think Jamie would fit right in. But whether he thought she'd fit in the company or in the family, Scott wasn't sure. And if he pushed the subject, he was going to look like he was protesting too much and Tommy Kincaid would latch on to that like a dog with a bone.

The cop show they both liked started, and that ended the conversation. By the time a commercial break rolled around, Jamie would be forgotten and his dad would move on to something else.

She'd be forgotten by Tommy, anyway. The episode wasn't good enough to keep Scott's attention and his mind wandered to earlier, in the supermarket. Obviously she'd been right about his family's inability to keep a secret.

Was she right about the fact she'd be the only one to face repercussions if their relationship became the talk of the station, too? He didn't like to think so, but he'd heard enough talk about women in general and female firefighters in particular over the years to know there would be dirt flung and none of it would hit him. Or if it did, it wouldn't stick. He was one of them—sixth-generation Boston Fire.

No matter how much he wanted her, he needed to pull back and leave Jamie Rutherford alone.

Jamie swung the ax, punching a hole to vent the roof of the two-story single-family home, cringing as she did it. It was a nice house, or had been, and she didn't like inflicting even more damage on it. What the fire didn't ruin, the water would, but at least nobody would get hurt and their neighbors would be spared.

The cause had come through with the call, since the homeowner watched the fire start. The origin was an overloaded power strip plugged into an overloaded circuit, and the strip had been sitting along the edge of the wall, under the long drapes.

The woman had grabbed her kids and her purse and run, which was the right thing to do. She'd called 911 from across the street and help had arrived a few minutes later. Unfortunately, it was a fast-moving fire thanks to flammable decor and an open floor plan, and all they could hope to do was knock it down before it spread. There wouldn't be much left inside for the family to salvage.

"I don't know what the hell they insulated the walls with, but the fire keeps popping up in random spots," she heard over the radio. There were multiple companies on the scene now, so containment wouldn't be an issue, but it was going to be a long day.

It took them hours to knock down the flames enough to sweep for hot spots and refires. It was hot, dirty work and there was a lot of climbing in and around charred piles of rubble. She knew, out on the street, there would be news cameras and cell phones capturing the drama. Their support volunteers with their truck stocked with beverages and high-energy snacks to keep the firefighters going. A cluster of guys around the incident command vehicle. None of that was her problem. Making sure there were no hot spots that would reignite when they turned their backs was her problem.

She did hope, however, that the Red Cross had already taken the family to the home of family or friends, or helped them find temporary shelter. They'd lost everything, and watching the firefighters poke around the remains of their home wouldn't help them feel any better.

Her guys had done a damn fine job, though, she thought as she took her helmet off to wipe at the sweat gathered across her hairline. She and Rick worked well together, so there were no bumps in the road when it came to the two companies' teamwork. While the majority of their calls might be medical or motor vehicle accidents, their first fire together was the true test, and she thought she'd passed it.

"We're about done here," Rick said from just behind her, and she turned to face him. "We'll keep at it while the other companies clear out, since the trucks are blocked in anyway, but there's nothing else we can do at this point."

She nodded and looked around the mess. "We should probably check that south wall one more time and then we'll start packing up."

It was a quiet ride back to the house, but she wasn't surprised. It had been a hot one, and between the sweat and the grime of crawling through a charred house, they were all pretty wiped out. When the trucks were parked and tended to and the gear stowed, they all trudged up the stairs.

"You want to shower first?" Rick asked her, but she shook her head.

"No sense in everybody sitting around getting the furniture dirty waiting on me. I'll throw that chicken stew in the freezer into the pot and get it started. When you guys are done, you can take over and it should be hot just about the time I'm done."

"Sounds like a plan."

She washed her hands and arms before taking a couple of containers of the stew out of the freezer. Jamie had been told they were a gift from Chris's wife, who would sometimes make extra of something and send it in for the station.

It took a long time for the guys to all shower, and she hoped there would be hot water left. She also felt as if every minute that went by increased the chances of the alarm sounding while she was in the shower. She'd gone on a call once, years before, with clothes yanked onto her wet body and the shampoo only half rinsed out of her hair. Her scalp had itched the entire afternoon.

When it was her turn, she hung the pink fabric wreath on the door of the shower room and went inside. She'd had it for so long she couldn't even remember where she'd gotten it, but it had come in handy over the course of her career. After showering as quickly as possible, she put on a clean uniform and dumped the dirty stuff into her basket.

They were serving the stew when she walked into the kitchen, and she took a bowl from Gavin. "Thanks. It smells delicious."

Since the seats around the table were full, she took her stew into the living room and sat in one of the chairs. Jeff had the other, and Aidan and Scott were on the couch. There was an old back-and-white Western on the television, which she'd already learned meant Jeff had the remote control.

"Glad you're here, Lieutenant Rutherford," Jeff said. "It was good today."

Jamie let the warm rush of pride she felt show in her smile. "Thank you. It *was* good today, and I feel pretty lucky to work with you guys."

"You fit in."

"With this bunch I don't know if that's a compliment or not," Scott said, and Jeff chuckled.

"Speaking of fitting in, Jamie," Aidan said, "Lydia wanted me to pass along an invitation to her dad's for dinner. Maybe Sunday. Tommy wants to meet you."

She wasn't sure what to say. Scott was focused on his chicken stew, and Jamie wasn't sure if it was because he didn't care that she'd been invited to his dad's, or if he was uncomfortable with the idea and didn't want to say it.

It wasn't quite a royal decree, but she knew Tommy was important to the local firefighters and she didn't really want to decline his invitation. And while Scott technically lived in the house, he had an apartment upstairs, so it really wasn't any of his business.

"Who will be there?" she asked, when she realized Aidan was waiting for her to say something.

"Tommy, me, Lydia, Danny and Ashley that I know of for sure. And you'll be there, Scotty?"

Scott lifted his gaze to meet Jamie's for a few seconds, his expression unreadable. "Yeah. I'll be there."

"It sounds like fun," she said to Aidan, since Scott was giving her nothing to work with as far as his thoughts on the matter. "Sunday works for me."

"We eat about five when we do family dinners. I'll text you the address later, and I think you're in easy walking distance."

"You guys in Boston have a weird sense of walking distance, though. Driving here is such a nightmare I think you've all convinced yourself that 'easy walking distance' and 'would be considered a marathon if you jogged it' are the same thing."

They all laughed, and then they watched some cowboys riding around fake cacti while they finished their stew. Chris walked in a little while later and took their bowls, since he was doing the dishes.

"You need help?" Jamie asked. She'd noticed some of the other guys going through to the bunk room or to the weight equipment, so he might be alone.

"After I wash these bowls, I'm taking a power nap. You can dry them and put them away if you want, or they can sit and drip dry. Either way."

"It would be nice to have a dishwasher," she said.

"Budget," all the guys said at the same time, and she laughed.

Old Westerns weren't her cup of tea, so she followed Chris into the kitchen and pulled a clean dish towel out of the drawer. After he'd pulled the plug in the sink, he gave her a mock salute and went to take his nap, leaving her alone with a pile of dishes and the sound of Hollywood gunfire from the other room.

She wasn't alone very long, though. Scott came in, and judging by how close he stood and the fact he was practically staring at the door, she knew he had something to say he didn't want anybody else overhearing.

Jamie hoped whatever it was wasn't very important, since she had trouble concentrating when he was so close to her. She could smell the soap and shampoo that all the guys used, but there was something about smelling it on him that made her want to tousle his hair and bury her face in his neck.

"You don't have to go to my dad's for dinner if you don't want to," he said in a low voice.

"I wouldn't have said yes if I didn't want to go. Do *you* not want me to go?"

"What do you mean?"

She kept wiping the bowl in her hand, even though it was already dry. "You didn't look too thrilled when Aidan offered the invitation, that's all."

"I just… I don't know. I'm not sure if the old man's up to something, that's all. Like maybe he has the wrong idea."

"Where would he get the wrong idea?"

"Because of the fight at the bar. Because I got so pissed that guy was disrespecting you, and then he thinks it's funny that you broke it up by pulling my hair, so who knows what thoughts he's got in his head."

"You're never going to live the hair thing down, are you?"

He grinned, which made her feel better. "Never."

"Maybe he just wants to meet me because you have a dangerous job and I'm a big part of it and of helping you go home safely at the end of each tour, so he wants to make sure I'm up to it."

"Maybe."

It was the nature of a firehouse that they weren't going to be alone very much longer, so she cut to the chase. "If you don't want me to go, I'll tell Aidan I just remembered something else I had to do. No hard feelings."

"No, I *do* want you to go, which is part of the problem. You know I'm attracted to you, and I'm doing my best to bury that. Us being possibly set up by my father for a family dinner makes that a little messy for me, but I'll handle it."

She looked into his dark eyes, surprised by his candor. He wasn't playing games, and she appreciated that. He wanted her, she'd told him why she didn't think it was a good idea, and he was trying to respect that. "I won't go. It's really not a big deal."

"I want you to go more than I don't want you to go." He ran a hand through his hair. "How's that for messed up?"

"I understand." She sighed and set the bowl on the counter to pick up another from the dish rack. "Trust me, I know what you mean."

Grant walked in then, rubbing his stomach. "Is there any stew left? I'm still hungry."

"You're *always* hungry," Scott said, picking the dried bowl up off the counter and turning toward the cabinet as if he'd been standing so close to her because he was putting the dishes away. "And no, there isn't any left."

"Should I bring anything Sunday?" she asked Scott while Grant rummaged around in the fridge. She was going to go because she *did* know exactly what he meant. She wanted to see him more than she feared what would happen if she saw him.

It was a mess, and all they'd done was kiss one time. But she didn't have the willpower to turn down an invitation to spend more time with him.

Chapter 6

Scott slapped the puck, and then groaned when it bounced off the goal crossbar with a solid and unmistakable clang.

"You are seriously off your game tonight, Kincaid."

"Screw you, Hunt." He flipped Aidan off as he skated by.

"Got something on your mind?" his friend called back to him. "Or somebody?"

The same somebody who'd been on his mind since the night of the wedding reception smoke machine, when Jamie had walked into the engine bay. "Just keeping Gullotti on his toes."

"On my toes?" Rick called from the net. "I could sit here on my ass and you couldn't get that puck by me tonight."

Trash-talking wasn't as fun when it was almost the

truth. Not quite the truth, though. He wasn't on his game, but if Rick sat down, he could probably score on him. Thankfully they weren't playing a game tonight. Grabbing some ice time was simply their favorite kind of workout and a bunch of them often got together to play outside of the fire department league. Tonight, only three of them had been able to make it but they were playing anyway because they had the ice, taking turns in the goal.

"How's the dating break going?" Rick asked when Aidan pointed at the clock to signal their time was up.

"I haven't been on a date, so I guess it's a big success," Scott said. He'd date Jamie in a second, of course, but since she was off-limits, the break lived on. "How are things with you?"

"Good. I'll be happy when Jessica's here for good and doesn't have to go back and forth to San Diego, but it's worth the separations. *She's* worth it. And this way she's building a great relationship with her grandparents without bailing on her relationship with her dad."

"You set a date yet?"

"Not yet. Once Danny's back, she and I will take Joe and Marie to California to see Davey. They've been estranged for so long, it won't be an easy reconciliation, but she wants them all there when we get married."

They sat on the bench to unlace their skates. "There's only one of him. Wouldn't it be easier for him to come here?"

"It would. And cheaper. But there are so many memories here and so many people who know them that it'll be easier on his turf. More neutral, especially since we'll all stay at a hotel. And Joe and Marie have never been to California, so at the very least, it'll be a nice vacation."

"How about you and Lydia?" Scott asked Aidan. "Set a date yet?"

"Soon. Maybe as soon as Danny gets his cast off and can be in the wedding photos without the crutches."

"Really?" Scott paused with one skate in his hand. "Is there a reason for that?"

Aidan laughed. "If Lydia gets pregnant, you'll be the second to know. Trust me."

"Who's going to be first?"

"Hopefully me." Aidan shrugged. "But with your family, I can never be sure."

"So why the rush?"

"I don't think it's a rush, exactly. She doesn't want a big, fancy wedding. Maybe because she doesn't have her mom...your mom. You know?"

Scott nodded, reaching down for his other skate. Losing their mom touched them all in a thousand different ways, but he'd always thought it was a little harder on his sisters. There were so many milestones and occasions a girl needed her mother for, and Tommy wasn't the kind of dad who could fill that role.

"Anyway," Aidan continued, "we want to be married more than we want to plan a wedding, so we're thinking of a civil ceremony at the bar with just family."

"Hey," Rick said.

"*All* of our family. You know we wouldn't get married without you guys."

They walked toward the locker rooms, Scott listening to the two guys talking about getting married. He didn't feel left out, exactly. He genuinely loved both guys and couldn't be happier for them. But before long he'd be choosing between being an extra wheel to the married couples or hanging out with Grant and Gavin, and he was over the club scene.

"I'm going to grab a shower at home," Rick said. "Jess sold her place so she stays at a hotel when she's in San Diego. The Wi-Fi's better at the office, so we usually chat before she leaves there and I'm already cutting it close."

"I'm going to shower at home because I forgot to throw clean clothes in my bag," Aidan said and they all laughed. "Scott?"

"I'm going to shower before I leave. I walked and you never know who you might run into on the way home."

"Hey, you could bump into your television wife," Rick said.

"My television wife? What the hell is that supposed to mean?"

"Oh, that's what Eriksson calls the woman you stopped dating to meet. Like an old sitcom wife or whatever. Aprons and baking and perfect children."

That made him laugh. "Perfect children? It would take one hell of a woman to bring perfect Kincaids into the world."

"I've been your best friend since we were teenagers and the fact my children will each have one foot in the same gene pool as you scares the crap out of me. I mean, think about it. Me and the Kincaid DNA means there's a possibility I'll have gorgeous, perfect daughters—like their mother—and then very attractive sons with bad tempers who kind of suck at hockey."

"Or they might take after me," Scott shot back.

The other two were still laughing when they left the rink, and Scott shook his head. It still blew his mind that Aidan was going to be his brother-in-law, but once he'd gotten over the initial shock, he had to admit he couldn't have picked a better husband for Lydia even if she'd let him.

He hit the shower before getting dressed and then slung his hockey bag over his shoulder. Maybe he should have done like the other guys and just showered at home, but the last time he'd done that, he'd run into some old friends and ended up in a bar in smelly workout clothes.

Walking was the right choice, though, he thought. Mother Nature had opted for a warm spring night, though there was another cold snap in the long-range forecast. A lot of people waved to him, and a couple of kids even recognized him from a Fire Prevention Week program he'd done with Chris and a few other guys at the elementary school. He talked to them for a few minutes.

After a couple of blocks, he turned down a side street to take a shortcut. The bag was heavy and he shifted it from one shoulder to the other. Sometimes he was tempted to drive to the rink because it was a long walk with a hockey bag, but he liked to think of each trek to the rink and back as one less hour he had to feel guilty about not being in the gym.

"Scott."

He looked to his left, at the woman he'd been about to pass by without really noticing, and stopped short. His tired legs and shoulders were forgotten as every nerve in his body seemed to spring to life.

She was wearing a long gray sweatshirt over black

leggings or yoga pants or whatever they called those things. Her feet were shoved bare into sneakers and her hair was caught in a messy knot on top of her head by one of those clips with the painful-looking teeth.

God, he wanted her. He wanted to squeeze the clip so it opened, watch her hair tumble down around her shoulders in waves, and then bury his face in it. "Hey, Jamie. What are you doing here?"

She nodded her head toward the building they were standing in front of. "I live here."

"Oh. That makes sense then."

"Had a craving for chocolate pudding." She held up a folded-over paper bag. "They sell this pudding at the corner that's amazing. The owner's wife makes it, I guess. Have you ever had it?"

"Nope."

She peered around his shoulder. "That's a pretty big bag."

"Hockey stuff," he said, and then he smiled. "And some free life advice—don't ever open a guy's hockey bag without a gas mask or a clothespin for your nose. I'm pretty sure women who think hockey players are sexy have never smelled one before he hits the showers."

"I'll keep that in mind. So what are *you* doing here?"

"I was playing some hockey with Aidan and Rick, and this street is a shortcut between the rink and home. I've been walking this way since I was so young my mom would hold my hand on the way to youth league practice."

She smiled. "I bet you were a cute kid."

"I was." He loved the sound of her laugh.

Then she sighed, and he realized they'd run out of standing-on-the-sidewalk small talk and were heading toward awkward silence.

He tried desperately to think of something to talk about—anything that would keep her there and give him an excuse to spend a few more minutes with her. But he'd already had this conversation with himself and he needed to do the right thing and say good-night.

Screw it, Jamie thought. She was done torturing herself, and the chocolate pudding in her hand was good, but it was no substitute for the man standing in front of her. She wanted him. She knew he wanted her. They were adults and they were both fully capable of showing up when scheduled and doing their jobs. Spending some time together off the clock wasn't going to change that.

So, before he could end the silence by telling her he'd see her around, she demolished the weak, teetering wall of professionalism she'd tried to build between them. "You want to come up? Maybe share my pudding?"

Something flickered in his expression, and then he gave her a wry smile. "Is this an offer you make to all of your coworkers?"

She assumed he was trying to feel out what kind of invitation she was offering. The "ran into a friend and why not share her pudding" kind? Or the "using the pudding as an excuse to get him alone" kind? "No. Sharing my chocolate pudding is a very exclusive offer, just for you."

He shoved his hands into his pockets, rocking back a little on his heels. "I've spent a lot of time this week trying *not* to imagine you inviting me up to your apartment because I don't want to be a problem for you."

"I appreciate that." And she really did. It meant a lot to her that he'd taken what she'd said to heart. "But having all this…tension between us is a problem for me, too. You and I have chemistry. It sure as hell isn't burning itself out, and it seems like everybody can see it and there's going to be speculation no matter what. If my sex life is going to be the subject of gossip for the next month and a half to two months, I'm going to damn well *have* a sex life."

She must have said it louder than she meant to, because a guy passing by paused to look at her. He looked like he was going to say something, but one look from Scott sent him on his way.

"Oops," she muttered.

"I'd love to come up and share your chocolate pudding," Scott said. "I've worked up an appetite."

As she unlocked the side door that gave residents access to the interior stairwell, Jamie decided that was the problem with innuendo. She didn't know if he'd worked up a sexual appetite for her, or if he'd literally worked up an appetite playing hockey with the guys and was going to try to eat all of her pudding.

They wound their way up the narrow staircases to the fourth floor, while she told him about the building. "Obviously you know there's a barber shop on the first floor, since you walk by here all the time and there's a sign. Then there's a two-bedroom apartment on the second floor and two one-bedroom apartments on the third. I've got the studio they managed to fit on the fourth floor."

"This explains why you haven't spent any time in the workout room," he said.

"I could afford the rent because they have a hard time finding people willing to climb this many stairs multiple times a day. There's no elevator, so this is it."

"Do you have decks off the back?"

"No, just a bare-minimum fire escape." At the top of the stairs, she unlocked her door and let Scott into her apartment.

Once inside, he set his hockey bag off to the side and made a relieved sound. "I need to get wheels for that thing."

"Or you could drive."

He shrugged, then unzipped his sweatshirt and tossed it on top of the bag. "The problem with driving is finding a place to park."

When she toed off her shoes, he did the same, but he didn't follow her when she walked to the counter to put down the bag from the market. She turned to face him, leaning the small of her back against the edge of the fake granite.

"Are you really sure about this?" he asked, his eyes serious as he looked at her from across the room.

"I wouldn't have invited you up if I wasn't. Are *you* sure about this?"

"I've been sure I want you since you first walked into the station. But you were right before, when you said it would be worse for you because you're a woman. I'd like to deny it because it sucks, but I've been around long enough to know it's the truth."

"My record speaks for itself. And if that's not enough… I don't care. I'm not going to spend the next six weeks being miserable because of other people's hang-ups." He didn't move, and she chuckled. "I swear. I'm very sure."

He moved then, crossing the room to her in long strides. When he reached her, he grabbed her hips and tugged so she was standing straight, almost pressed against him. "I swear I haven't been able to think about anything but you for days."

"I've been thinking about you, too, and I don't know why." When he arched an eyebrow, she laughed. "That didn't sound right. I just mean that I've never been this distracted by a guy before. Also, you smell delicious."

"I'm glad I took the time to shower after I left the ice or you'd be opening the windows right now. Or throwing me out."

"You're not going anywhere for a while."

He grinned and slipped his hands under the hem of her sweatshirt, pushing it up until his hands were at her waist. "I love these legging things. They make your legs look wicked long, and the elastic waist is nice, too."

As he said it, he dipped a finger under the waistband and she shuddered as his knuckle tickled her skin. But then she grasped his jaw with her fingers, tilting his face up until he met her gaze. "There's no home run if you skip first base."

He frowned. "I...don't know what that means."

"That's what I get for trying to use a sports analogy, because I'm not sure, either. It's supposed to mean you haven't kissed me since that night in your bar's storage room, and I like a little romance before a guy gets his hands down my pants."

His hands left her waist and he looked at her so intently, she was afraid for a minute that she'd turned him off and he might change his mind. But then his hands cupped her face and he smiled before his mouth claimed hers.

It wasn't a gentle kiss. It was hot and hungry, and she moaned as she buried her hands in his hair. His tongue danced over hers and she ran her heel up the back of his calf. When he nipped her bottom lip, she smiled against his mouth. His hands went underneath her sweatshirt again, but he didn't touch her waistband. His palms slid up her sides, stopping just below the bra she'd thrown on before running to the store.

He kissed her until her knees were weak and she wanted him inside of her so badly her entire body ached. Grasping the bottom of his T-shirt, she yanked it free of his jeans and slid it up over his abs.

"How much romance are you holding out for?" he murmured against her mouth.

"Being naked is romantic," she said, a little breathlessly.

He stepped back and lifted his arms, but before she could get his shirt off, he dropped them again. "This is kind of awkward, but before we start taking any clothes off, I should tell you I don't have any protection with me."

"Really? The grapevine would be so disappointed to hear you don't walk around fully prepared to have sex at any given moment with no advanced planning."

"In my defense, I went out tonight to play hockey with the guys. You're not supposed to keep condoms in your wallet and they'd probably disintegrate in five minutes if closed up in a hockey bag, so…yeah."

"I've got you covered." She paused, and then laughed. "No pun intended."

He groaned. "Really? That was pretty bad."

"Maybe. Why don't we move a few feet to the left, into the bedroom?"

"I kind of like the kitchen and the bedroom being all one like this," he said when they reached the bed. "And you can see the TV from both."

She sat on the edge of the bed and grinned up at him. "Yeah, so I can lie in bed and watch you make me a sandwich. Naked."

He pulled his T-shirt off and tossed it aside. "That's incredibly hot. You naked. Sandwiches. Maybe a hockey game on the TV, all at the same time. This is basically a perfect apartment."

Once she'd had her fill of looking at his chest and abs, which were impressive, she reached into the night-stand drawer for a condom and set it on the edge of the bed. Then she caught his hand and tugged as she lay back, so he fell over her on the mattress. She was done looking and wanted to touch. "Sex with a hockey game in the background?"

"Hey, a crowd cheering's good for a man's ego." He reached down for her sweatshirt and started working it up over her stomach. "You know, I've heard some women who work in male-dominated fields like to wear lacy lingerie under their clothes to remind them of their femininity."

She laughed and slapped his hand away. "I don't need to be reminded I'm a woman. And I'm not into climbing multiple flights of stairs in sixty-plus pounds of gear with a lace thong wedged up my ass, so if that's what you're hoping to find, you're going to be disappointed."

"You just smiling at me can make my whole fucking day." He pushed her hair away from her face, his gaze suddenly serious and intense. "There is *no* chance anything about you will disappoint me."

Emotion swelled in her chest and she lifted her head to kiss him so they would close their eyes and he wouldn't see it on her face. His kiss was as fierce as the look he'd given her and she ran her hands over his back, his muscles rippling under her palms.

Then he pulled back and hauled her to her feet. "I need to feel you against me."

She pulled the sweatshirt over her head and dropped it on the floor. His hands cupped the white cotton bra, his thumbs brushing over her nipples. Reaching behind her back, she unclasped the bra and let him slip it over her arms.

Scott made a low, growling sound of appreciation before unbuttoning his jeans. After kicking them off, he pulled off his socks and the white boxer briefs followed. Hooking the waistband of her underwear with her yoga pants, she pulled them off and then wrapped her hand around the back of his neck to pull him in for another kiss.

Without taking his mouth off of hers, Scott picked her up and set her on the bed. Jamie ran her hands down his back and over his ass, scraping lightly with her fingernails. He cupped one breast, rubbing his thumb over the nipple, and she moaned against his lips.

But when she rocked her hips up against his, he drew back to grin at her. "Pushy, aren't you?"

"I've been thinking about this for days. I don't want to wait anymore."

"Maybe just another minute," he said, his voice

rough as his palm skimmed over her stomach and between her legs.

She sucked in a breath as he pressed against her clit.
His fingers stroked her slick flesh and she buried her
hands in his hair, not wanting him to stop.

"God, you feel so good."

"I want you inside me now."

"You got somewhere to be?"

She growled, scraping her fingernails down his
arm. "You're killing me."

Finally, she heard him rip the condom wrapper
open. After a few seconds, he knelt between her thighs
and ran his hands down her calves. Smiling at him, she
spread her knees wider and lifted her hips.

He took his sweet time about it. Slowly, he entered
her, one hand gripping the back of her thigh while the
other supported his weight. Each time he pulled back,
he went a little bit deeper until he filled her completely.

"Damn," he whispered, a light sheen of sweat
gleaming at his hairline. "This has been building for
days, and I don't want it to be over."

"That's not the only condom," she said, rocking
against him.

He groaned and started moving, meeting each lift
of her hips. She wrapped her arms around his waist,
digging her fingertips into the middle of his back.
Stroke after stroke brought her closer to orgasm, and
she closed her eyes, savoring the sensations. He thrust
deeper and faster until her back arched and she bit
down on her lips to keep from crying out as the orgasm hit.

Only a moment later Scott groaned, his body jerking as he came, and she held him until his orgasm

passed. He lowered himself on top of her and kissed her neck as his body relaxed, and she sighed contentedly.

If there were consequences for tonight, she'd gladly accept them. It had been worth it.

Once they'd caught their breath, he kissed her again and then rolled away. "Since you only have one door, I guess that must be the bathroom."

"Mmm-hmm. But there's also a box of tissues on the nightstand and a wastebasket under it if you need it."

She closed her eyes as he disposed of the condom, and then smiled when he rolled back to her, his body spooning hers. "You're so warm. I might never move again."

"I guess I'll let you rest for a few minutes."

Laughing, she snuggled deeper against him. "A few minutes, huh? You sound pretty sure of yourself."

He lifted his head and kissed her neck before putting his mouth next to her ear. "I bet you think I forgot you offered to share that chocolate pudding with me, don't you?"

Chapter 7

Eating chocolate pudding naked in bed with Jamie Rutherford. Today was definitely ending a lot better than it had begun, Scott thought. And she'd been right about the pudding. It was damn good, and would have been worth climbing the stairs for even if she hadn't gotten him into her bed.

"What did you think?" she asked.

He looked over at her, smiling at the smudge of pudding at the corner of her mouth before she wiped it away with the tip of her finger. They were sitting up against her headboard, each with an empty bowl of pudding and, even though she'd pulled the sheet up over her breasts when she sat up, everything was pretty damn perfect.

"It was as good as you said it was. I don't know if I should start stopping at that market to get my own, or if I should find a new way to the rink so I'm not tempted by it."

"Tell me about it. It's just around the corner from me, so I have to depend on willpower." She took his bowl and set them on her nightstand before wiggling back down so her head was on her pillow. "I think you being naked in my bed says everything about how strong my willpower game is."

"You're the first woman who's ever given me chocolate pudding after sex. You do realize you might not get rid of me now."

She laughed. "That pudding was supposed be my reward for making it an entire week without having sex with you."

"You almost made it." He moved down on the bed and then rolled onto his side, propping his head on his hand so he could see her face. "What was your two-week reward going to be?"

"A Ferrari? I don't know, and I think the fact I can't think of anything says a lot about my faith in my ability to resist you."

"And that was with me deliberately trying to leave you alone."

"Which just made you even more attractive to me, by the way."

"So tell me something," he said, running his fingertip over her collarbone. "What made you want to be a firefighter?"

"You would think with all the times I've been asked that over the years, that I would have an easy answer for that question."

"Do you have family in the fire service?"

"Nobody. My dad sells insurance and my mom

owns a hair salon. One of my sisters works with her and will probably take over when my mom retires. My other sister teaches fourth grade. Both married with kids and all that. Then, when I was in middle school, we had a career day."

"Ah, yes. I've gotten sucked into doing a few of those. They're usually pretty fun, though, because let's face it, we have the coolest job. Maybe I'll do a few more of them if they actually work on kids."

"Actually, the guy who did it pissed me off."

"Really? You became a firefighter because the guy who did career day when you were a kid pissed you off?"

"Basically, yeah. He had this exciting presentation and he made it sound awesome, but he only talked to the boys. He talked about how real men took care of their communities with no thought to their own safety and—"

She paused when Scott snorted in derision. "Sorry, but sometimes it seems like *all* we think about is our own safety."

"Yeah, but preteen boys wouldn't find endless training classes and inspections exciting. So anyway, once he was done with his grandstanding, he was like, 'Oh, yeah, there's stuff for girls, too, like working in dispatch,' and his entire tone changed when he said it. I raised my hand and told him women can be firefighters, too."

"Of course you did." He tried to imagine a much younger version of her, and didn't doubt that even then, she wouldn't hesitate to set him straight. "I'm almost afraid to ask what he said."

"He said, 'But not good ones.'"

"Oh, ouch. So you've worked your ass off your entire life just to prove some sexist douche bag wrong?" When she blushed, he laughed. "That's one hell of a stubborn streak. I'm impressed."

Jamie slapped his shoulder. "It started out that way, yes. But the first time I went on a real call, I knew I was on the right road for me."

"Were you ever assigned to that guy's company? You said it was a small town."

"No. I would have been, but he was fired and sued for sexual harassment the year before I signed on." She smiled up at him. "Why did you become a firefighter? Because of Tommy?"

"Yeah, there's Tommy. And my grandfather. His father. I'm the sixth generation of Boston Fire in my family, so I'm not sure I even paid attention at career day. I remember back when my mom was alive and my dad was talking about his day, he'd think of some cautionary tale and say 'Someday when you're on the job, son...' and tell me what went wrong so it wouldn't happen to me. Nobody ever questioned that I'd follow in his footsteps."

"How old were you when your mom died? If you don't mind me asking."

"I was nine. Lydia was thirteen and Ashley was fourteen. They alternated between overmothering me to compensate and writing me off as too much like my dad to bother with. He threw himself into the job and, as soon as I was old enough, I did the same."

"Do you ever resent it?"

"Resent what?"

"That your life's path was some kind of foregone conclusion. It seems like you were destined from birth to be a firefighter. What if you wanted to build houses or work with computers or be a chef or something?"

He had to think about it for a minute because he couldn't remember anybody ever asking him that before. "Well, I didn't resent it before, but now that you mention it…"

She laughed, which made her breasts jiggle a little under the thin sheet. "I'm being serious."

"There have been times I resented my dad's job. It made my mom unhappy a lot and I don't think they would have stayed married much longer if she hadn't been diagnosed with breast cancer. But I never wanted to be anything but a firefighter. Even when I was little, I'd see a fire truck go by and feel a rush of pride. That was going to be me. They'd be my brothers and I'd take care of my neighbors just like my dad did. Like Fitz and my gramps. I guess being a firefighter isn't what I am. It's *who* I am."

"I get that," she said, and he knew it was the truth. Nobody would put in the amount of dedication and hard work it took to go from some small-town volunteer gig to being a Boston Fire lieutenant as young as she was unless it was a calling.

"Hey, how old are you?" he asked before his brain's filter could stop him and come up with a better way to phrase the question.

She arched an eyebrow at him. "Really?"

"Yeah, that wasn't very smooth. If it helps, I was thinking about how hard you must have worked to make lieutenant at a young age, and that made me realize I don't know how old you actually are."

"That does make me feel better, I have to admit. And I'm thirty-four." She winced. "Of course I already know you're only twenty-seven since I'm privy to more info about you than you are about me."

"That's not fair." He hooked his finger on the sheet and gave it a little tug. "Thirty-four is an incredibly sexy age."

"Lighting must be good," she said.

"The lighting isn't what's good." He lowered his mouth to her breast, nipping at her nipple before running his tongue over it.

She laughed and slid her arms around his waist, pulling him on top of her. They made love again, and he savored every minute of it. He loved the way she felt and tasted, and the way she unabashedly enjoyed his touch. Jamie was eye contact and naughty smiles and soft moans. With her sex was more than a primal urge to reach orgasm. It was something fun and yet intense they were doing together, exploring each other's bodies and finding those spots that amped up the pleasure, and he never wanted it to end.

When they finally collapsed on the pillows, panting and flushed and totally wrung out, he landed flat on his back and tried to catch his breath. He wanted to say something to her—something that let her know she was exceptional and how much she blew him away—but everything that ran through his mind sounded incredibly corny so he kept his mouth shut. He wrapped the condom in a tissue before dropping it in the basket under her nightstand, and then he rolled to face her.

Jamie's eyes were closed, but she must have felt the motion because she moved closer to him, so her arm and the length of her leg pressed against him. He kissed her, and then dropped his head back to the pillow. It didn't take long, though, for his body to relax to the point he knew he'd be nodding off. Already, Jamie's eyes were closed and her breathing was slowing as she drifted in and out.

"I really should go," he said, without much enthusiasm.

She opened her eyes and shifted her head so she could see him. "Or you could stay."

"I want to." She had no idea how much he wanted to. "But don't forget we're having dinner with my entire family tomorrow."

"Oh, yeah. I guess that just got a lot more complicated."

"And if I don't go home, my dad's the kind of tone-deaf guy who won't think anything of asking me where I spent the night while we're all sitting at the table."

"We really don't want that," she said, though she didn't do a good job of hiding how amusing she found the visual as she leaned over the side of the bed and snagged her sweatshirt off the floor.

While he got dressed, she carried the pudding bowls to the sink and rinsed them, and he watched her as she tossed the empty container in the trash. He kind of liked this all-one-room thing, although watching sports while somebody was trying to sleep wouldn't work out very well.

He took his time, but he only wore so many clothes, so the time to leave came too soon. She looked so inviting, wearing nothing but the long sweatshirt, with her hair free and tousled. When she slid her hands up over his abs to his chest and kissed him, he sighed.

She sighed and reached up to smooth the hair over his ear. "Just so we're on the same page, doing what they speculate we're doing doesn't mean I want to confirm the rumors. Gossip is one thing, but I'm *really* not supposed to be sleeping with you."

"It's nobody's business but ours." Before he left, though, he needed to know where her head was, as far as the whole sleeping-together thing. "So do you think we'll be breaking that rule again, or is there a chance you're going to wake up tomorrow and decide you made a mistake and we should pretend this never happened?"

"Oh, there's no way in hell I can pretend this never happened," she said. "And I intend to break rules with you whenever we have an opportunity. Since my time here has an expiration date, we can keep each other company until I move on and you go back to looking for your television wife."

"Oh, for the love of…" Sometimes the guys could be real pains in the ass. "You heard about that?"

"Of course I did."

"They're exaggerating for their own amusement." He winked at her. "Even I know you don't wear pearls with aprons anymore."

She laughed as they walked to the door, and he tried not to think about how much he *didn't* want to leave. In the past, sometimes he'd stay over and sometimes he'd leave, but it was always about convenience or whatever vibe the woman was giving off. It hadn't mattered to him one way or the other.

But he didn't want to leave Jamie. Over her shoulder he could see the bed with its messed-up covers, and he wanted to take her by the hand and lead her back there. He could wrap his body around hers and fall asleep with his face buried in her hair, and then kiss her awake in the morning.

"Aidan gave me directions to your dad's house. Well, your house, too, I guess. So I'll be there at five."

"I'll see you then. The door at the bottom of the stairs will lock behind me, right?"

"Yeah."

He kissed her, breaking it off before it could tempt either of them into going back to bed, and then put on his sweatshirt and picked up his hockey bag. "I'll see you tomorrow."

"Good night, Scott."

He was halfway down the stairs when it hit him how much he liked hearing her say his name. *Scott.* He wasn't sure if it was a Boston thing or a guy thing, but everybody loved to tack the *ee* sound on the end of any name they could, and he'd been called Scotty by almost everybody for his entire life.

The guys at the station did, but she hadn't fallen into using it, and he liked that. Maybe it was because he was trying to leave his old ways behind him— the merry-go-round of girlfriends and his temper— or maybe it was because it made her different, but he hoped she didn't stop.

Once he'd reached his apartment, he spent almost an hour picking up clutter. It was late and he should already be in bed. And there was almost no chance he'd come up with a plausible excuse for getting Jamie upstairs alone for even a few minutes, but he wanted the place to look decent just in case.

When he did finally lie down, he didn't sleep right away. Instead he stared at the ceiling, wishing Jamie was next to him instead of empty bed.

Jamie had never felt less ready for anything in her life than she did for having supper at the Kincaid house. Sitting down at a table, so soon after they had sex she'd rather everybody not know about, with the five people who could probably read Scott better than anybody else, probably wasn't the best timing ever.

But at two minutes before five, she walked up the steps of the deep front porch and knocked on Tommy's door. She was carrying a plastic container of store-bought assorted fruit pastries because she'd been raised to not show up as a dinner guest empty-handed. Unfortunately, she had no idea what they were having for dinner, so she wasn't sure what to bring to complement it. Bringing wine to the home of a guy who owned a bar didn't make a lot of sense to her. And her mother had once told her that bringing a fancy dessert was rude because it presumed there would actually be a dessert course.

Running short on time and patience, she'd finally grabbed the pastries. Pastries were flexible. They could be dessert, but they could also be an appetizer. Hell, Tommy could eat them all for breakfast the next morning for all she cared. She needed to bring something and they were handy. Now that she was standing on the porch, though, they seemed woefully inadequate.

Lydia answered the door, a smile on her face. "Hi, Jamie. Come on in. Did you have any trouble finding the house?"

"Not at all. Aidan's directions were perfect. And I suspect I could have knocked on any door and said I was looking for your dad and I would have been pointed in the right direction."

She laughed. "You're totally right."

Jamie held up the container from the market. "I brought some fruit pastries. They're store-bought, but trust me when I tell you it's better than if I'd made them myself."

"Those look delicious." Lydia took the box. "And I'm glad they're store-bought. If the guys start getting a taste for real homemade stuff…well, let's just say I don't want the bar set too high."

They were laughing together when they walked inside, and Jamie realized the front door led straight into the living room. The entire family stopped talking and looked when they entered. Of course her gaze went immediately to Scott and she returned the smile he gave her.

"Hey, Jamie."

"Hi," she replied, and then she tore her gaze away from him even though she could have happily looked at him for hours. Then she said hi to Aidan, who emerged from the kitchen long enough to wave to her.

"I'd stay and visit, but I've been assigned to lettuce shredding duty for the salad," he said before disappearing back into the kitchen.

A man who was obviously Scott's dad stood and walked toward her. "I'm Tommy Kincaid. Welcome to my home."

He was a big man and Jamie guessed that, even though he was going soft around the middle, he was probably still as strong as an ox. Most of Scott's looks had come from his dad, she saw, though Tommy's hair was mostly gray. "Thank you for inviting me."

"I've heard a lot about you."

She smiled. "Probably almost as much as I've heard about you."

"This is Ashley," Lydia said, and Jamie shook Scott's oldest sister's hand. Ashley had the same dark hair, though slightly lighter than Scott and Lydia's, and she was shorter, too. Probably took more after their mom. "And you've met Danny."

"Nice to see you again, Jamie. How's it going?"

"Pretty well, I think."

He smiled. "That's what I've heard."

She had no doubt he got daily updates. Not so much through any official channels, but from the other guys at the station and particularly from Scott and Aidan.

"We're going to eat in a few minutes," Ashley said. "I made a lasagna, but if you don't like that, I can whip up something else on the side."

"Who doesn't love lasagna?" Jamie replied.

"I knew I was going to like you," Tommy said.

The entire time, Jamie was keenly aware of Scott's presence in the room, so she actually jumped a little when she heard his voice. "How come you'll whip her up something on the side, but if I don't like something, I have to make a bologna sandwich?"

"Because you're a pain in the ass."

Tommy waved a hand at the couch. "Sit down, Jamie. Do you watch sports?"

"I'm not a big sports fan," she admitted, and she wasn't surprised when he frowned at her. "The guys have been trying to explain hockey to me, though, and I do own a Boston Bruins sweatshirt."

"Good enough. How long have you been in Boston?"

She had to think about it. "Almost two years, I guess. It doesn't feel like that long."

"Hell, you must be about ready to drive the truck."

"No," she and Scott said at the same time, and he chuckled.

"Oh, come on," Tommy said. "Boston's a fun place to drive."

"She finally stopped screaming when I make left turns," Scott said, winking at her.

She laughed, shaking her head. "I shouldn't be able to hear the tires squealing over the sound of the sirens."

"You going to sit down, son, or are you going to keep hovering?" Tommy demanded, craning his neck to look at Scott.

Since Tommy was in an old recliner and Danny was in an armchair with his leg up on an ottoman, the only place left to sit was on the couch with her. She shifted to one end, leaving plenty of room, and he really didn't have a choice but to sit at the other end.

Part of her wanted to laugh at the stupid situation they'd put themselves in. Less than twenty-four hours ago, they'd been naked in her bed. Now they were sitting on opposite ends of a couch, barely looking at each other.

The other part of her, of course, wanted to crawl across the couch and curl up on his lap.

"So tell me, what made you want to be a firefighter, Jamie? Family business?"

She shook her head. "I'm the first firefighter to shake out of the family tree. It was a career day presentation when I was in middle school, sir. A firefighter came in to talk to us about it and…the rest is history."

She glanced at Scott and he raised an eyebrow as if to ask if she was going to share the rest of the story. No, she wasn't about to go into how offensive men could be about female firefighters when talking to somebody of Tommy's generation. On the surface, he seemed perfectly happy to make her feel welcome, but in her experience, if given the chance they usually had a laundry list of concerns. And they quite often didn't realize those concerns—women weren't brave enough or strong enough or the guys would get in fights over her or they'd be bossy and make them clean too much—were offensive to the women they were talking about. The guys she served with didn't have a problem with her, so she didn't feel a need to open the door to Tommy wanting to justify that old-timer's attitude.

"You're not only the first woman in Engine Company 59," Tommy said, "but you're probably the first person who's ever told me those career day things were worth a damn. I remember the first time Ashley dragged me in for one of those."

Jamie listened to him tell the story, laughing in the right places, but she was conscious of Scott sitting only a few feet from her. He chuckled a couple of times, but mostly he was very quiet and still. It wasn't normal for Scott to be that still, so she assumed he was having as much trouble figuring what "act naturally" should be as she was.

And it was probably why Danny kept looking at Scott as though he was trying to figure out if something was wrong with him. Luckily, none of them knew Jamie well enough to know she probably looked a little off, too.

"Food's ready," Ashley called from the kitchen a few minutes later.

Scott and Tommy both stood and together hauled Danny to his feet. Once his crutches were tucked under his arms, he smiled at Jamie and rolled his eyes. "I can get up by myself, but they think it's funny to move me around like a doll."

They let Danny go first, and he thumped his way to the dining room with Tommy on his heels. Scott gestured for Jamie to go next, and as she passed by, he put his hand on the small of her back. She paused, very briefly, savoring the warm pressure for a few seconds.

"Thought about that pudding all day," he said in a voice barely above a whisper.

Before she could tell him he was welcome to stop by for chocolate pudding anytime, his hand fell away. Rather than risk a lull in the conversation in front of them coinciding with her saying something mildly suggestive to Scott, she kept her mouth shut and followed Tommy into the dining room.

Ashley was directing traffic around Tommy, who was already seated at the head of the table. The dining room wasn't very big, so there wasn't a lot of room to play with. "Danny, you sit on the end on that back side so your leg's out of the way. I'll put your crutches in the corner. Lydia and I will be getting up to serve, so we should be on this side."

"I'll sit in the middle on the far side, next to Danny, so I'm out of the way," Jamie said.

"I'll be the third," Scott said. "Aidan can sit next to Lydia."

Jamie walked behind Tommy's chair and pulled out the middle chair. As she sat, Scott pushed it in for her before sitting next to her. It was sweet, and she wondered if the others would notice the gesture, but then she saw Aidan doing the same for Lydia. Apparently it was how they did things.

There was a salad at every place setting and everybody dug in, so Jamie did the same. They all talked as much as they ate, and they made sure she was pulled into the conversations. Maybe because she was there, most of the talk was about the fire department, with Tommy occasionally breaking in to tell them how he did things back in the day.

The salad bowls were replaced by plates of the most amazing lasagna, and she looked across the table at Lydia and Ashley. "If you guys always eat like this, you're going to have to tell me your secret for still fitting in your jeans."

"We only eat like this when Ashley cooks for us," Lydia said. "Or, trust me, I wouldn't be able to."

"Ash won't be fitting in her jeans much longer," Danny said, and his wife blushed.

"Funny." She looked at Jamie, her cheeks faintly pink. "I don't know if anybody told you, but I'm pregnant."

"Congratulations! No, nobody told me. That's really wonderful news."

"It is. I originally didn't want anybody but Danny to know because I'm a little superstitious."

Lydia laughed. "Jamie's already noticed that about us."

"It's hard to keep secrets in a firehouse," Jamie said, hoping her cheeks didn't turn the same shade as Ashley's had.

"Well, I'm still not sure who knows and who doesn't."

"Rick knows," Scott said, and Jamie looked sideways at him when she heard the tension in his voice. "I don't know who else heard."

"It doesn't matter, anyway," Ashley said, her voice

high with a too-chipper, false note. "Superstitions don't trump science."

Jamie wasn't sure what was going on, but there was a low-level buzz of tension around the table that hadn't been there before. She put a forkful of lasagna in her mouth and chewed slowly so she couldn't unknowingly say something that made it worse.

Danny leaned closer to her. "We'd just found out when I got hurt. Tommy, Lydia and Scott were the only ones we told, partly because we didn't feel right not telling them and partly because she was having random any-time-of-day sickness and her shifts at the bar were becoming a problem."

She wasn't sure how that tied in with Scott sharing the news. "That must have been scary for everybody."

"It was," Scott said in a flat voice. "When Danny didn't come out, I tried to go back in and Rick wouldn't let me. I told him Ash was pregnant and I couldn't go home without Danny. He still didn't let me go back in."

"Enough," Tommy barked. "We're all here and we're having a nice meal. Put some in your mouths."

"Dad," Lydia said.

Scott turned slightly toward Jamie and she could see the anger in his expression. "We only talk about the good days."

The silence as everybody went back to the lasagna was deafening, and Jamie wished she could think of something to say that would restore the easy banter they'd started with. She shifted her right leg, though, moving it sideways until it pressed against the length of Scott's. He didn't pull away and, through the corner of her eye, she saw the muscles in his jaw relax.

"Hey, did you two pick a wedding date yet?" Ashley

asked, and everybody instantly picked up. Jamie knew she was the oldest of the three kids, so maybe she'd had to learn young how to keep the peace between two temperamental siblings and their dad.

"Not yet," Lydia said.

"You have to pick a date. People keep asking me and I have to tell them I don't know."

"I guess anybody who needs to know the date will know it when we do."

"Do you want a big wedding or a small one?" Jamie asked, because weddings were a fun thing to talk about.

"Small," Lydia and Aidan said at the same time Ashley said "Big," and they all laughed.

"So, Jamie, when are you going to come in the bar again?" Tommy asked, and Jamie felt as if she were under a spotlight when everybody looked at her. "I hear you've only been in once."

"I've actually been in three times, but the first two were quite a while ago and I didn't know anybody."

"And did the third time scare you off?"

"No, sir. I just haven't had a chance to come back."

He pushed back his empty plate and rested his hand on his stomach. "You'll have to come in more often."

"I might. I haven't had a burger yet and I've heard yours are good."

They sat around the table and talked while Ashley and Lydia cleared the plates and loaded up the dishwasher, refusing any help from Jamie. Tommy told them of the E59-L37 station's history, which she found interesting, even though it was obvious the others had heard the stories before.

After decaf coffees and pastries, Jamie cursed herself for eating so much lasagna. It was a good thing she'd decided to brave the roads and drive because it would have been a long, agonizing walk home. She didn't even want to think about the stairs.

When it was time to go, she thanked Tommy for the invitation and Ashley for making the lasagna. "It's a good thing we don't work tomorrow because I'll probably still be full."

"You're not walking, are you?" Tommy asked. "Scotty can walk you home. Make sure you get home safe."

Dammit. That would have been a great excuse to sneak some alone time with him. "I drove, but thanks."

Lydia walked to the door with her, so all she could get from Scott was a casual wave. "See you Tuesday."

"Thanks for coming," Lydia said when they were out on the porch. "The family can get a little hard to take at times, but we all mean well."

"I had a great time," Jamie said honestly. "I miss my family, so hanging out with yours was nice."

"You really should stop by the bar," she said. "It's pretty low-key when Scotty's not punching people, which he hardly ever does anymore."

Unless somebody insulted her, Jamie thought. "I will."

About fifteen minutes after she managed to drag herself up all the flights of stairs to her apartment, her cell phone chimed. She thought instantly of her friend Steph, and felt a pang of guilt. She needed to touch base with her, but usually Steph was the one to initiate the conversations because of her work hours and the customer traffic at the pizza shop.

But it wasn't from Steph. It was from Scott. I hope that wasn't too bad.

She wasn't sure if he meant being around all the Kincaids, or the strain of keeping up the appearance they hadn't recently had sex. I enjoyed tonight.

I wish I hadn't promised Rick I'd help him with a few things around his place tomorrow. I want to see you again.

She smiled, though she wished the same thing. You'll see me Tuesday.

It only took a few seconds for him to respond. You won't be naked.

Not on Tuesday.

Wednesday?

Some of her anxiety about how their tour on Tuesday would go had been eased by their success at getting through a family dinner without anybody seeming suspicious, so she didn't hesitate. Yes.

Good. The guys have the game paused for me, so I have to go. Good night.

Sweet dreams.

After setting a reminder on her phone to text Steph at a time the pizza shop was typically slow, she stretched out on her couch and hit the TV's power button on the remote control. There was no way she could go to bed after eating all that food, so she flipped through the channels, looking for something to catch her eye.

When she landed on a hockey game and some of the guys were wearing black and gold, she stopped channel surfing. It must be the game Scott was watching, which made her smile. Over the years she'd survived a lot of sports games on station televisions. Being a fan seemed to mean a lot of yelling and hand waving and cursing, so she'd usually used game time for catching up on paperwork or doing anything she could find to do in a room farthest from the TV. The E-59 guys, though, were taking it as a personal challenge to make her a hockey fan and they spent a lot of free time trying to tutor her.

After watching it for a few minutes, she laughed at herself and starting hitting the channel-up button again. It was hard enough to keep track of the guys flying around on the ice. She had no hope of figuring out where the puck was and the words the announcers were using still meant nothing to her.

After settling on a disaster movie she'd seen enough times that the fact she'd missed the first twenty minutes didn't matter, she pulled the knit throw off the back of the couch and got comfortable.

Her eyelids got heavy fast, though, and as she drifted off, her last thought was that she had to remember to ask Scott what kind of movies he liked.

Chapter 8

Scott frowned at the puzzle piece in his hand, then looked back at the picture on the box lid. "I think some dipshit mixed up the pieces of this puzzle with another one."

Jeff leaned over on the couch to look at the piece. "That looks like part of a Santa hat."

"We're doing a fall foliage puzzle."

Jeff shrugged. "Maybe it's like one of those *Where's Waldo* things and there's a Santa hat hiding in the leaves."

"Or maybe some dipshit mixed up the puzzles," Scott repeated under his breath.

"I've done that foliage puzzle about nineteen times," Chris said from across the room, where he'd been pretending to nap in a chair. "There's no Santa hat. It's probably the pointy part of a red leaf."

Scott tossed the piece back into the pile and picked up another one. It was a blur of red and orange, like 80 percent of the other pieces. He really hated jigsaw puzzles that were mostly scenery. "We need to put a puzzle fund jar on the table and buy some new ones."

Some tours, they busted their asses for hours without any rest beyond the short breaks necessary to keep them going. Most varied, with some medical emergencies and accidents and people smelling smoke, but plenty of downtime for meals, rest and getting stuff done around the station. And then there were days like today, when it seemed everybody in their neighborhood was feeling good, obeying traffic laws and not setting stuff on fire. They were good days for everybody but, holy crap, did the hours drag on when the chores were all checked off and the alarm didn't sound.

"Hey, Scotty, Ellen wants to set you up on a date," Jeff said.

"I'm not interested. Tell your wife I said thanks, though."

"She says this new girl at work would be perfect for you. Her dad's a firefighter in Philly, so she knows how it goes. Came up here for college and plans to stay. She's really pretty, smart, makes good money, and wants to get married and have kids in a few years."

"She sounds great, but I'm not into dating right now. Which you know."

"Yeah, but she's not the women you were dating when you decided to take a break. She's the kind of woman you're looking for."

Scott was glad Jamie had gone down to the second floor to do paperwork because he'd have a hard time not looking her way to see her reaction to this conversation. "I'm not looking for any women right now."

"I like pretty and smart women who make good money," Grant said from the kitchen doorway.

"Yeah, but my wife thinks you're a shithead because you flaked out on the charity breakfast last summer and you were supposed to be in charge of the bacon."

Grant sighed. "I was sick."

"You were hungover. And you can fudge a lot when it comes to breakfast, but you can't fake your way out of a bacon issue. It's bacon." Jeff pressed a yellow leaf into place in the puzzle. "Besides, her friend wants a guy who's ready to settle down. Rings. Strollers."

With a grimace, Grant disappeared back into the kitchen, which Scott hoped would end the issue. He didn't want to date Ellen's friend and Ellen wouldn't want her friend to date Grant or Gavin, who wasn't any more ready to settle down. Everybody else was taken, so both companies were a dead end on the road to finding Ellen's friend a husband.

"It's been a while since you talked about going out, Scotty," Jeff said. "You have to go on first dates to know who you want to go on a second date with, you know what I mean?"

He already knew he wanted to go on a second date with the woman who was one floor beneath them, either doing paperwork or asleep at her desk, but he couldn't say that. It was awkward because, if he hadn't met Jamie, it would have been in his nature to at least take Ellen's smart, pretty friend who made good money to dinner and they all knew it.

"Or maybe he's already found somebody to date and he's not telling us," Chris said, and Scott looked up from the puzzle to frown at him. Was he just messing with him, or was he fishing for information?

"Why wouldn't I tell you?" he asked, neither confirming or denying he actually *had* found a woman to date and wasn't telling them.

"I don't know. Maybe she's ninety-seven and you think she'll leave you her fortune."

Scott laughed. "If you don't tell anybody, I'll buy you a pony. And on that note, I'm sick of this puzzle. I'm going to go find Aidan. He said he was going to check the tanks and never came back."

"He's probably hiding in the cage, talking to Lydia," Gavin said as he walked out of the weight room with a towel draped around his neck. At least, unlike the rest of them, he'd worked up a sweat today.

Scott went down one flight of stairs and paused in the narrow hallway of the second floor. The door to the office Jamie and Rick shared was closed, but he could knock. He'd have to come up with a reason to want to talk to her if Rick was in there, but if she was alone, Scott could visit for a few minutes.

But showing up in her office their first tour after sleeping together might make her change her mind about their relationship. If there was any time besides on a run she would be most conscious of the fact they worked together, it would be when they were on opposite sides of her desk.

He continued down the other flight and checked the cage where they kept the air tanks, but it was locked. Then he heard a swishing sound and walked around the back of Engine 59 to see Aidan sweeping the floor with a wide push broom.

"Busywork?"

Aidan looked up and shrugged. "I just don't feel like sitting around today."

"Yeah, I know what you mean. I can only do the same jigsaw puzzle so many times." He went to the bench and grabbed a rag. Even though both trucks were clean, he went around theirs, rubbing the bits of chrome trim until they gleamed. The younger guys tended to do the bumpers and ignore the rest.

"Jeff was telling me Ellen wants to set me up with a new friend of hers from work."

"You going?"

He snorted. "No."

"I didn't think so. Seems like you've got your eye on a woman already and you might hold the record for the number of girlfriends for the company, but I've gotta hand it to you—they were never at the same time."

"I'm not dating anybody," he said, feeling as if he was walking a tightrope of semantics. Technically, he wasn't lying to his best friend. He and Jamie hadn't actually gone on a real date yet. "I'm on a break, remember?"

Aidan hung the big broom on its hook and pulled down the smaller broom and dustpan to pick up the piles he'd made. "Here's the thing. I'm not going to ask you any questions about a certain person that require an outright answer one way or the other because I don't want to force you into a situation where you have to lie to me to protect somebody else. But don't bullshit me."

Scott looked at Aidan for a minute, remembering how much anger and betrayal he'd felt when he found out his best friend had been seeing his sister without telling him. It had almost ended their friendship, but the bond between them was too strong. Even with that blowup only about six months behind them, Scott knew there was nobody in the world he could trust like he could this guy. But there was Jamie's trust to consider, too, so he was going to have to accept the compromise Aidan offered.

"Grant jumped at the chance to be set up with Ellen's friend, of course," he said, evading the issue of Jamie.

Aidan snorted. "Has she forgiven him for the bacon debacle yet?"

"Nope."

"Can't say as I blame her. It was the bacon."

Scott did a final walk around the engine, eyeballing not only the chrome, but every inch of her. She was probably his first love and he never told anybody, but he was secretly relieved when their house was passed over for new trucks every year.

"So Lydia and I set a date for the wedding so Ashley will stop bugging us about it. Fourteenth of May. It's a Saturday."

"No shit." Content now that there wasn't a water spot to be found on E-59's chrome, Scott tossed the cloth onto the workbench. "She's really going to go through with it, huh?"

"Have I told you lately how funny you are?" Aidan folded his arms and leaned against the engine. "No? I wonder why."

"That's pretty quick. What, a little over a month away?"

"Ashley's the matron of honor, of course, and she wants a killer dress for the pictures, I guess. So we either do it now or we wait until after the baby's born."

"And then, because she wants a killer dress, she'll want to lose the baby weight."

Aidan winced. "Yeah, I mentioned that during the discussion with Lydia and you shouldn't ever say that out loud again. It's probably safest to not even think it."

"I love my sisters, but I also know them really well and yeah, if the dress is an issue, you're going to want to get married sooner rather than later. Can you get a place that fast?"

"I know the guy who owns Kincaid's Pub."

"Seriously? You're going to get married at our bar?" It was all well and good to not want to drop a crap load of cash on a fancy wedding, but his sister was basically going to get married at work? "Wait. Does that mean we can wear jeans and T-shirts?"

"Nice try, but no. Suits for us. The aforementioned killer dresses for the bride and her matron of honor. The bar will be closed, obviously, and done up really nice."

"That doesn't sound too bad, really."

Aidan nodded. "Think about it. There's no place else in the world that means more to either of us. When we think about home and family, Lydia and I both think of the bar. All we want is a justice of the peace and a small party with our closest friends and family, so why not? And we're going to delay the honeymoon until fall when it's peak foliage, and then we're going to get a cabin in northern New Hampshire and hide out for a week."

"That's what you want?"

"Yeah, it's what we both want."

"Then I'm happy for you. And I'll try hard not to schedule anything else that day."

Aidan snorted. "I'll kick your ass if you do because I really want you to be my best man."

The punch of emotion in his gut surprised the hell out of Scott. It wasn't as if it was a surprise. They'd been best friends for so long, who else would they ask but each other? Aidan had a brother, but they weren't the *best man* kind of close. Over the years Scott and Aidan had even made passing references to future bachelor parties. Things like "when I get married, you better have smoking hot strippers at my bachelor party" or "you should probably leave that out of your speech when I get married."

But hearing it now, when they were adults and Aidan actually needed a best man, was different. Holy shit, Aidan Hunt was getting married.

"So you gonna be around that day?" Aidan asked when Scott didn't say anything.

"Yeah, I'll be around." He reached out to shake his friend's hand, and then pulled him in for a back-slapping hug. "I'm honored, and there's nowhere else I'd be."

"Your first act as my best man can be informing Tommy we'll need to use the pool table for the buffet."

"You rotten bastard."

There was a knock on the office door and Jamie looked up from her paperwork, her pulse ticking like an overwound clock. "Come in."

When Cobb poked his head in, she felt a rush of disappointment. Yes, it would be inappropriate for Scott to come lock himself in her office with her. Yes, it would be disastrous for her plan to keep their personal relationship and their work relationship separate. But she still thought it might be him.

"Hey, Chief."

"Where's Gullotti?"

"In his bunk. I guess his fiancée had some evening business meetings so they talked late. With the three-hour time difference between here and San Diego, it ended up being a little *too* late for him."

"That's gotta be tough on a relationship. But I know her grandparents. The Broussards are good people, and I'm happy for the kids."

It amused her to hear Rick called a kid, since he was older than all of them except Chris and Cobb himself. When she'd looked through their files prior to reporting the first day, she'd seen that Rick had been promoted over Chris because the latter hated paperwork and bureaucracy. He preferred being left alone to do his job.

"Do you want me to get Rick?" she asked.

"No, you can fill him in. I just wanted to let you guys know Danny had another appointment today and his leg's looking real good. He's still on track for another five to seven weeks."

"That's good news. I'll let Rick know, definitely."

"Thanks." Cobb started to leave, but then paused. "It *is* good news. Danny's a damn good firefighter and a great officer, but so are you. I'm bummed we only have you for a bit over a month left, and I wish E-59 could keep you both."

She recognized it as high praise from an old-school guy like Cobb, and gave him a warm smile. "Thanks, Chief. This is a great group of guys to work with."

"They're inspecting the equipment right now. The

lines and couplers mostly, just because they were starting to bicker like a bunch of kids with cabin fever. It's
a nice day so I told them to open the garage doors and
find something to do."

"You sent them outside to play, sir?"

He laughed. "Yeah, I guess I did. I would have told
them to clean their rooms, but they already did that.
I called them in as out of commission for an hour so
they could check the line and another house can cover
for us."

They definitely couldn't respond to an alarm when
the water hoses were spread out on the ground. "I
could use some fresh air myself, actually. Maybe I'll
go down and join in."

Cobb was right, she realized as soon as she stepped
into the engine bay. It was a gorgeous spring day and
there was just enough of a breeze so it brought fresh air
into the building. Her guys had lines laid out along the
floor while the ladder company had their own equipment strewn all over their half of the garage.

"Hey, Jamie," Grant said when he spotted her.

Through the corner of her eye, she saw Scott look
up from the coupler he was checking for any defects,
but she kept her gaze on the younger guy. "I heard you
were all getting some fresh air, so I decided to break
out of my office."

"You're just in time to help recoil the lines," Grant
told her. "Aidan was telling us about his wedding. He
and Lydia finally set a date."

"They did?" Ashley's prodding had paid off, then.
She looked at Aidan. "Congratulations. When's the
big day?"

"May fourteenth."

"*This* May fourteenth?"

"Yeah. Just a friends and family get-together at Kincaid's Pub with a JP."

"That sounds perfect."

"Hey, Scotty, are you going to bring a date to the wedding?" Grant asked.

Jamie didn't even flinch. She kept her focus on the line she was reeling in, but through the corner of her eye, she could see Scott glance over at her before shaking his head.

"No, I'm not."

"You know there won't be any single bridesmaids, right? Aidan said just a best man and a maid of honor. Or matron of honor or whatever, because Ashley's married."

"I'm going to watch my sister marry my best friend, not pick up women."

"Aw, that's sweet," Gavin chimed in. "But everybody knows women don't like going home alone after a wedding."

It was tempting for Jamie to interrupt and give the guy a verbal slap upside the head, but she'd learned long ago to pick her battles wisely when it came to being the only woman listening to men talk. Gavin was actually a good guy, and talking about hitting on single bridesmaids was how men got ready for weddings, in her experience.

"You should bring a date so you have somebody to dance with, though," Grant said. "You're the best man so you have to dance, but you can't dance with Rick's wife all night. I can hook you up if you want."

"Really, I'm all set," Scott insisted.

"Well, don't ask me to dance when you get sick of

standing against the wall watching everybody else
have fun," Grant said, and they all laughed.

"Maybe Jamie will take pity on Scotty the wall-
flower and dance with him," Gavin added.

She was worried enough about spending an evening
in front of all of his family and their friends without
touching. She didn't need the other guys setting them
up for a dance. "I'm not really much for dancing."

She realized Aidan was looking at her, and he held
her gaze for a second before turning back to the guys.
"We're not doing the whole plus-one thing. I think
Lydia's mailing the invitations this week, but basically we won't have room. I mean wives can come.
And a girlfriend if she's like…serious. Somebody we
know, like Jess. But we don't have the space for random dates. And we want to be surrounded by people
who are special to us, you know? Otherwise we'd do
the big wedding thing."

For a few seconds, Jamie wondered if Aidan's
strange look had been because she hadn't made the
invitation list, but that couldn't be it. Even though she'd
be handing the reins back to Danny about the time of
the wedding, she was part of the Engine 59 family
and he wouldn't leave her out. Plus Lydia seemed to
like her, so she was fairly confident she'd be getting
an invitation in the mail.

She couldn't help but wonder for a moment, though,
how much it would suck to be at a party with Scott—a
party with romance in the air and dancing—and pretend they were just coworkers.

But that was weeks away. For all she knew, the
sparks between them would burn out by then and that's
all that would be. Right now, the sparks were still siz-

zling, so she'd take each day as it came and enjoy the here and now.

When she turned to look at Grant's line, Scott caught her eye and gave her a look that made her shiver. Oh, yeah, she was definitely going to enjoy the hell out of the here and now.

After an entire day of doing nothing, it wasn't an hour after Cobb reported them back in service that the alarm sounded. A car had barreled into a deli and there were multiple casualties.

Scott sounded the horn in addition to the sirens as they pulled out onto the busy street. It was a shitty time of day to navigate the area, but he didn't yield and people got out of his way.

"They've got two employees unaccounted for," Jamie said. "A forty-year-old man and a seventeen-year-old girl."

"I know that deli," he said loud enough for everybody to hear. "It's an old building, so structural integrity's a concern."

He didn't need to say more. They knew that even going inside would be a risk, and it was the kind of risk they couldn't do a damn thing to mitigate. Fire was a fickle bitch and could turn on you in unexpected ways, but water, training and experience with its movements were weapons a good firefighter could use to knock the risk down. An unstable building could stand for years or it could collapse one minute after they went in. Short of waiting for engineers to go in, there was no way to know. But there were casualties and he knew they wouldn't hesitate.

They beat the EMS to the scene and hit the ground

running. There were three injured people on the sidewalk, two of whom had been inside but got out after the accident. None looked critical. He watched Rick send Gavin to check them over while the rest of them went in.

Jamie reached the driver of the car first and pulled her glove off before reaching through the smashed window. After a minute, she pulled her hand back and shoved it into the glove, shaking her head. "Elderly male, deceased."

A medical crisis behind the wheel, Scott thought as he lifted a broken table off of a crying woman. The driver probably had a heart attack or a stroke and his body stiffened, jamming the accelerator to the floor. It would explain why the car was so deep in the building.

The woman wasn't hurt badly, so he helped her to the opening as sirens announced the arrival of EMS. Sweeping the area, they found six more people and, miraculously, none of them were injured so badly they couldn't walk out with some assistance.

When Scott handed a badly shaken elderly woman over to the paramedics, he heard a man shouting at Rick. "They were in the back. Why didn't they come out?"

"We'll find them, sir."

They met up in front of the car, and Rick looked angry. "They haven't cut the power or the gas yet, and this building's creaking like an old bed frame, but there are two still unaccounted for. There may be a blockage somewhere, or they might have been knocked out if the impact knocked things off shelves. We don't know."

"With the gas on, I'd feel better if we at least have a line charged and ready to go," Aidan said.

"We have backup coming, but I don't want to wait," Jamie said. "You stay with the apparatus, Aidan, and we'll go in."

"We'll go around the back and try to come in from the other direction," Rick said. "Masks. We don't know what's going on with the gas piping, and if there's been any structural damage, who knows what shit's floating around in there."

Scott went in first, climbing over the smashed deli counter. He had the Halligan tool, essentially a huge crowbar with an adze head, so he could use it to pry or smash or prop things up, if necessary.

They found the man first, lying on the floor of a storage room with a shelving unit on his leg. He was overweight and sweating profusely, which was cause for concern.

"Do you have any injuries besides your leg, sir?" Jamie asked after looking him over. He shook his head. "Okay, we're going to get this off you and get you out of here."

"Mandy," he said in a hoarse voice. "She went to the bathroom, which is down the hall, and I heard her scream."

Scott and Grant looked over the metal shelving unit, as well as the boxes strewn around. To Scott, it looked as if the shelving had caught the victim's leg just right, breaking it with the weight of the boxes and momentum, but it wasn't heavy.

Jamie had obviously come to the same conclusion. "Sir, this is going to hurt a little, but they're going to lift the shelves and I'm going to slide your legs out to this side. If you can use your arms to move your butt at the same time, that would help."

"What if I can't? I don't feel very good."

"Then it'll take longer and might hurt more, but I'll move you because we're not leaving you here."

"Okay."

"Hold on just a second."

Scott listened as Jamie turned up her radio. The impact had shifted the building on its ancient foundation and the back of the structure had partially collapsed into the basement. Rick and the others could maybe get through, but it would be slow going.

"Let us see if we can get to her from this direction. She's possibly in the restroom, so have Aidan talk to the owner and see if he can give us a precise location relative to the collapse in the back."

She turned her attention back to the man and signaled to them. Scott and Grant lifted the shelving, and he watched as Jamie helped the man get out from under it. The effort of moving himself caused his face to darken to a scary shade of red, and Scott hoped like hell they could get him to the paramedics before he got any worse.

"Grant, go on his other side and let's see if we can get him up."

"I don't know if I can," the man said. "It hurts."

"Sir," Jamie said, "your leg is probably broken, though it's not a compound fracture. But this building isn't stable and we don't want you in here any longer than necessary. It'll take time to get a stretcher in here and guys to carry it out, and to be honest, it won't be a lot less painful for you."

"We'll support you," Scott said. "You won't have

to put much weight on that leg, if any. We'll get you out to the paramedics and they'll take care of you."

"Okay." The man took a deep breath. "I really want to get out of here."

As they got him to his feet and he looped one arm around Scott's shoulders and the other around Grant's, they all felt the subtle shift beneath their feet. *Shit*, Scott thought.

"Let's go."

It only took a few steps for them to find a rhythm, but Jamie stopped them. "You guys get him out. I'm going to look for Mandy."

"Let's get him outside and then we'll come back together."

"There might not be enough time." She pointed toward the front. "You go. If it looks hairy, I'll wait for you guys."

She turned and ducked down the hallway before Scott could come up with a good excuse why she shouldn't. Every muscle in his body tensed as his instincts screamed for him to go after her. He wanted to throw her over his shoulder and carry her out to the street.

Grant looked at him, his eyes wide behind the SCBA mask. Scott pointed him in the direction Jamie had told them to go. Grant shook his head.

"Your lieutenant gave you an order," Scott shouted.

"But she's alone."

God, he knew that. "Move your ass, Cutter. Let's get this gentleman some help."

By the time they got him to the sidewalk, Scott's back was screaming in protest, but all he could think about was Jamie. Once he was free of the guy with the broken leg, he took off his mask and drained half the water bottle Aidan handed him.

"The other guys are coming back around now," Aidan said. "They weren't getting anywhere and it won't be long before the building's in the basement."

"I'm going back in."

He got as far as the smashed car when Jamie came out of the back section with an unconscious teenager draped over her shoulders. Scott climbed the deli counter and put out his arms so Jamie could drop her head and kind of roll the girl to him. Once he had her, he backed up so Jamie could climb over.

"The floor was wet and there's blood on her head and the edge of the sink. I think she slipped and knocked herself out, but her vitals seem strong."

Once everybody was accounted for and in the care of EMS, the guys gathered around the trucks and waited to be cleared to return to quarters. The city inspector was on-site now and there were probably engineers on the way. They'd moved on to *not my job*, as far as Scott was concerned.

Jamie's phone rang and she moved away from them to a quiet spot in order to take the call. He watched her, hating all over again the memory of her going down the hallway. She shouldn't have gone alone and they all knew that, but it was her decision. Any one of them probably would have done the same.

But he still didn't like it and when she ended her call, he also couldn't help joining her away from the others.

"You shouldn't have gone alone," he said.

She looked at him, and he was surprised to see

amusement in her eyes. "Which I know, since I've actually been a firefighter longer than you have."

"Funny." He exhaled and ran his hand over his hair. "I hated that. I wanted to dump that guy on Grant and go with you."

"Which is why firefighters from the same company shouldn't sleep together. It can screw up priorities." She shrugged and took the bottle of water he'd been drinking out of his hand. "But it didn't because you let me do my job and you did yours."

He watched her drink his water, some of the tension easing from his body. "I really want to kiss you right now."

"Tomorrow," she said, screwing the cap back on his bottle and handing it back to him.

He watched her walk back to the others, shaking his head. This definitely wasn't going to be easy. But she was worth it.

Chapter 9

"I saw you on the news last night." Steph's face looked out at Jamie from her laptop screen. "They had a story about the car that ran into the deli."

"Did they at least get my good side?" Jamie joked. Steph always looked for her on the news but was usually disappointed, so she would at least text if she got a glimpse of her on the screen. Today they were video chatting because she'd been going on break just as Jamie sent her a text message, so she got her friend's excitement complete with facial expressions.

"They were getting a statement from some older guy, but you were in the background talking to some wicked cute guy. Dark hair. You took his water bottle away from him and drank it."

Of course they'd gotten that on film. "I was thirsty."

"Is there a reason you felt comfortable drinking out

of his water bottle, or do you get to drink out of everybody's because you're an officer?"

Jamie grinned at the monitor. "It's a perk. Came with the promotion."

And now she really hoped that not only was Steph one of the few people who'd noticed what was going on in the background of the interview, but that she would be the only one who asked about it. Her mouth had been dry and it had been pure reflex to take the water bottle, but no, she probably wouldn't have done it if it had been any of the other guys in the company.

"I only have a few minutes," Steph said, "but I'm taking Monday off. *Please* tell me you don't have any plans that day."

"Nothing I can think of. Do you want to meet somewhere?"

"No, I want to see your apartment. Plus it's far enough away so if somebody from the pizza shop calls me about a problem or because somebody didn't show up or a tour bus just dumped a shitload of people out front, I can be too far away to do anything."

"I'm so glad I don't work for my family. It must be twice as hard to say no when your parents are the boss."

"It does make it a lot harder to get fired." There was a noise offscreen and Steph turned toward a voice. Then she looked back at Jamie and rolled her eyes. "So I'll see you Monday, right?"

"Sounds great. Text me when you leave your place and give me an estimate on what time you think you'll get here."

"I can't wait. I really want to hear more about the cute guy with the water bottle."

"Nothing to tell."

Stephanie's eyes narrowed. "You're lying, but I don't have time to nag you right now. Monday."

Once Jamie closed out the chat window, she glanced at the clock and decided she had time for a quick run-through of Facebook. Scott had said he'd be over about one, which gave them both time to grab a few hours of sleep if they needed it. She'd taken a short nap, more out of habit than anything, since it had been slow after the deli situation and they hadn't been shorted much rest.

By the time she skimmed past political rants, funny or dramatic memes and everybody's game scores, there was a picture of her niece to like and a status update from her mom about cooking to read. Then she popped onto a few pages related to the fire department and caught up on the news there. Instead of following the pages, she liked to visit them independently of her feed just to keep her personal life more personal.

Her phone chimed and her pulse quickened as she reached for it. I'm here.

Another reason her rent was so cheap, relatively speaking, was the lack of a way to buzz in a guest. Whether it was company, food delivery or a package, she had to go all the way down the stairs and open the door herself. The place definitely didn't have much in the way of amenities, but she'd rather climb the stairs and have more money in her pocket at the end of the month.

When she got to the bottom of the last flight, she paused to watch him through the glass door. He was looking off down the street at something, and he had a shopping bag in his hand. He was so incredibly handsome, she thought, smiling to herself. His profile made her want to run her fingertip over his nose, down to his lips and over his slightly scruffy jawline.

Then, as if he felt her staring, he turned and their eyes met through the door. His mouth turned up in a smile and he held up the bag. "Food," he mouthed.

She pushed open the heavy door and let him in. "Are you trying to bribe your way into my building?"

"That's only phase one. Phase two we can't do here in the hallway."

They made the trek back up the stairs and Jamie unlocked the door. "What's in the bag?"

"I'm going to make you dinner."

She closed the door behind them and kicked off the slippers she'd shoved her feet into. "You get sexier by the minute. What are you making for us?"

"It's my sister's turkey tetrazzini recipe. You'll love it."

Jamie eyeballed the bag in his hand and shook her head. "Recipe? That bag doesn't look heavy enough to have a box of macaroni and cheese in it, never mind the ingredients for homemade turkey tetrazzini."

He gave her a sheepish grin. "Okay, fine. I was hanging out at Aidan and Lydia's earlier and she was making a double batch of it because she freezes individual servings for him to eat when she's at work. I made the sad puppy dog eyes at her and she gave me a couple of containers to take home."

"Microwaveable *and* no pots and pans to wash? Some magazine needs to make you sexiest man alive now." She took a step toward him, but he backed away.

"I need to put this in the fridge before I kiss you

hello, because once I start kissing you, I might not stop."

Jamie followed him to the refrigerator, unwilling to wait any longer than she had to. The second he closed the fridge door and turned, she was there, sliding her arms around his neck. "I missed you."

His mouth came down hard on hers, and she knew they were both releasing the frustration of going through their workdays pretending they felt nothing for each other. They were hungry for each other and she moaned as he buried his hands in her hair.

When she grabbed the hem of his T-shirt and lifted it, he broke off the kiss long enough for her to pull the shirt over his head and toss it aside. Then his lips were on hers again, demanding and hungry, as she ran her hands over the warm, bare flesh of his back.

"I haven't been able to think about anything but doing this since the last time we did this," he said against her mouth. "And that was too long ago."

They stopped again so he could pull her shirt over her head, but he didn't seem to have the patience for her bra. Instead of waiting for her to unclasp it, he pulled down the cups to expose her breasts. Bending his head, he ran his tongue over her nipple before dragging his teeth lightly over the taut skin. The fridge door was cold against her back and she had nowhere to go as he sucked hard enough to make her squirm.

Then she squealed so loudly she was thankful hers was the only apartment on her floor as he crouched and bent her over his shoulder. Before she could really register what he was doing, he straightened and carried her toward the bed.

"Put me down," she said, trying not to laugh. "What the hell are you doing?"

"I can't wait," he said, slapping her ass with the hand not braced around the backs of her knees.

She'd barely bounced off the mattress before he was peeling her pants down her legs. His urgency inflamed her, and she caught her lip between her teeth as he tossed her clothes to the floor and then stripped himself down to nothing just as quickly. He tossed a condom from the back pocket on the bed before tossing his jeans away.

Then he joined her on the bed, his naked body covering hers. She wrapped her arms around him and pulled him down for a kiss. His tongue dipped between hers and she raked her fingernails up his back.

"I haven't thought about anything but this all day," he said against her mouth.

"And it was a very long day. So long."

His hand slipped between her legs and she hissed when his thumb danced over her clit. "Do you like that?"

She moaned, parting her legs as he slipped two fingers inside of her. "I don't hate it."

He had just moved his mouth to her breast and his chuckle vibrated against the sensitive flesh. His erection was full and hard against her thigh, and his fingers weren't enough. But he bit down on her nipple, just enough to hurt slightly, and she arched her back.

"Are you going to come for me?" He ran his tongue from her nipple up her throat.

"I want you inside me."

He kissed her, almost savagely, before drawing back

so he could stand up. He pulled her to her feet and kissed her again before turning her to face the bed.

Splaying his fingers across the small of her back, he slowly pushed his hand up her spine with enough pressure to bend her over. She was aware of him grabbing the condom packet he'd tossed on the bed, and then his hand fisted in her hair and she moaned.

"Don't move," he said, his voice low and raspy.

Only a few seconds later, he ran his hands over her ass and she pushed back against them. She was running out of patience. Finally she felt the head of his cock against her, and she closed her eyes as he slowly filled her.

He scraped his fingernails down her back and she rocked slowly, taking him deeper each time. Then he braced one hand on her hip and bent down to kiss her spine. His other hand skimmed so lightly up her back it tickled, and she shivered. Then his fingers tightened in her hair again.

"Yes," she whispered. He drew back, almost fully, and then drove into her. She cried out, lowering her head. His hand was still clenching her hair, and it pulled with delicious pleasure. "Please, Scott."

He released her hair and straightened, bringing his hands back to her hips. She moved, meeting him stroke for stroke, and she breathed in small, ragged breaths as the orgasm built up inside of her.

The intensity of it made her gasp and her hands balled into fists, clutching the comforter. Scott's fingers dug into her hips as he thrust into her, and then his body jerked. He groaned and then said her name in a low, ragged voice as his orgasm shook him. His hands slid up her back to her shoulders for one last hard thrust before he collapsed on top of her.

Bent over her bed, with his weight on top of her, Jamie was content to catch her breath and bask in the pleasure for a few minutes. Eventually, though, she started to feel the strain on her legs. "We're going to fall on the floor any second. Which is totally okay with me, but I figured I'd give you a heads-up."

"Tuck and roll," he said, and then he chuckled. After kissing the middle of her back, he stood and disposed of the condom while she dragged herself onto the bed.

The mattress dipped under his weight and then he was next to her, hauling her into his embrace. Sighing, she closed her eyes and soaked in the heat of his body. He was just taller enough than her so their bodies fit perfectly together, and she loved being so close to him.

His hand skimmed down her side and came to rest on her hip as he pressed a kiss to her hair. "I don't really have words for how much I enjoyed that. My thoughts are like comic book bubbles right now. Wow! Bam!"

"Kapow!" she said, and they laughed together.

He was so fun, she thought. Scott liked to laugh, and it was just one more thing on the list of things she liked about him. The list that seemed to get longer every time she was with him. She was going to have to start keeping a mental list of things she *didn't* like about him just to balance things out. Later, though. Right now, she couldn't think of a single thing to put on it.

Scott couldn't remember a time he'd felt so content. One of his favorite movies on the television, his sister's turkey tetrazzini in his stomach and Jamie stretched out against him on the couch. Spooning was the only way they both fit, and he didn't mind a bit.

It wasn't originally how he'd pictured things between him and Jamie going, since he was pretty sure they'd both gone into it planning to orgasm and run, so to speak. But, as much as he enjoyed the sex—and he *really* enjoyed it—he also enjoyed talking to her and watching television with her and, yes, even cuddling.

When she was silent through a particularly funny part of the movie, though, he craned his head over hers to see if she'd fallen asleep. Her eyes were open, but she didn't look amused. "Oh, come on. That was funny."

She reached back and slapped her hand on his hip. "I'm sorry, but this is one of the worst movies I've ever seen."

"Oh, come on." Scott waved his hand at the television screen. "This is a classic. How can you not love *Spaceballs*?"

"Up to this point, probably because I hadn't seen it."

He chuckled. "I couldn't believe it when I heard you tell Aidan you'd never seen it."

"I hate to disappoint you, but I don't really get it."

"It's a spoof." He and Aidan had watched the movie so many times when they were younger, they could practically act out the entire thing in a two-man show.

"A spoof of what?"

"Star Wars."

"I've never seen that, either."

"Okay, now you're just messing with me." He didn't think he'd ever met anybody who hadn't seen *Star*

Wars. Maybe not all of them, and with varying opinions, but everybody had at least seen the original.

"I don't watch a lot of movies set in space, I guess. Although my dad loved that *Star Trek* series with the captain who always slept with the alien women even though it got him in trouble every single time."

"It's almost over, I promise." Which meant it was almost time for him to leave and he really didn't want to go.

"What time are you supposed to meet Aidan?" she asked, as if reading his mind.

"About nine." He tightened his arm around her waist and kissed her neck. "You should go with me."

"Yeah, right."

"Okay, not *with* me, but either a certain amount of time before or after me. We could have a beer. Shoot some pool."

She was quiet for a long moment. "I don't think we'd have a lot of luck hiding the afterglow from your family and your best friend right now."

Jamie was right, but he hated admitting it. And he wondered if this was how Aidan had felt when he first started seeing Lydia—having to hide out in his apartment because they didn't want anybody to see them and guess they'd been sleeping together. The difference, though, was that Aidan and Lydia had fallen in love and were going to be married in a few weeks. Maybe a casual fling was easier to hide.

"You sure you don't want to go?" he asked again forty minutes later, when he was standing at her door to kiss her goodbye.

"I'm sure."

"What are you doing tomorrow?" He was having a

hard time making himself leave until he knew when he'd see her again.

"I have some errands to do. And I might go see some friends."

He tucked a strand of hair behind her ear. "So you're busy, then?"

"Yeah." She sighed and then gave him a tiny smile. "I like having some time between you leaving my bed and me seeing you at work, you know? And before we know it, I'll be moving on and you'll be back on the search for your television wife. I don't want to get too used to having you around."

That, he understood. He could already feel himself getting used to being around her and it felt good. "Again with the television wife thing. The guys are idiots, I swear."

She laughed. "It's pretty funny, though, imagining you married to a June Cleaver type."

Rather than explain again that the guys had taken what he'd said and exaggerated it to a ridiculous degree, Scott just shrugged. "I should buy some button-down sweaters or whatever those things are called."

Smiling, she leaned forward and kissed him. He put his hands on her waist and held her for a moment, deepening the kiss and making it last until she pulled away. "You should go. Aidan's going to be wondering if you stood him up."

"I'll see you at work, then."

Scott walked to Kincaid's Pub, since he'd walked from home to Aidan's place, and then to Jamie's. It was definitely a lot more walking than he was used to, but he chalked it up as good exercise and it meant there was no chance of somebody seeing his car parked outside of her building. Several times, he thought about sending a text telling Aidan something had come up so he wouldn't make it and circling back to Jamie's. But then he'd have to come up with a lie when Aidan asked him what had come up, and Jamie might not welcome his return.

He paused with his hand on the door of the bar, taking a second to get his head straight. *I don't want to get too used to having you around.*

Her words echoing through his mind, along with remembering the look in her eyes when she said them, didn't help him sort out his own thoughts. It seemed as if she might be feeling the same thing he was— wanting to keep their relationship in a nice little box separate from the rest of their lives, but not finding the box so easy to seal and shove under the bed. He spent way too much time wishing he was with her for that to happen, and he wasn't sure if he hoped she felt the same, or if he needed her to have willpower for both of them.

The door opened and an exiting customer almost walked into him, putting an end to his sidewalk introspection. He stepped out of the way as three guys left, and then walked inside. Lydia was at the bar, and she lifted her hand in greeting when she saw him. He headed toward the bar, giving a wave to his dad and Fitz in the corner. They were deep in a conversation with some other old-timer, so they barely acknowledged him.

And Aidan was sitting at the end of the bar, as far from the old guys as he could get without turning the corner to the side with no stools. Scott sat next to him, smiling at his sister when she set a frosted mug of beer on a coaster in front of him.

"Thanks. Slow night?"

She shrugged. "Not busy, but we've had enough customers to make the time go by. Not that it matters since my guy's here with me."

He watched his sister give Aidan the kind of smile and eye contact that most men would have killed to be on the receiving end of, and then took a few gulps of his beer. The Celtics were playing, so he turned his attention to the basketball game on the big TV.

"They're not having a good night," Aidan said after Lydia walked away.

Scott snorted. "Yeah, because they're not playing hockey."

"You get all your stuff done this evening?"

For a few seconds, Scott was confused. But then he remembered he told them he had things to do when he left their apartment earlier, only saying he'd meet Aidan later at the bar. "Yeah."

His friend nodded, drumming his fingers on the bar. Scott knew it meant Aidan had something on his mind he was reluctant to talk about, and he knew it had to do with Jamie. And Aidan wouldn't ask and Scott wouldn't tell, so that conversational train had reached the end of the rails.

"I talked to my dad about the pool table," Scott said, hoping to change the subject.

Aidan chuckled and stopped drumming. "I heard all about it. We have to put some kind of insulation down to protect the felt from hot dishes, and then plastic to protect it from any spills. Then a tablecloth so it looks nice."

"He'll probably be the one spilling stuff because he keeps lifting the tablecloth to check on the felt."

They both laughed, and Aidan started telling him about some of the wedding plans. They'd decided on an open bar for beer, soft drinks and coffee, but a cash bar for anybody wanting liquor. And they were leaning toward a potluck situation rather than having the cook trying to keep the guests fed.

While Aidan talked, Scott thought about the day he'd figured out his best friend and his sister had been lying to him. Lying by omission, maybe, but he'd been hurt and pissed and felt stupid and betrayed. He'd gotten over it. He loved both of them too much not to, especially when he'd thought about how much Aidan had stood to lose. It was Lydia on one side, and the guy's best friend, his father figure and mentor, and possibly his ability to stay with his engine company on the other. It was hard to hold a grudge against a guy who loved a woman so much he'd risk everything important to him to be with her.

But it had hurt at the time, and he didn't want Aidan to be in that position. It wouldn't be as personal, because Aidan and Jamie didn't have a relationship other than at work, but hiding things from him didn't sit well with Scott.

"Hey, where'd you go?" Aidan asked, bumping his arm.

"Sorry, my mind wandered."

"I can't believe you have anything more important to think about than Lydia's concern that if we just put *potluck* on the invitation that we'll get fifteen slow cookers of chili and one pan of brownies." He rolled his eyes, but then threw an affectionate smile at his fiancée, who was pulling a pint of Guinness for a customer at the other end of the bar.

"That happened at Mrs. Eames's funeral, remember? Except it was like ten pots of baked beans and a vegetable platter." Scott grimaced. "That was a function hall that could have used better ventilation."

"We're open to suggestions."

He shrugged. "I'm the best man, not the wedding planner. But maybe if you add a note there aren't any outlets for Crock-Pots, you can avoid getting too much chili. Nobody's going to start stringing extension cords together at Tommy's bar."

The wedding talk went on for the rest of the night, with a few digressions into basketball, and Lydia joined in when she wasn't busy. They laughed a lot, and Scott found himself relaxing into the familiar rhythm of his life.

The only thing that would have made the night more enjoyable would be Jamie sitting next to him.

Chapter 10

Jamie skirted the edge of the scene, keeping an eye on the action around them as they worked on repacking their equipment. It hadn't been a particularly bad motor vehicle accident, but there were four cars involved and the intersection was a mess.

Police officers were managing to squeak one lane at a time around the two cars still waiting for tow trucks, and the ambulances had already departed. Jeff, Grant and Gavin were helping a couple of guys from the city who'd been nearby to sweep up broken glass, and she estimated they were only about twenty minutes from being able to return to quarters.

Usually she paid little attention to the clock other than taking note of the time for paperwork when necessary. Today, though, she was counting the hours until the tour was over. For the last two weeks, she and Scott had fallen into a comfortable rhythm of keeping their distance at work, and then hanging out in her apartment. Sex, talking, movies, food, books, music, card games, more sex.

But tomorrow they were going out on a date. A real date, not in her apartment, and she couldn't wait.

They were going on a nice, long drive to a South Shore restaurant Scott liked, right on the water. As much as she enjoyed curling up with him in sweatpants to watch television, getting to dress up a little and go out in public with him would be a welcome and long-overdue change.

She'd told him the night they'd watched that stupid space movie that she didn't want to get too used to having him around. She'd meant it at the time, but it hadn't worked. She'd not only gotten used to having him around, but she was happier when he was with her.

Only being with him in her apartment was growing old, though, so she hadn't even hesitated when he invited her to take a ride out of the city with him so they could go to a real restaurant.

Laughter drew her attention from what she was doing, and she looked over her shoulder to see Scott and Aidan laughing as they knelt next to the truck, repacking their first aid supplies. She wasn't close enough to hear what they were talking about, but it was obviously amusing.

She loved watching Scott with Aidan and the other guys. Mostly with Aidan, though. So many facets of his personality came through during his interactions with them, maybe because they worked together in a professional capacity, but the nature of their jobs made them almost family. He often played mentor to the younger guys, and he respected the older ones.

But it was seeing him with Aidan that always made her smile, even if she had to stifle it for work. They were a lot alike, though Scott was more intense while Aidan more laid-back. She wondered sometimes if Scott's reputation for being a hothead came mostly from being contrasted to his best friend.

Of course, there had been that fight the first night she went to Kincaid's Pub, but overall he'd either mellowed a lot lately or his temper hadn't been as bad as people said it was.

"Hey, LT," Aidan called, and she wasn't sure if he was talking to her or to Rick. Technically, she was their lieutenant and not him, but nobody had used the nickname for her yet.

Both of them were looking straight at her, though, so she walked over to them. "What's up?"

"What's your opinion on cake?" Aidan asked.

"I'm in favor of cake."

He laughed and stood, swinging one of the first aid bags over his shoulder while Scott did the same. "I mean wedding cake. Ashley wants to make a carrot cake because she says it's traditional."

She wrinkled her nose. "Chocolate coming from cocoa beans is as close as I like to come to vegetables in my desserts."

"See?" Scott nudged Aidan with his elbow. "I told you she had good taste in cake."

They both gave her approving looks and, even though it was stupid, it made her feel good. "Don't some couples do two cakes now? Like a big wedding cake and then a groom's cake?"

"I suggested that," Scott said. "And I got an earful about how all the men have to do is show up in suits and…there was more, but I tuned it out, to be honest."

"Every time I say that everybody would rather have chocolate cake than carrot cake," Aidan said, "Lydia shakes her head and mutters *men* under her breath."

The lightbulb went off in Jamie's head. "Ah. And because I'm a woman, you think if I suggest the chocolate cake, she might listen to me."

"At this point, I'm willing to do anything I have to do to keep my wedding cake from having shredded carrots in it."

"I'll do what I can."

"You're the best," Aidan said, grinning.

And Scott winked at her. "Definitely the best."

She rolled her eyes at them and went back to what she was doing, ready to get out of there and back to quarters. It was time for some food and some rest, in that order.

Later, she lay in her bunk, almost wishing the alarm would sound just to give her some way to pass the time other than staring at the ceiling. But if the alarm sounded, that meant somebody was having a bad night, so she stopped short of hoping it actually happened.

Eventually, it was time to go home. After a long, hot soak in the tub, she forced herself to stretch out on her bed. It had been a slow night, but she'd been restless, so she actually slept for a while. Then she packed a bag and waited for Scott to show up.

"I thought it would never be time," he said once she'd let him in and he'd kissed her senseless.

"I was beginning to wonder if all the clocks were broken because they didn't seem to be moving." When they reached the top of the stairs and stepped inside, she grabbed the front of the blue button-down shirt he was wearing and hauled him close to kiss him again.

"I want you so much, but we have reservations. And it's a really cool restaurant." He stepped back to look at her. She'd thrown on a simple plum maxi dress for the occasion, but it had a scooped neckline and a deep slit on one side. "There are other restaurants, though. Or takeout. Hell, you must have something in the fridge."

Laughing, she stepped out of his reach. "Oh, no you don't. I've been looking forward to this date too much to stay home tonight, even if it means staying here with you."

"Then let's go, because my resistance gets a little weaker with every minute I can see that bed over your shoulder."

They took her car, though Scott drove. He said it was just as easy to walk to her place and there was the better gas mileage to consider, but she knew he went out of his way to make it so his truck was never parked in front of her building for very long. There were enough businesses around so he could explain away being parked there for an hour or so, if anybody asked, but not after hours.

When she wasn't gasping and clutching the door handle as he worked through the city traffic, they spent the time talking, mostly about the television shows they both watched. A lot of couples probably would have talked about work, she thought, but they rarely did. She wasn't sure what was in his head, but for her it wasn't only the fact they worked together. Talking about work was a reminder to Jamie that they weren't supposed to be seeing each other, and the more time they spent together, the more that bothered her.

"I know it doesn't look like much," Scott said when he finally turned into the restaurant parking lot. "But trust me, the food is amazing. I don't get down here often, but it's my favorite place to eat."

It was one of the things she'd come to really like about Scott. He could have made a reservation at some fancy restaurant to impress her, but instead he was choosing to bring her to his favorite place, even if it looked a little sketchy from the outside.

Scott was that way about almost everything. He didn't pretend to like movies because he thought they were what she'd want to watch. The same with TV shows and magazines and food. He was willing to try almost anything, but his favorites were what they were and he didn't care what anybody thought of them.

Inside, the restaurant had a nice ambience, especially with the lights dimmed to help conceal the slightly shabby decor. But they were led to a private table at the back, in front of a bank of windows that overlooked the water, and she felt herself falling in love with the place.

"It's gorgeous," she said as the hostess put menus in front of them.

Scott grinned and looked out at the water. "I was young the first time we came here. My mom talked my dad into taking us all to the Cape for a weekend, because she was from there originally, and we stopped here on the way down. It was so good, we stopped on the way back, too. When I got my license, I couldn't remember the name to look up directions, but I came down and drove around until I found it."

"Seriously?" She leaned back in the booth, watching his face as he looked out the window. "Because the food was that good or because of your mom?"

He shrugged, turning back to her. "Both? I don't know. It was a happy memory. My parents got along for the whole weekend and it was the only family vacation I remember us ever taking. And the food was that good."

Jamie tried to imagine a teenage Scott, driving around looking for this place. His mom had died when he was nine and he would have been at least sixteen to have his license, so enough years had passed that she was surprised he'd found it. And it could have gone out of business or changed ownership and names. He must have really wanted to reconnect with the place.

"How often do you come here?"

"I try to get here a couple of times a year. It's been a while, though. The last time I was here I brought Ashley not long after she and Danny split up, just to get her out of the neighborhood for a day. The time before that I think it was me and Aidan and Rick."

"Family, huh? I thought maybe this was your hot date spot," she said, half-jokingly.

"Nope."

That was all he said, but the way he looked directly into her eyes when he said it seemed to give her the answer she'd been fishing for. He wasn't in the habit of bringing girlfriends here, then. So was this simply a two-birds-with-one-stone situation—take her on a date out of the city while revisiting a favorite restaurant?

Or did bringing her to this place that was so important to him he'd gone looking for it as a teenager mean something?

* * *

Scott looked across the table at Jamie and, maybe for the first time in his life except for his mom, wished everything could be different.

He wished he and Jamie didn't work together. That their relationship didn't have to be a secret. That he was the kind of guy she would want to have a real relationship with, and that she didn't think he was on the hunt for some kind of television wife who'd stay home and bake cookies while raising their children. When he looked into Jamie's eyes, he could almost see his future…if only their present wasn't so screwed up.

When she gave him a questioning look, he realized his thoughts might be showing on his face and smiled. All that mattered right now was the fact he was sitting in his favorite restaurant with a woman who could set his blood on fire with just a look or a single word.

"What's good here?" she asked, picking up one of the menus.

"Not to be unoriginal or anything, but definitely the seafood."

He already knew he was having that, so he watched Jamie as she read over the menu. Her face was expressive, and he could tell when something sounded appealing to her and when something didn't.

Their server arrived to introduce herself and take their drink orders. Jamie ordered a glass of white wine from their limited list, and Scott asked for an orange soda. While they waited for the drinks, they decided to split the seafood platter and a big basket of fries.

Once they'd placed their order, Jamie sipped her wine and looked out the window, her face relaxed and happy. "I can see why you like to come here. I'm surprised it's not overrun by tourists, though."

"It's just far enough off the beaten path, I guess. And it's a word-of-mouth kind of place. It's been busier since people started using those restaurant review apps, though. There's no hiding from the internet."

"I'm glad you were able to get a reservation for this table. It has the best view."

"It's too bad I have to go with Aidan tomorrow to pick out suits. Otherwise I would also have reserved us a nice hotel room down the street with a deck facing the ocean." He looked at her over the rim of his glass, wanting her so much his body ached. "Maybe I could tell him I'm sick."

"You can't call in sick to best-man duties for your best friend," she said, laughing. "Besides, I'm going shopping with your sisters tomorrow and I suspect I'm going to need a good night's sleep to get through that."

"Shopping? Didn't you just go shopping?"

"Yeah, but for groceries. We're going shopping for dresses."

He laughed and held up a hand. "Okay, I should have guessed that. How the hell did you get roped into dress shopping with my sisters?"

"I didn't get roped into anything. *My friend* invited me to help her and her sister pick out dresses for her wedding."

"That's weird."

She frowned at him. "Taking friends wedding dress shopping with you is weird? For a guy who grew up with two older sisters, sometimes you don't seem to know a lot about women."

"No, not the shopping. Women shop in packs. It's

just a little weird that Lydia's my sister. And Lydia's your friend. But there's no three of us together. Does that make sense?"

She nodded. "Yeah, it does. It's weird for me, too. It's like living two separate lives, but the lives intersect in multiple places."

"Yeah." He paused and then smiled at her. "Don't forget to mention the cake thing, okay?"

"I'll do my best to save us all from cake with vegetables in it. But in return I want you to tell me something. What made you decide to take a break from dating?"

The question seemed to come out of left field and he mentally flailed for a few seconds, trying to come up with an answer that might make sense. "It was a lot of things, I guess. Part of it's probably just a natural progression of life. I'm almost thirty, so there's that. It's time to starting thinking about the future and all that. But the last woman I had what I'd consider a real relationship with started asking a lot of questions about my benefits and whether they'd cover plastic surgery. And she said if she got pregnant, I'd have to marry her and put her on my bennies plan."

When Jamie's eyebrows shot up and her lips tightened, he almost laughed. She was angry on his behalf, and he liked knowing that. "Are you serious? Did she have absolutely no self-respect at all?"

"I don't know, but I do know she didn't respect *me*. And I do have some self-respect, so that was the end of that relationship. And I realized I didn't have a great track record when it came to asking out women who I'd want to spend more than a few weeks with. If that long."

"So you thought the best way to find the right woman was to stop dating?"

He laughed, feeling more than a little stupid. "I needed to take a step back and rethink how I went about dating, I guess. Stop hanging out in clubs and stuff like that. When spending the rest of your life with a woman is the objective instead of having sex with her that night, you have to break the behavior patterns and start over."

Jamie leaned forward and propped her chin on her hands, the candlelight reflecting in her eyes. "What made you break your temporary vow of abstinence for me?"

He froze, terrified by what might come out of his mouth. The seconds ticked by as he sorted words in his head, trying to separate what he wanted to say from what he didn't. What he didn't want to say was that, if their circumstances had been different, she might have been the woman he'd broken the cycle to find. That was a lot of depth to throw at a casual friends-with-benefits situation.

"Probably the same thing that made you break your rules about having sex with a guy in your company," he said finally. "We have insane chemistry and I wanted you so much I couldn't resist you."

The blush across her cheeks was faint, but he didn't miss it. "We certainly do have chemistry."

"Okay, fair's fair," he said, wanting to change the subject away from his feelings and more toward hers. "Lydia told me you moved here with a guy—and for the record, I didn't ask her and it just came up in conversation one day—so what made you stay in Boston when he left? Why wasn't he the one?"

She sighed and leaned back in her chair. "We started talking about the future and hypothetical kids. I said I thought eighteen months between having hypothetical number one and getting pregnant with hypothetical number two would be ideal. I'd have time to get back in shape and get back on the job for a while before having the second."

"And he disagreed?"

"He assumed I'd give up my career and stay home with the little hypotheticals."

"Was his expectation that you would have given up *any* career to be a stay-at-home mom, or was it because you're a firefighter?"

"It was mostly about me being a firefighter." She swirled the liquid in her glass, watching it with an expression he couldn't quite read. It wasn't sadness, really, or annoyance. Maybe both. "If I'd been a teacher or a lawyer or something, I think he might not have been so adamant about it."

"And you wouldn't quit if you had a baby?" He almost recoiled from the look she gave him. "I'm not saying I think you should. But you know I lost my mom when I was a kid. I know how shitty that is, so my kids having a mother in a high-risk job is something that would make me nervous."

She met his gaze across the table, her eyebrows furrowed. "I've heard it's pretty shitty for kids to have their dads die, too, but nobody thinks twice about guys running into a burning building."

"Is there any way for me to say I think it's different without sounding like a sexist asshole?"

"No, not really." After a few seconds, she leaned back and her expression softened. "I get it, though.

I know you're not a sexist asshole and I know most people have a harder time with moms having dangerous jobs. But I know how well I do my job and how safely I do it so, when I meet the right guy, I'm going to get married and have children without sacrificing my career."

When I meet the right guy. Because she hadn't yet, of course. If she had, she wouldn't be killing time with him. Ignoring the sharp jab of regret because this was what he'd signed up for, he looked at her across the table. She was staring at him, her gaze boring into him as if willing him to say something.

"He'll be a lucky guy," he said, lifting his glass in a mock toast.

She frowned slightly and her lips parted as if she was going to speak. Then she took a deep breath and lifted her own glass to take a sip of her wine.

The server arriving with their food put an end to their conversation and Scott wasn't sorry. It hadn't been going anywhere good, and he didn't want this night ruined by him being envious of a guy Jamie hadn't even met yet.

"There's no way we can eat all this," Jamie said.

He looked at the paper-lined baskets of all sorts of fried seafood and fries, and grinned. "Maybe not, but we can put one hell of a dent in it."

They talked while they ate. Not about anything serious, since they seemed to have both had their fill of that, but about the other guys in the company. The upcoming wedding. And, of course, about Ashley and Danny's pregnancy.

"I can't wait," he confessed. "They said they're not

going to find out if the baby's a boy or a girl, which is killing me."

"Are you hoping for a boy?" she asked. "The next generation of kick-ass, sports-loving, hot-tempered Kincaids?"

He grinned. "You think if I have a niece, she won't be a kick-ass, sports-loving, hot-tempered Kincaid?"

"True." She shook her head, laughing. "Maybe she'll be like her aunt Lydia."

"Danny's a pretty levelheaded guy, unless he's pushed too far. And Ashley's a lot more like Mom than Lydia and I are. We definitely got Tommy's genes in a higher concentration. But, boy or girl, I can't wait."

They lingered a lot longer over dinner than he'd anticipated, and by the time they were in her car and headed back into the city, it was late. Throw in traffic due to drivers rubbernecking a minor accident, and it was very late by the time they got off the highway.

"Your sisters want me ready at a ridiculously early hour," she said, and he could hear the regret in her voice. "I think Lydia has to work in the afternoon, which means morning shopping."

"We're not hitting the suit place early, but I told Aidan I'd meet him for breakfast."

"I hate the idea of you walking this late. Maybe we should head to your place and I'll drop you off there and drive myself home."

He wanted to make love to her in the worst way, but he knew she was right. If he went home with her, it was going to be at least a couple of hours before they were done for the night. And then he'd either have a late walk home or he'd have to get up very early in the morning to do it.

"I guess since it's our first date, I'll let you kiss me good-night," he said, turning his head to smile at her in the lights of the streetlamps.

He pulled up on the street behind his house. Not only would he have quick access to the stairs in the back, but she'd be pointed in the right direction to head home. After undoing his seat belt, he leaned across the center console to kiss her.

Ending the kiss was almost painful, but they'd both be sorry if they didn't go straight to bed and go to sleep. "Thanks for going down there with me."

"Thanks for inviting me." She smiled, running her thumb across his bottom lip. "It's a special place."

"Yeah." He put his hand on the door pull, since sitting on the side of the street wasn't any better a plan than going to her place. "Text me when you get home so I know you made it. And let me know how the shopping trip goes."

"I will." She got out of the car and walked around to the driver's side. After another kiss good-night, she slid into the seat.

"And, Jamie, don't forget the cake."

She was laughing when he closed the door, and he waited to duck between the buildings until she'd turned the corner. After a final wave, he walked to his dad's backyard and climbed the stairs to his apartment.

He should have left a light on for himself, he thought. Maybe then the place wouldn't feel so lonely.

Chapter 11

Since Lydia and Ashley both planned to make breakfast for their guys before hitting the mall, Jamie made herself a breakfast sandwich on an English muffin in the morning. She wasn't much of a breakfast eater and preferred to wait a few hours before a meal, but she'd learned on the job to eat when she had the chance.

After throwing on jeans and a T-shirt with a light hoodie, along with her comfortable walking sneakers, she steeled her nerves for the drive to the mall. She'd been tempted to ask them to swing by and pick her up, but then they would have had to backtrack. And she was trying to learn the neighborhood while sharpening her Boston driving skills. She couldn't do that while riding around as a passenger in somebody else's car, and even that was scary sometimes.

After parking in front of the store entrance they'd

told her to meet them at, she locked her car and headed across the parking lot. It was already more crowded than she'd expected, considering the mall had just opened. Lydia and Ashley were sitting on a bench, drinking out of paper cups, and they waved when they saw her.

"We weren't sure you were coming," Lydia said.

"Sorry I'm late," she said, thankful it was only by fifteen minutes. "I still don't have the hang of driving here. I swear, I can drive to the same place six times and it will take me a different amount of time to get there each time I go. Is there a bridal shop here?"

"Oh, I'm not doing a gown. I just want something nice, like a cocktail dress, maybe. Fancy, but not too formal. There are some high-end stores in this mall that might have something."

"We're trying *not* to do all the small boutique stores," Ashley said. "We don't have time for that and I don't want to walk that much."

In the second store, they found Ashley's dress. It was a fit-and-flare style in a dark emerald that suited her figure and coloring as though it had been designed just for her. They were about to give up on the mall when Lydia pulled a dress off a rack and they all sighed. A cream-colored sheath with a cream lace overlay, it was elegant and simple, but not plain. It was very Lydia and when she tried it on, Jamie wasn't surprised when Ashley got teary-eyed.

Jamie watched the sisters bond over the dress, remembering going through this moment with each of her sisters. They'd both had big weddings, so the process had been a lot more grueling for her, but the emotional payoff was the same.

"What are you wearing?" Ashley asked, looking at Jamie while they waited for the dress to be put into a garment bag.

Her eyes widened. "Me? I don't know yet. And nobody cares what I'm wearing."

"When's the last time you dressed up?" Lydia asked.

"I don't know. I went to a promotion ceremony not too long ago. And there was a plaque dedication."

"No," Lydia said. "I'm not talking about dressing up for work. I'm talking about dressing up for fun. My wedding's going to be fun."

"You know, I went to a firefighter's wedding once where they wore their Class A uniform," Jamie said. "Everybody matched. It was great, and I'm sure the pictures were stunning."

Lydia snorted. "Nobody's wearing their dress uniforms to my wedding. Even if the chief gave permission for the guys—and you, of course—to wear them, which even as a favor for my dad would be questionable because we're getting married in a bar and there will be drinking, we all live and breathe the fire department enough without it being the theme of my wedding."

"So what you're saying is that I need to start thinking about what I'm going to wear."

"Yes, you do." Lydia pointed a finger at her, which made her laugh. "You all have it easy every day. Your T-shirts and uniform pants and boots. Turnout gear. Even when you guys dress up, there are rules and a specific uniform. When you're off duty, you still wear the T-shirts and all you have to decide is sweatpants or jeans. Maybe cargo shorts in the summer. You're dressing up, Jamie."

"You should get a dress today," Ashley said.

"Yes," Lydia agreed. "And if I have to wear heels, you have to wear heels."

Half an hour later, Jamie stood in front of a mirror and frowned at the dark navy dress. It fit well and it was comfortable. It was made from some kind of jersey material that had a mock wrap waist and deep V-neck, with three-quarter sleeves she liked. Logically she knew it looked good on her and it certainly suited her more than the floral number Ashley made her try on or the red strapless number she'd vetoed while it was still on the hanger.

There was cleavage, though. And leg. A *lot* of leg.

She took a picture of her reflection with her phone and, after looking at it for a few seconds, texted it to her older sister, Carrie. Her younger sister, Tori, was probably the most fashionable of them, but Carrie was the most honest. Plus Tori and her family would probably be at church.

Yes or no?

Yes. The response was almost immediate. Definitely yes, but what's the occasion?

A wedding. It's not too fitted?

Enough time passed so she assumed Carrie gave the dress a second look. It looks perfect on you. Do you have a date for the wedding? If you don't, you will once you get there.

I'm shopping with friends, so can't talk now. I'll call soon.

I see that you dodged the question. Have fun and talk later.

"I can see under the door and your feet aren't moving, so I know you've got the dress on," Lydia said. "Stop looking in the mirror and come out here so we can tell you if you should like it."

Barely managing to keep from rolling her eyes, Jamie stepped out into the hall of the dressing room area. "Have I mentioned how much I hate dress shopping?"

"Oh, that's totally the one," Ashley said, and Lydia nodded. "You have the perfect body for that dress. You're in great shape, but not too thin. And you've got the boobs for it."

Jamie looked down at herself. "And everybody will know I have the boobs for it, too."

"That's the point. And I'm pretty sure everybody already knows you have breasts."

"I don't generally put them on display, though."

"Of course not, but you won't be at work," Lydia said. "And they're not really on display, since you only see a little bit of cleavage. I think it's just that the cut is really flattering on you and you're not used to that fit."

"You have great legs, too," Ashley added. "Scott would like that one on you."

Jamie froze, not sure what to say to that. Almost any denial of Scott's opinion being relevant would skirt too close to lying to them for her comfort. But as far she knew, Scott hadn't told his sisters anything about their relationship and, if they were fishing, she didn't want to take the bait.

"Stop, Ash," Lydia said. "We're all supposed to pretend we don't know she and Scott have been sleeping together for three weeks."

"Oh, that's right." Ashley looked at her, tilting her head as if giving the dress serious consideration. "That neckline means jewelry, though."

"Are you wearing your hair up or down?" Lydia asked.

"Down," Jamie said. She was confused, but she let them change the subject because it bought her time to figure out how she felt about Scott's sisters knowing what they were up to.

It was probably stupid or naive for them to think Lydia and Ashley hadn't caught on to their relationship. Even though they were rarely all together, they saw Scott often enough to guess he had somebody in his life he wasn't talking about. And she was pretty sure Aidan knew—or at least had strong suspicions—but based on Lydia's silence on the issue, Jamie had assumed he hadn't shared them with her.

"Do you know what the mother of the groom is wearing?" she asked Lydia. "I know you're not really doing colors, but I don't want to step on anybody's look."

There was an awkward pause, and then Lydia waved off the question. "Aidan didn't invite his family. We're going to tell them we eloped and do a wedding brunch or something with them later."

"Oh." Jamie wasn't sure what she was supposed to say to that. He was always so solid and laid-back that she'd never guessed Aidan might have family issues. "Sorry about that."

"It's nothing bad. They're very...*very* white-collar and don't understand why Aidan took the career path he did and they're not shy about voicing their feelings. We don't think they'd enjoy themselves."

"They're really snotty and treat him like crap," Ashley said. "And his whole family would just sit in the corner of the bar all night and judge everybody Aidan loves."

"That's it in a nutshell," Lydia said. "He gave it a lot of thought and decided it would be easier on everybody and better for their relationship in the long run if we fudge the truth just a little."

Jamie couldn't imagine getting married without her family, but they didn't treat her like crap over a job, either. "And you'll get a free brunch out of it, since it would be poor form of them not to pay the bill."

Lydia laughed. "That's what Scotty said, too. Free food."

"I want free food. I'm starving," Ashley said, putting an end to the conversation. "After you pay for that dress, because you're totally buying it, we should have an early lunch before Lydia has to go back to work."

"You're always starving," Lydia replied. "And don't even tell me you're eating for two. The only way that excuse works for your current appetite is if you're having septuplets."

They decided on a burger place in the food court for convenience's sake, all of them laughing when Lydia pointed out they couldn't do it often or they wouldn't fit in the new dresses they'd run out to the cars.

"I'm not very hungry, anyway," Jamie said, once

they'd carried their trays to a nearby table. "I had the best seafood ever last night and I ate so much, I swear I'm still full."

They both paused in the act of putting condiments on their burgers to stare at her. Jamie replayed the words in her head, but she didn't think she'd said anything remotely stareworthy. She'd had seafood for dinner. So what?

Ashley replaced her top bun, but didn't pick up her burger. "Nice little place? South Shore? On the water?"

She should have known spending half the day with Scott's sisters wasn't going to end well. But she'd hoped they'd be so wrapped up in dresses and wedding plans that they'd barely pay attention to her. "I... Crap. Please don't make this a thing."

"It could be a thing," Lydia said. "In fact, we can't figure out why it's *not* a thing."

"Because sometimes there's chemistry between two people who, number one, shouldn't have a relationship for professional reasons and, number two, have different ideas of what their futures will hold."

"You don't want a family?" Ashley asked. "Not that there's anything wrong with that. I guess we just make assumptions, you know."

"I do want a family. But I don't intend to give up my career when I have kids." She shrugged and dipped a French fry in the small paper cup of ketchup on her tray. "Other people think mothers shouldn't risk themselves in dangerous jobs, even though it's okay for fathers to do it."

"You already know he mostly grew up without our mother," Lydia said. "That's probably a big part of it. But it's kind of a pervasive way of thinking in the neighborhood, too, you know? It's old-fashioned and tightly knit. He was raised in a community of alpha guys, really, where the wives and children kept the home fires burning."

"That's not a great metaphor," Ashley said, and they all laughed. "I do agree with it, though. He probably has certain expectations of his future wife, but expectations change. He respects the hell out of you, Jamie. All the guys do."

"We can be a stubborn family," Lydia said, "but we come around."

"Danny getting hurt hit all the guys pretty hard, but Scott was the worst. It's all tangled up, you know? The brotherhood, the friendship and the family ties." Ashley paused, running her finger around the rim of her water glass. "You wouldn't believe how happy and excited he was when we told him I was pregnant. Seriously, it's like being an uncle is going to be the best thing that ever happened to him."

Jamie smiled, not having any trouble imagining his joy. He lit up whenever he talked about his sisters, and whenever he mentioned his future niece or nephew, he practically beamed. She'd seen it last night at the restaurant, and she would have loved to have seen his reaction when he first heard the news.

"I think that's why he had such a hard time," Ashley continued. "Because the fire was so soon after we told him. When he realized Danny hadn't come out of the structure with the rest of the company, I guess it was pretty bad and it stuck with him for a while. I mean, he's Scotty, so he tried to hide it and crack jokes and stuff, but it was there. He didn't want my baby coming into the world without a dad, I guess."

"It weighed on his mind a lot," Lydia agreed. "Losing Mom and the possibility of that little peanut losing its daddy before he or she's even born shook him up. Hell, it shook all of us up, but Scotty's a smart guy. When push comes to shove, he's not going to walk away from something he wants because of the risk. If that was in his nature, he wouldn't be a firefighter."

"We haven't seen you guys together as a couple, obviously," Ashley said. "But we like you. And we like how Scotty is right now. As his oldest sister, it's a big deal when I say I'd really like to see you guys be a thing."

But how hard was Jamie willing to push? And did he want a future with her enough to compromise, or was she simply a spill he'd taken off the no-dating bandwagon?

Her phone chimed, saving her from having to respond to Ashley. But she sighed when she saw the message from Scott. The guy had seriously bad timing. Are you done shopping yet?

God, she hoped so. If she didn't get out of here soon, she was going to end up spilling her guts to his sisters and then things would get messy. We found dresses. Refueling now. You?

We didn't have to shop because Lydia picked our suits. But we've been measured in uncomfortable places and won't look like ragamuffins at the wedding.

She laughed, belatedly realizing Scott's sisters were both watching her. "Sorry."

"If that's my brother, ask him if they're done with the suits," Lydia said.

"Uh." Jamie hesitated before the realization sunk in that it would be nothing short of stupid to even try to pretend at this point. With them, anyway. "He said they won't look like ragamuffins, so I assume they're all set."

"Tell him they need ties, too. They're going to try to sneak parts of their uniform past me because they're lazy."

Your sister said to get a tie. No uniform ties.

There was a long pause before the response came through. She knows I'm texting you?

Please. Have you met your sisters? She appreciated that the two women had obviously gone out of their way to play along and give them space, but the gig was up.

Fine. We'll get ties. Call me later. Oh, and don't forget the cake.

Smiling, she tucked her phone away. "So, Lydia, have you done any cake tastings?"

"Oh, for God's sake, carrot cake is not a vegetable." She pointed a French fry at Jamie. "You might be part of the whole firefighter brotherhood thing, but don't let those two yahoos drag you onto their side."

"Can I ask why you just don't have a chocolate groom's cake?"

She blew out an exasperated breath. "Because that will be the groom's cake, not my wedding cake. I want my husband to share our wedding cake with me, but he's not going to if there's a chocolate cake sitting next to it."

"Okay." Jamie nodded slowly. "So this is one of those stubborn Kincaid things and Aidan's going to eat his vegetables and like it."

"Yes." Lydia shrugged. "He knew what he was getting into."

Ashley laughed, and then waved her hand at them. "I love this. This dynamic, I guess you could say. Jamie's our perfect third."

Below the warm feeling that came from being so openly accepted was a cold jangle of nerves. The genie was out of the bottle now, and she wasn't going to be able to shove him back in. Her and Scott's time of quietly, privately enjoying each other's company with no expectations was over.

She had no doubt his sisters were going to try to make it a *thing*.

My dad's off with Fitz somewhere until late. Want to come to my place for a change?

Scott sent the text and tried not to hold his breath as he waited for Jamie's answer. He knew she'd had an exhausting morning with his sisters, and they'd just seen each other the night before, but he really wanted to see her again. And he wanted to see her in his apartment for some reason he didn't care to analyze too closely.

Sounds good. It'll be about an hour, though, if that works.

Perfect. See you then.

He exhaled and then looked around. Luckily, the place didn't look too bad since he didn't have a lot of clutter and he'd learned over the years of sharing a small space with a lot of guys to pick up after himself. But he did change the sheets because it seemed like the gentlemanly thing to do.

Then he dropped onto the couch and started flipping through channels so when she did show up, she wouldn't catch him with his face pressed to the glass sliding door, waiting for her. Even when he heard her footsteps on the wooden deck, he kept his eyes on the screen until she knocked on the glass.

He wasn't sure what he trying to prove to himself by acting casual, because on the inside he was jumping up and down like a black Lab whose human had finally come home.

"Hey, come on in," he said, pulling open the slider for her. Before closing it, he peeked down into the driveway. "You didn't walk, did you?"

"You walk all the time. But no, I drove. Unlike your jacked-up truck with the fancy chrome and firefighter plate, my car's just another gray compact job parked on the street. It blends in with the crowd."

After he closed the slider, he took her hand and pulled her close. "My truck is not jacked up."

"It came that way?"

"It's a stock three-quarter-ton pickup and the chrome came with the package that included the heated seats and remote start."

"Okay, so you're not one of those macho truck guys. Just spoiled a little bit."

He laughed. "Macho truck guys? No, I'm not. And as for being spoiled, I spend enough time freezing my ass off on the job. When I get in my truck, my ass is warm."

She ran her hands down his back and then tucked her fingers into the back pockets of his jeans. "It's definitely an ass worth pampering a little."

He kissed her, feeling the curve of her smile against his lips. Her hair was up in a ponytail, but without taking his mouth off hers, he pulled the fabric-covered elastic free so he could bury his hand in the soft strands. He loved her hair and it would probably have been the hardest part of her to resist touching at work if she didn't keep it braided whenever they were on duty.

When the kiss was over, she sidestepped him and looked around the apartment. "You don't really have a lot of knickknack-type stuff, do you?"

"No, but neither do you."

She ran her hand over the granite bar, looking at the kitchen. "I've moved so many times, I've learned to travel light. But you've lived in this house for your entire life. Maybe not on this floor, but still."

"Trust me, there are boxes and boxes with my name written on them down in the cellar. You want a drink?"

"I'll have a soda. Whatever you've got."

He took out a couple of cans and popped the top on hers before holding it out to her. "How was dress shopping?"

"It was more fun than I thought it would be, actually. I'm not big on shopping, but Lydia and Ashley are a lot of fun."

He winced. "I guess they're also more intuitive than I gave them credit for."

"There wasn't much point in denying anything, although I did manage to avoid being pinned down too much, conversationally."

Scott really wanted to know what they'd said, but then again a part of him didn't. If they'd done a full-court press on her and wanted to talk love and marriage, pushing her for details might get awkward. He didn't want her first time in his apartment to go sideways on him.

"I honestly don't know if I've ever successfully kept a secret from those two," he said.

"So everybody must know, then, if they do. At the station, I mean."

"I don't think so. Aidan and Danny, probably." He paused. "Okay, Aidan almost definitely, though he's never asked and I've never confirmed or denied. But if you're worried they're all talking about us, don't. Family loyalty still comes first."

"Do you think Tommy knows? He's family."

"I doubt it. He'd have to figure it out on his own because he's the last person my sisters would talk to about my personal life. He can be a bit of a bull in a china shop when it comes to shit like that, and Lydia and Ashley don't usually throw me under the bus with him."

She sighed, and then gave a little shrug. "It doesn't matter. People can say what they want."

Wanting to bring the mood back to where it had started, Scott set his soda on the counter and moved closer to her. She took a long sip of hers, and after she put down the can, he pulled her hard up against his body.

"You gonna dance with me at the wedding?"

She smiled at him, and he felt the familiar rush of pleasure he got every time she looked at him like that. "I don't know. What do you think the chances are you can keep your hands where they're supposed to be?"

He cupped her ass, squeezing a little. "I can behave."

"That's probably the one thing I *haven't* heard about you, Scott Kincaid."

"I should give you the grand tour."

She looked around his shoulder. "I can see most of the apartment from right here."

Since her head was cocked sideways, he took advantage of the opportunity to kiss her neck. "You can't see the best part, though."

"You mean the gigantic television?"

He grinned and, with his hands still on her ass, pulled her close enough so she could feel his erection press against her. "I have a gigantic bed, too."

"I'd hate to miss the main attraction."

Letting go of her with some reluctance, he took her hand and led her into the bedroom. The bed was big, though hardly gigantic, but it dominated the room. He didn't have a TV in here because he tried to be strict about his sleep schedule and the bed meant sleep.

Today, though, the bed meant Jamie. She looked around the room, which wasn't any more cluttered than the rest of the place, and then at the bed. He wondered if she noticed the condom packet on the nightstand, kind of tucked beside the lamp. "Nice bed. Definitely bigger than mine."

Laughing, he stepped close enough to kiss her. "We don't need a lot of space for what I have in mind."

He slid his hands under her shirt, cupping her breasts and rolling her nipples between his thumbs and forefingers. Even through the fabric of her bra, his touch made her squirm. They stripped quickly and he admired the view as she climbed onto his bed. Then she held out her hand to him and he knew he should be reciting box scores or algebra problems or something in his head. But the only thing in his head right now was the sight of her, naked and beckoning to him.

Once he was on the bed, she shoved him backward and laughed when he splayed out on his back. He opened his mouth to make a smart-ass comment, but Jamie threw one leg over his hips and nothing came out of his mouth but a guttural sound.

She bent low so she could kiss him, her hands holding his wrists over his head. The position pressed her breasts against his chest and he groaned, fighting the temptation to prove which of them was stronger by flipping her onto her back and driving into her.

Then she kissed his chin. His Adam's apple. First one nipple and then the other, sucking just hard enough to make him hiss. Then she started making her way down his abdomen, punctuating her kisses with flicks of her tongue, and he held his breath.

When she wrapped her fingers around his dick, Scott thought he might never breathe again. She stroked him, lightly at first, but then her grip tightened as she flicked her tongue over her lips.

He couldn't look away from her mouth, but he still jumped when she closed her lips around the head of his cock. She lowered her head until her mouth bumped into her fingers, and then kept going. Her hand slid down the length of his shaft, along with her mouth, and his hips arched up off the bed.

Then she took away her hand and took him only with her mouth. The wet heat scrambled his senses and he fisted his hand in her hair. Not resisting or forcing. Just clenching the strands as he struggled to think of anything but how much he wanted to come in her mouth.

Only a few more strokes and he pulled her hair slightly, holding her head still. "You have to stop, honey. I can't…"

Jamie kissed her way back up his body to his mouth, and then he had to release her hair so she could reach for the condom to hand to him. She kissed him hungrily while he put it on, and then gave him a saucy smile as she straddled him. Taking him in hand, she lowered herself onto his erection with excruciating slowness.

His breathing turned ragged as she rocked her hips, taking him deeper inside of her with each stroke.

She arched her back and he reached up, cupping her breasts. Her neck was exposed and he wanted to kiss that hollow at the base, but he couldn't reach it with his mouth. He settled for stroking her neck with one hand, sliding his fingers over her jaw until she turned her head and sucked lightly on the end of his finger.

When he groaned, her rhythm changed. Each rise and fall of her body was faster and harder, and he knew she was close. Since he was on the ragged edge himself, he lifted his hips to meet each stroke, driving up into her. Reaching down, he rubbed his thumb over her clit and watched her body jerk.

He felt her muscles clench as she came with a small cry that seemed to set his blood on fire. Grabbing her hips, he rocked her body, harder and faster until his orgasm hit like a wrecking ball knocking him senseless. Losing himself in the intense sensation, he rode it out and was glad he was lying down because it seemed like his entire body was boneless.

Jamie collapsed on top of him, turning her head so it was on his shoulder. He kissed her hair and wrapped his arms around her back to hold her tight.

After a few minutes, when they'd caught their breath, he reached between them and held the condom as he pulled out of her. She shifted slightly to one side, but didn't get up, so he was content to stay right where he was for a little bit longer.

"I almost didn't send you a text because I thought you'd be tired out from shopping," he said. "I'm glad I did."

"Me, too. Very glad."

"I did a little shopping today, too. Guess what I bought?"

She lifted her head to look at him and he took the opportunity to grab a quick kiss. He could never get enough of kissing her.

"I'm almost afraid to ask," she said, amusement shining in her eyes.

"I stopped at the market over by your place and bought some chocolate pudding."

"Ooh." She made a sound he'd previously only heard during sex. "You didn't mention that in your text."

He gave a mock sigh. "Then I would have wondered if you were only here for my pudding. I needed to know if I was enough."

She laughed and pushed away from him. "Trust me, you're enough. Sometimes I wonder if you're *too* much."

He wasn't sure what that meant, exactly, but she hadn't said it in a particularly negative way, so he shrugged it off. She was here. That was exactly enough.

Chapter 12

"Why do I have five gloves?" Scott tossed them into the growing pile of locker debris on the floor behind him. "Did I have six and lose one, or did I have four and stole one of somebody else's?"

"If anybody's missing one," Aidan said, "they'll know who to go after."

"I have five gloves," Grant said. "But I don't know if I started with four or six."

Scott heard Jamie's laughter behind them. "Maybe you should just have a big basket of gloves and share them all."

He didn't turn and face her, but he felt the familiar warmth at the sound of her voice. They hadn't been able to spend a lot of time together in the three days since he took her out to dinner, but at least he was guaranteed forty-eight hours per week with her.

Unfortunately, he couldn't touch her or kiss her or check out how amazing her ass looked during those forty-eight hours. But he could hear her voice and listen to her laugh and talk about all the inane things people talked about at work. And every once in a while, there would be an opportunity for his hand to brush hers, or even for him to press his palm to the small of her back. But never more than that.

It was a warm and dry day, so they had the engine bay doors open and were cleaning out all the cold-weather things they'd collected over the course of a winter. There was a lot of foot traffic on the street as people embraced spring, and their work was constantly interrupted as they waved to little kids and even let a few of them look at the apparatuses. They didn't mind, though. There wasn't a single one of them who didn't remember feeling the wonder of the fire station as a child.

But part of his attention was on the stairs in the back, waiting to hear Danny Walsh come thumping back down on his crutches. The cast was gone and he was doing physical therapy, but they still wanted him to use the crutches if there would be strain on the leg for a little while longer.

He'd shown up about half an hour ago and, after spending some time catching up with the guys, had gone upstairs to see Cobb. Scott guessed he was probably giving an update on his progress and he might even have a tentative date for his return.

And that screwed with Scott's head in a way he didn't like. He liked Walsh and always had. The guy was a damn good LT who took good care of Engine 59. He was also Ashley's husband and the father of Scott's future niece or nephew. Scott wanted nothing but a full recovery for his brother-in-law, as soon as possible.

But his return meant there was no room for Jamie and she would leave. It had been inevitable from the first, and maybe even for the best considering they didn't see eye to eye when it came to two firefighters having a family together. But he couldn't imagine not having her in his life, and his mind shied away from even trying.

With his locker emptied out for the most part, he turned to start sorting through the pile of gloves, intending to at least see if the colors or sizes would help identify them. He doubted it, since they were all black wool and the only one of them who didn't wear a standard men's size was Jeff, but it was worth a shot.

But when he turned, he got distracted by Jamie. She'd been at the workbench, doing an inventory of the miscellaneous small supplies lying around, but now she was staring in the direction of the staircase, as if her mind had wandered.

So she was waiting, too, he thought. They both knew Danny coming to the station marked the beginning of the end of her time there, and she didn't look any happier about it than he felt.

He scooped up the gloves and carried them to the bench, dumping them beside her clipboard. "The light's better over here."

She looked at the gloves and then at him, one eyebrow arched. "You need light to see that you have five black gloves?"

"To read the tags, maybe." It was a thin excuse, to be sure, but he wanted to be near her.

"Are you aware you have five gloves, but four of them are for the left hand?"

He scowled at the pile, then cursed under his breath. "I guess it's time for a glove swap because somebody has too many right hands. Remember when we were kids and they had those mittens with the long string between them so you couldn't lose one?"

"Yeah, I do. But I don't think they make those in adult male sizes."

He didn't miss the amusement in her voice, and it made him want to lean closer to her, but he forced himself to keep a normal amount of distance between them. "Maybe I'll get lucky and Grant's mommy wrote his initials inside his gloves."

"Hey, I heard that," Grant said, and most of the guys laughed.

He took his time checking the gloves over for any identifying marks. The fact there weren't any wasn't a surprise, but it gave him an excuse to be near Jamie.

"You okay?" he asked in a low voice.

"I keep wondering if I should go upstairs and be nosy, but if there's something I need to know, I guess they'll tell me." She shrugged. "I guess they're probably talking about when Danny's coming back, though."

He was going to ask her how she felt about leaving—if she would be sorry to leave them or if she was looking forward to landing someplace on a more permanent basis—when Ashley walked through the open bay door.

He grinned at his sister. She wasn't showing yet, but if you knew to look for it, she was already starting to waddle a little bit when she walked. "Hey, Ash."

"Hi, guys," she said, giving a wave that encompassed all of them. She didn't stop by the station very often, but between being Tommy's daughter, Scott's sister and Danny's wife while running the bar, there was almost nobody in the firefighting community she didn't know. "Is Danny still upstairs?"

"Yeah," Scott responded. "I was thinking about texting him to see if he was still with Cobb or if he was stuck at the top of the stairs and can't get down."

"I'll text him." She pulled out her phone and typed as she spoke. "He has an appointment and we're not running late, but we will be if he doesn't get his ass down here. He was supposed to come back to the market and meet me ten minutes ago."

Because of the appointment, Danny didn't waste any time talking to them when he finally made his way down the stairs. While everybody was focused on saying goodbye to him, Scott looked at Jamie and saw the tension in her face. It mirrored the tension he felt.

She met his gaze and forced a smile before giving a little shrug. Whatever was going to happen would happen, and it wouldn't be a surprise. They'd known all along there was an expiration date on her presence in his life.

But now that it was imminent, Scott dreaded knowing what that date was. He didn't want to know when his time with Jamie was coming to an end.

An hour later, Jamie was surprised when the intercom system in the engine bay crackled to life. It wasn't something they used often, since most of them just used text messaging if they had something to say to somebody not in the room.

"Rutherford, I'd like to see you in my office for a minute."

Jamie tensed at the use of her last name. It was something they all did with each other, switching between first names and surnames and nicknames, but Cobb had always called her by her first. But she pushed the button on the wall and spoke into the speaker. "Right away, sir."

Several of the guys were in the bay and looked at her as she went toward the stairs, but it was Grant who spoke. "What did you do now?"

She gave him a grin that belied the nerves dancing around in her stomach. Even though it was probably an update on Danny's return, she couldn't deny she was nervous about the way she was being summoned. "Probably a meeting about all the complaints we've received about your socks smelling."

Once she'd stepped inside Cobb's office, he gestured for her to close the door and sit down. Judging by his expression, she would have preferred to stand. It was less awkward to take an ass chewing for something standing at attention and staring at something over and behind the boss's head. Sitting was more intimate and involved eye contact.

But he had rank, so she sat. He sighed, staring at the pen he was fiddling with and shifting his weight in his chair, so she remained silent. Clearly he was uncomfortable and trying to figure out how to start, and she got a bad feeling in the pit of her stomach. This wasn't going anywhere good.

Finally he straightened up and looked at her. "Are you involved in a personal way with Scott Kincaid?"

Her gut was rarely wrong. "Respectfully, sir, that's none of your business."

"It really is my business, actually."

"Have I performed any of my duties in a less than satisfactory manner?"

He sighed and rubbed the bridge of his nose. "Hell, no. You know I think highly of you."

"Then, again with all due respect, I don't believe we need to have this conversation."

"Stop with the—" he waved his hand, as if trying to summon the right word out of thin air "—formality or whatever. This isn't an inquisition, it's a conversation."

"And are you having this conversation with Scott?"

"The standard's different for you."

She narrowed her eyes. "Because I'm a woman?"

"Because you're a goddamned officer," he snapped. Then he blew out a long breath and leaned back in his chair. "This is going all kinds of wrong on me."

"As it will when a male superior asks a woman under his authority about her sex life."

"Is there a threat buried in there, Rutherford?"

She looked him in the eye, and then shook her head. "No. I'm just on the defensive, I guess."

"Okay." He leaned forward and slapped his palms on the desk. "Let's start this over so I can come at it from a different direction because you and I like and respect each other and that wasn't the conversation I was trying to have."

"Thank you, sir. Can I ask if the timing of this conversation and the fact Danny Walsh just left are connected?"

He looked startled by the question. "What? Oh, no. He interrupted what I was doing and then I figured I should get this out of the way before I went back to it. Just a coincidence."

That made her feel a little better, at least. She hadn't been burned by his family. "I'd like to know where this accusation came from."

"It's not an accusation. It's just scuttlebutt. I went to a memorial ceremony yesterday and afterward went to a diner with some guys I've known for decades. Shit, we were probably putting out fires before you were born."

She laughed. "Not quite, sir."

"A long time, anyway. They know Tommy, of course, and he came up in a story one of the guys was telling. That was the opening for the gossip about Tommy's kid and the female lieutenant in my company. I guess there was a fight at Tommy's bar?"

"It's not the first time I've been subject to that kind of speculation, sir. People talk."

"I'm not going to ask you if what they're saying is true. Quite frankly, as long as nobody's job suffers and there's no hanky-panky under this roof, I *don't* consider it any of my business. But I called you in here because I wanted you to know there's talk. Whether or not you care is up to you."

"I do care. People talking about me like that can affect my career. Where I'm assigned can be changed because somebody's worried about the dynamic in the house or a sexual harassment suit or jealous wives hanging around. If they perceive me as being a certain way, I might not even get the chance to prove myself. It's not fair, but when you're a woman, your personal life is questioned as well as your ability to do the job."

"Have you had to deal with that?"

"I've been luckier than some women in the fire service. Back in my early days, I had a group of wives petition to have me transferred because they didn't like me spending so much time with their husbands. I was in the process of moving to a new city, anyway, so nothing came of it. And there was an older guy who refused to go out on a call if I was along because he said women couldn't fight fires and he didn't have time to take care of me. In that case, he was transitioned into a desk job, but I believe he had other infractions going on his record about the same time. Overall, men have treated me with varying degrees of acceptance in their companies, but I haven't had many out-and-out jerks."

"I had some concerns in the beginning," he said. "My initial reaction was what if she can't pull her weight? Or what if one of the guys refuses to work with her or she wants her own bathroom all to herself or somebody says something stupid or tells a joke that gets us slapped with a sexual harassment suit. But your record speaks for itself and, like you said, there's a good group of guys here."

"I appreciate you giving me a chance to prove myself."

"Speaking of this being a good group of guys, I'm going to jump the gun and give you a heads-up before you get the official notification. You'll be with Ladder Company 41, effective immediately upon Danny Walsh's return to duty."

Ladder 41. She closed her eyes for a moment, visualizing the map of stations in her head. It was on the western fringe of the city, maybe twenty minutes away on a decent traffic day, in an affluent neighborhood. More single-family homes, office buildings and upscale shopping, which probably meant fewer fires and more medical calls. It would be an adjustment.

Jamie gave herself a few seconds to process the information and her emotional response to it. She thought she'd managed to keep the fact this was temporary in the back of her mind the entire time she'd been with E-59, but the knot of emotion in her throat and gut told her she hadn't done a very good job of it, after all. And it wasn't only Scott. She'd really felt at home not only with the entire engine company, but the ladder company, too.

"You won't be filling in," Cobb said. "Their LT is moving out of state for family reasons and the district chief wants you. The timing's perfect, too. I'm guessing you heard that there's no reason Walsh shouldn't be able to resume his duties on the twentieth," Cobb continued.

"I'm sure everybody will be glad to have him back," she said, her voice sounding a little hoarse to her own ears. Only two more weeks and she'd have to say goodbye.

"They will. But that doesn't mean any of us want to see you go."

"I understand." She was afraid she was going to cry, and she focused on keeping her back straight and her eyes dry. "Thank you for letting me know."

"They're decent guys, too. I think you'll be a good fit there."

"I've met some of them, sir, and I don't anticipate any problems." And if there were any, she'd deal with them. Being the new "guy" was a situation she'd had a lot of experience with.

"I'll leave it to you whether you want to share the news or not," he said.

"I will when it's a little closer to the date. After the wedding, maybe." She wanted some time to come to grips with the transfer before she was presented with the feelings of all of the other guys. And Scott. She couldn't imagine not working with him anymore, and it was going to take a lot of self-control to keep her emotions in check when she told him she had a transfer date.

Cobb stood, so she did the same, and then he extended his hand. "I stayed awake in the training seminars long enough to know I'm not allowed to hug you."

When she walked out of his office, Jamie felt the first stirrings of a headache and decided a cup of coffee was in order. She climbed the stairs to the third floor rather than going back to her office, with its single-cup brewer, because she felt restless. If she went and sat at her desk, she'd probably do more brooding than she did work.

She wasn't surprised when, after the few guys hanging around the television waved at her, Scott got up and followed her into the kitchen. There was nobody else in there, so he stood close while she grabbed her mug and made herself a coffee.

"Is everything okay?" he asked. She nodded, but didn't volunteer any more information. "Was it about me? About us, I mean?"

She didn't really want to talk about it here, but he looked so worried, she didn't have the heart to put it off. Part of it, at least. "Some gossip got back to Cobb from another house."

"Shit." He leaned against the wall and ran his hands over his hair. "How bad is it?"

"Not bad. He's not concerned about us doing our jobs, but he wanted me to know it was out there."

"Does it bother you?"

"Of course it bothers me." She took a sip of her coffee and wished she'd grabbed some ibuprofen from her desk before coming up. "But we already talked about that. I knew it might happen and I'm okay with it."

"Was that it? He just wanted you to know there's talk?"

She didn't want to lie to him, but she also didn't want to tell him her transfer was in place yet. Not until she'd settled her own feelings about it, and not until they were alone and there wasn't a chance one of the other guys could walk in at any second.

"Mostly. And some administrative stuff," she hedged.

He snorted. "Bureaucracy is one of the reasons I'm not in any hurry to take the lieutenant exam. I might be like Eriksson. Show up, do my job and go home until it's time to retire."

"I've seen your paperwork, so I'll thank you on behalf of everybody who won't have to deal with extra piles of it in the future."

He leaned close, chuckling, and she knew from his body language that if they were anywhere else, he'd grab her and they'd tussle until they ended up kissing. "You're a pretty funny lady, ma'am. We should talk more about my paperwork inadequacies later, when we have more privacy."

She should admonish him for not only the suggestive words, but the way his voice dropped into that low, sexy range that made her toes curl. Instead, she just gave him a stern look and then took her coffee into the TV room before he could say anything else that might tempt her into doing something stupid.

Especially when she was feeling vulnerable because, unless Scott's vision of his future had drastically changed, the clock was now undeniably ticking on the time they had left together.

"How are things going with that woman of yours?"

Scott set the clipboard bearing Lydia and Ashley's lists on a shelf and pulled the wheeled cart closer. "What woman of mine?"

Tommy gave him a look that let Scott know exactly what he thought of the evasion. "I'm a lot of things, son, and perfect definitely ain't one of them. But stupid or blind, I'm not. And I'm not deaf, either. You know as well as I do that the firefighting community is like a small town unto itself, no matter how big the city is."

"Unless my best friend's seeing my sister. Then everybody has better things to talk about."

"Don't go dragging that shit up the night before their wedding just because you don't want to talk about what's going on with you."

"I'm not dragging anything up. You know I'm happy for them and I wouldn't have agreed to be Aidan's best man if I still had a problem with him. I'm just sick of the way everybody protected him and Lydia but aren't shy about running their mouths about me and… I'm just sick of it."

"Maybe people were afraid that temper of yours would destroy your friendship and maybe even your family."

Scott grabbed a box off the shelf and set it on the cart with a thump. "Maybe they should be that concerned about a woman's career, too."

He could feel his mood going sideways on him, and he tried to rein it in. They were doing the prep work for the wedding tomorrow, which meant he and his old man were going to be stuck in the storage room together for a while. He didn't want to butt heads with him the entire time they were getting ready for a celebration.

When he reached for another box, Tommy reached out a hand to stop him. "We're supposed to check each box off the list."

"Shit." He looked at the end of the box for the label and then picked up the checklist. "These are the coasters."

Once Tommy had accepted the bar would be hosting his daughter's wedding and that his beloved pool table would be used as a buffet, he'd thrown himself into making sure it would be special. And he'd started with special coasters listing Aidan's and Lydia's names, along with the date. There were also napkins and plates for the buffet, along with a variety of other things.

"What exactly are you doing in here?" he asked his dad. "I'm doing the boxes and the checklist."

"I'm supervising."

Scott laughed. "Yeah, my ass you are. You do the checklist."

They were supposed to be consolidating the wedding supplies Tommy had ordered on the cart so the staff could set up the place before the wedding. The bar would be closed, but the staff would work and they'd be getting double time. Karen Shea, an emergency room nurse who filled in now and then on a part-time basis, would be working behind the bar. Scott had wondered how that would work, since she and Rick Gullotti had once dated. But Jessica, Rick's fiancée, had met her and didn't mind at all, according to Lydia.

"Seriously, son, how are things with you? I've spent a lot of time worrying about you over the years, and you've seemed different the last few weeks. More settled. Happy, even."

"Happy maybe, but not more settled."

Especially over the last week. Something had been different since Jamie's meeting with Cobb the week before, but he couldn't put his finger on a reason. He kept telling himself it was simply a matter of the gossip bothering her a little more than she'd anticipated it would, but his gut told him there was more to it.

"Ashley told me Danny's recovery is going well and he shouldn't be out much longer."

"That's what I hear. It's good news."

"Is it?"

He looked at his dad, scowling. "Of course it is. Jesus, he's my brother-in-law. He's my friend. Of course I want him recovered and back on the job."

"Does Jamie know where she's going yet?"

"I don't know. I haven't asked her."

"How come?"

Because he didn't want to know. He didn't want to think about what was going to happen when Danny returned and she left the company. He didn't want to think about her moving away and not being around anymore. "If she wants me to know, she'll tell me."

His father gave him a long look he couldn't quite

decipher, and then slowly shook his head. "That's a good way to go about it, if you want to end up old and alone like me."

There was no way in hell Scott wanted that. If he did, he wouldn't have taken a break from dating in the first place. He would have just kept on having company when he felt like it and being alone when that's what he was in the mood for.

"What if a guy doesn't want to end up alone raising kids because their mother got killed on the job?"

Tommy slid a crate over and sat down on it, gesturing for Scott to do the same. He regretted asking the question, if it was going to lead to a lecture. But the question was one he'd been thinking about a lot lately. Was there any sense in trying to extend his relationship with Jamie past her departure from the company if it was doomed to end in failure, anyway?

"Son, you're talking to a man who was left to raise kids alone. I certainly don't have to tell you I screwed it up nine ways to Sunday, but you all made it to adulthood and you're all doing well in life, if I do say so myself."

"But Mom died from breast cancer. It wasn't a choice she made."

"No, it wasn't." His dad sighed. "I don't know that a well-trained, smart firefighter is that much more at risk on the job than she would be doing anything else, to be honest. It's dangerous, sure, but not enough to miss out on a good life together."

"It's hard," Scott said in a low voice. "Growing up without a mom. Not having her anymore still hurts in so many ways even though it's been almost twenty years."

"I know it's hard. I miss her, too. But look at the bigger

picture, son. Lydia's getting married tomorrow. Ashley's having a baby. This life your mother and I made together goes on and it's still a beautiful thing, even though she's not here with us. The thought of missing out on all this because of fear of the what-ifs is sad as hell."

Maybe his old man was right, but Scott knew it was a lot more complicated than him coming to grips with Jamie's job. He knew as well as his dad did that they did everything possible to minimize the risk every time that alarm sounded.

Mostly he was hung up on the fact she hadn't talked about the future with him. If she knew where she was going to be transferred, she hadn't told him. And she hadn't talked about Danny's return or how she felt about that with him. He could only assume it was because she didn't see any of that being particularly relevant to their relationship because it was coming to an end along with her time at Engine Company 59.

The last thing he wanted to do was make things messy by throwing his feelings into the mix. He was still trying to sort through them himself, and he didn't want to ruin the time they had left together by making things awkward.

"Maybe after the wedding's behind us," he told his dad. "I want to enjoy Aidan and Lydia's wedding and then I'll talk to her about her transfer."

"And you'll tell her how you feel about her."

Scott shrugged and got up, picking up the clipboard to give himself something to focus on besides the fear that knotted up in his gut at the thought of telling Jamie he didn't want to give her up when Danny came back, transfer be damned.

"Yeah. After the wedding."

Chapter 13

Jamie looked at herself in the mirror and decided what she saw in the reflection was as good as it was going to get. Even though she didn't have a full-length mirror in the apartment and could only see herself from the waist up in the mirror over the bathroom sink, she thought she looked pretty damn good tonight.

Despite Ashley's declaration that the neckline required jewelry, Jamie wasn't wearing any with the dress. Maybe the neckline demanded it, whatever that meant, but she'd never been a fan of necklaces. She'd put the small diamond studs her dad had bought her when she graduated from high school in her ears and that was as fancy as she got.

Her hair looked good, too. Because she wore it in a French braid to work and often threw it in a ponytail, she wasn't in the habit of styling it, and she didn't really have a knack for it. But she'd gotten lucky today and it was smooth and shiny, hanging slightly past her shoulders. Makeup was another thing she was woefully out of practice with, but she managed to do up her face without getting lipstick on her teeth or poking herself in the eye with the mascara wand. That was a huge win in her book.

The shoes were an issue, and after much deliberation, she'd decided to take a cab to the bar. It wouldn't cost much, and would pay for itself in saving her the hassle of finding a place to park. Walking was out of the question. She'd be lucky if she could walk across the bar without falling on her face, never mind walking *to* the bar.

When the cab pulled up in front of Kincaid's Pub, she was surprised to see a few people waiting on the sidewalk. She paid the driver, watching the line slowly move inside. Hopefully it would move a little faster, she thought as she got out of the cab. It was a little chillier than she'd anticipated and nobody liked to ruin a good look with a hoodie.

The reason for the line became obvious as she stepped into the doorway. Aidan and Scott were greeting people as they entered, and there were a lot of hugs and words being exchanged.

"Hey, Jamie," Aidan said when it was her turn, and she was glad to see he was positively beaming. No nerves or cold feet for this guy. He was unabashedly happy and excited tonight. "Thanks for coming."

She hugged him quickly, finding it a little awkward because her subconscious was always monitoring her interactions with the guys she worked with and hugging didn't usually happen. "Thanks for inviting me."

When she moved on to Scott, her subconscious

perked up again, in an entirely different way. Him, she liked touching and she had to remind herself before stepping into his embrace that they were surrounded by people. A quick in and out, and she couldn't let her breasts make contact with his chest.

"It's good to see you," he murmured against her ear, holding her for a few seconds longer than was probably appropriate.

She shivered and made sure a polite smile was fixed on her face before pulling back. "You guys look sharp in your suits."

"My sisters have good taste." He swept her body with a look that was not even in the neighborhood of polite, and while his expression didn't change, she didn't miss the way his jaw clenched for a second or the very slight flush of heat over his face. "That dress is… I like the… Damn, woman, you are going to kill me tonight."

Very aware that Aidan and the guest he was welcoming behind her were wrapping up their chitchat, Jamie just smiled. "Like you said, your sisters have good taste. They made me buy it."

"I'll thank them later."

She would have liked nothing more than to stand there and talk to Scott for the rest of the night, but there were still people arriving and she didn't want to hold up the line. After looking around, she walked to Rick Gullotti, who was standing with Jeff and Chris, along with two women Jamie assumed were their wives.

"Hey, Jamie." Rick smiled when she stepped into the circle. He introduced the other two women, and then smiled at the pretty blonde woman next to him. "And this is my fiancée, Jessica."

"It's nice to meet you." Jamie shook her hand. "I've heard a lot about you, so it's nice to finally meet you in person. Rick said you were coming back from San Diego for the wedding."

Jessica nodded. "For two weeks, actually. I've decided I want an office space separate from the house so I don't follow in my dad's workaholic footsteps, so I'm going to scout some locations."

"When do you think you'll make the move permanent? If you don't mind my asking."

"At least two more months," she said, wrinkling her nose. "My dad and I have been working on building a client base here, but it's a tight market. Soon, though. And it's worth it."

"Yes, it is," Rick said, and Jamie watched L-37's lieutenant give his future wife such a sappy look she almost laughed.

"Did you see the cake?" Ellen Porter asked. "It's gorgeous!"

"I haven't seen it yet," Jamie said, and before she knew it, Jeff's wife was leading her through the crowd to the pool table room.

She stopped several times to introduce Jamie to different people, though she luckily knew quite a few of them. Jamie didn't mind putting herself in the other woman's hands. Being in a social setting with the guys' wives and having them not regard her with subtle suspicion or, even worse, overt jealously, was a pleasant surprise and she was a lot more relaxed than she'd thought she would be.

"You're right. It's gorgeous," she said when they finally reached the alcove. The pool table had been covered with a protective cloth and had so much food on it, Jamie was surprised the wooden frame wasn't groaning under the weight.

But on a table off to the side, which had been decked out in a white cloth with ribbons, was a three-tiered wedding cake. She wasn't surprised it was a traditional style, with fondant roses around the edges and a porcelain couple on top.

What did surprise her was the second table in the corner. There were at least two dozen chocolate cupcakes on a platter, with two in the middle that had tiny cardboard cutouts of hockey players in Boston Bruins jerseys on top. One had Aidan's name in small script and the other had Scott's.

"Even Kincaids can be reasonable once in a while," Scott said from just behind her, and she turned. He kept about a foot between them, maybe because Ellen and a few others were milling around, looking at the buffet. "It was Ashley's idea, actually. She's always been the family peacemaker—the one who handles negotiations when one of us digs in our heels."

"Technically he's not betraying the actual wedding cake?" When he nodded, Jamie laughed. "Of course not. They're just cupcakes."

"He has to eat the carrot cake, though. That was the deal. He shares the wedding cake with her and does the ceremonial first bite and all that. Then he's free to stuff his face with chocolate cupcakes."

"So it is possible to budge a Kincaid who's being stubborn," she mused. "Good to know."

She heard his phone chime and grinned when he rolled his eyes. "It's a good thing I have unlimited text messages or I'd have to charge a fee for being best man. I thought we'd just take some friends to a bar and have a good time, but there are so many details."

"You had Aidan's bachelor party at a *bar*?"

"Yeah, but it wasn't *this* bar." When she snorted, he looked up from his phone to smile at her. "Okay, when I say bar, I really mean it was a strip club."

"Ah. That explains why I didn't hear anything about it."

"That and the fact it appears men reach an age where shoving money at women just to watch them dance in thongs doesn't seem like all that good a deal anymore, you know?" He shrugged. "Gavin had a good time. The rest of us watched a game on the TV over the bar and occasionally remembered to roast Aidan."

"Sounds like a good time." She'd gone to Lydia's bachelorette party, which had been hosted by Ashley at a bowling alley that had glow bowling, a private room and a bar. They'd had a few drinks, snacked on fried foods and bowled under black lights, and Jamie had a good time, despite not really knowing any of the women besides Lydia and her sister.

"What?" Scott prompted. "No lecture on how barbaric male wedding traditions are?"

She laughed. "Yeah, because I do that so often. And women usually have their traditions, too. Like spending ridiculous amounts of money on raunchy lingerie the bride-to-be is forced to hold up in front of her mother and future mother-in-law, and that she'll never wear because it's all scratching and uncomfortable and she'd rather wear her husband's T-shirts."

"At least bachelor parties usually take place at a venue with some kind of sports on a screen." He leaned a little closer. "And as much as I like you in that dress, I like you in my T-shirts even more."

Her face flamed and she turned back to the tray of cupcakes so nobody would wonder what he'd said that made her blush so badly. "I knew you couldn't behave yourself for an entire night."

"I have to go wrangle wedding things," he said, and then in a lower voice, "but make sure you save me a dance."

She used her cell phone to take a picture of the cupcakes to have an excuse to regain her composure, and then turned back to the pool table. Ellen was taking a photo of it, and something about her demeanor made Jamie think she was going out of her way to look like she hadn't been paying attention, rather than she simply hadn't noticed the exchange between Jamie and Scott.

Great, she thought. At this rate, there wouldn't be anybody left in Boston who didn't know they were a thing before the reception was over.

Scott was in the kitchen with Aidan when he got the text from Ashley that they were about five minutes away and would be coming through the back door. There was a follow-up text threatening bodily harm to Scott if he didn't keep Aidan out front where he couldn't see the bride before Tommy walked her up the makeshift aisle.

He reminded himself this was still twice as relaxed as the show the Kincaid family had put on when Ashley married Danny, and kept his return text short. I've got this.

"Is that Ashley?" Aidan asked, craning his neck to see the screen.

"Five-minute warning."

"We should go out front, I guess. Lydia will kick my ass if I screw up and see her before I'm supposed to. I guess it's the kind of bad luck even Bobby Orr's picture can't fix."

"There's a line for taking a beating if we screw this up. I think Ashley has me in front, since I'm the best man."

Aidan laughed, but for the first time, he looked a little shaky. "I can't believe it's finally time. And, God, I'm so glad she said we didn't have to write our own vows. I don't even remember my own name right now."

"You're not going to pass out on me, like all those guys in the funny videos online, are you?"

Aidan grimaced. "I hope not, but thanks for making sure I worry about that, too."

"Don't lock your knees when you're standing there and you'll be fine." Scott laughed, and reached out to adjust Aidan's tie. "You clean up nice, at least."

"Before we go back out front, I just want to tell you this wouldn't be the happiest day of my life if you weren't standing next to me as my best man."

"You've been like a brother to me since we were kids. Now you'll actually *be* my brother. I'm glad I got my head out of my ass so you didn't have to ask somebody else."

"I don't know if I could have asked anybody else," Aidan said, and then he sighed. "I don't know if I could stand out there and marry Lydia if I didn't have your blessing."

"This is the happiest day of my life, too, so far. I mean that." He hugged Aidan, slapping him on the back. "You haven't been keeping track of how long this little love fest has taken, have you?"

"You're the best man. Throwing yourself in front of the bus is implied if we run out of time."

Scott laughed, but stopped when Tommy turned the corner. His dad looked dapper as hell in his suit, and he grinned when he saw Scott and Aidan. "You boys better hustle. She's coming through that door in about two minutes."

They hustled because the last thing either of them wanted to do was cause Lydia even a second of stress on her wedding day.

The guests quieted for a few seconds when they walked into the bar, and then the excitement level in the room ratcheted up a notch when they realized it was almost time. Scott walked with Aidan to the far end of the bar, where the justice of the peace was waiting.

His phone chimed and he read the text message. "They're inside. Danny's getting the flowers out of the walk-in and then they'll be ready."

As they'd planned in advance, Grant was watching and as soon as Danny emerged from the hall and gave him a thumbs-up, he hit a button on the phone he'd docked in a portable speaker system. Wedding-sounding music filled the bar and everybody quieted.

He couldn't help looking for Jamie in the small crowd, and he found her in the back. She was sitting with Cobb and his wife, and she smiled at him when their gazes met. Since Cobb wasn't looking, he winked at her. Then he cursed silently when a few heads turned toward the back. Since he and Aidan were at the front, people had been watching them and naturally wanted to know who he'd winked at. Luckily, there were a lot of people between him and Jamie.

Scott heard Aidan take a really deep breath before slowly exhaling, and he reached over to squeeze his friend's shoulder as Ashley turned the corner into the bar. She'd definitely gotten her wish as far as wearing a killer dress, he thought, and he struggled not to chuckle at the way Danny looked as he watched his wife walk up the aisle.

When Ashley reached them, she stood on her toes to kiss Aidan's cheek before stepping into her place on the other side of the JP. She gave a quick nod to Grant and a few seconds later the music faded out and then the traditional "Wedding March" began to play.

Seconds later, his sister walked into the bar with her arm tucked under their father's arm. Tommy was standing tall and proud, but Scott could see the emotion in his eyes. The man loved all of his kids, but Scott and Ashley had always known Lydia was his favorite. And they hadn't minded because it diverted his attention away from them.

Lydia looked beautiful. Her dress was amazing and he wasn't surprised to see that she'd worn her hair down. It was thick and wavy and didn't behave very well, so it was usually in a ponytail. But down like it was, the dark curls framed her face perfectly and contrasted the cream-colored dress.

It all paled in comparison to her expression, though. She only had eyes for Aidan and she looked so happy walking toward him, Scott had to clear his throat and blink a couple of times to avoid embarrassing himself. Then she smiled at her almost-husband and Scott almost felt like he was intruding on a private moment by staring, so he let his gaze wander over the crowd.

Jamie's eyes were on the bride, of course. Everybody's were, so he let himself look at her for a few seconds. Her expression was soft, almost dreamy, as she watched his sister walk down the aisle, and she looked beautiful. Then there was the dress, of course. The dress made him think all sorts of indecent thoughts that could get him in trouble when he was standing up in front of his friends and family.

When Lydia reached them, Scott turned and watched his dad kiss her hand before handing it over to Aidan. Then he watched his best friend and his sister exchange an excited, love-filled look that sent envy burning through his veins. He wanted a woman to look at him like that.

The justice of the peace started to talk and Scott had to stifle a snort when he saw Aidan shift his weight so he wasn't locking his knees. He and Ashley handed the rings over when they were called for, and Aidan got through his vows without so much as a hesitation.

"I now pronounce you man and wife. You may kiss the bride."

The cheers and applause could have shaken Bobby Orr's picture right off the wall if the frame wasn't bolted to the brick. He grinned, clapping his hands as Aidan dipped Lydia so deeply for a kiss that she lifted her leg for balance. Behind them, Scott saw Jeff's wife look at her camera's LCD screen and do a small fist pump. She was the best amateur photographer in the community and she'd volunteered to take the photos.

Once he'd set his wife on her feet, Aidan turned to Scott and pulled him in for a hug. Tears burned in Scott's eyes, but he laughed when Lydia wiggled her way into the embrace. He kissed her cheek. "Congratulations, Mr. and Mrs. Hunt."

Chapter 14

Once the ceremony was over, Jamie practically made a beeline for the bar. She knew she couldn't drink enough to blot out the memory of Scott's face when he embraced his best friend as his brother-in-law for the first time, but maybe she could take the edge off the extreme case of warm and fuzzy it had given her.

And maybe a little indigestion, because she knew someday Scott would have that look on his face for his own bride, and Jamie hated that unknown woman with a burning passion.

The woman behind the bar, who was a friend of Rick's, gestured to the lineup of glasses when she approached. "We have beer, champagne and soda. There's a coffee urn over there, with all the fixings, and I can get you water with ice. If you want hard liquor or a cocktail, I can make you one, but Tommy's a cheap bastard so those you have to pay for."

Jamie laughed and took a flute of champagne. "I think I'm in the mood for bubbles tonight."

"Everybody!" Grant stood on a chair and clapped his hands. "Lydia wants Ellen to take some pictures before we eat because some of you eat like toddlers."

The crowd, including Jamie, laughed. There was a lot of milling around as Ellen directed people in front of the bar. With the brick backdrop, and Bobby Orr, along with the old-style lighting, Jamie had to admit it was a good spot. Perfect, really, considering the emotional attachment both the bride and groom felt for the building.

"Hey."

Jamie was surprised to find Lydia at her elbow. She gave her a quick hug. "Congratulations and that was so beautiful and aren't you supposed to be having your picture taken right now?"

"No, *we* are. Come on."

Jamie balked. "What are you talking about?"

"We're starting with the big group pictures because everybody's here. If we start with just me and Aidan, people will get bored and wander off and Ellen will never round them up again. So probably us and the two companies first, like a big old family picture."

"I'll just watch. I can make funny faces if Ellen has trouble getting somebody to smile."

"Shut up. Of course you're going to be in the picture."

"It's not a good idea." She resisted when Lydia tugged at her hand. "I don't belong in a family wedding photo."

"You guys *are* family."

"They are, but I'm moving on. Every time somebody looks at the pictures, I'd just be that woman who filled in for him while he was on medical leave."

Because Lydia and her brother were so much alike, and Jamie knew Scott so well, she didn't have any trouble recognizing the temper rising in the bride. "That's bullshit, Jamie. You think when you peel the name tape off your locker door, we're going to forget who you are? That you've been a part of this family?"

"Do you want me in the picture because I'm part of Engine Company 59 or because of Scott?" When Lydia hesitated, uncertainty flickering in her eyes, Jamie knew she'd hit on the truth. "I *am* moving on and maybe I'll always feel a connection with this fire company, but you don't want to have a family photograph with your brother's ex-girlfriend in it. Or ex-whatever."

Lydia sighed, shaking her head. "Okay, fine. But I want a picture with you and me and Ashley because moving on or not, you won't be my ex-friend."

"Absolutely."

Ellen was starting to get annoyed, judging by the pitch of her voice and the way she was waving her hand, so Lydia gave her a final *I mean it* look and walked away. They started lining up, but when Scott sent a questioning look in Jamie's direction, she shook her head.

Then she sighed when Scott pulled his sister off to one side. She watched him and Lydia talking, their conversation obviously intense, while she sipped her drink. He looked mad, and his sister was obviously trying to calm him down. If Jamie had to guess, she'd say Scott thought Lydia had made a decision to exclude Jamie from the photograph.

She'd just decided to go over and tell him what was going on—or just be in the damn picture if that's what it took—when the fight went out of Scott. She didn't know what Lydia said but, after a quick look in Jamie's direction, he shrugged and got in line where he was told.

Once the bride and the photographer were content with the shots they had, Grant put on some dance music and the party started. They ate, drank and made merry as hell, and Jamie moved from group to group. There were stories and laughter, and the more drinks that were served, the more people danced.

And maybe because Aidan and Lydia had limited the guest list to friends and family who mostly all knew each other, there was no drama and everybody was having a good time.

She might have had a better time if she wasn't trying to stay one step ahead of Scott, Jamie thought. Or, more accurately, many steps away from him. He wasn't drinking tonight because he'd volunteered to make sure everybody who left the reception had a designated driver or a cab waiting, but he was enjoying himself and she wouldn't put it past him to forget himself if he got within arm's reach of her.

Rick Gullotti stepped over to her, so close their elbows were almost touching. "Hey, Jamie."

"Hey, Rick. You having a good time?"

"Yeah. How about you?"

She nodded, looking around the room. "I am."

"You are, or you could be?"

She frowned, turning slightly to face him. "What do you mean?"

"I'm not sure how to say this without overstepping,

but this is…a safe place. Everybody in this bar right now has your back. We have Scotty's back. Dance with the man. Hold his hand. Enjoy your night."

And again she was put in a position of not wanting to either deny or confirm. She sipped her drink and looked at Scott across the room, wondering what the hell she was supposed to do now.

"It's not something you can hide, you know," he continued. "It's the small things. Glances. The way you talk to each other. You're both more relaxed when you're together. Couple shit, you know?"

"Couple shit?" She laughed. "So tell me, if everybody thinks Scott and I are involved, why were Grant and Gavin trying to hook him up with a date for the wedding?"

"Yeah, those two aren't exactly relationship experts. I don't think either of them knew back then. But Gavin came to me a few days ago with some rumors he heard while taking a shift for a guy in another ladder company. Nothing too bad, but bored guys will talk about anything."

"And what did you tell him?"

"I told you both show up for every tour and do your jobs, and unless it affects the companies, it's not really our business. Of course, when you don't deny something outright, people usually take it as a confirmation. But Gavin told me that his response when asked if it was true Tommy's son was messing around with his lieutenant was basically that you're a great firefighter and he couldn't give a shit less who you sleep with."

She looked him in the eye because he was a man she had a lot of respect for professionally, besides liking him personally. "What's your opinion of the situation?"

"If I thought you and Scotty being involved would cloud your judgment and put a single firefighter at risk, you'd be gone already. And if I thought it would cause friction in the house, we would already have had a discussion." He didn't even blink as he spoke, and she knew he meant every word. "But it hasn't been a problem. Trust me, I had to deal with the fallout when Scotty found out Aidan had been seeing Lydia behind his back, so I can tell you whatever you two are doing isn't even a blip on my potential problem radar."

"And I'll be leaving soon, so it would be a temporary situation anyway," she said, and no matter how many times she verbalized the inevitable, she felt the sharp pang of sadness.

"You'll be transferring to another station. But you'll still be in Boston, so you're not really leaving us." He sighed. "You know, if the situation was different and it wasn't Danny Walsh's chair you've been sitting in, I would push Cobb to keep you here. I really hate seeing you go and I want you to know that no matter where you end up, you have my respect and support. Danny's, too. And Cobb's. Hell, everybody's."

Tears burned Jamie's eyes. "That means a lot to me. Thank you."

"Jesus, go dance with Scotty before he thinks I made you cry and tries to kick my ass."

She laughed and saw Scott's head turn until he located her and their gazes locked across the room. "I think I will."

Scott watched her approach, his gaze sweeping down her body and back up before locking with hers.

As she passed a table bearing a tray, she set her empty glass on it and kept walking. His eyebrow arched and she guessed her intent must have shown on her face.

"Hey, gorgeous," he said when she walked up close enough to him to leave no doubt.

"I was told I should dance with you and hold your hand."

"Really?" He scanned the crowd, then looked back at her. "I saw you talking to Rick."

"Yeah. And Rick suggested that everybody in this bar has our backs and we should just enjoy this night."

He laced the fingers of one hand through hers while twisting to set his glass down. "I always did like Rick."

His other hand wrapped around her waist before coming to rest at the small of her back, and she lifted her arms to cup the back of his neck in her hands. Then they were swaying to the music. Maybe they were in time or maybe they weren't. Jamie barely even noticed the song.

She was finally in Scott's arms, and nobody around them cared.

Scott turned the lock on the front door and collapsed against it with a sigh. "I thought they'd never leave."

Jamie laughed and then looked around at the debris from what had been one hell of a good party. As wedding receptions went, it had definitely been one of her favorites. "In all of the details they sent you by text, did your sisters happen to tell you how much of this you have to clean up before you go home?"

"We've got this," Karen called from behind the bar. "I actually have some friends arriving in about half an hour who Tommy is going to pay a crap ton of money to play cleaning fairies. A few hours from now, it'll be like it never happened."

"That's my kind of magic," Scott said. "I'm beat."

"But it was fun," Jamie said. She'd definitely never believe this night had never happened. And it had already been magical, as far as she was concerned.

"How many drinks did you have?" he asked, pushing her hair back behind her ear.

"Not enough so I'm drunk, but definitely enough so I'm not sober. But I took a cab here, so I wouldn't be driving anyway."

"I'll bring you home."

"You just said you were beat." She put up the token protest because he did look tired.

"Not *that* beat." He grinned. "Besides, making sure everybody had a designated driver was one of the duties assigned to me, remember?"

"Great. I just need to find my shoes. I think they got kicked under the pool table earlier."

"I'll grab them."

She made herself useful while she waited, dumping plastic glasses into a huge lined garbage can on wheels that somebody from the kitchen had brought out. It hadn't escaped her notice that, after the reception had begun and the formalities and photographs were taken care of, all of the glassware had been swapped out for plastic stemware and cups. Nice ones, but still disposable.

"Okay, I found your shoes." Scott dangled her heels from one hand. But then he held up the other hand, from which a pair of cream pumps hung. "I don't know whose these are, but somebody left here barefoot."

Karen laughed. "This wouldn't be the first wedding venue to have a lost and found. I'll put them here behind the bar and stick a note on the register for Ashley."

"I can't believe she has to work tomorrow," Jamie said. "I know she didn't drink because of the baby, but being in a bridal party is exhausting even if you're not pregnant."

"Yeah, but I worked tonight and won't be leaving for several more hours." Karen shrugged. "And we all thought it would be nice to give Lydia the day off. Now go on, you two. Let us get to work."

"Are you giving me a ride home?" Jamie asked, taking her shoes from him and then groaning as she stepped into them. No wonder one of the other guests chose to leave with bare feet.

"I'm sure as hell not letting you walk. And, no, you're not taking a cab, either, so let's go."

He was parked out in the back lot, so they said good-night to Karen and then stopped in the kitchen to say thank-you and good-night to the staff who'd remained to help. They'd stay until Karen's cleaning fairies showed up because no employees were ever left totally alone at Kincaid's, especially the women.

Then they went out into the brisk night, the chill setting in immediately. Screw the hoodie, she should have ruined the dressy look with a parka. But he'd hit the remote start at some point because the engine was running and the parking lights were on.

He opened her door first, and then laughed when she looked from the ground to the running board and up to the seat. "Here, let me help you up."

His hands slid under her armpits and he lifted just

enough so she could get her foot onto the running board without tearing her dress or flashing any surveillance cameras monitoring the parking lot. Then she turned and sank onto the warm leather seat.

She sighed, closing her eyes, and heard him chuckle. "Guess you're glad I'm spoiled right about now."

"I take it all back. Also, I'm buying a truck."

He was laughing as he closed her door, and a moment later, he climbed into the driver's seat and inserted the key. "You can get heated seats in a car, you know."

She opened her eyes and turned her head in his direction, suddenly very tired. "Yeah, I know. I hate spending a lot of money on vehicles, though. I just need to get from point A to point B."

"Yeah, but I'm taking you to point B with a nice, warm backside."

It didn't take long for them to get to that point B, but parking was a bit of an issue. "You can just drive by and push me out if you want."

"You've been drinking. I'm walking you to your door."

"I told you I'm not drunk."

Scott nodded, then suddenly whipped the truck down a side street so fast she almost smacked her head on the window. "Yeah, and you also told me you're not sober."

He pulled into a space she wasn't sure actually *was* a space and killed the engine. She knew that, as long as he wasn't parked in a way that was blatantly illegal or caused complaints, he'd get a little more leeway than other drivers because of his job. Besides the Firefighters Memorial license plate framed by a Boston

Fire holder and the sticker in the back window, most of the police officers in the neighborhood knew him and would recognize his truck.

Her door opened and he put his arms up to help her out. She clutched his shoulders and was thankful he held on to her a few extra seconds so she could find her balance on the heels. Maybe she'd had a drink or two more than she thought she had.

He laced his fingers through hers and they walked down the sidewalk together in silence. The neighborhood was quiet and she might have enjoyed the stroll if she wasn't freezing. And if her feet didn't hurt so much she could feel each impact with the concrete up into her shins.

Once they were inside the front door, she stopped and stepped out of the heels. Walking up barefoot wasn't ideal, but she wasn't going to make it up all those flights of stairs in the shoes.

"Do you want me to carry you?" he asked. She imagined him draping her body over his shoulders and laughed. "I'm serious. I know how to do that, you know."

She laughed harder, until he actually shushed her. "You're going to wake up the whole building. Start climbing, Rutherford."

By the time they reached the top of the stairs and entered her apartment, Jamie was ready to just fall on the floor and sleep there. And Scott didn't look much better, despite the fact he hadn't had anything to drink.

"Are you staying?" she asked, tossing the heels into the shoe pile. She'd put them back in their box under the bed tomorrow and maybe add a sticky note to the lid noting she shouldn't try to wear them for more than two or three hours, and even then only if there were a lot of opportunities for sitting.

"I'd like to." He looked down at himself. "I'll have to do the walk of shame in the morning."

"If you're going to do the walk of shame, you may as well do it in a fine-looking suit."

He pulled her close and kissed her until the chill of the night had been chased away and replaced by heat. "I had a good time tonight."

"It was a beautiful wedding and a great party."

"I had a good time *with you* tonight. It was nice to touch you and hold your hand and laugh with you without worrying about it being a secret."

"It was." She wasn't sure how she'd feel walking into the station for their next tour, but she had no regrets. Even if it turned out to be awkward, she didn't have a lot of time left there.

"What just happened?" He put his finger under her chin and tilted her head back a little so he could see her face. "You looked sad for a minute."

"I'm not sad." She smiled to prove her point. "Just tired."

He hooked his finger into the neckline of her dress and slid it up until he could pull the fabric off her shoulder. "We should get you out of this dress, then, and get you into bed."

They made love slowly—almost tenderly—and afterward Jamie curled into his embrace. It was nice, she thought, that he wasn't going anywhere. She could close her eyes and drift off with his arms wrapped around her.

And in the morning she would tell him about the transfer.

Chapter 15

Scott slowly opened his eyes, not surprised by his urge to smile into Jamie's hair. He wasn't much of a morning person, but waking up with her curled against him was definitely getting the day off to a good start.

He kissed her hair, pretty sure she was awake since she wasn't snoring. Her bunk might be on the second floor, but she'd nodded off on the couch or in the chair on the third floor often enough for him to know she snored like the rest of them. It just annoyed him less when she did it.

"Good morning," he said when she tried to burrow deeper into her pillow.

"Coffee."

"Are you hungover or is that how you greet every new day?"

"Coffee."

He chuckled and brushed her hair away from her neck so he could kiss her nape. "Five more minutes."

She rolled over so she was facing him, also managing to move a little farther away in the process. Her eyelids were not only very heavy this morning, but still bore some traces of last night's makeup since they'd been so tired they made love and fell asleep almost immediately.

"Good morning," she mumbled.

"Do you have stuff to make breakfast or should we go out?"

She shrugged one shoulder, making the comforter slip a little. "I don't know. I have coffee, though."

He realized that she might not want to go out to a restaurant, despite the fact they'd obviously been a couple last night. Rick had told her everybody in the bar had their backs, but the reception was over. But what could it hurt to be seen sharing a meal at this point? Everybody who really mattered to him had been at the wedding and they already knew there was a good chance they'd spent the night together.

"What are you thinking about?" she asked, her voice more clear as she shook off sleep. "You look very serious all of a sudden."

"I was wondering if we could go out to a restaurant or if we're back to hiding in your apartment."

"We might as well go out." She pulled up on the sheet to cover her mouth while she yawned. "The only people who don't know are people who don't matter much, especially since I already know what's going to happen."

He frowned. "What's going to happen with what?"

Her eyes widened and he realized she hadn't meant

to say that. She was probably still groggy and her think-first filter wasn't awake yet. "With my transfer."

"You found out the day Danny stopped in, didn't you?" It made sense to him now. "It wasn't only the conversation with Cobb that made you seem off. You found out where you're transferring."

"Yeah. I didn't want to say anything until after the wedding."

Because it was bad news. Or at least news that didn't bode well for them, he thought, if she was worried it would be a damper on the celebration. "Where are you going?"

"I'm transferring to Ladder 41, effective immediately upon Danny's return to full duty."

"Ladder 41. They're good guys."

"Yeah, I've met some of them at different events and they seem to be. I know they have a good record."

"They're not close, but I guess they're not that far away, either. Are you going to move?"

She shrugged. "Not right away, if at all. I might see how the commute goes for a while because I like my apartment. Plus L-41 is in a pretty swanky neighborhood, so I'm not sure I can afford to live close enough to work to make it worth moving again, anyway."

He waited a few seconds, wondering if she'd give him some kind of clue that he might factor into her decision, too. Maybe a comment about how staying in her apartment meant they'd be able to continue seeing each other. A joke about her still being on his route to the ice rink, at least.

But the words he wanted to hear from her didn't come. He rolled over to sit on the edge of the bed and scrubbed his hands over his face.

He'd known it would happen. Their relationship was never meant to be anything but temporary. He couldn't have gotten any bigger a clue they were nearing the end than he had last night.

Denying the bride's request to be in a wedding photo was kind of a big deal, so Jamie must have felt pretty strongly about not being in what Lydia considered the family picture. It was awkward when the formal family shot had an ex-girlfriend in it, she had said according to his sister.

Ex-girlfriend. She already thought of herself as his ex and they hadn't even broken off the relationship yet. He'd put it out of his mind, especially when she'd walked across the bar and into his arms, but now the pain of hearing that explanation from Lydia returned with such a vengeance, it made his stomach hurt.

"Danny said he's on track to return to duty next Friday," she said, her voice very quiet.

"Yeah, that's what he told us."

"Scott." He didn't respond right away, and then he jumped when he felt her hand on his back. "Hey."

All he could think about was how glad he was that he'd put off taking his dad's advice to tell Jamie how he felt about her. While he'd been falling in love with her and trying to wrap his mind around how their future would look together, she'd known the details of her departure and hadn't even bothered to tell him.

At least he'd be spared the embarrassment of having his feelings rejected. The pain would be bad enough. He didn't need humiliation piled on top of it.

After making sure his expression wouldn't reveal any of his emotional turmoil, he shifted on the bed so he could see her. "We'll miss you around the station."

He could tell by her eyes that the words had hit their target and she hadn't missed the far less personal *we*. "I'll miss you...all, too."

"It's not time to say goodbye yet," he said, as much for himself as for her. "I'm going to make coffee and then we can figure out what we want to do about breakfast."

She smiled, but it didn't quite reach her eyes. "That sounds like a plan."

Scott was brewing the first cup when he heard her get up and go into the bathroom. Blowing out a long, slow breath, he leaned his hip against the counter and tried to get his head on straight.

He could end it today, he thought. The door was open to a *hey, it's been fun but you need to focus on moving on* talk. Sure, they still had a couple of shifts left to work together, but their relationship hadn't been a factor on the job up to this point, anyway.

But the idea made him almost physically ill and he knew he wouldn't be able to say the words. Not today, anyway. Even after the double whammy of the ex-girlfriend comment last night and learning she hadn't told him about her transfer this morning, he wasn't ready.

He wasn't sure he'd ever be ready, actually. But he knew the moment wasn't now, so he'd keep on going the way they had been and hope she didn't see the truth in his eyes.

Jamie sat down at her table, tucking one leg under herself, and opened her laptop. She hated sitting in the kitchen chair when she talked to her mom, but the alternative was standing at the counter. She'd learned the hard way curling up with her laptop on the couch led to some unflattering camera angles.

She poked around Facebook until she got the text from her mom that she was ready whenever Jamie was. After taking a sip of her coffee, she initiated a video chat. And when her mom's face appeared on the screen, she smiled. The Rutherford household had a desktop with a large monitor that her mom had angled so it was flattering, but she was fussing with her hair when it went live.

"You look beautiful, Mom. As always."

"Oh, hi, honey." She leaned forward, peering at her monitor. "You look a little tired."

Jamie smiled because she knew her mom said it out of concern and not criticism. "Restless night, I guess."

"Is everything okay?"

"Yeah. Probably something I ate." She didn't like lying to her mother, but the truth would worry her a lot more than thinking her daughter ate something too rich before going to bed.

She'd screwed up by not telling Scott about the transfer right away. He hadn't said anything, but his mood had changed and she didn't think it was the transfer itself. They'd both known that was going to happen.

After far too much time tossing and turning, alone in her bed last night, she'd decided it had to be the timing. She'd wanted to wait until after the wedding to start the process of saying goodbye, but because of their relationship, she should have confided in him the day she found out where she was going.

Their relationship. She wished she knew what that meant.

"Jamie?" Her mom's voice broke into her thoughts. "What's wrong?"

"Nothing." She forced herself to sit up and look chipper. "So when do you think I should come home?"

"Is it that young man you've been seeing?"

"We're not really seeing each other." Jamie sighed. She really didn't want to try to explain Scott to her mother.

"You told me you'd gone on a date. But I heard a man laughing once while I was on the phone with you, and assumed he was watching television. And when you sent me a picture of how you organized those baskets in your living room, there was a hockey stick leaned up against the wall. Since you can't ice-skate *or* roller-skate, I assume it wasn't yours."

"And yet you didn't ask."

"You're my private one, sweetie, and you talk when you're ready. I took for granted you'd tell me if it got serious." Jamie looked away, taking a sip of her coffee, and she heard her mom sigh. "Uh-oh."

Looking into her mug, Jamie mimicked the sound. "So I kind of love him, I think."

"Oh, that's wonderful."

She looked at the screen, knowing she was about to disappoint her mom. "Not really. We're not…it's not. Dammit. We work together, so it's awkward."

She wasn't surprised when her mother's eyebrows shot up. She knew how her daughter felt—or *had* felt—about becoming involved with fellow firefighters. "He's in your company?"

"Yeah."

"How does he feel about you?"

She shrugged one shoulder, leaning back in the

chair as she untucked her leg before it went to sleep. "We have a good time together, but that's it. And I'm leaving anyway, so it's a moot point."

"Your text said you'd be working in a different part of the city, but that you're not giving up your apartment. Maybe not working together will be a good thing."

"We're not really marriage compatible. We kind of have different views of raising a family, I guess."

"Because of your job?"

Jamie nodded. "Yeah. Plus, it was always kind of meant to be temporary. It wouldn't be fair to spring something more on him at this point."

Her mom pointed a finger at her computer's camera, which made Jamie smile. "It wouldn't be fair to *you* to walk away from a man you *kind of love, you think* just because coming to a compromise might be hard work."

"I know he likes me, Mom. We like being together."

"You should tell him how you feel, Jamie."

She nodded, though the thought made her stomach hurt. "I should. But I should wait until I'm done at that station in case things get awkward. I don't want it to spill over into work."

Her mom narrowed her eyes. "You mean you want to wait until after this casual thing of yours should be over because then if he calls you or stops by, you'll take it as a sign he might want it to continue."

She chuckled, not bothering to deny it. "Maybe. But also because I don't want things to be messy at work. Now, when do you think is a good time for me to visit? I'd like to wait until at least July so I'm settled in at the new station before I take a couple of tours off."

As she hoped, the prospect of nailing down details distracted her mom from Jamie's *kind of* love life. She looked down, frowning, and she knew her mom had her planner open on the desk.

"I think Tori's planning a family vacation the week after July Fourth, so maybe later in July? Let me look."

While her mother looked at the calendar on which she tracked four households in two states, Jamie drank her coffee and thought about what her mother had said. While she was serious about not wanting to take the chance of souring their relationship while they still worked together, her mom knew her better than anybody and she probably wasn't wrong about waiting to see if Scott wanted to keep seeing her once she'd transferred.

Maybe working beside her for weeks had changed his mind about her job being too risky for a mother. It was one thing to imagine a woman rushing into a burning building when she had kids at home. But he knew her. He knew she was damn good at her job.

"Maybe the third week of July?"

Jamie pulled up the calendar on her phone to see if she had anything scheduled for then, though she was sure she didn't. It was time to give her mom her full attention and put Scott out of her head. They had two more tours together and then they'd see if the end of her time at Engine Company 59 was also the end of their time together.

Chapter 16

"You look tired, Hunt. Maybe you should go take a nap and catch up on sleep."

Scott laughed at the ribbing Jeff was giving Aidan. They'd been at it most of the day, giving the newlywed a hard time about everything from looking sleep deprived to trying to get him to do an air management test with his SCBA and tank now that he was dragging around a ball and chain.

Jamie laughed, too, and he tried hard not to look at her. She was sitting in one of the chairs, a book in her lap, but he hadn't seen her actually turn a page for at least fifteen minutes.

They hadn't seen each other since he left her place the morning after the wedding, and they'd seemed okay then. Yesterday, he'd gotten sucked into doing errands and chores for his old man, and she'd promised her mom they'd do a video chat to talk about when would be a good time for Jamie to go home for a visit. Other than a few text messages, they hadn't spoken until they arrived for their tour today.

She'd smiled and said good-morning, as she always did, and they'd gone about their usual routine. He also noticed that none of the guys acted any differently toward her or made remarks about her relationship with him, which was good. He knew she'd been worried about that, no matter how much Rick had assured her it wouldn't be an issue.

So everything was the same. And yet everything was different. Because now he knew when she was leaving and where she was going. And he also knew she hadn't cared enough to share the information with him. He was just a guy she was killing time and having a good time with.

Just like he'd offered to be.

Tossing the magazine he'd been flipping through onto the coffee table, he stood and headed for the weight room. He couldn't stand sitting around anymore while his mind ran in circles. He might not be able to stop thinking about Jamie, but he could wear out his body.

He wasn't surprised when Aidan followed him in. Besides the fact the poor guy probably wanted a break from the teasing, they usually spotted each other. Aidan kicked the door closed behind them and hit the button to turn the radio on.

Scott grabbed a pair of gloves from the shelf and walked over to the heavy bag because he felt more like hitting something than lifting weights. Aidan positioned himself on the other side of it, ready to hold it for him.

"You're not going to knock me on my ass, are you?" he asked, peering around the black bag.

"Only if you're weak."

Aidan laughed. "That's it. Make it my fault you're in a bad mood and want to beat the shit out of something."

"Who says I'm in a bad mood?" He'd gone out of his way to make sure he didn't act any differently today than he did any other day.

"You might be able to bullshit them, but you can't bullshit me."

Scott fidgeted with the closure on the left glove until it was as tight as he liked it, and then shoved his right hand into the glove. Then he held it out to Aidan so he could fasten it for him. "Jamie's going to Ladder 41. The end of this week when Danny comes back."

Aidan nodded, pressing the Velcro down to secure it. "That's pretty quick."

"I guess, although we knew from day one she'd transfer out of here. She's temporary."

Aidan couldn't have looked more serious if he'd been at a funeral. "Is she?"

"Is she what?"

"Temporary."

Scott growled and hit the bag. "I just said she was. She was just filling in for Danny."

"What about you guys? She's not temporary to you, is she?"

He hit with the left, getting into a rhythm of solid jabs to warm up. "Did Lydia tell you why Jamie wasn't in the pictures?"

"Yeah, she did. But how does she know your feelings about the relationship have changed if you don't tell her?"

He threw some hooks, mixing it up a little. The blows were hard enough so Aidan had to brace himself to avoid getting knocked around on the other side. "Who says they have?"

"Seriously, why do you even *try* to bullshit me? I know you, Scotty."

Scott was winding up to take a swing at the bag that just might knock Aidan back against the wall when the alarm sounded. He ripped off the gloves and tossed them aside as they ran for the door.

"Three-story, multifamily residence. Juveniles reported trapped on third floor."

Shit. They went for the pole. It was rarely used anymore because it wasn't the safest way to get to the ground floor, but every second counted.

He barely paused long enough to shove his feet into his boots and pull up the bibs. The coat and helmet he took with him and he ran around the truck to climb into the cab. Firing the engine, he immediately hit the sirens so by the time the rest of the company was on board, he was ready to roll and—hopefully—drivers and pedestrians on the street had ample warning to get the hell out of the way.

The second E-59's nose cleared the door enough for Jamie to see and tell him he was clear, he hit the gas pedal hard. Usually he noticed her reactions to corners and his aggressive way of getting through intersections, but today he had no attention to spare.

He brushed a car, parked illegally too close to a corner. "Fuck."

Jamie pulled out her phone, but didn't make a call

as they approached another intersection. Once she'd let him know the side street was clear, she slipped it back into its pouch. They'd report the damage and drown in the paperwork later.

They pulled up in front of the address, both drivers having to lay on the horns to get the idiot bystanders out of the way. There was plenty of flame and smoke for them to capture on their cell phones, but they needed to do it from well across the street.

The guys were spilling out before the trucks even stopped and he pulled his coat on as he climbed down. The ladder company was busting ass getting their landing pads down so they could raise the ladder, and he joined his guys, who were pulling out the line. Jeff had the spanner wrench to open the hydrant.

"Are there any adults up there with the kids?" he yelled to Jamie.

She shook her head. "They don't think so. Latchkey kids, home alone. Oldest is ten."

"Shit. Any visual confirmation?"

"No. The neighbors are sure they're in there, though."

Probably hiding. Maybe under the beds or maybe in a closet. Best-case scenario, they were all together and as soon as the ladder was up, a shout would have the oldest guiding them to the window.

"Fire started on the first floor. Cigarette and oxygen tank." Jamie cast a quick glance around to make sure they were ready. "All right. We need to keep those flames down until they get those kids out."

As they moved onto the porch, ready to blast the first floor with water, Scott registered movement on the ladder. Gavin was on his way up, scrambling toward the window. He could hear the crowd across the street, shouting pleas for them to find the kids. Sirens blaring as more police officers and fire companies and the EMS arrived. The incident command SUV skidding to a stop.

He was about to step from chaos into hell, and as he always did when it looked like things might get rough, he sent up a quick and silent prayer to his guardian angel.

Okay, Mom. I need you to watch my back. He grabbed on to the line behind Aidan and tapped his shoulder to tell him to go. *And today watch out for Jamie, too, okay?*

Jamie hit Aidan's shoulder to get his attention because either it was too loud for him to hear her or her radio was cutting in and out. She hadn't taken the time to figure out which. "We need to get up to the second floor. Flames in the back and they don't have the kids yet. Another company's at the rear, but they don't have a good angle."

He nodded, and they moved toward the stairs at the front. She hated moving floors before the fire was contained to at least a minimum degree, but they had guys on the third floor. Since she knew they wouldn't retreat without finding the children, they had to do everything they could to keep the fire from breaching that floor for as long as possible.

She didn't know if the entire building was decorated in cheap synthetic fabrics or if there were chemicals they didn't know about, but the smoke was thick and dark. It played hell on visibility, but they got the line to the second floor and turned the water on the flames. If they could beat it down from this direction while the other companies attacked it from the rear, they might be able to keep it from spreading any further.

Static crackled in her ear and she wanted to shake her head to clear it. Something was definitely wrong with her radio and it was an extremely shitty time to have a malfunction. Gullotti's voice came through in pieces, though.

They had the oldest and middle children. The toddler had been down for a nap and by the time they realized what was happening and went to find her, she'd already hidden. While the flames hadn't reached them yet, smoke had, and they'd gotten disoriented. They were being treated and the L-37 was going to have to do a room-by-room sweep, looking in every nook and cranny until they found the little girl.

"We have to keep this contained," she shouted, and her crew acknowledged.

She lost track of how long they worked, beating back the flames only to have them jump or reflame. It wasn't exactly a hoarding situation, but the apartment was full enough to offer plenty of fuel for the fire while hampering their movements.

It would have been tempting to back down and get her guys out of harm's way, but she couldn't surrender the third floor to the fire.

"Shit!"

She turned in time to see a beam fall, narrowly missing Grant's helmet. He reacted, jumping to the right, but then went right back to the line. Looking past him, Jamie saw the old furniture surrounded by stacks of magazines and swore under her breath.

"You need to find that kid *now*," she shouted into

her radio. Not that they weren't trying their best, but they were losing ground and she needed him to pick up on the sense of urgency.

It was at least five more minutes before they found the toddler hiding in a lower kitchen cabinet and got her out onto the ladder.

"We're pulling back," Gullotti reported. "Ladder 37 is clear of the structure."

"Let's get the hell out of here," Jamie shouted. The fire could have the building and the piles of junk somebody had been collecting since probably before she was even born.

They started their retreat, which wasn't easy since they had to manage the line as they went. And they were halfway back to the stairs when the building shifted and a ceiling joist dropped onto Grant, whose knees buckled.

Shit. Jamie moved to his side, wondering why the hell this house had it out for the young guy. He was already trying to get back on his feet, but he was wobbly and she could see the joist had damaged his tank connections.

They had to get him out of there.

"Go," she yelled, gesturing at the other guys. They could handle the line and make sure she didn't run into a dead end of flame. "Make sure the exit's clear."

She grabbed Grant's coat, pulling him close. But before she could get into position to hoist him up onto her shoulders, Scott was there. "I'll take him."

"I told you to clear the exit." The smoke was seriously hampering visibility now, and she knew the flames were devouring the place almost unchecked at this point.

"Aidan's got it, and there's another company in support. Let me carry him down the stairs."

She was so angry she couldn't even speak for a few seconds. Carrying Grant down the stairs she could do. Physically it was harder for her to backtrack out of the structure while wrestling with the line, and therefore more dangerous for everybody. "I gave you an order."

He ignored her and hauled Grant onto his shoulder. The younger guy struggled, trying to tell them he could walk, but he was so shaky and disoriented, it would be faster to carry him.

The building shifted again with a creaking groan, and she knew they couldn't spare even another second to have a pissing match about who was in charge. She took off toward the stairs, staying just far enough ahead to make sure their path was clear without losing sight of Scott and Grant.

They caught Aidan, and Jamie grabbed the line behind him as he sprayed what had to be a reignition point. She waved for Scott to take Grant behind them and then pointed at a window. It had already been smashed out, probably by another engine company, and it was only a few seconds before guys appeared on the other side to take Grant.

Scott didn't go out, though. He came back and tapped her on the shoulder. "I've got this. You should get out."

She ignored him and shouted to Aidan. "We're clear, Hunt. Let's get clear."

Once outside, they grabbed waters and protein bars from the volunteers and walked as a group to check on Grant.

He was sitting up on the stretcher in the back of the ambulance with a white collar on, looking annoyed.

The paramedic who seemed to be in charge looked at them and, noting the rank on her helmet, addressed her comments to Jamie.

"He says he's fine." She rolled her eyes. "I think he might have a mild concussion. Initial smoke inhalation, but he snapped out of that pretty quickly when we put the oxygen mask on him. We're taking him in to have a look at his neck and spine just to make sure there aren't any hairline fractures in there. It looks like his tank took the brunt of it, but his tank's on his back, so we want to be cautious."

"I'm fine," Grant called, trying to catch Jamie's eye.

She pointed a finger at him, having had her fill of people not doing what they were told. "You're going to the hospital. When they say you can leave, you can leave. Do you understand?"

"Yes, ma'am."

Once the ambulance doors were closed, they walked back to the truck to start getting their equipment together and repacked. They'd hang around for a while in case it took a long time to burn down, but for now they could rest for a few minutes.

"Jamie." She heard Scott's voice and turned to face him, giving him *the look*. It was the look she'd been about to unleash on the guy in the bar before Scott punched him instead. He stopped in his tracks, his eyes widening.

"I gave you an order and you disobeyed it." She didn't want to do this in front of both companies, but if he wasn't going to give her a choice, at least she could steer him toward keeping the conversation about the job.

"For a good reason."

"The only good reason for you to disregard what

I say is if you think I'm unfit for duty or command. You didn't indicate to me or to anybody else that you believed that to be so."

"I had personal reasons," he said, not giving up.

Keenly aware of the fact they had an audience, Jamie made sure her voice was low. "Your personal reasons have no place here."

She turned to walk away, which, in hindsight, was probably a mistake. Scott grabbed her arm, spinning her to face him. In her peripheral vision, she saw the other guys stop trying to pretend they couldn't hear as they all turned to look. Aidan even took a step forward, but Rick held out his hand to stop him.

"I couldn't do it," he said in a hoarse voice. "I couldn't stand there and do nothing but listen to the radio, praying to hear your voice. I did that with Danny and I knew I couldn't leave without you. And if you think I was disrespecting your ability to do your job, then I'm sorry. But I love you, Jamie. I fell in love with you and I couldn't stand by and do nothing."

His words fell on her like blows. At any other time, in any other place, those words might have made her the happiest woman on the planet. But not here, on an active scene in front of the guys in her command.

She jerked her arm away. "If you loved me— hell, if you really knew anything about me and paid attention—you would never have done this here."

Without giving him a chance to say anything more, Jamie turned and walked away with her back straight, her eyes dry and her heart splintering into ruin.

Scott looked up when the swinging doors to the emergency room opened, but the nurse walked to a family sitting across the hallway from them. Since it wasn't anybody about Grant, he dropped his head back against the wall and stared at the ceiling tiles some more.

He'd blown it. His temper and lack of impulse control had gotten him into a lot of trouble over the course of his life, but he'd never sabotaged his own happiness the way he had today.

"Stop beating yourself up."

Scott wanted to ignore Aidan, but right now he was the only person Scott had to talk to. The others were back at the station, since Jamie had volunteered the two of them to go to the hospital and wait for news on Grant. Or to bring him back if he was released.

He knew she'd just wanted him out of her sight.

"Why the hell did I do that? I mean, I know why I disobeyed her. It was wrong and stupid, but I know what happened. But telling her I did it because I love her in front of everybody? I opened my mouth and it came out."

"I have to ask. Is it true?"

"That I love her?" He sighed. "Yeah. I do love her. But I also know that wasn't the time or place to tell her that. And I knew it when I was saying it."

"I have a theory, but it's probably best if you figure it out on your own."

"Really?" Scott swiveled his head so he was looking at his best friend. "What the hell is that supposed to mean?"

"It means just that. I have a theory, but I think you should figure it out on your own because I might be wrong and then I'd just look like an asshole."

"You can't look more like an asshole than I do."

"That's pretty much been my life motto since the day we met. I can't look like more of an asshole than Scotty Kincaid does."

Scott actually chuckled, which he knew was Aidan's intention with the insults. But his amusement was short-lived. "Even if you're wrong, at least you have a theory. I can't wrap my head around why I would pull a stunt like that. I *knew* she wouldn't forgive that."

"Because you're scared." Aidan's voice was very serious now. "You're scared of taking a chance on Jamie, so you did something you knew would make her walk away and not come back."

Scott swallowed past the lump in his throat and shrugged. *And not come back.*

"Why am I scared?" Deep in his gut, he suspected Aidan's theory might be right. "We're great together. We have a good time and we enjoy each other's company. We laugh and talk. I mean, I love her. I know I do. How can I love her and be scared of being with her?"

"I don't know. I think if you want to dig deeper into that psyche of yours, you'll need a professional. Or Lydia."

"I don't even want to think about telling Lydia what happened. Don't tell her."

"Really?" Aidan shifted in his chair, leaning forward with his elbows propped on his knees. "I knew there would come a time when my loyalty to you would conflict with my loyalty to my wife, but I thought I'd have more than three days."

The swinging doors opened again and this time

Grant walked out. He looked annoyed and slightly chagrined, but whole. "Hey, guys."

A doctor was with him, and he looked at them over the top of his glasses. "Mr. Cutter here will be fine. He was lucky and escaped with a very minor concussion. He needs to rest for a couple of days, but as long as he remains symptom free and pays attention to any messages his body might send him, there's no reason he can't resume his duties on his next shift."

"Thanks, Doc." Aidan looked around the waiting room. "Can I take him out in a wheelchair?"

The doctor didn't even crack a smile. "He can walk. You guys have a good day and be safe."

They rode back to the station in silence. Grant probably because he had a raging headache. Scott because he was still trying to make sense of his moment of stunning stupidity, and Aidan because nobody else was talking.

Everybody was on the third floor when they got back, except for Cobb and Jamie. He went into the kitchen to make Grant a cup of coffee, which he probably wasn't supposed to have but really wanted, while the kid shared the diagnosis. Because it was good news, Grant took a ration of shit, which would have made Scott laugh if he wasn't so focused on Jamie's absence.

When he saw Rick by himself, Scott walked over to him. "Where's Jamie? She'll want to know that Grant's back."

Rick gave him a look that could have set a glass of water on fire. "The lieutenant's in her office, doing paperwork. Not the least of which has to do with the car you hit today. And she already knows Cutter is back."

Temper at being iced out by a guy who'd known him as long as Rick had flared in Scott, but he shoved it back. This wasn't personal. Scott hadn't done what he was told to do. Firefighters doing whatever the hell they wanted put their companies at risk. And anything that put Engine 59 at risk was probably going to put Ladder 37 at risk, too.

"Yes, sir." It killed him to say it and not try to defend himself, but he didn't have anything to say that would make it okay.

But as he turned away, he caught a flicker of something on Rick's face. "Scotty."

He turned, bracing himself for more censure. "If Jamie wasn't leaving this week, we'd have a problem."

"I know. But I'm the root of the problem, not her. What happened today shouldn't reflect poorly on her at all."

"Oh, I'll make sure it doesn't." Rick gave him a humorless smile. "Luckily, I think the only guys paying attention were our own, so that issue's moot. But on a personal level that's none of my business, you need to make this right. Not only for her sake, but for yours. Even if it's over, this isn't the way you want it to end."

"I don't want it to end at all," he said, though his subconscious must have differed for him to so blatantly shoot himself in the foot. "I'll talk to her. Maybe try to make her understand."

"You should. But not here and not today. I've got a couple of guys coming in. I want you to take Grant home and make sure he has whatever he needs to keep him on the couch for a couple of days. And then you can head home, too."

"Am I being suspended?"

Rick shook his head. "Not in an official capacity, that I know of. But she doesn't need you here. And if we have to go on a run, everybody's going to be distracted and less confident. Go home. Or go see your old man. Have a beer with Tommy and see if he can help you figure this out."

Scott snorted, not really able to picture his dad giving him advice. "Okay. I guess space is best for everybody."

"Yeah, but not too much. And not for too long." Rick slapped him in the shoulder. "I'm rooting for you, you know. Even if you are a dumbass."

Once Grant was ready to go, Scott followed him down the stairs, but he paused on the second floor. Maybe he should knock on her door and at least apologize briefly. He could test the waters, so to speak, and see how open she would be to seeing him later, when he could really apologize. Leaving without saying anything at all didn't sit well with him.

But they were still at work. He'd disrespected her once already and there was a good chance she'd see him knocking on her door as more of the same. She didn't want to talk about their personal lives at work.

With a last glance at Jamie's office door—which remained firmly closed—Scott shoved his hands into his pockets and followed Grant down the last flight of stairs.

Chapter 17

Jamie sat with her elbows braced on her desk and the heels of her hands pressed to her eyes, praying like hell the alarm didn't sound. Red, puffy eyes and a stuffy nose from crying wouldn't do much to inspire confidence.

He loved her.

Even now, when everything had gone to crap and she'd shut him down before sending him away, her pulse quickened at the thought. She'd known he cared about her more than he let on. She felt it in the way he touched her and the way he looked at her.

And when a woman was in love with a man, she was sensitive to those kinds of things.

He could have told her he loved her when they were tangled up in her sheets, hot and out of breath. He could have told her while they were curled up on the couch watching one of his stupid movies. But not Scott.

Instead he'd pissed her off by defying her orders and then he'd turned what should have been the sweetest words she'd ever hear into professional embarrassment. He knew what that scene would do to her—that he was pushing one of her biggest hot buttons—and he'd done it anyway.

And that made her doubt that what he had said was actually the truth.

And damn, there were more tears again. She rubbed at her eyes and then pressed the wet washcloth she'd grabbed from the bathroom to her face. It wasn't cold enough to help anymore, but it calmed her a little.

He loved her. He'd told her he loved her and she'd rejected it. Coldly and as publicly as he'd thrown it out there. It was over. Her time at E59-L37 was over and her time with Scott was over.

Rather than give in to more tears, Jamie pushed back from her desk and looked around the office. There were very few personal items in it. Most belonged to Danny, and the stuff that was hers would barely cover the bottom of a box. But she had things in the officer's bunk room to pack. And she'd have to remember to take the box of tampons from under the bathroom sink so nobody was traumatized by it after she left.

That thought made her smile. She probably wouldn't feel like laughing any time soon, but she wasn't going to curl into a ball and weep for hours, either. At least not here.

Too many hours later, she left the awkward silences and too-polite conversations behind her and went home. Her apartment felt emptier than usual. Quieter. And she knew it would feel that way for a while because Scott wouldn't be filling it with his energy and big personality. She was alone again.

After forcing herself to take a shower, she put on her comfort pajamas—old sweats she'd stolen from a college boyfriend—and crawled into bed. If she slept a few hours, maybe things wouldn't look so depressing when she woke up.

But life didn't look any better when she finally decided to roll out of bed and force herself to eat something. Sleep hadn't been easy, and the nodding off and waking up and trying not to cry had given her a headache.

She was halfway through a bowl of cereal she didn't want when her phone chimed. She really wanted to ignore it, but there was a good chance if it was a well-meaning friend who knew what had happened, that friend would show up at her door.

It wasn't, though. It was Scott. Can we talk for a few minutes? I'm downstairs, but I can keep walking if you want.

It was tempting to tell him to keep moving, but she couldn't do it. I'll be right down.

She took a few seconds to look in the mirror, and then wished she hadn't. Her hair wasn't awful, but her face had the look of a brokenhearted woman who'd cried too many tears and not slept enough hours.

There was no help for it, though, so she forced herself to go down the stairs to get some closure. She saw him through the glass door and her heart ached so badly she had to resist the urge to raise her hand to her chest to rub the spot.

At least he looked almost as miserable as she did, but without the red eyes.

She pushed open the door and stepped back to let him in. Once the door swung shut, she leaned against the wall and folded her arms. "I'm not going to invite you upstairs."

"I understand." He paused, staring down at the bag in his hands before lifting his gaze to meet hers. "I'm sorry."

The sincerity came through so strongly, she wanted to wrap her arms around him and hold him close. He looked sad and tired, and she couldn't help but contrast it to the fire scene, when his expression had burned with intensity as he told her he loved her.

"I'm not sure what else I can say," he said. "I know that…what I said before wasn't what you wanted to hear, but—"

"You're wrong. I did want to hear you say those words to me. I *really* did."

He was silent for a few seconds, probably realizing what that meant, and then he cleared his throat. "I shouldn't have said them there or then. And I shouldn't have used my feelings for you as an excuse for disrespecting you professionally."

At least he got it. "You had to know I wouldn't want that in front of everybody."

"I did." He shifted his weight, sighing heavily. "I did know that, and I think subconsciously I did it on purpose. Talking about your transfer and everything made me think about the future, but we weren't really supposed to have a future together. We're just not on the same page. But I fell in love with you and I was starting to wonder if we could make it work. In the fire, in the structure after Grant got hit, I just... I panicked. I didn't want you in there and that scared me. And I imagined how that would feel day after day and I guess I sabotaged whatever we had."

Jamie processed his words, letting them sink in. They made sense to her. He'd lost his mom so young and then had to live with a father who was a firefighter and had survived a heart attack. And Ashley had told her how shaken he'd been by Danny's accident.

At least it had come from a place he couldn't quite control, because love and fear weren't always rational, and that was a comfort. It helped to know he hadn't simply been acting with blatant disregard for her feelings.

"You proved that you can't really handle letting me do my job. I'm not the television wife you're looking for, Scott."

She watched the impact the words had on him. He paled slightly and his jaw clenched. "You're the woman I fell in love with."

Curling her hands into fists so tight her fingernails bit into her palms, Jamie absorbed the blow of the words. "I fell in love with you, too. But I won't be happy in the box you want to put me in."

"I don't want to put you in a goddamned box."

"You *did* put me in a goddamned box. You already did it. You decided you knew better than I did what was good for me, and even if I *wasn't* your lieutenant and we weren't on the job, that's not something I'm going to accept in *any* part of my life." She looked up for a few seconds, blinking rapidly to keep the sheen of tears at bay. "Imagine how much stronger that fear would have been if I was also the mother of your children."

He nodded, so much sorrow in his eyes, she couldn't stop her own tears from spilling over onto her cheeks. "I love you, Jamie. I respect you. I really do respect the hell out of you. I want you to know that."

"I know you do. And that makes this so much harder."

"I didn't want this." He blew out a breath and ran a hand over his hair. "I should go. I hope you like being with Ladder 41 and that it all works out for you. I'm sure I'll run into you at events and stuff. And I, uh, brought you something."

When he held out the bag, she took it and peered inside. The little tub of chocolate pudding from the market made her breath catch in her chest and the tears kicked it up a notch.

"I only got a single serving," he said. "So you wouldn't think I was trying anything. But I thought it might help you feel better later."

Jamie couldn't talk, so she just nodded, clutching the bag. After a few seconds, he put his hand on her arm and leaned forward to kiss her cheek. She turned her face into it, the contact lingering for a few seconds.

And then he stepped back. "I'm sorry, Jamie."

He pushed open the door and walked away. She watched him shove his hands into the pockets of his sweatshirt, his shoulders hunched as if to fend off a cold wind. And once he was out of sight, she walked back up the stairs and set the bag on the counter.

It was over. Not just a bump in the road and *maybe we can get through this* over. But a *hey, enjoy your new assignment and I'll see you around* kind of over.

She should throw the pudding in the garbage and forget he ever existed.

She didn't have the strength to do, either, though. Instead she pulled out a spoon and cried her way through the sweetest, most painful parting gift she'd ever gotten.

Scott slapped the puck and watched it sail between the pipes. Then he slapped the next one. Taking shots on an empty goal wasn't much of a challenge and barely qualified as exercise, but it was somewhat satisfying when he hit them and they shot like bullets into the net.

The ice was the only place he'd ever been able to work out his feelings without getting himself in trouble. Even then, his temper sometimes got the best of him, but it wasn't the same as getting into a fight or kicking the crap out of his truck because he was pissed. Times like this, when it was just him on the ice and a line of pucks, were almost like meditation sessions for him. Usually they cleared his mind.

His mind was refusing to clear today, though.

Jamie loved him, too. That's why he hadn't slept worth a damn. Why he couldn't stand the thought of eating. Why half the pucks he shot were bouncing off the pipes and coming back at him. He'd gone over there to try to apologize and try to end things on a more positive note and hearing her say that had driven home just how badly he'd screwed up. He'd thrown everything away.

The click of a blade on ice broke into his thoughts and he turned toward the bench area, expecting to see one of the other guys or maybe the kid who was working that day. But it was Ashley, wearing jeans and a fleece pullover, along with ice skates she'd obviously gotten at the desk.

"Jesus, Ash. What the hell are you doing?"

"What do you mean?"

"You're pregnant. You can't just go flinging yourself around on ice skates."

She laughed and ignored him, skating toward him. "I don't really intend to fling myself at anything. And I might not be very good at hockey, but I'm the one who taught you to skate, dumbass."

"Slow down, at least."

"I'm barely moving. And the baby is fine. I've got plenty of built-in padding for safety."

He shook his head, knowing it was futile to argue with her. "What are you doing here?"

"I was going by and saw your truck. And I just asked Danny the other day if he'd been on skates yet and he said you guys haven't planned any ice time, so I figured you were in here alone. Probably brooding."

"I think better on skates."

"You always did." Sighing, she looked at the pile of pucks in and around the net. "Figure out the solution yet?"

"Solution to what?"

"Don't play dumb with me, Scotty."

"There is no solution. Or I guess you could say it already resolved itself. I was an asshole and that's not a quality she's looking for in a man."

"So stop being an asshole."

He clenched his jaw, wishing he could unleash his temper on a puck, but he wasn't taking the chance of it taking a weird turn and hitting his sister. "If it was a switch I could turn on and off, I would have done it years ago. Maybe."

"You can't let her go because you're afraid to love her. It's too late, you know. You *already* love her, so why be miserable?"

"How do I live with that fear every day?" He heard his voice rising, echoing through the rink. "I was so afraid for her that I did something stupid and we're not even... I hadn't even told her I loved her yet. We don't share our lives. There are no kids waiting at home for their mom. How would I handle that?"

She looked at him, her expression slightly sad, but also bemused. "The same way we all do. You've seen this your entire life, Scotty. You're just on the other side of it and you don't know how to handle it. But you deal with the fear the same way I do and the same way Lydia does and that Mom did and that this baby will. You trust your firefighter will be safe and smart and come home to you."

"And what if she doesn't? Come home, I mean."

"Then you keep going. If Danny had died that day—"

"Don't say that."

"No, I *do* get to say that, Scotty, because it's my reality. That possibility is something I live with every time he walks out the door. And if someday he doesn't come home, I won't regret loving him. I won't regret having his child. The baby and I will keep going. Just like we all did when Mom died, except I won't do like Dad and tell my kid to suck it up and get on with life. There would be counseling and support, like we should have had."

"Dad did the best he could," Scott said, defending

the old man out of sheer reflex. "It was never the same after, though."

"Of course it wasn't." She sighed, and he couldn't help but feel like he was missing something. "I'm not going to give you the speech about how Jamie could get hit by a car or fall down the stairs or be the first victim of the zombie apocalypse. But you need to ask yourself why you wouldn't think twice about asking a woman to spend the rest of her life taking it on faith you'll come home from work, but you won't do the same for her."

"I don't know how to stop wanting to take care of her."

"That's part of the way you're wired. You keep people safe." Ashley sighed again and took his hand. "And you're supposed to want to take care of her. You take care of each other. But wanting her to be something she's not isn't taking care of her."

"I miss her so much my stomach hurts and it's only been a day."

"I know what that feels like," she said. "After I told Danny we were done, I cried so hard I puked and then cried some more. But we worked through it. And that's your second mistake. You guys hit a wall and instead of looking for a way over or around it, you said *fuck it* and went home."

"I didn't say *fuck it*. I just decided not to hurt her any more than I already had."

"If she does love you, this—the emptiness—hurts more than anything you could say to her." She squeezed his hand. "Pick up your pucks and let's go. You can buy your niece or nephew some ice cream."

Once they were back in sneakers and he'd put everything away, he took her hand and they walked out of the rink together. The sun was warm and being outside with Ashley made him feel better. Less hopeless at least, and he knew he needed to get out of his own head for a while.

"Thanks for coming, Ash. Somehow you always know what to say. Sometimes it doesn't sink into my thick skull for a while, but I don't know what I'd do without you."

"That's what big sisters are for. And you're lucky to have two. Lydia to kick you in the ass and me to give you a hug."

He laughed and put his arm around her shoulders. "Let's get some ice cream."

She grinned. "I want a small scoop of chocolate with a pound of whipped cream and jimmies on it. And half a jar of cherries."

"That baby's got good taste." He squeezed her hand and they started walking toward the ice cream shop. For now, he'd shove his pain and confusion into the dark corners of his mind and enjoy an hour or so with his sister.

It seemed like just Jamie's luck that the guys got called out on a run just before she finished packing the few things left in her office and the bunk room, and emptying out her locker.

Maybe it was for the best, she thought, looking around the empty engine bay. She hated goodbyes and she'd been especially nervous about this one because she was afraid she'd cry again.

She'd spoken to each of the guys at some point during the morning, anyway. They'd all wished her luck and there had been jokes and promises to keep in touch. She could tell they were thrilled to have Danny back, which made it slightly easier for her to move on. This had never been her place, really.

She'd barely seen Scott. He kept himself busy down in the bays, taking inventories and cleaning the trucks and chatting with people who walked by and stopped to talk. Every time she saw him, even from across the room, the pain was so sharp she struggled not to let it show.

It was definitely time to go. There was no way she could hang around, caught up in her own thoughts, and not bawl at having to say goodbye and hug each one of them. And she would either have to say goodbye to Scott again, or she'd have to ignore him.

She put the last box in her car, which she'd managed to get reasonably close to the station, and then took one last look around. All traces of her were gone, so after sending a mental goodbye to Engine 59 and all the guys, she got in her car and drove away from the curb.

Jamie hadn't intended to go to Kincaid's Pub when she pulled away from the station, but she wasn't surprised when she found herself on the sidewalk, staring at the door. Her mind had been totally wrapped up with Scott, and here she was at his family's bar. As if coming here would somehow offer up a clue to what had gone so horribly wrong or how to fix it.

Everything had changed when she told him she was transferring to Ladder Company 41. It hadn't been an easy thing to tell him because she'd hated saying the words out loud. She'd known that things were going to change and that meant their relationship would change.

She'd been right. Except their relationship hadn't

just changed. It had crumbled like a dried-out sand castle.

Jerking open the door, she went inside. She was pretty well braced against the memories that threatened to emotionally overwhelm her, but she got a little shaky when Lydia saw her and smiled.

"Hey, you." Lydia looked at the clock hanging on the wall. "I've never seen you in here at this time of day, but it's five o'clock somewhere, right?"

"It's definitely five o'clock." She climbed up onto a bar stool, thankful the place was practically empty.

Lydia tilted her head, frowning as she looked at her. "You want a beer or do you want me to break out the good stuff?"

"I'd actually love a coffee. I'm not much of a beer drinker and I'm not doing cocktails on an empty stomach."

"Coming right up."

When Lydia set a huge mug of coffee in front of her, along with a small dish of creamer cups, Jamie smiled her thanks. She wasn't sure what, if anything, Scott had told his sister, but she didn't seem to be acting any differently toward her.

"Do you want something to eat?"

Jamie shook her head. She knew she should eat, but she wasn't hungry and was afraid if she forced herself, she'd only make herself sick. "No, thanks. Just the coffee, I guess."

"Okay." But Lydia reached under the counter and dropped a few packages of oyster crackers in front of her. "Do you want to talk about it?"

Tears prickled her eyes and she tried to blink them away. "Not really."

"Neither did he." Lydia sighed and leaned against the counter. "That's probably half the damn problem, you know. If you guys would talk to each other, neither of you would be so miserable."

"Some things just aren't meant to be," Jamie said. Saying it to Lydia was a good reminder for herself, and she forced herself to sit up straight.

"Things don't just *be*." Lydia paused, then shook her head. "Okay, that made a lot more sense in my head. But some things *are* meant to be, but you have to work for them and not expect all the pieces to magically fall into place."

Jamie fiddled with a package of crackers to give her hands something to do. Part of her resented the lecture, but she knew her subconscious hadn't come here accidentally. She'd pulled up a stool in front of one of the two women who cared about both her and Scott, and one who wasn't shy about telling a person what she thought.

"You know, I didn't want to come back to Boston," Lydia said. "I got out and I intended to stay out. I was done with firefighters. I was done with the entire firefighting community and my dad and this bar. I wanted no part of it."

"Since I was here when you married a firefighter *in* this bar, I guess you changed your mind."

"We talked."

"That's it? You talked?"

Lydia shrugged. "Basically. I mean, he *was* willing to walk away from everything for me, but I guess knowing I meant that much to him was enough for me. But if he hadn't come and talked to me, I would have been gone and I probably wouldn't have come back."

Jamie ripped the end of the package open and popped an oyster cracker into her mouth. Chewing and swallowing gave her time to think about how much she wanted to say, because this was her friend. She was also Scott's sister and Jamie knew that relationship trumped hers.

"We did talk," she said finally. "And this is where we ended up, so there's really nothing more to say."

"At this time of day, to come in here and not want a beer or food, you must have come here for another reason, Jamie. You're not ready to give up on him yet."

"I came to say goodbye." As much as she hated saying the words, she knew they were the right ones to say. "I cleaned out my office and my locker this morning. I'm officially done with Engine Company 59."

Wow, that hurt to say. And it wasn't only because of Scott. She would genuinely miss all of them.

"I know everybody's sad to see you leave the company, but what the hell is this goodbye bullshit? You're going to Ladder 41, not Michigan."

Jamie gave a short laugh, which surprised her. "Why Michigan?"

"I don't know." Lydia shrugged. "I don't know anybody who's ever gone to Michigan, so it seems like you moving there would merit a goodbye."

"You'd never met anybody from Nebraska before me, either. I guess I'm all about broadening your horizons."

"No, you're all about trying to change the subject. I'm a bartender. I can sense these things."

"I know I'm not moving to Michigan. I don't know if or when I'll move at all. But I don't think I'll be

coming in here for a good long while. This is pretty
undeniably his turf, you know?"

"You're my friend. I'm not letting you disappear
on me."

Jamie's throat tightened and she prayed she
wouldn't burst into a full-on bout of tears. "And I'll
see you when you're not working, like most people
see their friends."

"I can't accept that you're not meant to be together."

"I'm having a hard time accepting it myself." Jamie
wished Lydia would move on. Unfortunately, if she
kept pushing at her about Scott, Jamie knew their
friendship would eventually wither and die because
she wasn't going to rehash it every time they spoke.
"I should probably go home. I've got my stuff in the
car and I want to go through it and see what I'm taking with me to L-41."

"The coffee's on the house today. I know you won't
stop in, but text me or call me and we can get together,
okay? I want to hear about your new assignment."

"I will."

The phone rang and Lydia gave her hand a squeeze
before walking to the register end of the bar to answer it. Jamie saw her chance to escape without further drama and slid off the stool, but the picture on
the wall caught her eye.

She stared at the photo of Bobby Orr, the light reflecting off the glass highlighting the many—possibly
even hundreds—of fingerprints smudging it. There
had probably been a lot of broken glasses over the
years. Kincaid's Pub had probably seen its share of
broken hearts, too.

"I don't know if you do broken hearts," she said to

the man in the picture. "But I feel like my heart shattered like glass, so you're worth a shot, right?"

She kissed the tips of her fingers and pressed them to the picture, holding them there until the glass warmed under her touch. And then she laughed at herself and walked out of the bar.

Chapter 18

Jamie stopped by to say goodbye. Are you okay?

Scott read the text from his sister twice, wishing she'd left well enough alone. It was hard enough sitting on the couch feeling as if he'd lost everything while the guys went on with their lives around him.

They'd come back from a call and every trace of Jamie was gone, as if she'd never been there. The others were in good spirits, glad to have Danny back, and he tried. He was genuinely happy to have Danny back, too, but there was a void in Scott's world he couldn't ignore.

He typed in his response to Lydia. Yeah, I'm fine. Busy. Call you later.

Okay.

He wouldn't call her later. Right now, he didn't want sympathy *or* a lecture and he knew she'd give him one or the other.

The couch creaked as Danny sat down next to him and propped his legs up on the coffee table with a sigh.

"How's the leg?" Scott asked.

"It's good. It'll probably ache a little later, but it's better than I'd hoped. Mostly it's just being up and around for so many hours. I had too many weeks of sitting on my ass, watching television."

"Says the guy sitting on his ass in front of the television," Scott said, and they both laughed.

"How are *you* doing?"

"Fine." That was going to be his party line for the foreseeable future. He was fine. Life was fine. Work was fine. Everything was fine.

Maybe if he repeated the lie often enough, it would eventually become the truth.

"You want to talk?"

Scott realized it was quiet and the other guys had all found someplace else to be. "Not really."

Danny leaned his head back against the couch, pinching the bridge of his nose between his fingers. "I'm your lieutenant. I'm your brother-in-law. I'm your friend. I get to worry about you from all different angles."

"You heard what happened, then."

Danny snorted. "Was that in question? If anybody should know you can't keep a secret around here, it's you."

"Yeah. Nothing like embarrassing yourself in front of everybody."

"Embarrassing yourself? Nobody's laughing at you, Scotty."

He snorted. "No, but they're talking."

"Of course they are. Number one, they all consider you a friend and nobody likes seeing you hurting. And nobody wants to say or do the wrong thing and set you off."

"I'm not going to go off." The only person he was mad at was himself.

"And I won't lie to you. Everybody respects the hell out of Jamie Rutherford, so it also made them all a little uncomfortable."

"Sorry to cause them discomfort." He started to get up, but Danny put a hand on his shoulder and shoved him back.

"Scotty, don't be a dick. As your friend, I just want to know if you're okay. And as your LT, I want to know if you're okay to be here or if you want to take some time off."

Time off to what? Wander around his apartment and take stock of how empty his life was? To think about how full it had been for a few weeks before he'd thrown it all away? Maybe he could hit some clubs and hook up with somebody who could never be Jamie just to hate himself a little more.

"I need to work." He said the words quietly, afraid to show just how badly he needed to be anywhere but alone at home. "I might even cover for some other companies. Lots of guys looking for some time off with summer coming."

"If she was the one, you won't be able to work hard enough to forget her," Danny said. "That's not how to fix this."

"I'll never forget her," Scott said, clearing his throat when his voice almost betrayed him. "I just want to work hard enough to sleep at night."

Jamie couldn't handle being in her apartment and she had no idea what to do about it. She'd already escaped the loneliness that seemed to echo through the place by going to Kincaid's to see Lydia. She'd even done a few errands. But with hours stretching ahead of her, she was afraid she'd do nothing but flop on her bed and cry until she made herself sick.

She thought about reaching out to her family but, as much as she loved them, they wouldn't give her what she needed and might even make it worse. There would be sympathy and gentle advice that would feel like empty platitudes. And she would cry, which would wreck her mother. Not being able to hug over the computer would be too hard.

Grabbing her car keys from the kitchen drawer, she put on her shoes and gave herself a pep talk before heading deeper into the city. She took a couple of wrong turns, almost went the wrong way down a one-way street, and got flipped the bird at least twice, but finally managed to land a parking space within walking distance of the pizza place Steph's family owned.

When she walked inside, assaulted by the delicious aroma of food she had no appetite for, she was glad to see it wasn't too busy. She might be able to steal Steph for a few minutes. Walking up to the counter, she smiled at Steph's dad.

"Hi, Mr. Lawson. Is Steph around tonight?"

"She's out back, chopping veggies," he said.

Mrs. Lawson looked up from the pizza she was boxing and, after a look at Jamie, waved her around the counter. "I'll take over for her for a few minutes. You girls go have a break for a little bit."

She could have cried tears of gratitude for Mrs. Lawson's *mom radar*, but she just smiled. "Thanks."

When Steph looked up from the line of tomatoes she was slicing, her expression made Jamie laugh. "Hey, what are you doing here? Did you drive?"

"I drove. And your mom said she'd take over the veggies so we can visit for a few minutes."

"If you'd told me you were coming this way, I would have tried to get somebody to cover for me."

"It was kind of a last-minute, impulse thing."

Steph looked at her, and then waved for her to follow. Winding through the busy kitchen, they dodged the three employees assembling orders and went into the break room. After closing the door behind them, Steph gestured for her to sit at the small table.

"What happened?" she asked. "You look exhausted and sad."

"Scott and I broke up."

"I'm sorry." Steph tilted her head. "I hate to be dense, but wasn't that the plan all along?"

"It was, but the plan fell apart when I fell in love with him."

"Oh, honey." She stood. "Hold on two seconds."

It was more like two minutes, but since Steph came back carrying a big basket of French fries and a dish of cheese sauce, she forgave her. Jamie hadn't thought she'd be able to eat anything tonight, but that was serious comfort food.

"Okay," Steph said, once they'd each had a few fries dripping with cheese sauce. "Tell me what happened."

Jamie told the story, starting with her chat with her mom, during which she'd decided to wait until they were no longer with the same company before figuring out if they had a future. And then she walked Steph through the fire and Scott disrespecting her authority in an attempt to keep her safe, despite the fact she knew exactly what she was doing.

Steph held up her hand, shaking her head. "He did that to you? What an asshole."

It wasn't until she heard the words come out of Steph's mouth that Jamie realized why she'd come here. It wasn't just visiting a friend so she wasn't alone. She'd wanted somebody to be pissed off with her. Because she *was* pissed. She was hurt and sad and lonely, but she was also mad as hell at Scott.

"And then he told me he did it because he's in love with me."

Steph sat back in her chair, eyes wide. "Are you serious?"

"Yeah. We were still on the scene with both companies right there."

"He's in love with you?"

"That's not really the point."

After dredging a fry in cheese sauce, Steph popped it into her mouth, frowning. Considering how long she chewed, Jamie knew she was just buying herself time to think.

"So you fell in love with him. And then he said he's in love with you... And?"

"He said it in front of everybody," Jamie clarified for her. "Even knowing how important it was to me to keep our personal and professional relationships very separate."

"But he was scared for you."

"And *that* is the point. He got scared for me and interfered with my job and then embarrassed me in front of guys under my command."

"Because he loves you," Steph pointed out. "Did he apologize?"

"Yes. And he brought me chocolate pudding."

"Aw." Jamie must have made a face because Steph straightened up and scowled. "He's still an asshole, though."

That made her laugh, but it was short-lived. "That's the problem. He's really not. He knows he screwed up, but it doesn't change the fact he'd probably do it again. No matter what he says, his actions spoke louder than his words. And I'm not changing how I live my life."

"I'm sorry, honey." Steph slid the dish with the last bit of cheese sauce across the table to her. "What are you going to do now?"

"I'm going to focus on being the best damn fire lieutenant that Ladder 41 has ever had."

She said it hoping to lighten the mood, but Steph didn't laugh. "You don't think you can fix things with Scott? I mean, you love each other. Doesn't that mean you're supposed to be able to get through stuff together?"

"I'm not giving up my career and I can't change who he is or how he feels about my job, so it's better to recognize it won't work now, rather than down the road."

She said the words without her voice choking off, and she really believed them, but it would take time for her to accept that it was really over. They were done. Tears welled in her eyes and she swiped at them with her sleeve before they could fall.

"I'd get you a beer," Steph said, "but you can't drive for shit sober. I'm not giving you alcohol."

"Hey! I'm a great driver. It's this city. Nobody can drive in Boston."

Steph snorted. "So it's not you. It's *all* of us?"

"Yes." Jamie nodded. "I know you have to get back to work, but thanks for the talk. And the cheesy fries."

"Why don't you hang out and have some real food to eat? Once the late dinner rush is over, we'll head to my place. Watch a movie. Drink some wine. You can crash on my couch."

Jamie thought about how painful it was to think about Scott every time she walked into her apartment and knew she'd have to get over it at some point. But not tonight. "That sounds wicked awesome."

"*Wicked* awesome," Steph said, and then she laughed. "You're starting to sound like us now, Jamie."

"That's okay. As long as I don't start driving like you."

Chapter 19

Two weeks. Scott sat at the bar, nursing a beer and watching the evening news on the big screen with no sound. Two weeks with no Jamie. With no love and no laughter.

And then, suddenly, she appeared on the screen, with her helmet gleaming in the sun and smiling at the reporter who had a microphone in her face. Her name was on the bottom of the screen, along with a caption. *Happy ending for child who climbed a tree to rescue kitten.*

He stared at her face, drinking in the sight of her, as his heart ached in his chest. God, he missed her. He missed her face and her laugh and her touch and every damn thing about her. He missed the sound of her voice.

"Hey, Lydia. Turn up the TV for a second?"

She looked up at the screen as she moved toward the remote control next to the register and then stopped. "No. If you want to hear Jamie's voice, you can grow some balls and go talk to her like a man."

"Jesus, you can really be a bitch."

"Nothing warms a man's heart like the love his children have for one another," Tommy said from the corner.

"I love them." He glared at Lydia. "I just love Ashley more."

She laughed at him. "Because she coddles you and gives you ice cream."

"Hey, the ice cream's for the baby."

"Sure it is. Because every growing baby in the womb needs ice cream three times in a week." She stepped closer, a bar rag dangling from her hand. "Go talk to her."

He pointed at the screen. "She's rescuing children who rescue kittens."

"That was yesterday afternoon. Slow news day, I guess, so they're replaying the feel-good stuff." She sighed and shook her head. "I happen to know she's home and was planning to clean out her refrigerator today. I know this because I tried to talk her into coming in to visit and that's what she told me."

"How often do you talk to her?"

"Almost every day."

That hurt—the reminder that she wasn't really gone. She was only gone from *his* life. And it was his own damn fault. "How is she?"

"She's fine. She's really happy at Ladder 41 and the commute isn't too bad."

"That's not what I mean and you know it."

"I do know what you mean, but this is one of those fuzzy boundary things. I'm her friend."

"You're my sister."

"Yes, I am. And if you weren't such a dumbass, you might have caught on to the fact I've told you *twice* to go talk to her since you walked in."

"Oh." Hope flared to life as he realized if Lydia thought he should go talk to her, that meant Jamie hadn't totally put him in the rearview mirror. There was a chance.

"Yeah, *oh.* I think you should lay off the hockey for a while. You've taken too many hits to the head."

He drained the rest of his beer and then slid off the stool. "I'm leaving now. You can save your abuse for the paying customers."

"Are you going there now?"

"I think so, before I chicken out. If I don't go straight there, I might talk myself out of it."

"Don't." She reached across the bar to take his hand. "Leave your pride at the door and talk to her."

He lifted her hand and kissed the back of it. "Just so you know, I don't really love Ashley more than you. You're both equally pains in my ass."

"You might want to come up with other ways to express your feelings before you get to Jamie's." She smiled. "Call me later."

Hope buoyed him for most of the trip to her apartment building, but he felt himself faltering when he stood on the sidewalk in front. He had no idea what he could say, other than he loved her. He still loved her and that was all he had, but it didn't feel like enough.

But he knew if he walked away right now, he wouldn't come back. Seeing her face on the television and Lydia letting him know he still had a chance had given him the courage he needed, but it was fading.

And he wished the damn downstairs door didn't lock. It seemed like being able to knock on her door would make it easier. Asking her if she'd come down three flights of stairs to let him in was a lot more awkward.

I'm outside your door. Can I see you for a minute?

The wait for a response was probably only thirty seconds, but it felt like hours. Did you bring pudding?

The last thing he thought he'd do standing outside her door, about to beg for another chance, was laugh. But he did, and he remembered how much he loved that about her—about them. They laughed a lot.

No. He sent that and then typed again. But I'll go get some.

I'll be right down.

The grip he had on his phone made him realize his hands were shaking, and he put the thing in his pocket. Every minute he waited seemed like an eternity but then, finally, he saw her through the door.

His heart pounded and he felt the hair stand up on his arms and neck as he watched her come toward him. God, he'd missed her so much. His hands were still shaking and he didn't want to put them in his pockets, so he curled them into fists so maybe she wouldn't see how nervous he was.

She pushed open the door, and his heart skipped a beat when she smiled at him. "Hey, you. Come on in."

Scott wanted to touch her. He wanted to wrap his arms around her and squeeze her and not let go until they physically couldn't stand there anymore. "Thanks."

"You want to come up for a few minutes?" The smile was still there, but her eyes were sad.

"Even though I didn't bring pudding?"

"Normally I wouldn't offer hospitality to somebody showing up empty-handed like this," she joked. Then her lip quivered and she gave a tiny one-shouldered shrug that almost killed him. "But I've missed you, so I'll make an exception."

He followed her up the stairs, trying to think of the right words to say to her. But he also didn't want to overthink it because the only way he was going to get Jamie back was if he spoke from the heart. She wasn't going to settle for any less.

"I saw you on the news," he said when they reached the last flight, just because he couldn't stand the silence anymore.

"I couldn't believe it when the news crew showed up. A kid climbed a big-ass tree to rescue the neighbor's cat." She unlocked her door and pushed it open. "Needless to say, once the kid got up there, the cat came down. The boy didn't. But there are worse days, so I don't mind those kinds of calls."

Walking into her apartment was like coming home. They'd spent so much time here that everywhere he looked, he was reminded of the weeks he'd had with her—the best weeks of his life.

"I've missed you, and when I saw you on the television, I couldn't... I had to come, you know?"

"How have you been?"

"Shitty." There was no point in sugarcoating it. "I screwed up again by just walking away. I don't know if giving you space was the right thing or if I should have pushed and tried to get you to forgive me. I don't know and I took what I thought was the easy way out."

"It hasn't been easy."

"No. So I'm here and I'm still in love with you and I'm still sorry." He realized they were both standing there in the living room, and he wished they could sit down. His knees felt a little wobbly. He changed his stance so his knees weren't locked because passing out wasn't going to impress her any. "I don't want to put you in a box, Jamie. I want you to be you because you're the person I love. I don't want to change anything about you."

She folded her arms over her chest, her lips pressed together for a few seconds. "I feel like it's easy for you to say that now because I'm not going through the door with you anymore. I'm at Ladder 41 and you're not there when I'm in situations you don't want me to be in. Removing the situation doesn't mean the feelings that trigger the behavior are gone, too."

"Maybe that's part of it. But there's a chance we'll end up working a fire together someday and if we do, it's because they struck a shitload of alarms, so it'll be a bad one. If that happens, I swear to God I will not get in your way. I'll worry about you. Hell, I'll be scared shitless for you, but I won't ever disrespect you again."

"I want to believe that. I want to so badly."

"I've mourned, Jamie. I lost you and I've grieved for you and I hate that it was my own damn fault. I lost my mom to something she couldn't control, but she fought it. And we've lost brothers who were doing what they were called to do. I didn't even give you that. I thought it wouldn't hurt as much to lose you now, but it's even worse because I wasted what we had. I want to make memories with you. I want to grab every single day we can together."

The tears shining in her eyes ripped his heart to pieces, but he forced himself to stand where he was and not try to wipe them away. "I want that, too."

"We can do it, Jamie. We'll make a life together and we'll figure it out. We can have kids and they'll have days with me and days with you and then we'll have, what, three days a week all together? And we can chat and text and video chat during downtime. We can have it all."

She laughed, the sound a bubble of happiness through her tears. "I can almost see it."

"I *can* see it. And we'll worry about each other, but we'll be strong." He moved toward her, unable to help himself. "I'll go see the therapist that Ashley and Danny go to if you want me to. If we have a problem, we'll figure it out together. I don't ever want to walk away from you again."

"You better not." She looked him in the eye as she closed the distance between them. "Don't ever push me away like that again."

Burying his hands in her hair, he rested his forehead against hers, blinking against the tears that blurred his vision. "I swear I won't. I love you, Jamie."

"I love you, too."

Scott felt like all the broken pieces inside of him knit back together again, and he kissed her. Slowly and tenderly because he wanted to savor this gift he'd been given. Then he wrapped his arms around her and squeezed.

"You're everything to me," he whispered. "I'm going to spend the rest of our lives making sure you know it."

"I can't wait." She tilted her head back to smile at him. "It's still early. What do you say we take a drive down to this little place I know on the South Shore and catch up. They have great seafood."

Three months later...

The flames grew taller as smoke billowed around them. The smoke was thick and black, smelling like burnt meat and barbecue sauce.

"Turn the gas off," Jamie yelled.

"Hey," Scott said, turning and waving a spatula at her. "You're not in charge of *this* company."

"Obviously not, because if I was, that grill wouldn't be sending up smoke signals to the neighbors to call 911 right now."

"This is like a bad joke," Lydia said. "How many firefighters does it take to put out a grill fire?"

There were half a dozen of them standing around the grill, so more than six, Jamie thought. Grant and Gavin were just laughing but the others ignored them.

"Maybe I should get a fire extinguisher," Ellen Porter said.

"We'd never get that taste out of anything we cooked after that," Aidan argued.

"Turn the gas off," Jamie repeated.

"If we turn the gas off," Scott said, "then the fire will go out."

"I can't believe they haven't let you skip the exam and just made you an honorary officer," Jamie said.

He waved the spatula at her again. "You're going to pay for that later, funny lady."

"If the fire goes out, how will we cook off the gunk so we can make the steaks?" Aidan shook his head, and then jumped back when something—probably left-over fat stuck to the grill plate—sizzled and popped. "Joey, you always man the grill when we do charity cookouts. Explain this to her."

Joe, one of the guys from Ladder 41, shook his head. "Hell, no. I'm not here to explain anything to my LT. I'm just here for the beer and the steak, and it's probably a good thing I like mine more on the well-done side."

"If you turn the burners on full, that shit'll burn off faster and we can eat sometime today," Tommy said from his lounge chair in the shade.

"Dad!" Ashley walked out onto the back deck, one hand on her baby bump. "You of all people should know better than to say that to them."

Jamie laughed and turned back to the folding table that was practically groaning under the weight of pot-luck food. They'd all come together to christen Aidan and Lydia's new house with a backyard barbecue, and all she could do was hope the guys didn't burn down their backyard. That would just be embarrassing, both personally and professionally.

Jess stepped out onto the deck, carrying a tray of condiments. "I don't even know if there's room for these on that table."

"We'll make room." Jamie started shifting dishes

around. "I heard you officially opened the Boston branch of Broussard Financial Services last week."

"I did!" Jess set the tray down in the clearing Jamie had made. "It's scary, but so exciting. And I'll still fly to San Diego now and then, but being home with Rick all the time is amazing."

"How are your grandparents doing?"

"They're doing great. They love where they're living and they've made a lot of friends there. I swear, they're always doing something. And my dad's going to fly out later this month."

"Really? That's awesome, Jess." Jess's father had been estranged from his parents for all of her life, so getting him to Boston was a big deal.

"I'm nervous, but I think it's going to be good. Seeing the office is an excuse, but part of rebuilding their relationship is him facing where he came from. We're going to have them all over for dinner, of course."

"That'll be good because it's the house he grew up in, so the memories will be there, but you guys have changed it enough so they won't be overwhelming."

Jess smiled. "Exactly. I think after this visit, if it goes well, we'll probably start planning our wedding. It won't be at Kincaid's Pub, but we'll try to make a decent party."

"Cavemen cooked dinosaur meat over open fires, didn't they?" she heard Rick say. "Why can't we just throw the damn steaks on?"

"Evolution," Jess called to him. "Embrace it, honey."

Inevitably, the flames ran out of caked-on food to burn off and the guys were able to throw steaks and chicken on the grill. Aidan and Lydia didn't have a lot of outdoor furniture yet, but they all stood around or perched on whatever they could find to eat. There was a lot of laughter, and Jamie basked in the glow of more happiness than she'd ever believed she'd find.

This was an amazing family she'd found for herself. It was unfortunate that Joey was the only guy from her company who'd been able to make it, but they'd all been together for a charity half marathon the month before. There was great chemistry between the companies and she didn't think it would be too long before she'd be looking at another promotion. And the separation from Scott was just right. They had the common bond of their career, but each had the space to do their jobs without distraction. Everything was perfect.

Once everybody had eaten, she helped carry the leftover food inside. Luckily, they'd eaten almost all of it and the dishes had been brought in disposable containers, so there wasn't a lot of cleanup. But she took the time to wash up the few dishes and barbecue tools they'd used.

She heard the footsteps behind her just a few seconds before Scott's arms wrapped around her waist. He kissed the back of her neck and then she leaned back against him.

"Nice party," she said.

"Yeah. They've got a nice place here. Worth having to drive to work for them, I guess."

"It's not that far to drive. And it's definitely worth it."

He hugged her close, resting his chin on her shoulder. "Are houses something you think about?"

She'd finally given up her apartment a few weeks ago. After spending a couple of months practically living together, it hadn't taken much for her to officially move in with him. "Not really. I like our place, and I like the fact we can walk so many places. And being around for Tommy so he's not alone."

Her personal life was as perfect as her professional one, finally. She and Scott were happy. He'd gone home to Nebraska with her in July, and her family had loved him. Her niece had been fascinated by his accent and made him repeat things over and over so she could laugh. *Say* car *again! Say* park*!*

"I already have everything I want," she said, turning her head so she could kiss his cheek.

"Everything?"

"Well, I still don't have a car with heated seats but other than that, yes."

"Don't think I haven't noticed how often you take my truck because it's easier to get out of the driveway. Or so you claim."

Laughing, she pulled the plug in the sink and dried her hands on the towel so she could turn and wrap her arms around his neck. "It's not my fault your big truck hogs all the space. My poor car barely fits in the corner."

"Why do I feel like I'm going to start getting links to property listings with big driveways?"

She laughed and gave him a quick kiss. "I'm serious about being happy where we are. You're all I need."

"And maybe this?" He held up his hand, the diamond ring between his fingers sparkling under the overhead light.

Her breath caught in her throat, and she couldn't speak.

"I love you, Jamie Rutherford. Will you marry me?"

She nodded, hating the tears blurring her vision because she couldn't see the ring. While he took her left hand and slid it onto her finger, she used her right to swipe at her eyes. "It's beautiful."

"You're beautiful."

She kissed him and then looked into his eyes. "I love you so much."

"Let's go tell everybody."

Jamie knew as soon as they walked out the door that at least some of them had known this moment was coming. If not today, then soon, because Aidan and his sisters all turned to look in their direction and Lydia's eyes went directly to her left hand.

She held it up so the stones could sparkle in the light, and there was a lot of squealing and hugging from the women and backslapping from the guys. The tears came back when Ashley squeezed her extra hard before handing her over to Lydia for the same treatment.

"I told you," Ashley said, "that Jamie is our perfect third."

She had, the day they'd shopped for dresses for Lydia's wedding. Smiling, she looked at the guys, who were standing with Scott and saying who knew what to make him laugh. Then Tommy pulled her into his arms for a hug that almost squeezed the air out of her.

"Welcome to the family," he said, his gruff voice choked with emotion. "You're everything I ever wanted for my boy."

She probably would have cried some more, but Ashley clapped her hands for everybody's attention. "This seems like a perfect time to bring out the desserts, doesn't it?"

There were cheers and Lydia waved her hand at her husband. "Hey, come help me cut the carrot cake."

As the cheers died abruptly, Scott leaned close to whisper in her ear. "You sure you're ready to be a part of this forever?"

"I can't wait."

* * * * *

We hope you enjoyed reading
WANTED: PERFECT PARTNER
by *New York Times* bestselling author
DEBBIE MACOMBER
&
FULLY IGNITED
by *New York Times* bestselling author
SHANNON STACEY

They were originally MIRA® and
Carina Press stories!

SPECIAL EXCERPT FROM

Can't get enough of Boston Fire?

Read on for a short excerpt from
Under Control, *Derek and Olivia's story,*
by New York Times *bestselling author Shannon Stacey.*

As he lowered his mouth to hers, Derek felt the same fear and exhilaration he'd felt the one and only time he'd jumped out of an airplane. If it ended badly, it was really going to hurt, but he knew the experience would be worth the risk.

Tentatively at first, to give her the space to back out if she wanted to, he brushed his lips across Olivia's.

She didn't back out. She put her hands on his shoulders and rose up, pressing her mouth against his. Relief and hunger swept through him as he kissed her, and he wrapped his arms around her, pulling her close as his tongue dipped between her lips.

Her fingertips brushed over his back and then her hands curled, bunching his shirt in her fists. He cupped her face, deepening the kiss. Her skin was damp from the rain and he knew he should stop and let her go, but he didn't want it to end.

Then she made a sound deep in her throat, a hungry sound that told Derek she didn't give a damn about the rain. She wanted him.

And he wanted her so badly it hurt, but it wouldn't be tonight—it was too soon and the first date, and he didn't want to screw it up by going too fast—so he was going to take every second of this kiss he could get.

It was definitely too soon when she pulled back, breaking the contact. "I'm pretty sure that car just sitting there, with the driver trying really hard not to look at us, is my ride."

Her voice sounded as shaky as he felt inside. It was hard not to ask her to send the driver away and let him drive her home, but he was trying damn hard to remember the reasons he didn't think they were compatible. In the aftermath of that kiss, though, he couldn't come up with a single one.

"Thank you for dinner," she said.

"It was definitely a pleasure." He opened the back door of the car for her, but she paused with one leg inside and they locked eyes over the top of the door.

"Definitely," she whispered.

He winked at her as she got into the car. "Sweet dreams, Olivia."

The look she gave him just before he closed the door confirmed that he wasn't the only one who knew sleep might be hard to come by tonight.

Don't miss Under Control,
available August 28, in print and ebook wherever
Carina Press and Harlequin books are sold.

www.CarinaPress.com